Anna Jefferson is a fiction writer and playwright. She has written for stage and screen since 2005 and has toured her work through the UK. Born in Scunthorpe, Lincolnshire, her work draws on her abiding love of northern England.

Winging It is her first novel and is inspired by her blog. Anna lives in Brighton with her husband and two children.

www.annajefferson.co.uk
🐦 @annajefferson
📘 @youcantakeherhomenow

Winging It

ANNA JEFFERSON

ORION

An Orion paperback

First published in eBook as *You Can Take Her Home Now*
in Great Britain in 2019 by Orion Fiction,
This paperback edition published in 2020 by Orion Fiction,
an imprint of The Orion Publishing Group Ltd,
Carmelite House, 50 Victoria Embankment
London EC4Y 0DZ

An Hachette UK company

1 3 5 7 9 10 8 6 4 2

A CIP catalogue record for this book
is available from the British Library.

ISBN 978 1 4091 8598 7

Typeset by Input Data Services Ltd, Somerset

Printed and bound in Great Britain by Clays Ltd, Elcograf S.p.A.

MIX
Paper from
responsible sources
FSC® C104740

www.orionbooks.co.uk

To Ben, Nancy and Thomas

Part One

'Having a baby won't change me. It will have to fit in with me, not the other way around.'

Chapter One

Our baby is stuck. The previously calm birthing room is full of doctors shouting at the midwives.

'We need to get her to the operating theatre, now!' one yells. 'Why the hell isn't she there already?'

I strain to see behind me as the pain grips and twists. 'Nick? NICK? Where are you?'

'Here,' Nick says. His hand firmly grabs mine.

'What's happening?' I shrill, my voice not sounding like my own.

'It's OK, Emily,' my midwife reassures me, 'you've been in second stage labour for some time now. We are going to help you get your baby out.' She squeezes my shoulder and hurries out of the room.

'Nick, what's happening? What does she mean?' I demand as my entire innards crunch and tighten in the world's strongest vice.

'It's going to be alright,' Nick says.

'How do you know?' I screech at him. The mother of all contractions takes hold as I'm wheeled down the corridor. 'Holy fuck!' I hear myself scream.

The porters push the trolley through the swing doors and the waiting doctor greets me, 'Hello, Emily, I'm Doctor Marston. We're going to move you into a sitting position and ask you to keep very still as I insert a spinal drip into your back. Do you understand?'

'Yes,' I respond, as the contraction eases and I get my breath back.

'OK, Emily, you need to keep still. That's it, remain absolutely still.'

Can he stop asking me to stay still? It's like asking a boxer to remain static as his opponent repeatedly punches him in the face. My body wants to push our baby out.

'Right, it's in!' he says triumphantly, and my midwife appears, guiding me back into a horizontal position on the bed.

'You're so close, Emily, you can do this,' my midwife encourages.

'I can do this,' I agree weakly.

'You're doing brilliantly.' Nick wipes my sweaty forehead with the sleeve of his jumper.

This isn't how it's meant to happen. I wanted 'Here Comes the Sun', the Nina Simone version, playing triumphantly as my child effortlessly slipped into the world. I'd imagined doing the whole thing drug-free; that I would get the baby out on willpower alone. It's all typed up in the birth plan. Why isn't it happening like the birth plan?

'Get my baby OUT!' The wave of another knee-shaking contraction is starting to rumble. I can hear a low, Maori-like wail, which I assume is coming from one of the other rooms but as I draw breath, I'm surprised to find it's me making the noise.

'What are you doing?' I ask as a doctor straps monitors to me linked up to big beeping machines. 'Is there something wrong with the baby?' I panic. Where's Nick? He's not next to me anymore.

'Nothing's wrong. You've been crowning for a while now and your baby has just become a bit distressed so we need to monitor the heart rate. Just try to relax,' the doctor explains.

'Nick? Nick?' Where has he gone?

'I'm here. I'm right here,' he soothes as I grab for his hand and pull him close to me. He's changed. He's wearing blue scrubs, George Clooney in *ER* style, and a net that tames his uncontrollable curly hair; he looks like he works in a chip shop. Where did he get the outfit from?

'They know what they're doing, Em.' His voice is calm but his eyes look wild with fear. My breath is becoming shallow and panting. People sound like they are talking underwater and the skin on my face feels like it is about three sizes too small for my skull. I squeeze Nick's fingers together so tightly that his hand starts to twitch.

I close my eyes and try to take in a deep breath but only feel as if I can fill about ten per cent of my lungs.

'Just breathe, breathe, Emily. Release it slowly like we practised. Make your lips really tight. Like a cat's bum, remember?' Nick's voice sounds far away and echoey.

I exhale and open my eyes. My vision has altered, the harsh strip lights have developed a seventies porno soft-focus quality; the doctors busy around me through a frosted pane of glass. Nick grins at me and I know he is trying to mask his panic. He's squatting down so he's at eye level but his face is too close to mine. I can feel his warm breath on my cheek and it smells like Cornish pasties.

'I love you. I love you so much. You're doing so brilliantly. You're amazing. Keep going, keep going. You're nearly there.' He squeezes my hand and emphasises every word.

I try to reply but no sound comes out. He tucks a sweaty clump of hair behind my ear and I momentarily close my eyes. When I open them, my legs are in stirrups. I hadn't even felt them move. These drugs are brilliant. Why hadn't I asked for them sooner? Stupid, self-righteous birth plan.

I start to melt into a drug-fuelled bliss. My head feels like it is full of cotton wool; sentences drift off unfinished. I try to smile at Nick but only half my face moves, like a kind of Anne Robinson wink.

'That's my girl.' He leans over and kisses my forehead. 'We're nearly there,' he whispers, 'we're so nearly there. I'm so proud of you.'

I reach out to touch his face but my arm feels like it weighs a ton so I drop it back down onto the bed.

My midwife has both her hands pressed deep into my stomach to feel when I am contracting; I can't feel anything at all now – thank fuck for drugs. 'OK, OK, this is it. I can feel another contraction coming, Emily. I need you to do one last big push for me, can you do that?'

'How? I can't feel anything. How do I push?' My body is completely numb from my lower chest downwards.

'Imagine you're doing a poo. Push like you think you're doing a poo, Emily,' she orders. 'NOW! DO IT NOW!'

The world suddenly stands still. I'm looking at the silent, scarlet-faced midwife barking orders at me. Her mouth is moving but I can't hear her. I am utterly gripped by fear. I can't do this, I can't do this. I want all this to stop. I can't do this. I'm not ready. I scrunch my eyes shut as the tears spill down my cheeks. Can all this just stop for a moment? I'm not ready.

Then quick as a flash I'm back in the room like I've been given a shot of adrenaline. A glob of spit sprays out the midwife's mouth as she screams, 'I SAID NOW, EMILY!'

I shut my eyes again, but this time, a sheer determination takes over my whole body. I tense every muscle I can feel and focus on tensing all those that are numb. I imagine myself sat on the toilet and then push. And push. And push. And push.

'And PUSH. Keep going. The head is almost out. Your baby is almost here. ONE MORE BIG PUSH, EMILY!'

The doctor standing between my legs is nodding frantically at the midwife. Fuck. This is it. Come on, Emily, you can do this. Let's get this baby out.

I gulp in another huge breath, grip Nick's hand with all my might and scream a deep, powerful scream from somewhere right down in my solar plexus.

'That's it, Emily, that's it, keep going. This is the one, we're going to get your baby out on this one, KEEP GOING,' she bellows.

I gasp for another lungful of air and use the last bit of upper body strength to bend forward, imagining I'm doing the biggest poo of my life.

Suddenly there's a sharp tug between my legs followed by what sounds like someone spilling a pint of water on the floor.

'Yes! Well done, Emily, your baby is here.'

Our baby is here.

Everything pauses. There is a collective intake of breath followed by an ear-bleedingly loud wail and the room becomes a hive of activity again. I flop back on the bed, sweat dripping in my eyes.

'Daddy, do you want to come and see what sex it is?' It takes me a moment to realise the doctor is talking to Nick.

'Oh my God, Emily . . .' His voice cracks. 'It's a girl, she's a girl!'

'Can I see her?' I croak.

The doctor carefully places her on my chest. I'm stunned by the alien feeling of having the weight of a one-breath-old human being on top of me. She has tiny, tiny fingers with titchy fingernails and a mouth the size of an old five pence, opening and closing like a goldfish.

We have a daughter. All slippery, a full head of black hair matted to her purple scalp with blood and discharge.

I look up at Nick, who is taking a picture of us both on his phone, and say in a voice that comes out so deep it sounds more like a burp: 'It's our baby.'

Later, we look back at that photograph which he immediately texts to everyone we know, and both comment on how much I look like a transvestite.

'Do you have a name?' a nurse asks.

Nick and I look at each other and without hesitation, proudly say, 'Lucy', in unison. Of the five million names we toyed with, we always came back to Lucy. We don't agree on a lot of things, but thankfully we agreed on this.

There is another tug between my legs. I've been so busy staring at our baby, I hadn't noticed the doctor was still ferreting around down there. She looks up at me and says, 'Would you like to see your placenta?'

I nod before I've really had a chance to think it through and she passes it to the midwife who presents me with what looks like a massive bloody steak.

'Are you keeping it?' she asks.

'Am I what?'

'Some people like to keep them, have it dried and made into capsules, or necklaces.' She's still holding the meat tray of bloody flesh.

'Err . . . No, no, I'm fine thanks.'

'Yes, it's not everyone's cup of tea.' She shrugs, putting it down.

'Can I hold her?' Nick whispers.

'You can do better than that, would you like to cut the cord, Daddy?'

I wish she'd stop calling him 'Daddy'. It's totally creeping me out.

Nick looks terrified as the midwife gently takes Lucy from me and hands him a pair of scissors. He says afterwards how he wished the midwife had done it.

'It was horrible.' he explains.' 'Like sawing through really gristly cheap meat, knowing that you might slip and stab your newborn baby.'

Nick picks her up tenderly and holds her in the crook of his arm. He reminds me of the Athena poster, if the guy was dressed like he worked in a chippy. A wave of emotion shudders through me. This is my family now.

Nick passes Lucy back and I wrap a sheet around us both. A purple, wrinkly hand rests on my chest territorially and I think, I'm your mum. I'm your mum. I'm your mum.

The room has emptied so it's just me, Lucy, Nick, the midwife and one doctor, who looks at me reassuringly as she settles on the stool between my legs, which are still strung up in the stirrups.

'Just relax,' the doctor says perkily. 'We had to cut through several layers of your vaginal wall to get your baby out, so I'm going to sew it up for you. You won't feel a thing for now. I'll tidy it up as best I can so it'll be nearly as good as new.' I don't think I ever want to use my vagina again. She might as well just sew the whole thing up.

'Would you like some tea and toast?' the midwife asks in a kind voice that makes me want to cry. I am suddenly the hungriest I've been in my entire life, having done the whole labour on two peanut Tracker bars and a Milky Way. Under normal circumstances, that would be an in-between-snack snack. I give my brand-new baby a big sniff on the top of her sticky head, and gratefully say, 'Yes please.'

'I'll go and put that toast on for you. Just relax, you've done the hard work now.' She smiles. Those words stick with me, and later I will think how cruel it is to mislead someone so much, so early on.

The hard work has only just begun.

Chapter Two

How am I meant to go to the loo? I'm desperate for a wee but my legs still don't feel like my own and I'm unsure if I'll make it out of bed. Nick has gone home as he's not allowed to stay on the maternity ward overnight. He promised to be back first thing in the morning and left on a wave of kisses and 'I love you's. I try to shuffle closer to the edge of the hospital bed but my vagina throbs deep inside with every movement. I eventually ease my feet down onto the ice-cold floor. As I tug back the curtains, I see a woman with blonde plaited hair in an oversized Ramones T-shirt sitting cross-legged on her bed, feeding her baby while flicking through *Grazia*. It isn't very sisterly of me but I fucking hate her. How is she sitting like that? I'm never going to be able to sit cross-legged again.

She looks up and smiles and I instantly feel guilty.

'How are you doing?' she whispers in a voice so loud she might as well be talking normally.

'I feel a bit broken.'

'Not surprising, you have just pushed an entire human into the world.' She smiles. 'What did you have?'

'A girl, Lucy.' I point to my beautiful sleeping baby in the cot next to my bed. 'You?'

'Gorgeous name. This is Bodhi,' and before I have a chance to comment she groans, 'it wasn't my choice. My boyfriend's obsessed with Point Break and I'd promised him if we had a boy he could choose the name, as I'd chosen our daughter's name, Charlie. I was convinced I was having another girl, so you can imagine how disappointed I was when they said he was a boy.' She shakes her head. 'Never mind.'

'Do you know where the toilets are?' My legs start to shake under the weight of standing up.

'Down the corridor and on your right. Leave the cot here if you want, I'll keep an eye on her.' She nods at Lucy in the transparent crib. Fuck. I hadn't even thought about taking Lucy with me, is that what you're meant to do? Do cots even have wheels?

'Thank you, I'll just be a minute.' I hobble towards the door.

'You won't, you'll be ages. Don't forget to take your pads.' She indicates the maternity bag. 'And lean forward when you go for a wee like you're touching your toes.'

'Why?'

'Because otherwise it will sting like fuck, that's why,' she nods knowingly. This turns out to be one of the best pieces of advice I have ever been given.

I lie in bed on my side staring at Lucy through the perspex, knowing I should sleep but utterly mesmerised by her. As my eyelids start to feel heavy and I let my body relax, Lucy wakes and I kick myself for not dozing earlier. I ring the buzzer as I can't reach over to her.

'Aha, I think she's done a poo,' the nurse tells me. 'Would you like to change her nappy?'

'Alright, yes please. I've no idea what I'm doing, though.'

'Don't worry, you'll get the hang of it pretty quickly, and I'll stay with you.' She adjusts the bed to a semi sitting position and places Lucy between my legs along with wipes and a clean nappy.

11

The first thing I notice is the umbilical cord. It looks absolutely disgusting, like a long bit of cured meat that's been lurking at the bottom of the fridge for weeks. It is virtually impossible to take the nappy off without knocking it.

'It won't hurt her, and it should fall off in a few days,' the nurse reassures me. 'Some people like to have them made into keepsakes, you know?' I must look absolutely appalled, as she mutters, 'It's not for everyone, of course.' What's the deal with drying out bits of your body and having them made into ornaments and jewellery, why can't someone give you a good old-fashioned diamond when you've given birth?

The nappy is full of what can only be described as tar. Black and sticky.

'That's great,' the nurse coos. 'A lovely black poo, that's what we want, isn't it? Good girl. It will just get lighter in colour now until it settles into a rich yummy yellow like Dijon mustard, that's what we're aiming for.'

The nurse puts Lucy back in the cot and she immediately closes her eyes and falls straight back to sleep, like some kind of magic trick. I lie down and try to sleep as well but I can't stop thinking about eating mustard and how I may never do it again now. I pull the sheet up to under my chin and try and get comfy but I miss my bed and my duvet. This mattress is wafer thin and I can feel the steel struts holding it together. The nurse didn't readjust the bed back to flat and I can't find the lever to change it, so I'm attempting to sleep in a sitting position. I must ask Nick to bring in my pillow when he comes today. I'm completely wired and absolutely knackered in equal measure. Every bit of my body aches in ways I never thought possible, but my brain won't stop turning over and over. Muscles that I didn't know existed throb and creak. I'm looking out from a body that won't do anything I tell it to. I don't think I will ever feel normal again.

Chapter Three

I want to go home. The hospital has kept us in for forty-eight hours so far as Lucy isn't latching on properly and they won't let us leave until they've seen her feed for more than three seconds. If I hear 'tummy to mummy' or 'nose to nipple' one more time, I'm going to kill someone. I don't think I've had more than about five minutes consecutive sleep since she was born, as every time I close my eyes she starts crying, so I take her out of the cot and the cycle of unsuccessful feeding starts again.

'Why don't you try squirting it over her face near her mouth and see if any of it drips in?' Nick suggests unhelpfully. He's brought in a bag of clothes from home that are all totally useless and unwearable. I'm trying my hardest not to be mardy with him, as I don't want to start family life being cross. But seriously, who packs non-maternity skinny jeans that I haven't been able to fit into for the best part of a year and my best cream-coloured cashmere jumper? And to top it all off he's forgotten the pillow, again, even though I texted him about it three times after he forgot it yesterday.

He notices me eyeballing the clothes again with ill-disguised fury. 'I didn't know what to bring.' He shrugs apologetically. 'So I just picked up the stuff I know you like wearing . . .'

'Forget it,' I snap, making myself take a breath. 'Did you get any chocolate?'

He digs into the front pocket of his hoodie and produces two Twirls. 'Ta daaaa!'

All is forgiven, for now. 'I just want us to go home,' I sigh as I rip open the wrapper. I don't think I've ever felt so tired and desperate to leave somewhere, but I can't even get off the bed unaided as my vagina hurts so much. I'm not going to be making a quick escape any time soon.

The breastfeeding specialist pulls back the blue plastic curtain that's surrounding my bed. 'So, how's it going in here? Have you managed to get her to latch on yet?'

'A bit,' I lie.

'Well let's see then, shall we?' She leans right over me, her face inches away from my boob, hands on hips, as I try and get my nipple in Lucy's mouth.

'Nearly. Remember, nose to nipple.'

I shoot a look at Nick who quickly shakes his head and mouths, 'It's OK.'

'Here, let me try.' She takes the back of Lucy's head and confidently moves her to start feeding. She makes it look so easy. 'There, she is hungry isn't she? I'll pop back in a bit and see how you're getting on. It just takes practice.'

She closes the curtain around us again and the moment she leaves, Lucy unlatches, her head flops back and she starts wailing.

'I know how you feel Lucy,' I whisper to her, avoiding the terrifying throbbing fontanelle as I lean down to kiss the top of her perfect tiny head.

I'm starting to get a bit desperate. The woman opposite went home late yesterday evening. She strode over and hugged me, wished me well and left her copy of *Grazia*, which made me cry uncontrollably for no reason. I think it's partly because this is the least amount of sleep I have ever had in my whole life.

The sense of desperation isn't helped by Nick hovering over me all the time, asking, 'Is she doing it now? Is that it? She looks like she's feeding from where I'm standing.'

'I know what you're trying to do, but please just be quiet for five seconds.'

'I'm only trying to help, Em.'

'I know, it's just . . .'

'Annoying?' he suggests. I nod and he grins back at me. 'What can I do, then? I feel like I'm just getting on your nerves.'

'Just sit.'

'Alright, but I'm here if you need me to . . . anything really,' and he sits in the plastic-coated chair, face immediately illuminated by his phone.

'Don't send your mum any pictures of me with my tits out.'

'Shit, sorry, Em. It's just the one.'

'Nick!'

'Sorry.' He puts his phone in his pocket. 'Is she . . .'

'No. I'll tell you when she is,' I snap.

When Lucy does finally feed, there is no one official here to see it happen.

'Look, Nick, this is it, right? Can you see? Am I doing it? Is she feeding?'

He scrambles up. 'I think so, hang on,' and he attempts to record it on his mobile to show the doctor when she next does her rounds. Unfortunately it turns out amateur film footage doesn't qualify for discharging patients.

Nick is eating my lunch of bangers and mash when Lucy does eventually latch on properly. He gets his phone out again. 'Put it away, Nick!'

'I thought . . .' he starts to say with a mouthful of mash.

Just then the doctor opens the curtain. I'm so relieved that I burst into shoulder-shaking tears and she bounces right off again.

'That counts, that counts, that's got to count, right?' Nick stands up in protest, arms wide, begging the doctor.

She looks at her notes, gives an *X-Factor*-length pause and then finally nods, 'I think that'll do nicely. You can take her home now.'

That's it then.

We're going home.

Nick pulls up outside the flat. A car slows down and the driver shouts 'fucking granny driver!' out the window at him as he cruises past. The guy's been behind our car for the last five miles without an opportunity to overtake and Nick's been driving through the city at an average speed of about fifteen miles an hour all the way, hands gripping the steering wheel tightly and checking on Lucy in the mirror every four seconds.

'Dick,' he mutters.

I open the car door and start heaving myself out.

'No! Stay where you are, I'll help you out.' He trots round to my side, opens the door as wide as it will go and grips me too tightly under the armpit. 'Right, put your weight on me and shuffle out.'

'Thanks. Is the flat tidy?'

'Yes, 'course.'

'Properly tidy, not Nick tidy?'

'Yes! Look, let's just all get in, shall we?' He leans into the back and gently lifts the car seat out. Lucy is fast asleep. Her hat has fallen down over her eyes and I notice for the first time that she's inherited my bum chin.

16

Nick turns the house key in the lock and gives the door a kick to open it. 'Welcome home, Lucy!'

I shuffle into the front room and Nick places the car seat in the middle of the carpet. I sit down on the sofa, precariously balancing on one bum cheek and clinging on to the arm while wincing through the pain. We both stare at her.

I know I should feel prepared for this moment after nine months of carrying her and three days of getting to know her in the hospital, but that now feels almost like someone else's life, like a weird and very realistic dream, so it's come as a total shock to be sat in my front room with a baby, and we created her.

I look at my daughter and wonder how I'll even be able to lean forward to pick her up. I haven't been for a poo since giving birth. The nurse gave me a box of stool-softening sachets to drink, but the thought of having to push anything out again is too much to bear. I'm terrified that I'm going to prolapse and I'll do a poo swiftly followed by my womb falling out and I'll bleed to death in the most undignified shit-filled way before Lucy is even a week old.

So, instead I've just been regularly letting out little toxic farts in the hope that it will relieve some of the pressure. I lean to one side and try to discreetly let one out now.

'What are you thinking about?' Nick asks.

'About how beautiful our baby is,' I lie.

We carry on sitting in silence, looking at her, ignoring the smell that has started to engulf us.

'So, what do we do now?' Nick whispers.

I'm not sure whether Nick is genuinely looking for a response, but I don't have an answer. This is the 64,000-dollar question, isn't it?

Since we'd found out I was pregnant, we'd started to get our shit together without even realising we were doing it.

We bought our flat, which, disappointingly, had stunk of fags and wet dog when we first moved in. But we'd cleaned it and painted it, bought new carpets, learnt how to bleed a radiator and bought a Quentin Blake print of the BFG for the nursery. And this was what it was all for. So we could bring our new baby home.

But what are we actually meant to do now? Nick and I look at each other and smile weakly as I shrug at him. 'I have absolutely no idea.'

Chapter Four

I'm standing in front of the full-length mirror in our bedroom feeling like Sam in *Quantum Leap*. It is literally like living inside the body of a stranger. I peel off my jogging bottoms, T-shirt, size eighteen pants and milk-soaked bra, and stare at a body I no longer recognise. What has happened to my stomach? It has turned into a kind of human stress ball. What had been a taut, baby-filled orb for months is suddenly empty, like a half-deflated water balloon. My boobs don't look like my own anymore; my nipples are huge and a completely different colour than normal.

I have no idea what condition my vagina is in, but it feels like someone has punched me with a fist full of rusty nails, then made me bathe in lemon juice. I am going through maternity pads like there is no tomorrow; is it normal to be leaking so much blood? I decide to further investigate the situation. I unhook the mirror from its peg on the wall and lie it down on the floor and straddle it. Without my glasses on I can't see much, so I attempt to lower myself down into a kind of lunge, which is no mean feat given that the stitches feel so tight I have taken to shuffling around like an elderly woman.

'Emily? What are you doing?' asks Nick inquisitively as he leans against the doorframe, arms folded, grinning.

I jump. 'Why are you creeping up on me?'

'I just came to ask if you wanted a cuppa?'

'Yes please. And one of those posh ginger biscuits that work sent.'

'I ate the last one. You said you didn't like them.'

'I didn't like them after I'd brushed my teeth, but I fancy one now. Fuck's sake, Nick.'

Just then a big clot of blood drips out of me onto the mirror with a splat.

'Shit. Please can you pass me the wet wipes?' I whisper.

Nick leaves the room and comes back with a handful of toilet paper. 'I'll do it.'

'Oh, Nick, it's grim.'

'Seriously, it's just blood,' he comments as he helps me step precariously over the mirror and chucks my jogging bottoms at me. 'I've seen a whole lot worse over the last few days.'

I knew it. I was sure I had shit myself while giving birth. I asked Nick and he said he hadn't noticed but I could tell he was lying.

I gently pull on my jogging bottoms and T-shirt, lower myself down onto the soft bed and ease myself into a lying position.

'I'm so tired, Nick. I don't think I've ever been this tired before.'

'It can't be like this forever, can it?' he responds from somewhere on the floor.

'I don't know. Probably.' I reach out for the milk book, which has pages of handwritten lists of the times and lengths of feeds throughout the night, as well as which boob she fed from. The list goes on for pages and that's just from last night. 'She fed all night long, Nick. 1 a.m., 1.23 a.m., 1.58 a.m., 2.26 a.m.'

'I know, Em, I was there. You don't have to read them all out.'

'I'm just saying, no one can get any meaningful sleep for twelve minutes at a time. I'm losing my mind, Nick.'

'Just try and shut your eyes for a bit now, Em. You'll hear her if she wakes.'

I peer over at Lucy who is fast asleep in her Moses basket, her arms above her head, looking a bit like a highlighter pen in a hideous acid-green hat my mum had knitted for her.

'Why is she always asleep when I'm wide awake?' I mutter to myself.

She is unquestionably the most beautiful, perfect thing I have ever seen. I cannot believe, with all the things I have tried and failed at in my life, that I have made her. That my body put all the pieces in the right place, from fingers to lungs to eyelashes, and that she's here, sleeping and breathing in our bedroom as if she's always lived here.

I feel like I'm watching a scene play out from behind a window, like I'm peeping into someone else's life. I'm looking at a beautiful baby and a man squatting down clutching handfuls of toilet roll and I have to remind myself that this is my life. She is my baby. I am a mum.

It hadn't really dawned on me that she was going to be here forever. When I left the flat a few days ago to go to the hospital, there were two of us, and now there are three. Three people living in our tiny flat, occupying the space, calling it home. And out of the three of us, the smallest has the most stuff.

I watch Nick kneeling down and wonder what's going on in his head right now. He's the most laid-back man I know, which has always been one of his attractions. But this is different. It isn't like being unphased because your card has just been declined at the supermarket or taking a job knock-back in your stride. Something major must have shifted in him: he has a daughter now. But he is trying to

21

keep everything as 'normal' as it can be and I don't know if that's for his sake or mine.

I watch him smearing bright red blood all over the mirror and think, God I love him so much for doing that.

That thought is quickly followed by: he needs to use Flash not just water on that or he'll be here all day.

'OK, I'm going to get a rest in before the next feed.' I sink into the pillow and pull the duvet up around my chin. Right on cue, Lucy starts to stir. 'It's like she knows,' I whisper, as I will my prickling eyes to open again.

Chapter Five

The extremes of emotions I am experiencing are off the Richter scale. From an all-consuming love that feels almost physical when I look at my old-man-faced baby sleeping, to uncontrollable tears. I can't stop crying. I started sobbing to Elaine Page when I heard 'Memory' on the radio the other afternoon. I just can't get any sense of perspective. I can't tell the difference between something that's a big deal or a small deal, or no deal at all for that matter. Do I actually care that I've felted my old pink wool jumper that I haven't worn in years by putting it on the wrong cycle in the washing machine? Is it the end of the world that Nick has bought me a Fruit and Nut Dairy Milk and not a plain milk chocolate one as requested? Do these things warrant the depths of despair I suddenly experience? I have no idea anymore. Everything is just a bit much at the moment. I thought I knew tiredness before, but if I saw the pre-baby me whingeing about being worn out, I would tell her to fuck right off, that she doesn't have the first clue about what it is to be bone-tired.

It's not that I'm a complete control freak but I do generally like to know what I'm doing that day or week. Since Lucy, though, we are literally living minute by minute. Days are spilling into nights spilling into days and our only real connection with the outside world is through Ken Bruce on Radio 2 or the health visitor.

She's a small woman in her sixties with wild, uncontrollable hair that she tries to tame into a crocodile clip. She is eighty per cent torso with short, stout legs that have to do double the work due to their size; like Fred Flintstone driving his car. On her first visit, she'd left her weighing scales behind and had to return for them, and this time she's forgotten her pad, so is writing our notes up on the back of her hand.

'Can I get you some paper?' Nick asks.

'Oh no, no I'm fine.' She shakes her head and her hair escapes. She scrapes it back into her clip again. 'I'll only lose it.'

I don't feel very confident in her ability to get home unaided, let alone look after Lucy and me.

'Now, before I get started, can you point me towards your loo?' Nick points her in the right direction and as she leaves the room I suddenly start to feel chilly, like I am sitting in a breeze.

'Did she leave the front door open?'

'Nope. Are you OK, Em? You don't look great.'

'Cheers, Nick.'

'No, it's just you look a bit off colour.'

I'm sweating buckets. I wipe my face on the sleeve of my cardigan and catch a drip off the end of my nose. Now, no one tells you how absolutely rancid new mother BO is. It's disgusting. Like the inside of a marathon runner's trainer disgusting. Apparently it's so your baby can identify you by scent, but in reality, when is Lucy ever going to have to pick me out of a BO line-up with loads of other sweating mothers?

'You've gone grey, Em.' Nick sounds concerned.

'Yeah, I don't feel great, as it happens.'

I look at my tits. They are engorged, larger than I've ever

seen them before but also totally misshapen. My nipples resemble half-chewed pink bubble gum.

The health visitor returns, 'Actually, Rick—'

'Nick.'

'Nick, I will have that sheet of paper, I've washed off my scribbles, stupid woman. Now, Ellie—'

'Emily.'

'Emily, how are you getting on?' she asks, while unpacking her scales.

'Absolutely brilliant!' I chirp, as I wipe the sweat from my eyes.

'Great. Well, latch your baby on and I'll see how she's feeding.'

I burst into full-on, ugly-face tears. 'Please, don't make me do it right now.' The thought of having Lucy anywhere near my excruciatingly painful breasts is enough to make me want to throw myself out of the window.

'Ah.' She nods, taking my damp, grey face in properly for the first time. 'I see what's happening here. Can you feel lumps under your armpit?'

I uncomfortably prod around. 'Yes, it feels like loads of ball bearings.'

'And can I look at your breasts?' She looks down my top. 'Yes, yes, you've got mastitis, Ellie.' I let that one go. 'It's very common with a newborn. Just give me a minute.' She pushes herself off the floor and retrieves her mobile.

She wanders into the hall. One phone call later she's booked me a doctor's appointment.

'In the meantime, Rick, you can make yourself useful by going and buying some Savoy cabbage from the greengrocer's.' She ushers Nick towards to the door, then explains to me how the cabbage breaks down the enzymes and reduces milk production, and so should help ease the mastitis.

25

'You just shove two leaves straight from the fridge into your bra. The grim part is that it works best when they're wilted, so you'll end up smelling a bit like a kitchen composter on top of everything else, but could be worse, hey?' she singsongs.

Nick dutifully departs, and the health visitor assures me that I will be feeling much more like myself, whoever she is, by the evening.

Sure enough by the end of the day I am full of antibiotics with a calm, mewing, newborn snuffling like a small pig on my cabbage-covered chest. I don't trust the health visitor to remember her own birthday, but she's completely sorted us out and, for that, I am totally in love with her.

Nick is doing everything and nothing. He is constantly busy: picking things up, putting the kettle on, making toast, sticking Babygros in the washing machine, but nothing seems to actually get done. We're surviving on an average of three hours broken sleep and I think we're both losing the plot. The flat looks like we've been burgled. We are a mess. Our baby is running out of nappies and the thought of having to venture out to Boots feels about as achievable as climbing Mount Everest in high heels.

This isn't how I pictured motherhood. The Mamas and Papas catalogue shows parents sitting in the sunshine sipping lattes while their newborns sleep peacefully in their arms. I think they should be prosecuted under some kind of trade description act: when is it ever like that?

'Come on.' Nick passes me my coat. 'We need to get out before we go crazy. Let's nip to the café at the top of the road, what do you think?'

I think of the catalogue parents, joyfully drinking their fancy coffees.

'I'm exhausted, Nick, I just can't imagine being outside. Let's do it tomorrow.'

Lucy currently feeds on and off throughout the entire night. It feels like I've only just put her down after her last feed when she starts hungry mewing again. I don't think I have had more than about fifteen minutes continuous sleep since she has been born. And it hurts to feed her, my God my nipples hurt. Is that how it's meant to feel?

'Scize the moment, Em. Come on, we don't have to be out for long.'

'But what about Lucy?'

'I was thinking she could come too,' he teases.

'No, I mean, we need to get all of her stuff together to go out,' I reply discouragingly.

'Then let's do it, Em. Just tell me what we need and I'll get it.'

Nearly an hour later and we are ready to 'nip out'. I catch a glimpse of myself in the hallway mirror. I look a complete shambles. My long brown hair is tied back into a greasy bun. I have food stains down my top, which I've been wearing for the last two days, and slept in last night. I wrap my knee-length coat around me. I'll just have to keep it on inside.

'You look beautiful,' Nick lies and gently kisses me. 'Now, let's do this.'

He pushes the pram onto the pavement. I shuffle behind like a geisha. It takes about ten hours to get there and when we finally arrive all the tables inside are occupied.

'You can wait, or there's tables outside on the pavement?' the waitress offers.

The world feels bigger. Noisier. Everything seems to be happening on a larger scale. The cars seem to be travelling faster. The sun feels brighter. The waitress is talking more loudly than normal.

'Shall we wait, Em? I don't mind?'

'No, let's sit outside.'

Nick parks up the pram next to the table and I skim over the laminated menu.

'A latte and a slice of chocolate cake,' he says to the waitress.

'Make that two.' I hand her the menu and smile at Nick, who's gently rocking the pram with his foot. 'OK, so this is alright, isn't it?'

'It's fab, Em. Small steps, right? Today it's the café, next time it might be town.'

This is alright, isn't it? This is good, we're out. Together. I grab a paper-thin cushion from another chair and add it to mine, as protection from the wire frame that is pushing against my stitches.

'Lean in,' Nick requests. I move my head a bit closer to the pram. 'Bit more,' he says as he takes an awkward picture of me and the hood of the pram. 'That's brilliant.' He shows me the screen with my painted-on smile wincing through the pain, then starts tapping away.

'Please don't send it to your mum.'

'Oh.' He looks up from his phone guiltily. 'Sorry, I've just sent it. You look great though,' he lies.

'Right, I'm going to nip to the loo. I'll be back in . . . a bit.' I steady myself as I stand and use the backs of chairs to weave my way towards the toilet. It's unisex, and smells strongly of urine. 'Yuck,' I mutter to myself.

Once in the single cubicle (why do busy cafés always have only one loo right next to the kitchen?) I shakily peel off my maternity leggings and XXL pants. I should have brought a maternity pad in with me but I forgot, obviously. I simply can't retain any thoughts in my head and the idea of having to pull my pants back up, shuffle back outside, root around

28

in the maternity bag and shuffle in again is too much to bear. I'll have to wait until I get home. I sit on the cold seat, lean forward as best as I can and attempt to touch my toes, silently willing the direction of wee away from my stitches as I briefly think about the Ramones woman from the hospital. She's probably out on the piss at the moment, having just shagged her husband and gone back to work, not necessarily in that order. Whereas I still haven't been for a proper poo yet, just little pellets like the kind guinea pigs do.

I'm beginning to think it's never going to happen. I read an article in *That's Life* magazine once about a girl who wanted to get IBS like her friend so she could get time off work, so purposefully didn't go for a poo. For a whole year. By which time she was, I can only imagine, more shit than person. Anyway, her intestines exploded, like literally erupted. She had to have most of them cut out and wear a colostomy bag for the rest of her life. And she lost her job. And her friend thought she was a dick when she found out what she'd done and didn't visit her in hospital because she was so cross.

That's going to be me: ninety per cent shit, sitting around waiting for my stomach to explode.

The toilet walls are covered in vintage posters for club nights, gigs and festivals. It's like looking at an archive of my former life. I scan them to see if there's any I recognise, and there, tucked underneath the window, is an A4 print-out of Glastonbury 1997. Mine and Rachel's year. I still have the ticket in a clip frame on my bedroom wall at Mum's house. I scan through the names, and try to remember us as sixteen-year-olds, carefree and wearing too much tie dye. God, what I'd do to see her now. I could desperately do with a good talking-to, a reality check from my oldest friend. She'd pop out and get me a clean sanitary pad, no questions asked. But she's not going to be here anytime soon.

That's the sacrifice I made, fucking idiot that I am.

'Is there anyone in there?' The hammering on the door drags me from my thoughts.

'Sorry, I'll just be a minute.'

'OK, it's just my three-year-old is going to burst.'

I pull myself off the toilet, carefully dab myself with scratchy paper, and hoik my trousers up. I wash my hands and look at myself in the mirror above the sink. I haven't seen my face this close up in days, and the harsh strip light highlights every new line, every crease, every dark ring under my eyes.

I dry my hands on my leggings and open the door.

'Finally,' The woman rolls her eyes as the little girl pushes past me and hops on the toilet, calling out to her mum, 'Yuck, it smells horrible!'

'I did that,' I reassure the woman. It is only once I'm half-way back to Nick and Lucy that I realise what I meant was I also said yuck, whereas she will have thought I meant I made that revolting smell. Great.

'All good? I was worried. You were gone ages.'

'Yep, everything just takes a bit longer at the moment,' and I tell Nick about the 'yuck' mix up.

He guffaws with laughter and I'm starting to relax into being out a bit more. The waitress brings over our coffees and cakes and I shut my eyes, letting the autumn sun warm my face. This feels good.

Just then a group of builders on their lunch hour sit at the table next to us and all spark up. This would have been me not so long ago, so I can't judge, but I start fretting that Lucy is going to get lung cancer before she's a month old from secondary smoke. The anxiety is creeping in again, twisting and tightening around my chest.

I try to neck the coffee. It's scalding hot, and I'm

30

having to down it in uncomfortable gulps.

'There's no hurry, Em.'

'It's fine, she's just going to need a feed soon, so maybe we should think about getting off?' I wrap my cake in a napkin. 'We can eat these at home, can't we?'

'Seriously, Em.'

'Seriously Em nothing. Come on, let's go,' I bark.

Nick takes a mouthful of his drink. Shakes his head slowly in disapproval and leaves a tenner on the table.

'Sure, let's go then.' He shrugs and we retrace our very slow steps back to the flat.

At home we sit in silence. I feed Lucy while scattering cake crumbs over her head as Nick flicks through last week's Sunday supplement.

I just want to enjoy being a new mum without assessing every situation with a new-found sense of impending doom, without aching all over, or generally feeling like I am two breaths away from a panic attack. That isn't too much to ask, is it?

I suddenly get a pang of loneliness. Nick clearly doesn't feel like this at all. He's tired, yes, and he is a dad now, granted, but nothing has actually changed for him. He'll be going back to work soon, being busy and using his brain and drinking hot cups of tea at leisure. His body looks exactly the same as it did last week or the week before. He can go for a poo whenever he wants without the fear that his bum might rip in two. I want him to understand all this, but I want him to understand instinctively. I don't want to have to explain it.

There are only two people in the world that would really know how I feel and I've already spoken to Mum this morning.

I'm just not quite brave enough to ring the other one up yet.

Chapter Six

Nick is going back to work today. I have no idea how I'm ever going to get Lucy and me out of the flat without help. I'll just have to start getting everything delivered to the flat and when Lucy's older I'll homeschool her. I'll be one of those recluses they make Channel 5 documentaries about.

He's flapping around, rooting through his leather-look man bag that his mum bought him for Christmas last year. I can't think what he needs it for; he only takes his wallet and phone to work.

'How are you feeling about going back?' By this, I obviously mean, 'I'm feeling worried about being left alone.'

'Fine. Fine. It's going to be completely fine.' Does he mean fine for me or him?

'Look on the bright side, at least you'll be able to drink a coffee while it's still warm.'

'At least.' He smiles weakly. I must have looked questioningly at him as he continues, 'I'm just going to miss you guys, that's all,' and he kisses me on the top of my head from behind the sofa. 'And you know things are a bit tricky at work at the mo.' I had actually completely forgotten. My memory only seems to stretch back as far as Lucy's birth. 'I could just do without it and would prefer to be with you girls really,' he sighs. He gets lost in his thoughts for a moment and then as if coming out of a trance, enthuses: 'But you two, you're going to have a great time!'

'As you say, it's going to be completely fine. I'm looking forward to it in fact,' I lie.

'And I can FaceTime you both from work,' he reassures me. 'It's going to be great, Em. I can pick up something nice for tea from Sainsbury's on the way home. You two don't need me hanging around, cramping your style.'

There's a nervousness to his voice. I think he's going to miss us more than he's letting on.

'Look, just ring me anytime, OK? I'll keep my phone by me all day, so it doesn't matter when. Do you know what you're going to do?'

'No plans, but it'll be great. We'll go out. Meet some other mums. That's what being on maternity leave is all about, right?'

'OK, cool, keep in radio contact.' He leans over and kisses Lucy's head and my cheek. 'Em, you might want to think about having a bath today maybe.'

'Have a good day at work, darling,' I mock.

'Right, I'm off then. See you both later!' There's an urgency in his voice but not in his movements as he slopes out of the room.

'What does Daddy mean by tricky?' I ask Lucy. 'What is Daddy's job, sweetheart? What does your daddy do?'

I know it's something to do with recruitment, and training. Or headhunting: he says headhunting a lot like I should know what that means, but in reality, I'm not actually a hundred per cent sure at all what he does every day. He works for a company that's a series of posh names like Allterton, Fawcett and Gladstone. Or Middleton, Buckingham and Norfolk, or something like that. We both went through a 'portfolio career' period of working in a variety of mismatched offices a few years back, panic-buying smart shirts and pencil skirts from Primark in an attempt to match the clothes with the grown-up job descriptions. And somewhere along the way one of the temp jobs became permanent for Nick, but they all sounded so similar, so pressurised, yet so dull that I can't remember which one stuck. I know it's close enough to the council offices where I work to meet for the occasional overpriced panini, but that's about it. I'll google it, make it a side project while I'm on leave: learn what your partner does for a living, step one. And I'll definitely remember to ask him about 'tricky' when he gets home.

He's right about needing a bath though. My maternity bra is so soaked in milk that I'm starting to smell a bit like mature cheddar.

I wait until I hear the front door slam before turning on *Lorraine*. I'll shower in a bit.

The truth is it all feels massively overwhelming. The amount of paraphernalia that accompanies a newborn baby is utterly ridiculous: two clean sleep suits, a stack of nappies, Sudocrem, cotton wool, wet wipes, muslin cloths, scratch mitts, nappy bags, a sun hat, a warm coat, a blanket, a cuddly toy. And for me: breast pads, nipple cream, lip balm, maternity pads, spare pair of massive pants, bottle of water, purse, mobile, house keys.

By the time I've packed everything in the changing bag, Lucy needs another feed, so I'm struggling to see the point in going out at all. I still can't sit down properly and have to precariously balance on one bum cheek. You only realise once your vaginal wall has been cut through how very uncomfortable most seats are, other than your own sofa.

And as for breastfeeding in public? Well you might as well just ask me to sit topless in Costa as I don't think it's ever going to be possible to 'discreetly' feed a baby who prefers to hang painfully off the end of my nipple instead of doing any meaningful feeding, so I can't really see the point in going out. Not at the moment, anyway.

Lorraine is discussing whether women should be encouraged to grow their armpit hair and pubes. This should fill a good hour.

I look around our front room. It's full of bunches of flowers people have sent us, which has been extraordinarily kind, but we only have one vase, so the rest are shoved into pint glasses and plastic milk bottles with the tops cut off. They have all started to wilt and die and the flat carries a distinctive rotting smell. Every surface is also covered in cards. I don't know what to do with them all, or for that matter, who sent a lot of them. I imagine they're from people Mum has been broadcasting Lucy's birth to as she liberally hands out our address during her volunteering shift at the library. There is zero storage in our flat, but is it bad form to chuck out all the new baby cards? And do I have to send cards back to people to thank them for their cards, or is that then starting a never-ending cycle of them having to thank me for my thank you card, and repeat until someone moves or dies?

I should really get out of the flat before I go mental, even if it's just to the shop around the corner. Memorising the daytime TV schedule between 9 a.m. and 6 p.m., which includes lusting after Luke from *One Tree Hill* and watching *Neighbours* twice, is not a productive use of my time. I've got to venture out, to re-engage with the real world, which frankly feels utterly terrifying at the moment.

I will obviously wait until *Lorraine*'s finished and possibly *Frasier*, but then I'm definitely going to start to have a really serious think about going out.

*

Who in their right mind would consider leaving the house when *Twins* is the afternoon film on ITV2? That would be a crime against TV. As a consequence, yesterday didn't go according to plan. I did, at least, wash.

But today is going to be different. The arty cinema down the bottom of the road opens its doors every Tuesday morning to mums with babies under the age of one. They screen all the current films, with the addition of turning the lights up so you can see your child, and cranking up the sound, so you can hear what is being said over the noise of everyone's crying babies.

I have also told Nick that we're going as a fail-safe, so I definitely have to do it or I'll be met with his 'sympathetic' face when he gets in from work, which frankly makes me want to punch him in the nuts.

The walk, which normally takes about fifteen minutes, takes nearly half an hour and I'm panicking that the film has already started. I am using the pram as a kind of Zimmer frame as my vagina still doesn't feel quite right. I think if I take too big a stride I might split right up the middle like an overripe melon.

But as I turn the corner, there is a sprawling metropolis of prams spilling out of the cinema and onto the pavement. Mums standing around with babies strapped to their chests, takeaway coffee in hand. It hadn't really dawned on me that I'd see other actual people.

I recognise one woman, Tania, my old pregnancy yoga teacher. Tania was heavily pregnant when she taught the class, but maintained her size eight figure apart from a compact bump, whereas the rest of us were massive, mottled skin like ham hocks, and sweating even though all we did was lie around on cushions and breathe deeply.

I catch her eye and wave. She waves back so I negotiate

the pram through the sea of buggies to her.

'Emily, hi! So, what did you have?'

'A girl – Lucy.'

'She's beautiful.' She peers into the pram. 'And this,' – she leans forward so I can see the baby strapped to her chest – 'is Falcon.'

Now, nature can be brutal sometimes. Falcon looks like Chairman Mao.

I must have looked surprised, as she explains, 'I was convinced I was going to have a home birth, but Falcon had different ideas. Two weeks after my due date the doctors said that I had to go to hospital to be induced as it was getting dangerous for the baby.' She sighs heavily.

'God, poor you.'

'I know. We live in a tiny flat. Can you imagine being that fucking pregnant and having to negotiate around a birthing pool in your front room every day for a fucking fortnight. And for nothing?'

I don't remember her being so sweary at yoga.

'Anyway, he came out in the end. But his head's a weird shape because he was also breech, not that anyone fucking noticed beforehand. Everyone keeps asking if he's half Chinese. My husband's bloody Cornish.'

'Bloody hell,' I'm thinking of her vagina now. I wonder if this will happen whenever anyone talks about childbirth from now on.

We stand in silence for a bit.

'Can I give you a flyer for my new post-natal yoga class?' She hands me a slip of paper, squeezes my arm a bit too tightly.

'Yes, 'course.' I look at the flyer: it's a picture of a load of heavily pregnant women lying on the floor. 'Is that me?' I ask, pointing at a particularly large, out-of-focus woman

37

wearing my yellow maternity dress in the background.

Tania holds the flyer up closely to her face. 'Maybe. It's hard to tell.'

'When did you take that?'

'I don't know, must have been when you were all sleeping at the end of the class . . . it's hard to get good publicity shots.' She looks around at the gaggle of women. 'I know this is bad form, but I can't be fucked with meeting any new mums. I've had enough of them through work, but it would be good to have someone to meet up with for coffee now and then. Preferably someone who's not going to just lie around whingeing about how they think they're getting varicose veins through pregnancy.' I have a quick flashback to having that very conversation with her in her class and wonder if she is talking about me. 'So if you fancy meeting up, you know, anytime soon, my number is on the flyer.'

'Yes, yes that would be amazing!' I almost squeal with enthusiasm and she raises her eyebrows.

'Wow, OK, look forward to it.' I'm not sure if she's taking the piss or not. 'See you soon,' and she wades through the crowds, pushing her flyers aggressively into women's hands as she goes.

I suddenly feel overwhelmingly self-conscious; looking around, everyone appears to know each other. Pre-Lucy, I'd be totally unphased walking into a crowd of strangers. I'd happily strike up a conversation with anyone, but my world has now shrunk to the size of our front room and the newsagent's two streets away. The longest conversations I've had in the past three weeks have been on the phone with Mum and that's because she's conditioned to love me even if I can't string a sentence together. Her and the Hermes delivery guy who drops off all my middle-of-the-night eBay purchases.

What would Rachel say? She'd probably tell me to pull my socks up and stop being so wet.

'Do you want to go in on my two-for-one voucher?'

The voice belongs to the woman behind me in the queue, who I seem to have inadvertently pushed in front of.

'Yes. Yes!' my voice comes out much higher than usual.

I think she's regretting asking, her eyes darting around nervously to see if there's anyone else who might be interested. But I only want to sit next to her, not go for dinner. Bloody hell, what's happening to me, why can't I just play it cool?

This is a pinnacle moment for me: unbeknownst to the woman with the coupons, this is my first official 'meeting a new mum' encounter. Her daughter, Polly, is two weeks older than Lucy and was born in the same hospital. The film starts but we're too busy to notice, talking about how brilliant Infacol is for wind; how her baby has a high palate so breastfeeding leaves her nipple looking like a lipstick; the benefits of baby massage, and how quickly you forget about going to work. Eventually she also tells me her name is Helen.

'What do you do, you know, in real life?' I ask and she looks at me blankly.

'You know, your job before Polly.'

'Oh, right, yes. I kind of shut down that bit of my brain when I had her. I worked in a bank.'

I wish I hadn't asked.

'And you?'

'I work in Arts Education for the council and write a bit for theatre.' We look at each other, uncomfortably scrabbling about for things to say. I hope she doesn't ask about the writing bit. Aspiring playwright, with the emphasis on aspiring, would probably be more accurate.

Then she asks, 'Don't think me rude but did you have an episiotomy?'

'Yes, yes,' I sigh with relief, 'you?' And we are chatting away like old friends again.

The film ends and we exchange numbers. Helen looks kind of familiar and I wonder if we've met before, but then I don't trust my brain to recall anything useful. On top of that I don't want her to think I'm some kind of weird stalker. The chances are it's because she looks like someone from *Homes Under the Hammer*. I once accosted someone in Brighton during my second year of university, who I was convinced I knew. I was sure we must have been on a night out together as she looked so familiar. She was hugely patient as I wittered on about what I'd been doing during my summer holidays. I kissed her and gave her a big hug and it was only when I'd got around the corner that it dawned on me that I didn't know her at all. She was Anna the Nun, the previous year's *Big Brother* winner so I did in fact know her face, but only because I'd been watching her sleep on telly for hours on end.

It's all going brilliantly with my new friend. I almost ruin it a bit by giving her a tight hug while she has Polly strapped to her in the sling. But it's a start.

I wonder how soon I can text her without her realising how desperate I am?

Part Two

'I'll be back in my old Levi's before you know it.'

Chapter Seven

Disaster has struck. I've worn my maternity jeans so much that the crotch has worn through. To be honest, I had completely unrealistic expectations of how quickly I'd get back into my pre-pregnancy clothes after having Lucy. I was so convinced that I'd be trotting out in a pair of size twelve jeans within weeks of having her that I ruthlessly bagged up all my maternity clothes bar one pair of trousers and sent them up north to someone Mum knows through the library, virtually before I'd unpacked my hospital bag. I spent a good part of my last trimester buying unrealistically titchy, trendy clothes off eBay, having visions of meeting friends for coffee looking all shiny, straightened hair and skinny jeans.

The reality, of course, is that I had a baby just over a month ago and my body is still unrecognisable. My boobs fluctuate from being Lolo Ferrari-size to resembling empty rubber gloves, depending on where we are in the feeding cycle. I can squeeze my stomach into a doughnut and I have stretch marks that no amount of Bio Oil is ever going to fix. I tried on a pair of my old jeans and managed, with a lot of brute strength, to pull them halfway up my thighs before giving up and having to seek assistance to get them off again.

The thing is, when I was pregnant, everyone was like, 'Wow, you're just bump, aren't you?' and 'You don't look like you've put on any weight other than the baby', etc.,

etc. Now, I had in fact put on the best part of three and a half stone through pregnancy and, while I'm no mathematician, I think if that was all baby, then Lucy would be a child worthy of the *Guinness Book of Records*. So, the maternity jeans have become a wardrobe staple, until this afternoon when I bent down too enthusiastically to pick up the Sudocrem from under the sofa and heard the rip.

I am loath to buy any new clothes that are bigger than my pre-baby size but can't go around in a pair of crotchless trousers, so I've made a mercy dash into town. By dash, I mean it has taken us over an hour to leave the flat, and forty minutes to get on a bus because the first two wouldn't let us on as they were already carrying three buggies.

I'm in the changing room with the pram wedged halfway in so all the other customers can see me getting changed.

'Excuse me!' I shout for the shop assistant. 'Sorry, these ones don't fit either, could you get me the next size up?' This is the fourth time she has had to bring me larger and larger sizes of various different ninety per cent elastic jeggings.

She reluctantly shoves another pair through the curtain. I manage with some effort to squeeze myself into this pair, three sizes bigger than I normally wear. I look horrendous. As I stare at the podgy, soft version of myself in the mirror, Lucy starts to stir. She stretches with a shudder in the pram and I lock eyes with her for what feels like an eternity. It's amazing how long a baby can stare without blinking.

I take one last look at my battle-scarred body in the full-length mirror in my size sixteen jeggings, and ask the shop assistant if I can pay for them at the till so I can wear them out.

I'm desperate to shed the body insecurities I wear like armour, the poisonous little voice in my head that tells me I would be so much happier if I was slimmer. That's not going to happen overnight: I know that. But I've been listening to that voice for the best part of twenty years so she's not going to shut up just because I tell her to now. For Lucy's sake, I can at least try to ignore her from time to time.

Nick rings as Lucy and I are heading for the bus. Town has suddenly got busier and I realise it's 5 p.m. – normal people are leaving work for the day.

'How are you girls doing?'

'Good, just got myself some massive leggings in town.'

'You're in town? Did you get the bus?'

'Yep, 'course.' I'm playing this casually but this is a big deal. I need to give Nick a blow-by-blow account of the whole trip when he gets home, so I don't want to tell him too much about it now, although there is really very little more to tell. We got on a bus. We got off a bus. I bought some jeggings. Nick rang me. But still, this is huge progress.

'Well done, Em.' I can hear him chewing down the phone.

'What are you eating?'

'Oh, just club sandwich from the deli.'

'That's a late lunch, Nick.'

'Early tea actually . . . Look, I'm going to have to stay late at work, I shouldn't be too long but I've just got to clear my desk before coming home.'

'But what about Lucy?'

'Obviously I'd prefer to be heading home, but this is my second week back, no one's picked up any of my leads so I've got to get on top of everything.'

'Do you know when you'll be home?' The thought of Lucy and me coming into the same empty flat we left makes my heart sink a bit.

'I'll just get back as soon as I can, OK? This is a total ball-ache for me, I'd much rather be with you than here,

45

but I've got to put the hours in at the moment.'

I'm about to say something really clever in response that would not only remind Nick of how much he loves me and misses us both, but would propel him into throwing away the rest of his club sandwich, ordering a posh takeaway and jumping in a taxi home, when I spot Helen outside Card Factory. It's been three unanswered texts and two straight-to-voicemail phone calls since I met her at the cinema. Nick had suggested that maybe she'd given me the wrong number, but I am undeterred. We definitely hit it off, I know we did, and in lieu of not meeting hoards of mums with children of a similar age, I am keen to pursue her in a non-creepy way.

'OK, fine, I've got to go. I've just seen Helen.'

'Who?'

'Helen.'

'Who's Helen?'

'Never mind. See you at home.'

'Bye, give Lucy a kiss from me.'

'Will do,' and I frantically hang up and shout, 'HELEN! HELEN!'

She doesn't react. Shit, maybe that's not even her name. I push Lucy over the road and catch up with her before she disappears inside the shop. Up close she looks like shit. Now, I know I'm not exactly Kate Middleton, but all Helen's buttons are done up wrong on her blouse, her hair looks like it could do with a good brush and she's got toothpaste or Sudocrem smeared all over her left cheek.

She looks at me blankly.

'It's Emily. From the cinema.'

'Shit. Of course. I'm so sorry I haven't responded to any of your messages.'

I knew she'd given me the right number. In your face, Nick.

'I'm just so tired.' It's like she's looking through me instead of at me. 'Polly doesn't sleep. Ever.' She zones out for a second like she's lost her train of thought.

'There's a reason they use sleep deprivation as a form of torture. Why didn't anyone mention this beforehand? I feel like the walking dead.'

'I know. I knew it would be knackering, but this is something else.'

'It's good to see you though, have you been shopping?' I nod at her bag, desperate to continue the conversation, to make her my friend.

'Oh, this . . .' She shakes the bag. 'Polly's such a hungry baby, I just can't make enough milk. I'm trying her on formula but she doesn't like any of the bottles. I've just bought a load more.' She opens her Boots bag to reveal seven or eight different varieties. 'It's costing me a fortune.'

At which point she drops her head in defeat and starts to cry, nose-dripping tears. I steer her out of the Card Factory doorway and into an Italian coffee shop.

'The doctor wants to put me on anti depressants, but I've said to him, I don't need tablets, I just need a fucking good night's sleep.' I'm relieved to hear her swear. She didn't strike me as a swearer at the cinema.

I sit her down in a window seat. 'Right, what do you want to drink?' I take control.

'Oh, just a strong black coffee. Thank you,' she sniffs.

I order and by the time I sit down with the drinks, she's texting and looking calmer.

'Sorry about that, I don't normally fall to pieces in the street.'

'It's completely fine, a relief actually.'

She raises a questioning eyebrow at me.

'I mean you just seemed so together at the cinema, it's

good that . . .' Oh, fuck me, good that what? This isn't how I meant for the conversation to go.

'I should be getting Polly back in a minute.' She smiles politely at me.

'Shit, I just mean it's not as easy as I thought it was going to be, and it makes me feel slightly less shit to see someone else thinking the same.' I wipe my forehead; why am I always sweating these days? I don't think I used to be a sweaty person.

Helen takes a thoughtful sip of her coffee and I briefly wonder if I should ask her for the £2.60 as that's a third of my £7.50-a-day budget, but then think better of it.

'I know what you mean,' she sighs and takes another gulp of her drink. 'I started an NCT group before Polly was born but everyone seemed to already know what they were doing and instead of it reassuring me, I found it a bit intimidating, so I only went to one session.'

'Me too! Well we signed up to it, but then Nick said we don't really have the time to see our proper mates so why would we sign up to something where we've got to go to the pub with a bunch of strangers? Which made sense at the time. I cancelled the course but they'd only give us half the money back, so I spent fifty quid to make a point that I already have enough mates. But then none of them have kids so no one's really been in touch much since Lucy was born as people don't seem to know how to act with me now I've got a baby.' She's nodding in agreement so I venture on with a deep breath: 'I don't know whether it's OK to say this as I should feel massively lucky that Lucy's here and healthy and everything, but so far I have, a lot of the time, just felt . . .' just say it Emily '. . . a bit lonely.' Lucy's sleeping in the pram and I immediately feel guilty and look out the window, thinking I probably would have had more chance of being friends with Helen if I hadn't bumped into her today and just continued with my barrage of unanswered texts and calls.

'I know what you mean. That was my husband Chris texting a minute ago. He works on an oil rig so is home for a few weeks then offshore again. He'd been around for the lead-up to Polly's birth and then the first couple of weeks of her life, but then went back to work. I've been telling him everything's going brilliantly' – I think about the conversation I had with Nick as he left for work on the first day – 'but the reality is I have no idea what day it is. I speak to him on the phone and tell him everything's fine, but the flat is a wreck. I'm a wreck. I don't even think Polly likes me and my mum lives in the bloody Costa Del Sol.' She lets out a little sob laugh.

She rummages around in her handbag and pulls out a Twix, rips it open and offers half to me, which I gratefully accept. I'm impressed how she eats hers in two big mouthfuls.

'I just need some structure. Anything. My day is pretty much shaped around *One Tree Hill*.'

Bingo! I knew we had stuff in common. We discuss whether Luke or Nathan is hotter, and I watch how she, without pausing for breath, cradles Polly in one arm, hoiks up her top, pulls out her boob and guides it professionally into Polly's mouth, who holds it with both hands like an old man downing a pint, and latches on and starts suckling.

I'm not sure if it's acceptable to feel massive jealousy towards a woman who may or may not be suffering from post-natal depression, but I would give literally anything to get Lucy to feed like that.

The health visitor came round yesterday and told me that Lucy needs to be gaining more weight. She said it in a way that suggested I'd been withholding food, or putting her on a diet, but I genuinely don't know what to do. It's so unbelievably painful. My nipples are covered in small blisters and Lucy only seems to want to feed from the right breast. I don't think she's had a decent meal in her whole little life, which probably accounts for her being up most of the night. She's absolutely famished.

Lucy is stirring so I take her out of the pram and attempt to feed her. Helen looks over at me sitting with my tits out, my shoulders hunched up to my ears in pain and Lucy nibbling on the end of my blisters.

'Fucking hell. Are you OK?'

'Yes,' I wince. 'Doing fine.'

'That looks excruciating. Have you tried her in a different position?'

I know she's trying to be helpful, but this kind of obvious advice from a woman whose baby is making audible gulping noises is not constructive. As if reading my thoughts she changes tack. 'There's a breastfeeding support group in the community centre round the corner from my house on a Tuesday morning. They're meant to be really good.'

'I don't need a support group, I just need her to feed properly.'

'I know, I know, I don't think it's like therapy. It's more practical stuff. That looks so sore.' She leans in to get a good look at my boobs and sucks in her breath.

'Well maybe I'll give it a go next Tuesday. I'm OK though, it's no big deal.'

Helen doesn't look convinced.

Although that sounds like the worst possible way to spend a morning, I feel I might have to give it a try before either a) Lucy starves to death or b) my tits fall off, whichever comes first.

'OK, I'll try it.'

'Brilliant, then you can come round to mine for a coffee afterwards.'

I'm air-punching inside but using every inch of my theatre degree to play it cool on the outside. Don't fuck it up now, Emily. 'Yep, sounds good. Do you have to rush off now or do you fancy another coffee?'

'That sounds great.' Result. 'Another Americano would be fab, thanks so much.' Helen smiles gratefully and I realise I'm getting these ones as well. That's tomorrow's budget blown then, but on the plus side I have definitely made a new friend and I've got an invite to her house. That's surely worth a fiver of anyone's child benefit.

Chapter Eight

Mum and Dad are on their way. They'd come all the way down from Lincolnshire when Lucy was first born but only long enough for a hug with their only grandchild and a cup of tea. This time they're staying at the Travelodge around the corner so they're calling it their 'official visit' like royalty. Dad loves a good Travelodge, as 'you always know what you're getting'. This passion for hotel continuity is shared by Nick. An all-time relationship low was looking at the Travelodge map with him while we were staying at one in Peterborough and Nick enthusiastically ticking off all those we'd been to.

Mum has been regularly texting me updates of their driving progress.

'ON M1. BUSY.'

'STOPPED AT CAMBRIDGE SERVICES. DAD'S OR-DERED A BIG MAC. I'M JUST HAVING A COFFEE.'

'ON M23. RADIO SAYS THERE'S AN ACCIDENT BUT IT MUST HAVE CLEARED UP.'

'STUCK IN TRAFFIC. THERE IS AN ACCIDENT.'

'SAT NAV SAYS 45 MINUTES AWAY. DAD THINKS NEARER 1 HOUR.'

How can she manage to press my buttons when all she's done is send a shit-load of texts in caps lock?

'AT TRAVELODGE. DAD'S HAVING A SHOWER AS HE'S SWEATY FROM THE DRIVE THEN WE'LL HEAD UP TO YOU.'

Nick sits on the sofa with Lucy asleep on his chest.

'You don't have to keep tidying.'

'I'm not!'

'And you don't have to be shitty with me, it's just your mum and dad coming.'

'I know it's just Mum and Dad, but I can still make the flat nice, can't I?'

He rolls his eyes at me and I immediately dislike him. Not only did I want the flat to look clean, but I also wanted us to be a team and now I wish he'd gone to watch whatever football match he was banging on about this morning instead of sitting on the sofa like a big judgey idiot. I wouldn't mind if he helped a bit, but he doesn't. I want Mum to think that I'm coping, that we're all coping as a family. Today isn't going to plan so far. Not at all.

On top of that my boobs feel like they're going to fall clean off. I need to go to the boob group Helen told me about but I don't think I can bear anyone else seeing them. They really do look a state.

I retrieve the Lansinoh from the bathroom cabinet and cautiously apply it to both nipples, then notice that Nick has made his mark like a tom cat: there's a strong smell of urine and skid marks in the loo.

'NICK, FOR FUCK'S SAKE, WHY CAN'T YOU JUST CLEAN UP AFTER YOURSELF?' I bellow, waking Lucy.

'NICE ONE, EM. WHY DO YOU ALWAYS HAVE TO MAKE A MASSIVE DEAL ABOUT EVERYTHING?' he shouts back over Lucy's cries.

'Knock, knock, the front door was open.' They've arrived. Mum has a bunch of flowers in one hand and a Waitrose bag in the other. I'm stood in the bathroom with the door wide open, one cream-covered breast out, clutching the toilet brush like a weapon.

'Should we come back later?' Dad asks, not quite sure where to look.

'No. Just go through. I'll be with you in a minute,' I say too sharply, then close the bathroom door, sit on the loo and have a quick weep.

Dad is looking out onto the garden with his hands on his hips. 'You really need to trim that bush, Nick, or it'll bolt. I can do it while I'm here if you have some secateurs?'

Nick looks at him blankly.

'Never mind, I've got a pair in the boot just in case.'

This is probably the most Dad will say during the whole visit.

Mum has Lucy in the crook of her arm; Lucy is clutching her finger and cooing. 'She's grown so much, Emily. She's not a newborn anymore, is she?' She doesn't look up from Lucy when talking; it's amazing how hypnotic a baby can be. 'And how are you? How are your stitches?'

Dad's shoulders shoot up to his ears; he's in denial that I've ever had sex, let alone have an actual vagina that I squeezed Lucy out of, poor man.

'Fine, fine. It's all fine,' I say, uncomfortably perching on the sofa next to Nick.

'And the feeding, how's that going?'

Why can't she ask me about something that is actually going well, like how many Twirls I can consume in a day, or how good I've got at last-minute eBay purchases?

'That's good too, just . . . you know, everything's going well.'

Nick raises his eyebrows at me. I just find it easier to speak to Mum on the phone sometimes rather than face to face, that's all.

'And is that bindweed you've got growing at the bottom

of the garden, Nick?' Clearly this is much safer territory for Dad than talk of my intimate parts.

'I'm not sure.'

'It's evil, Nick. It'll strangle all your other plants; literally squeeze the life out of them. You need to get rid of it but it's a bugger. You should have told me, Emily, I would have brought some weedkiller down with me.'

They're just trying to help, they're just trying to help, I repeat the mantra in my head.

'Rachel's mum popped into the library the other day, she gave me a little present to bring down from Rachel. I think it's a Babygro from the feel of it.'

My skin prickles at the mention of her name.

'Spoiler alert, Jennifer,' Nick chuckles, breaking the increasing atmosphere.

'Spoiler what, Nick? You should send her a note to let her know it's arrived though, Emily, I'd hate people to think I didn't pass it on.'

'Alright, Mum. I will do, let's change the subject.'

'Well, she'd have gone to a lot of trouble to get it and then for her mum to bring it to the library, it's not necessarily on her route.'

'I said I will and I will, OK?'

'I really don't know why you're always so funny about her, Emily. You used to be such good friends growing up.'

'Give it a rest, Mum, will you?' I snap. God, I'm starting to sound like my fourteen-year-old self. What's happening to me?

'I think she's hungry, Emily, she's trying to latch on to my finger,' Mum says dispiritedly.

I know I've upset her but she should, after all these years, know better. Even Dad doesn't bring it up now, and he has the emotional intelligence of a piece of paper.

Mum passes Emily over and then hovers. I don't want to get my boob out because I don't want her to see how sore it is and I don't want her to say anything. I'm feeling all out of sorts and emotional even though there's no real reason to feel like this. That makes it a million times worse, that I might just cry, just start any second and not know how to stop and then Mum would think it's because she mentioned Rachel. Or worse, she would think that it's a sign that I'm definitely not coping when, actually I definitely am coping. I'm coping just fine. I really am.

She finally drifts into the kitchenette to put the kettle on.

'Why don't you tell her you're struggling?' Nick whispers.

'Because I'm not,' I hiss.

'Got any biscuits to go with a cuppa?' Dad sits down in the armchair, which has quickly become 'his' chair.

'I bought some from Waitrose at Cambridge services,' Mum answers, 'and I got a few bits I've put in the freezer for you both.'

'You didn't have to.'

'Well we don't want to eat you out of house and home.' She leans over to hug me from behind. 'My goodness, that looks sore.'

'It's fine, I told you I'm fine.'

'Richard, why don't you take Nick out for a pint and I can put something on for tea?'

'They're showing the match in the Jolly Brewer if you fancy it?' Nick can't contain his excitement.

Dad doesn't need any encouragement and they're out of the door in less than a minute.

Mum sits down next to me.

'I don't want to talk about it.'

'You don't have to,' Mum replies and simply puts her arm around me as I painfully feed Lucy. We sit like that for an age. I hadn't even realised that tears were streaming down my cheeks.

'I'm so proud of you,' Mum whispers and for the first time since Lucy was born, I feel myself relaxing. She strokes my hair like she did when I was a child and I close my eyes and breathe in the smell of Oil of Olay. My shoulders slowly lose their tension and I start to drift off to sleep.

I wake in a panic. Where's Lucy? Did I drop her? Did Nick and Dad leave the front door open and someone's come in and pinched her? Then I hear Mum quietly singing 'Show me the way to go home', from our bedroom.

'Mum, is she OK?'

'She's an absolute dream is what she is,' Mum says as she walks back in, bobbing Lucy on her shoulder. She's changed her clothes into something new. 'I hope you don't mind, I brought her a few bits and wanted to see what she looked like in them. And Dawn, you know Dawn, she volunteers with me at the library? Anyway, she knitted the hat and booties.' I swear I've never met Dawn before in my life. 'Your phone's been buzzing, but I didn't want to mess around with it.' She passes it to me.

Helen Cinema: Fancy a coffee soon, my treat?
Me: Yes. Would love to, anytime. My social calendar is quite flexible.

The dots appear, she's typing. Then she's not typing. Then nothing. I read and reread what I've written to her. I'm obviously trying too hard. I should have given it a few minutes. Fuck.

Helen Cinema: Sorry. Polly puked on me. Reflux. How's about tomorrow?

'Who's that you're text-messaging?' Mum asks. Is it wrong that I find it annoying that she has to say everything in full? Text messaging. Mobile phones. Boots the Pharmacy.

'Just a friend.'

'Ooh, you've got a new friend? Good for you, love.'

Me: Sounds fab. Just tell me when and where. X

'I'm meeting her tomorrow, Mum, do you mind?'

'Of course not. I'd love to meet your new friend, what's she called?'

No. Absolutely not. Categorically no. I am not taking my own mum on my second mum date with Helen. That's absolutely not what's going to happen.

Helen is already sitting down feeding Polly in the window seat of the Italian café we'd hung out in before when we arrive. I wave at her and try and mouth 'sorry', gesticulating towards Mum.

'What?' she shouts.

'Never mind, do you want a drink or are you OK?'

She peers in her cup and says, 'Yes, a skinny latte, please. Mix it up a bit!'

'What do you want, Mum?'

'Ooh, a cappuccino with chocolate sprinkles please, love, that's very kind of you,' and she pulls up the seat next to Helen. 'I can mind Lucy, Emily.'

I begrudgingly head up to the counter, hearing Mum and Helen laugh unselfconsciously about something.

As I come back with the drinks on a tray I catch the end of Mum's sentence: '. . . so we were delighted when Emily brought Nick back instead.'

'What are you two talking about?'

'Oh, I was just telling Helen about that awful boyfriend you used to have at school with the dreadlocks.'

'Why are you talking about that?'

'I don't know really' – Mum briefly touches Helen's arm – 'can you remember?'

'I think it was because I was talking about going through IVF for Polly, and I'd mentioned that the consultant had dreadlocks and then you said—'

'That's right, and then I said you used to have a boyfriend with dreadlocks.'

I pull up an extra chair and sit down with a louder-than-anticipated huff. I've only been gone long enough to buy three bloody coffees (which no one has offered me any money for I might add) and they're chatting like old friends, finding out brand-new information about each other. Helen had IVF? How come she didn't tell me about that before she told my mum?

'What's happened to him now?'

'Who?'

'The old boyfriend with the dreadlocks?' Helen enquires.

'Ryan? Oh, God knows, he either went on to be a chef or he's dead in a ditch, it could have gone either way.' This is meant to be a joke, but Helen pulls an 'awkward' face at Mum.

'Ryan. Yes that was his name. And then you met Nick in Thailand though, didn't you, thank goodness,' Mum chips in. 'It was just after you'd finished university, wasn't it? She went with some friends she was living with,' Mum explains, 'quite a motley crew!'

'Oh that sounds fantastic, Chris and I went there for our honeymoon, whereabouts did you go?'

'Mainly Koh Phangan, but we travelled about a bit.'

'Oh, lovely. So how did you meet Nick?'

'You met him at a party, didn't you, Emily?'

'Yes. A full moon party.'

'Sounds so romantic,' Mum adds.

It wasn't. We were both high as kites on magic mushroom pancakes and bumped into each other on the beach. Nick spilt his bang lassi all down my top so chivalrously lent me the T-shirt he was wearing, but by the time the sun came up he'd forgotten and accused me of stealing it from him. We had a huge row and I thought he was a massive dick. But over the course of the subsequent 24-hour drinking session he slowly grew on me, his Midlands and my Northern sense of humour complementing each other as we ripped the piss out of each other unmercifully. Before I knew it, we were travelling together to another island but this time as a couple. I came back to Brighton to get a job, and several weeks later Nick returned to England and showed up unexpectedly at my door, big grin on his gorgeous face, demanding his T-shirt back. He was the most beautiful visitor I'd ever received, with his wild curly hair and suntanned body. Fast-forward eleven years and here we were with a mortgage and a new baby.

'What about you though, Helen?' Mum asks. 'How did you meet your husband?'

'Oh, I met him online.'

This is so far out of Mum's comfort zone she doesn't know how to respond.

'And how long have you been together?' I take up the questions.

'On and off for about ten years, I'd say.'

This whole meeting is underlined with awkwardness. I felt like we were making great progress as friends over our last coffee date but the dynamic seems all wrong now. I'm not sure whether it's because Mum's here or because we genuinely have no common ground other than a mild connection of sorts from both having our vaginas ripped open then stitched up again. The whole conversation has turned into a not very interesting episode of *This is Your Life*. I quietly blame Mum.

Mum has just asked Helen if Polly is 'short for something' and I know where this conversation is going. Mum has a real chip on her shoulder when it comes to abbreviating names without the full name being registered on the birth certificate. I know what she's going to say next: it will be something about not giving a child the 'right to choose' when they're an adult. This is almost certainly going to be the death of my new friendship, but just then I spot Tania stomping past with Falcon strapped to her. I bang on the window, startling Polly and making her cry. Tania sees me, bows with her hands together in prayer pose and comes in to join us.

'Am I relieved to see you! I've just had the yoga session from hell. Spiral couldn't look after Falcon so I had to bring him with me and he's basically put all my pregnant clients off having their own babies now, what with his screaming and shitting.' She looks at Mum and offers a hand. 'Sorry, I'm Tania.'

'I'm Emily's mum, Jennifer.'

'Lovely to meet you, Jennifer.' She offers her hand to Helen. 'And . . .?'

'Helen,' and then pointing to her still-feeding baby, 'and Polly. Short for Pollyanna, after my grandma.' Mum appreciatively squeezes her arm as Helen winks at me. She tells me later this is utter bollocks – that's the kind of shit I would pull to shut my mum up, I knew we were destined to be friends!

'Helen. Polly. Great to meet you both too.' She waves to

get the attention of one of the staff and shouts, 'Can you bring me a double espresso?' She gives them a double thumbs up and turns back round to face us. I think I need to be more Tania in my approach to life.

'So. It's so nice that you go out with your mum, Emily. I can't remember the last time I saw my mum, let alone had a coffee with her.'

'That's a shame,' Mum consoles.

'No, not really, she's a total nightmare. Are people eating here or are you just having a coffee?'

'Just coffee, I was thinking.' If I have something to eat then that's the budget gone for the whole month at this rate.

'I could eat.' Helen shrugs.

'I'm quite peckish,' Mum pipes up. 'What about we eat, Emily; my treat?'

'OK, sounds fab, Mum.' At last, someone else is paying.

'Should I get us all a bottle of something nice to accompany it, what do you think?' Mum's suggestion is greeted with a round of applause.

Four calzones and two bottles of Prosecco later and we all stumble out of the café with our babies.

I have, in that time, found out that Helen had two ectopic pregnancies before her course of IVF, and so Polly is seen very much as the miracle baby. Even the doctors were convinced it would never happen.

Tania was christened Arabella and her parents own a very successful hotel chain. She'd been brought up in absolute wealth but met Spiral and decided to turn her back on her privilege and live a simple life with a man with a tattoo on his head, much to her parents' huge disappointment.

And the most shocking discovery of all, that Mum and Dad still have sex regularly. As the subject of when to have sex after birth came up, Mum chipped in with, 'Get back in the saddle, girls,' as she drained then refilled her champagne flute: 'Sex only gets better as you get older, take me and your dad, for example.' Tania and Helen roared with laughter.

'Mum!' I squealed with embarrassment.

'Well how do you think you were made, Emily Jones?' and the table fell about laughing again.

As the cold air hits us I feel every one of the three glasses of fizz going to my head and it's wonderful.

Tania and Helen kiss both me and Mum and thank us for a lovely afternoon.

'You've got some nice friends there, Emily.' Mum links arms with me as we trundle along with Lucy. 'I'm pleased I got to meet them before your dad and I head off.'

'Thanks, Mum.'

'And thank you for inviting me along, I don't know the last time I had so much fun.'

I hadn't meant to invite her at all, but now I'm so very pleased she came.

Chapter Nine

The breastfeeding support group is a bit like AA for boobs. Based in an old community hall, there is a welcoming circle of colourful plastic children's chairs in the centre of the room. Twenty or so women huddle round in little groups talking quietly.

I make my way to the snacks table and help myself to an instant coffee and a Rich Tea biscuit, popping 50p in the suggestion box. I step aside to let another woman fill her cup from the urn. She smiles sympathetically at me as she puts a two-pound coin in the box.

'Is that your little treasure?' She nods towards Lucy, who is fast asleep in the pram I'm clutching like a security blanket.

'Yes, yes, this is Lucy.'

'They're so precious, aren't they, when they're sleeping?' She's talking in a creepy meditative voice. I hope she's not one of the boob nurses.

'Yes, a nightmare when they're awake though, hey?' I snort. I wish I could play it cooler when nervous. 'Are you here for . . .?' I leave the question open-ended for her to finish but she simply raises her eyebrows. 'For your boobs?'

She dunks her green tea bag in the hot water and puts it in a bowl with the other used tea bags. 'Yes, of sorts. Horatio is a very hungry baby, so I'm combination feeding. I want to check that I'm doing the best by him. He's feeding so much, the weight is just falling off me, literally slipping off me like melting butter.'

I suddenly feel my full eleven stone bursting out of my new jeans next to her svelte size eight. I'm not sure I've come to the right place, to be honest. She maintains eye contact so I comment, 'What an unusual name. I went to university with a boy called Horatio.'

'Oh, really?'

'Yes. He was a complete dick, now I think about it but—'

'Can everyone take a seat, please!' a voice calls out. Thank fuck. Saved by the bell. Horatio's mum pushes her pram to the furthest point away from me and sits down.

Carol and Karen are the breastfeeding specialists. They make their way around to talk to each person individually about the challenges we're facing. Nothing's a problem. Everything's a challenge.

'OK. Do you want to get her out so that we can have a look at her latch?' Karen asks me once I've briefed her on the situation.

'Umm, OK. Yes of course.' I don't. Lucy is asleep in the pram so I'm loath to wake her, but the alternative of us having to go through another eye-wateringly painful feed is too much.

The moment I get her out, she lets out a loud wail. Karen is standing behind me and swoops in to look in her mouth.

'Aha,' she says in a Poirot-esque voice and raises her finger to fully emphasise her discovery. 'She's got thrush.'

The two women either side of me lean in to have a look and I want to cover her mouth with my hand. How do you get thrush in your mouth anyway? The only time I've ever had thrush was from having sex with Nick in a hot tent after a day on the beers. It was so itchy the next day that I wanted

65

to climb inside my own vagina and scratch it. Surely this isn't what we're talking about here, ladies?

'Sorry? She's got what?'

'Do you feel sharp pains in your breasts when you feed?'

'Well, yes.'

'Do they tingle uncomfortably when your milk comes in?'

'A bit.' I shrug.

'A bit?' she questions.

'Yes, every time. Is that not how it's meant to feel?'

She smiles at me reassuringly. 'No, love. No, it's not. I think you're just passing thrush between the two of you, and you both need antibiotics to clear it up.'

I'm so impressed by her lightning-quick diagnosis that in a flash I unbutton my shirt and whip out both blister-encrusted breasts.

'And there's these.' I point to my nipples. 'They're pretty painful too, is that anything to do with the thrush?' I've lost all dignity now. I'm sure I just saw Horatio's mum disapprovingly shake her head in my direction but that's probably because I've stolen her weight-loss-story limelight.

There is a collective intake of breath from the circle of boobs.

'Now that looks painful.' Karen winces. 'Have you shown your doctor?'

Another mum from the circle gets up to have a closer look.

'That looks really sore,' she remarks. 'Have you tried bottle feeding instead?'

'Lucy would prefer to live on thin air than take a bottle.'

Following her lead, a second mum gets up to take a closer look. 'Ah, my son's like that. He's attached to me twenty-four-seven, it's a nightmare. I don't get a moment to myself, not even when he's sleeping.'

'It's hard, isn't it?' I agree.

Another mum gets up and comes over. 'You're so brave to continue, it must be so uncomfortable.'

'It's the challenge with the first child, isn't it?' says another mum who's joined the growing crowd. 'It's all about the pregnancy or birth. No one tells you about this bit.'

'Exactly! Where's the books about never having sex again and feeling like your tits are going to fall off?' I point my finger at my chest in emphasis and the woman all nod in agreement with me. I now have a semi-circle of new mums crowding around me to take a look at my breasts and offer their advice.

Then from the back of the group a woman shouts over the din, 'He's tongue-tied.'

The women part like the Red Sea to let her through, and she leans in to have a proper inspection of my nipples. 'Yep. My sister-in-law's baby was and her nipples went that weird shape like yours have as well. It means your baby can't open his mouth wide enough to get the nipple in so he's—'

'She.'

'Sorry, she's hanging off the end of your nipple instead of feeding properly.'

Karen is nodding in agreement. 'I think she could be right. You're going to do me out of a job, Ruth!'

Ruth shrugs off the compliment but she's glowing and her neck has gone all blotchy. The women all return to their seats and I put my boobs away.

'You should talk to your doctor who can make a referral to the hospital to look at Lucy's tongue.' Karen squeezes my shoulders.

'Thank you,' I whisper. I am overcome with relief. As I clip my bra back on I realise I've spent the majority of the meeting topless and hope I never have to see any of these women ever again.

Karen starts packing away the biscuits and rinsing the cups to signify the end of the session, and I pack up my things, put Lucy into the pram and push her out of the dimly lit hall into the bright, crisp morning. The air feels cold and refreshing and I make myself take a deep, calming breath. I'm moving things along, I'm taking responsibility. I quietly congratulate myself for being so adult.

I ring the bell twice and knock on the door and the window. I check and recheck the text message. This is definitely Helen's address unless she texted it to me incorrectly.

'Well she did say to come over, didn't she, Lucy? Shall we try her again? Just once more and then we'll go home?' My hand is poised to knock again when the door swings open.

'Emily!' Helen greets me enthusiastically. She is looking dishevelled again, her hair looks like it needs a brush and her buttons are done up wrong, poor woman. She's obviously having a bad day and really does need me in her life, I think.

'I thought you'd forgotten.' I take the brakes off the pram, ready to drag it inside.

'Sorry, Emily, it's just . . .'

'Who is it?' a man's voice bellows from inside.

'My new friend,' she calls back. 'Chris,' she says by way of explanation, 'my husband, he came back unexpectedly to surprise us.'

A gorgeous man of at least 6′4″ with blonde hair that's in need of a cut appears behind her, curling his arms around her waist. He's topless and tanned.

'Hello, Helen's new friend!' He grins, offering me a hand to shake. He has a gentle Liverpudlian accent.

'Emily, I'm Emily, and this is Lucy.' My cheeks burn

with embarrassment as I realise I'm staring at his naked, toned chest.

'Well, absolutely wonderful to meet you both.'

We all stare at each other for a minute until the slow-motion train hits me. I've interrupted them shagging. It hadn't occurred to me that anyone in their right mind would be having sex after having a baby, and in the afternoon at that. I momentarily imagine them having sex and then try to shake off the image.

'Right, OK, well lovely to see you,' I mumble, 'and great to meet you, Chris. Let's hang out soon, Helen.'

'That would be great. I'll text you,' she replies. As if remembering when closing the door, she adds, 'Oh, how did the group go?'

'Brilliant! It was fantastic! I got my tits out in front of everyone. That wasn't the fantastic bit, obviously. But, you know, other than that I think it went really well,' I ramble. 'Right, then. I'd better get off and leave you guys to do it.' I fluster. 'I mean to it. Bye, then.'

Fuck. Someone kill me now.

'I'd be delighted if I got to stare at your tits for a whole afternoon.' Nick is trying to talk with a mouthful of tinned spaghetti hoops.

'Yes, but that's different. Is this warm enough?' I point at our revolting dinner.

'Oh, I thought we were meant to be eating it cold. It's fine. So, did you go round to Helen's then?'

'Oh no, we popped over, but she was busy.'

'That's a shame. Is there any more of this or was that the last?'

'I think we've got another tin. Just stick it in the microwave.'

'No don't worry, I'll just have it cold.' He gets up to retrieve it from the tin cupboard and it dawns on me that our standards have dropped to complete survival levels. Neither of us was ever going to be the next Gordon Ramsey, but we at least used to heat stuff up as a matter of course.

'So what was she up to?'

'Who?'

'Helen, you said she was busy. Was it anything you and Lucy could get involved in?' He sits back at the table with the can and tin opener and starts to get to work.

'Sorry?' I splutter.

'I mean you said you wanted to do some stuff during the day, start a class or something with Lucy. What was Helen doing? Was it something you could do with her?'

'Oh, God. I see what you mean. No. Absolutely not,' I shake my head in disbelief. 'She was having sex, Nick.'

'Oh wow. Fuck.'

'Exactly,' and we sit in uncomfortable silence slurping on our hoops. We haven't so much as dry rutted since Lucy arrived; I'd kind of half accepted that we were never going to have sex again, or not until Lucy was at least one. And there Helen was, shagging in the middle of the day, and more to the point, looking like she was really enjoying it.

'Wow,' Nick says again and tips the entire tin of hoops onto his plate.

So it turns out some of us are doing it after all.

Chapter Ten

'OK, so you're here for Lucy's jabs, is that right?' My hot doctor looks up from his notes; he looks a bit like the guy from *Prison Break* but with a beard. His eyelashes are so long, like a cow's. A really attractive cow, I think.

'Yes, and also about the . . . thrush.'

'Ah yes. So what shall we do first?' I momentarily imagine him asking me that in the bedroom and then feel immediately shameful. 'Thrush first, then jabs?' He probably wouldn't say that, though.

'Great.' I nod.

He looks into Lucy's mouth.

'Yes, that looks suspiciously like thrush. And you? How are you feeling?'

'Absolutely fine. You?' It's not a date. It's not a date. It's not a date.

'I'm fine thanks, Emily, but I'm not the one with thrush and blistered breasts.'

Fair enough. I let out a long breath and with it the tears start to roll down my cheeks. 'I'm in constant pain. All the mums on parenting forums go on about how much they enjoy feeding their babies, the closeness and everything, and I think, how? How can you enjoy this? This is fucking excruciating. Sorry for swearing.'

'I don't give a shit,' he jokes. I think I'm a bit in love with him. 'Here's what we'll do. I will prescribe a spray for

Lucy, tablets and a cream for you. That should clear up the thrush.'

'Thank you,' I wipe my eyes on the back of my cardigan sleeve, and Hot Doctor passes me a tissue from the box on his desk.

'Now' – he looks at his screen – 'the notes say you also wanted me to look at Lucy's tongue?'

'Yes please. The women at breastfeeding group said she was tongue-tied.'

'OK, little one, can I have look?' I pass him Lucy and he stares in her mouth for what feels like an age, then says confidently, 'Yes, yes, I think they're right. No wonder you've been in such pain. Here.' He passes Lucy back and starts typing on his computer. I notice the family photograph on the windowsill: it is him with an equally attractive woman and three young children.

'You have three?' I exclaim.

'Ah, yes' – he points at the picture – 'three boys, aged four, five and six now.'

'Wow!'

'I know. I come to work for a break.' He smiles weakly, clearly not joking. 'OK, you should now get a referral in the post for a hospital appointment, and once Lucy has had the snip' – just the word makes my uterus contract and every hair stand on end – 'you should be much more comfortable.'

'Thanks.'

'Right, that was the easy bit out the way. Are you ready for the jab?'

'Yes, you are, aren't you, Lucy,' my voice sounds thin and uncertain.

'I meant you actually. In my experience, it's far worse for the mums. Now could you take her arm out of her sleeve? Right that's great, if you can hold her arm firmly?'

I pull Lucy's chubby arm from her sleep suit, holding her close to me, her head lolling on my chest. She's sleepy and warm.

'OK, this is only going to hurt for a second, Lucy. Mum, can you hold her arm tighter? That's it.'

As the needle pierces her skin, Lucy's eyes open wide with fear and she lets out the most blood-curdling scream. A choking lump of emotions rises in my throat. She screams in pain, twisting and bucking.

The doctor quickly sticks a cotton wool ball to her arm: 'That's you done.'

Tears, actual human tears roll down Lucy's face as she screams and sobs. Why did I put her through this? She trusted me, and I looked her in the eye as someone stabbed her with a needle.

'You did really well, both of you,' the doctor reassures us as I strap Lucy to me. She's squirming like she doesn't want to be close to me anymore and feels heavier as I hug her and do up the clips. I wonder if it is actually the emotional weight of the guilt I'm now carrying, having purposefully maimed my only, until then, perfect child?

'If she starts to feel hot just give her a dose of Calpol and make sure she's hydrated.' He's having to raise his voice over Lucy's loud screams. 'You'll both be feeling much better before you know it.'

'Thank you for everything.'

He raises his hand in a kind of 'no worries' gesture but I totally misread the situation and high five him.

'Well that's never happened before,' he remarks.

I think I'm going to have to change my doctor.

'And there's definitely not an alternative?'

A week later and Lucy is sleeping in the crook of Nick's

arm while he paces around the clinic's waiting room.

The letter came through two days ago. This is all happening so quickly, we've kind of got carried along without having chance to speak about it properly, but something in Nick's tone really annoys me, like somehow this is my fault. Nick is still unconvinced that getting her tongue snipped is totally necessary. I've scoured the internet researching this and apparently babies can't feel it at all, but I don't know if that's just something they tell parents to ease the massive guilt.

I have tried to explain to Nick how hugely uncomfortable it is to feed her, but just because I don't bring it up every time I feed her, he assumes it's got better, and when I mention it the next time he says, 'Does it still hurt?' like I'm just making a fuss. It makes me want to grab his balls really, really tightly and ask, 'Does *that* hurt?'

I pick up the pamphlet on ectopic pregnancies and pretend I'm reading it.

'You've got to let me ask questions, Emily. You can't have the monopoly on Lucy's welfare just because you spend the most time with her.'

I'm about to paper-cut his forehead with the pamphlet when I think, maybe, just maybe, he might have a small seed of a point. Lucy and I are together every waking moment of the day and night. I'm so familiar with all her little movements and sounds, I feel like we almost have our own language. Nick will come in from work and cuddle her and without thinking I'll say something like, 'Don't hold her like that, she doesn't like it.' Or he'll be changing her nappy and I'll comment, 'You've done it up a bit too tightly; here, let me do it,' and I'll totally take over. I don't mean to, but I sometimes feel like I have a shortcut to how to make Lucy stop crying, or laugh or go to sleep, and instead of letting

Nick find his own way with her, I try to make him do it my way.

I put the pamphlet back on the table and give his hand a quick squeeze. I tell him everything Karen and the doctor had told me and answer his questions. I even let him peer down my top to see how bad my tits look, at which point the consultant comes over to us.

'Sorry to interrupt . . .'

The top of Nick's head cracks my chin as he tries to move quickly away from my chest.

'I need to talk through the procedure with you.' The doctor sits on the edge of the table with his hands clasped between his knees and tells us how they will make a quick incision of the flap of skin under Lucy's tongue, and that it will only take a matter of seconds. Then he says, 'Ready?'

'What, now?' I don't know when I was expecting it to happen.

'Yes, now. Dad, would you bring her through?'

'Sure, of course.' Nick clears his throat and I see how nervous he is.

He carries Lucy into the small consultation room where two other medics are waiting, putting her down gently on the table. We're ushered back out the door and asked to take a seat in the waiting room again. The door is shut and I can only imagine the awful things they are doing to my daughter in there. I start to rise and Nick gently pulls me back down.

'They know what they're doing, Emily, let them just do their job.'

I sit back down and try to distract myself with a copy of *Country Living* until moments later the door opens again, and the doctor brings a screaming Lucy out. He passes her to me, and I can see there's blood in her mouth. Holy shit.

'You should feed her straight away, so she gets used to the new sensation.'

I pull up my T-shirt and guide my nipple into her mouth. I get ready for the rush of pain, the hair standing up on the back of my neck, the intake of breath and biting my lip bloody.

But no, it feels different: it still hurts like mad but that's because my tits are ninety per cent blister; the actual feeling of her feeding is different. Almost comfortable. I can feel my shoulders drop about a foot and I breathe for what feels like the first time in two months.

I can do this. We can do this.

Chapter Eleven

I've just fed Lucy to bursting. This is almost as liberating as skinny-dipping in the sea after a night clubbing, except thankfully without the two-week flu that followed. I can feed her without willing the pain to stop, without holding my breath for thirty-second intervals or pinching my thigh so my brain concentrates on a different type of pain. My nipples have started to scab over; a phrase I never thought I'd hear myself say. They look revolting, like they're covered in lesions, but they are getting better.

I don't think Lucy will ever take a bottle, but that's fine, I will just continue to breastfeed her until she goes to secondary school or gets married. I am just so relieved.

As a treat, I am taking myself into town in the middle of the day on a Saturday on my own. This is the first time I have been out without Lucy for longer than it takes to have a shower or go to the loo. As I say goodbye to Nick, Lucy starts to grumble. I think of suggesting he sings 'Twinkle Twinkle Little Star' to her but decide he won't appreciate the advice. I feel quietly pleased with myself for being so thoughtful and adult. I have a two-hour window before the next feed, so time is of the essence.

I head out with only my handbag, which is beyond liberating. While waiting at the bus stop I find myself doing the baby rock, which, without a child, just makes you look a bit mental. I sit on the top deck at the front, just because I can, and head to the leisure centre.

And now I'm swimming. And it is amazing.

The size twelve Asda swimsuit is a tad ambitious and I can't push off from the side of the pool as my boobs fall out the top every time. Also a bikini wax wouldn't have gone amiss, but all in all I feel pretty chuffed with myself. I've done twenty minutes of peaceful mum-swimming: breast-stroke while keeping your head firmly above water so as not to get your hair wet. The peace has only partially been disrupted by Noddy Holder shouting 'It's Chriiiiiiiiiiistmas' over the sound system, but I could try to be less bah-humbug about the whole festive affair which has somewhat crept up on me; how can it only be four weeks away?

As I heave myself out of the pool, I realise how hugely unfit I am. I've only done fifteen lengths but I feel completely light-headed, like I've just smoked a massive spliff. I sit down on the slimy bench by the side of the pool and try to regulate my breathing. Someone is waving in my direction from the baby pool, but without my contacts in I can't be certain it's me they're waving at. I risk it and wave back.

The figure emerging from the pool with a large baby turns out to be Tania, who joins me on the bench. She tries to give me a hug, but it's all a bit awkward as we're both wearing soggy swimming costumes and Falcon gets sandwiched between us and starts squealing.

'Where's your one?'

'She's at home with Nick.'

'Oh my God, you're so lucky. Spiral would never do that for me, he's so fucking lazy. I never realised it until we had Falcon. How's your mum doing?'

'She's good,' and I remind myself to give her a ring on the bus home to check.

'I liked her. You're lucky to have a good mum.'

'Thanks. She liked you and Helen too.'

'Did she? That's brilliant, I've been told I don't always make a good first impression, that I can be a bit abrasive, which is a nightmare as a yoga teacher.'

The lifeguard blows his whistle to stop a pair getting off with each other in the shallow end. Imagine being that attracted to each other that you can't keep your hands off each other at the municipal pool.

'Is Spiral really his name?'

'Oh God, 'course not. He's called Peter. But then he got a massive swirly tattoo on his scalp when he was eighteen and then everyone started calling him Spiral.'

'How long does it take to tattoo your whole head?'

'Ages. Absolutely ages apparently. He's tried to tell me it's more painful than childbirth but you can imagine how well that went down with someone who's had a ten-pound baby.' She shifts Falcon onto the other knee while he intertwines his fingers in her hair. 'He used to be really proactive in those days, always out on demos and chaining himself to things. We just seem to be in the fallow years now.' She sighs and we both watch the copulating couple who have taken no notice of the warning from the lifeguard. 'It's just that he doesn't do anything now, but he's so self-righteous with it. I wish I'd known all this beforehand.'

'What do you mean?'

'Well he insists that we only use reusable nappies but doesn't help with washing them out, so our flat is full of buckets of shitty nappies. I can't fucking bear it.' She's talking really fast like she's a balloon with a small hole in it and I wonder when she last had a proper conversation with an adult who wasn't lying down on a cushion.

'Our flat smells like shit and we use disposable ones.' I shrug.

Falcon leans over, grabs the strap of my costume and whips it down. My right breast falls out and I hastily tuck it back in.

She continues without missing a beat, 'Sorry, he's so strong, I already feel like I'm totally controlled by him. What's it going to be like when he can speak? I'm going to be like one of those women you read about in *Take a Break* who are terrorised by their children.'

Tania doesn't strike me as the kind of woman who'd read *Take a Break*. She is a constant surprise.

Falcon has settled into his face now. He looks more like a baby and less like a grown-up Chinese communist. But he's big; he looks like he could eat Lucy.

'He's on the hundredth percentile,' Tania explains, as if reading my mind. 'I know. He's massive.'

'He's solid,' I suggest.

'That's how you describe shot-putters. No one wants to be solid, do they?'

But he is. His legs and arms have deep chubby creases, which give the illusion of huge muscles. We sit in silence, dripping, for a moment and Tania lets out a long exhalation that sounds like she's deflating.

'You are so lucky to have a girl, you know.'

'Well as long as they're healthy, it doesn't really matter what they are, does it?' I offer up.

'That's bullshit. Boys are disgusting. That's a fact. And it's not like Spiral is going to teach him to grow up to have good manners. He thinks we should follow our animal instincts. And that involves only washing with water so as not to wash away our natural oils. I used to agree with him but now I just wish he'd put on some fucking deodorant.'

80

Falcon grabs a clump of Tania's hair and pulls it with such force that he ends up headbutting her, then starts wailing.

'God, he can be such a dick sometimes.'

I don't know whether she's talking about Falcon or Spiral.

'You doing anything nice for Christmas?' I ask.

'We haven't decided yet; probably nothing. Which is a shame as I really like Christmas.' She's holding Falcon in a kind of headlock. 'You?'

'We've got to drive about a thousand miles seeing all the relatives, which is going to be a total ball-ache, and I guess we'll be up there for New Year. I haven't really given it that much thought, to be honest. All I really want to do is stay at home, drink Baileys and watch telly for our first Christmas together.'

'Ooh, when are you back? I was just thinking how nice it would be to have you over for some festive drinks. Or in the New Year, if you're not back until then. Or any time, really. We could do pretty much any time. But our flat's not big enough to have people round.'

The silence that follows is almost palpable. My mind is blank. Tania looks at me expectantly and eventually I respond, 'Well . . . you could always come to ours?'

'Oh, if you're sure. That sounds fantastic. As I say, we don't really have anything planned. Falcon doesn't travel well so we can't go to Spiral's folks in Cornwall and I don't see much of my parents, so, brilliant! I'll really look forward to that.'

'Yes, brilliant! Me too.'

'Right, that's me done for activities for today then. I'm going to go home and see if I can watch a bit of *Judge Judy* on the iPad before Spiral gets in. Text me about New Year.'

'Yep, of course.' We settle on a handshake to say goodbye.

'I'm still doing the post-natal yoga classes at the Brighthelm

Centre every Tuesday morning at ten if you fancy it? There hasn't been a huge take-up so there's still drop-in spaces.'

'Sounds good,' I say, knowing I'll probably never actually go.

I watch her juggle Falcon from one hip to the other as she negotiates the verruca footbath to get into the changing rooms and feel grateful for small mercies. I might want to punch Nick in the face about ten times a day, but at least he has a bath once in a while.

Chapter Twelve

I'm trying not to use the C-word at home. It's a nightmare. I've no idea how we are going to get Lucy around all the relatives this Christmas, so it's easier to just not talk about it. There's Nick's family in the Midlands and mine in the North East, and everyone wants a piece of her. If I don't speak of it, maybe it will just cease to exist.

Pre-Lucy, Nick and I would do the family thing separately and then come together at New Year's Eve to get hammered. Which brings me to the worst C-word of all. Compromise.

'You can't bagsy the good dates,' Nick mutters over our dinner of Happy Shopper veggie lasagne.

'I'm not trying to. I just think my family are more . . .' tread carefully '. . . able to accommodate us all.'

'Come on, Emily, you know my mum has been looking forward to this since the moment she found out we were pregnant.'

Correction, Nick, I was pregnant. I don't remember you waddling round like a duck with ankles the size of your neck.

'You know how much they like to make a fuss, Emily — it'll be great. They'll just take care of us and you can relax. We might even get a chance to catch up on some sleep; how brilliant would that be? And we haven't seen much of them at all since she was born.'

We mostly speak on FaceTime, which is unbearable.

Their internet is so slow that most of the time we're looking at a frozen image of Dennis and Cathleen's grinning faces while hearing the pair of them bickering over who's broken the 'device' this time. I know it's not fair, but other people's parents are just generally more annoying than your own.

The bottom line is I know we'll have more fun at my parents for Christmas. Nick's parents are a bit stuffy and it's not as if they've really embraced their role as doting grandparents. Even on FaceTime they seem to get bored of Lucy quite quickly and instead take the computer outside to show us what they've been doing in the garden, until, thankfully, the Wi-Fi completely cuts out.

'But if we go to my parents for Christmas Day then there might be a chance I can see Rachel.' I hold my breath. This is a very low blow. I have pulled out my absolute emotional Top Trump card. I fizz with guilt as I say her name and wonder what I would actually do if I saw her.

'Oh. OK. Alright then, I can't argue with that, can I?' he gives a defeated shrug. 'But if we're going to your folks for Christmas, then we have to go to mine for New Year.'

Oh, Nick, fair fucking play to you. I genuinely didn't see that one coming. Try as I might, I just can't hide my disappointment.

'It's not like we're going to go out and get wasted this year, is it?'

'I guess not.'

'And Dad's always got a shit-tonne of booze, and they buy out M and S in snacks. It's going to be brilliant.' His eyes light up and I can imagine him as a boy stuffing his face with Quality Streets as Cathleen fusses over him like a pet.

The thought of having a sherry with Dennis and Cathleen

to welcome in the New Year makes me want to shoot myself in the face. And then I remember Tania and our post-New Year drinks arrangement.

'Oh, I forgot to mention, I've invited a mum friend over for drinks in the New Year.'

'Who?'

'Tania.'

'Who?'

'Tania.'

'That's literally the first time I've ever heard you mention her.'

'She was my old pregnancy yoga teacher.' He's looking at me blankly. 'I went out for lunch with her and Mum.' Nothing. 'Anyway, it doesn't matter, I thought they could come over when we get back in the New Year. I could invite Helen and her family too.'

'Who?'

'Helen. Fucking Helen. You remember, the woman from the cinema.'

'Ah, the one who was shagging when you turned up for a playdate?'

'Yes. That's her.'

'Well if you're inviting your mates, then shall I invite some of mine too?'

'No way. Absolutely no way. These aren't my mates; these are mum friends, women who have babies the same age as Lucy. This is what you do when you have kids, you hang out with other people with kids, it's just what you do, Nick.' I've got myself so worked up I feel a bit flushed and think I might burst into tears. 'Fuck's sake,' I mutter.

'OK. Fair enough. I don't know why we'd hang out with people we don't know though when we don't really get to see our proper friends anymore.' He shrugs. 'But if that's

85

what you do then fair enough. It just doesn't sound like much fun though.'

'Thank you!' I concede. Exhausted.

He does have a very good point.

Chapter Thirteen

I've forgotten to buy Christmas presents for Dennis and Cathleen. Nick is finishing packing the car up. I was just checking I'd locked all the windows and unplugged the sockets when it dawned on me. I am so used to buying for my own family and friends that it completely slipped my mind, so while the car boot is loaded with presents not a single one of them is for my beloved in-laws. Shit.

'Ready?' Nick pops his head round the bedroom door as I am lying flat on the floor under the bed attempting to unplug the bedside lamp.

'Just wondering, what have you got for your folks?' I enquire.

'We always buy each other a present for a fiver, it's a bit of a tradition to see who can get the most imaginative gift. I told you about it, remember? Don't tell me you've forgotten.'

''Course not.' This, among about a thousand other factors, is why my family Christmases are way more fun. I am filled with joy all over again that we're spending Christmas Day with my folks.

As Nick is putting Lucy in the car seat I make a quick dash to the shop around the corner. Even shit presents will be better than no presents at all.

'Merry Christmas,' Mr Patel announces loudly from

behind the counter, open-armed, like Kate Winslet in *Titanic*.

'To you too.'

'And the first Christmas for your son, yes?'

He has, from the first time I brought Lucy in the shop, assumed she was a boy and too much time has elapsed now to correct him.

'That's right. Now, I need a present for five pounds, what would you suggest?'

He thoughtfully searches around the shop, picking up and examining international plug adapters and shower caps before putting them back on the shelf. We settle on the Christmas edition of the *Radio Times* and a kingsize Mars bar for Cathleen, and a car air freshener and a large bottle of dandelion and burdock for Dennis.

'All set?' Nick enquires as I return laden with thin blue plastic bags.

'Yep, ready to go.'

This is going to be one spectacular Christmas.

It's taken eight and a half hours to get to Mum and Dad's. That's 510 minutes. 30,600 seconds. We could have flown to Delhi in that time. However you look at it, it's a bloody long time to be in a car. Thankfully Lucy has, on the whole, slept whenever we were moving but it's so mind-numbingly boring and Nick is driving at a frustratingly cautious speed.

'I'm going sixty-five, Em, that's almost the speed limit,' he snaps when I point out that yet another car with a trailer has overtaken us. The thing I've realised is, he can't do more than one thing at the same time, so if we're talking about something, then the car will incrementally slow down. I'm not suggesting we drive like Michael Schumacher, but we're never going to get to my parents' if every time Nick opens his mouth we trundle along the motorway at fifty.

And on top of that, we've left all the CDs on the doorstep at home. It was, of course, my job to put the bag in the car but I must have stepped straight over them. The only CD we have is Now 34 that the previous car owner had left in the glove compartment, so the choice is that, or Michael Ball on Radio 2. We used to punctuate long journeys with smoking fags: it gave it a bit of a structure and the passenger a purpose with having to roll one every few miles, but that's a thing of the past now obviously.

Every stop at a service station involves panic eating a packet sandwich, a grab-bag of crisps, a packet of Maltesers and a bottle of pop, because we're not sure when we will stop again. Only to pull over thirty minutes later when one of us needs a wee or has done a poo, and we repeat the whole gluttony again.

But as we finally get closer to Mum and Dad's, I can feel myself relaxing. We pass the village pub I first got served in, then Costcutters where I used to spend my pocket money on Refreshers and Mojos and later on, bought fags. Fifteen-year-old Rachel and I would lurk down the alley round the corner and accost adults as they walked by, asking them if they'd buy them for us. We had most success with the middle-aged single men, which looking back is definitely a bit creepy.

As we pull up to my parents' house, Mum comes bounding out the front door before Nick's even finished his thirty-four-point parking manoeuvre and walks out in front of the bonnet.

'Does she *want* me to run her over?'

I suddenly feel really deflated, like Nick is going to change Christmas and not in a good way.

Mum opens the passenger door.

'My brilliant girl!' she shrills, before sticking her head past me to grab Lucy's hand in her car seat and I realise she's not talking to me.

As Nick unpacks the car, I carry Lucy into my childhood home. Everywhere I look there are memories of pre-Lucy. The piano I was made to play from when I was nine, which I hated but then loved when I was allowed to bring my own sheet music to lessons aged thirteen and learnt how to play 'Manchild' by Neneh Cherry. It turns out it doesn't translate very well to the piano, but I thought I was a rock star none-theless. Through the living-room window I can see into the garden, where little bushes are scattered around to mark the graves of each treasured guinea pig – twenty-seven in total. I tried and failed to tell the difference between a girl and a boy, and as a consequence they bred like mad.

Everything's the same. But I feel different.

'You got everything you need?' Dad asks as he walks out of the bathroom doing his flies up. At least he shuts the door.

'Yes, thanks, Dad.'

He walks into my room where I'm holding Lucy on my hip and kisses her first on the top of her head and then me. Mum has borrowed a travel cot from her mate for Lucy; it looks out of place here in my old bedroom, weird somehow, as if it doesn't belong. It's like being someone's daughter and someone's mum at the same time.

'It's good to have you home, Emily.'

'It's good to be home.'

'I'll leave you to get settled in. If you need anything, ask your mum.' He pulls the door to and walks down the stairs. I listen to the familiar creaks of his steps.

I sit down to breastfeed Lucy on the bed where I cried myself to sleep when I discovered my first boyfriend had got off with someone else at the school disco.

The bookshelves are full of GCSE Oxford School Shakespeare books, Judy Blumes from the early years (including a well-leafed copy of *Forever* with that sex scene that turned the air blue at primary school) and Irvine Welsh, from when I was older and considered myself cutting edge and very modern. On the wall is the clip-framed Glastonbury ticket. I wipe off the dust with my sleeve and wonder what Rachel's doing this year for Christmas.

When we were young, before everything changed, we used to spend every Christmas Eve together. We matured from watching *A Muppet Christmas Carol* to drinking sherry we'd pinched from her dad's drinks cabinet and dancing to Michael Jackson in someone's front room before we'd stumble in at about 5 a.m.-ish. But I remind myself that hasn't been the case for a long time. That me having a child wasn't the reason that stopped, and how I will be getting up with Lucy at that hour now instead.

'Where do you want this?' Nick's struggling with the door handle, a travel cot in his arms.

'Mum's already put one up.'

'Are you serious?' he says in an annoyingly high voice and I imagine throwing *Are You There God? It's Me, Margaret* directly at his head.

'It's fine. Just put it down there.'

He chucks it down with undue force and an unnecessary groan then stomps back down the stairs.

'Knock knock.' Mum pops her head around the door. 'Have you got everything you need? Can I get you a cup of tea? Glass of water? I made some cheese straws if you need to keep your energy up?'

I blink back the tears but it's too late, the wave has already taken hold. Mum puts her arm around me and I rest my head on her shoulder while Lucy peacefully suckles.

Three generations of women sat on the bed where I gave my first blow job when Mum and Dad had gone to Whitby for the night.

'It does get easier.'

'When?' I lean into Mum gratefully. She always smells exactly the same, a mixture of Oil of Olay and Coal Tar soap.

'Every day. You just don't realise it because you're doing it.'

I hear Nick huffing his way up the stairs with another load of bags and my shoulders tense. He dumps them on the floor and Lucy jumps with the sound.

'Sorry. Just one more load then everything's in.'

As he sets off back downstairs, Mum strokes my head. 'I used to scream into a pillow,' she says wistfully, almost to herself.

'Sorry?'

'When you were a baby. I'd get so tired, and your dad was no help at all, and sometimes I'd get so frustrated I'd just scream into a pillow. I'd feel much better after that. And people didn't frown on smoking with small children so much then, so that helped.'

'Some days it's OK. We get on just fine. But other times I want to kill him. I don't think I've ever felt so annoyed by another person.'

'I used to dream about being with someone else when you were little.' I can't believe Mum is saying this to me when Dad is sitting in his armchair downstairs. 'He was called Mario and he was Spanish. He looked like a cross between Julio Iglesias and a young Cliff Richard.'

'Really?' I can't quite picture what that face would look like. Perma-tanned, for sure.

'At the moments when everything was getting on top of me, I'd think about my alternative life with Mario in our villa, with the pool and the sunshine, and it would calm me down.'

I wind Lucy over my shoulder; I'm not really sure where to go conversationally from here. Maybe I should reciprocate and tell her how I daydream about having sex with our Hot Doctor, but I'm not quite ready to cross that line with her yet.

'The reason I tell you this is because the fantasy is never as good as real life. If I actually ever met Mario, he would almost certainly be an utter disappointment. Nick will wind you up, as I'm sure you do him, but you'll find your way. Of course you will, because you love each other. And you have this beautiful girl to think of.' Mum takes Lucy from me and gently rubs her back as she does a big milky burp.

'It's not easy, but I promise you, it does get easier. It has to. Otherwise no one would ever have more children.'

'But you only had me.'

'We only needed you, sweetheart.' She passes Lucy back to me and squeezes my knee as she hoists herself up.

She passes Nick on the stairs and I hear her say, 'I think your girls need a hug.'

I don't think I have ever loved Mum more than I do right now.

Nick pops his head around the bedroom door. 'Is it OK to come in?'

'Of course,' and I pat the space next to me on the bed.

He lowers himself down slowly. 'Is it weird being in here?'

'A bit.'

He picks a book up off the shelf next to my bed. It's the Mel and Kim unofficial biography.

'Which one . . .'

'It was Mel.'

'And . . .'

'Cancer I think.'

'Oh right,' he absent-mindedly flicks through it then returns it to the shelf. 'Look, sorry for being a dick,' he whispers.

'That's OK.'

He takes Lucy from me; she stretches her legs like a cat, smacks her lips then shuts her eyes. Nick puts his arm around me and I rest my head on his shoulder. I feel tired. Heavy. Like my legs are filled with lead and I might never have the energy to get up again.

'It's going to be a brilliant Christmas, Em, I can just feel it.'

I can hear the comforting sounds downstairs of Mum and Dad arguing over whose turn it is to empty the dishwasher and think, maybe he's right. If not brilliant, this will at least be different. Good different.

*

It's Christmas morning, and we have just finished 'helping' Lucy unwrap all her presents from Father Christmas. I know she has no idea what has just happened, but for me, I feel hugely grown up. Last night we put out the mince pie and sherry, both of which Dad has eaten and drunk as his contribution to the festivities, then we stuffed Lucy's stocking with gifts I've spent the last three months lovingly selecting.

Normally I would be waiting for my turn to see what I'd been given, but this year I'm not so bothered. Well, I will of course be furious if Nick has forgotten to get me the Chanel No.5 I requested, but it just doesn't feel so much about me this year, which is a strange and unexpected transition.

'And here's another for our favourite girl,' Mum trills as she passes Lucy yet another present.

I wonder if I'll ever get used to that not being me. I'm sat cross-legged with Lucy propped up between my knees, which at least means I get the pleasure of unwrapping all these gifts – even if they aren't for me. I've taken so many pictures of her that I have used all the storage on my camera and am now resorting to alternating between mine, Nick's and Mum's phones.

'Before I forget, I bumped into Rachel in the Co-op yesterday. She was visiting her mum and I said you guys were heading up for Christmas.'

I pretend I can't hear her.

'Why don't you take Lucy up to meet her in a bit?'

'Because it's Christmas Day.'

'Yes, but she's only up the road, isn't she, if she's at her mum's. Why don't you pop up for a quick cuppa after we've opened these?'

'That's a great idea, Em, you were saying you'd hoped to see her while you were up here,' Nick encourages.

I fire Nick my worst look. 'That's not exactly what I said.'

'But, I thought . . .' he starts to protest.

'Come on, Emily, I bet she'd love to—'

'Can we all just drop it?' I take the bit of wrapping paper Lucy's sucking out of her mouth. Mum goes to say something else but Dad gently touches her arm. For a man who didn't notice when I got my nose pierced, he can be hugely observant sometimes.

'Once your mum has put the dinner in, we were thinking we could take Lucy for a stroll around the village, give you guys a chance to have a rest. Would that help?'

Good gear change, Dad.

I dream of having half an hour to sleep; my eyes prickle from tiredness.

'Yes, please!' I catch Nick's eye and he gives me a wink so quickly it could have been a tic. Hang on, he can't really be thinking that, can he?

'No problem, you guys can have some chill-out time.' I stifle a laugh as the phrase sounds so unnatural coming from Dad.

My parents have barely closed the front door when Nick whispers in my ear, 'Shall we go upstairs?' His outstretched hand hovers in front of me. 'We don't have to do anything. We can just cuddle. I just want to be naked with you, Emily.'

But that's the problem, that's exactly what I don't want. I don't think I ever want to be seen naked again, unless I'm having some kind of major surgery and I'm under general anesthetic, then perhaps I won't be so bothered.

'Come on, Em. Don't think about it, just come upstairs.'

I clutch his hand and he pulls me to standing. Why do I feel nervous? This is ridiculous, it's just Nick.

I push open my bedroom door and as Nick takes off his shoes, I close the curtains and switch the light off.

'What are you doing?'

'Just making it cosy.'

'Or totally pitch-black. I have seen you naked before, Em.' Nick reaches over and turns the bedside lamp on.

I slump down onto the bed.

Nick wraps his arms around me from behind. 'You know you are still the sexiest woman I know.'

I try and remember if I've even shaved my legs since Lucy was born. I must have, surely, but definitely not recently.

He kisses the nape of my neck. It feels so alien. I genuinely can't remember the last time I've been touched by someone who doesn't want a boob full of milk.

'OK, let's get under the duvet, but don't touch my boobs.'

'Deal.'

'Or my stomach.'

'Gotcha.'

'Or . . .'

'How's about you tell me what I can touch instead?'

'Righto.' I don't remember Pussy Galore saying 'righto' before she seduced Bond, but today she did.

I'm lying naked in my teenage bed and I've just had sex for the first time in six months. Nick lies next to me with his arm draped around my stomach, quietly snoring. I lift up the duvet and take a peek at our bodies. Nick's looks exactly the same as it always has. His taut stomach rises and falls as he breathes. Sleeping, his face looks younger, like all the lines have fallen away.

Mine, on the other hand, still looks almost unrecognisable. My stomach has zero muscles. As I lie on my side, it has kind of slipped down onto the mattress like warm lard. I fed Lucy before Mum and Dad took her out so my boobs are empty. The scabs have finally healed, but the skin looks older, like it doesn't belong to me.

I feel overwhelmingly relieved. I haven't been able to get past the thought that my womb might fall out if I had sex, or that my innards may have somehow collapsed in on themselves since giving birth to Lucy. Or that my stitches haven't healed properly or, worse still, I'd been sewn up too tightly and it would be like having an episiotomy all over again if I tried to push a penis in there.

I think I'd come to the conclusion that, since Lucy had come out of my vagina, it was safe to say that nothing, really, should go back up there again.

I take another look under the duvet. It's not just that my

body looks so different, it's that it doesn't really feel like mine at all at the moment. I'm a walking feeding-machine for Lucy so the thought of having my boobs touched in any other way than to provide milk at the moment just feels . . . wrong.

Sex just feels a bit, well, biological.

'How's about this?' Nick had enquired politely as he'd shifted his weight on top of me.

'No, that hurts.'

'Right, what about this?' as he attempted to lift one of my legs up.

'It doesn't bend that way!'

In the end we settled for him kind of spooning, with a strict set of rules about which bits of my body he could and couldn't touch.

'That was nice,' Nick had whispered as he'd rolled over.

It wasn't. It was worse than losing my virginity, because we both have the experience to know when the sex is rubbish. But it's done. We have now officially broken the seal.

And I know it will get easier. It has to. Katie Price has had four children and I'm always reading about how much sex she gets, so if she can push out four humans and do it loads, I can surely birth one and have sex more than once a year, can't I? But the truth is, if I was given the choice again between sex and a nap, I'd choose a nap every time at the moment. Can Nick and I be a couple and never have sex? Or does that make us more mates? Maybe I could just give him the occasional blow job to keep things fresh, would that be OK? Who can I ask these questions? Maybe I should google it.

As if reading my thoughts, Nick mutters, 'Stop overthinking things.'

'How do you know what I'm thinking?'

'Your breathing changes when you're worrying about stuff, it goes all panty.'

He pulls me to him and wraps his leg around me and buries his face into the crook of my neck. 'This is my favourite bit,' he purrs, and I think, we're OK. This is going to be OK.

Just then I hear the front door rattle and I freeze. Downstairs Mum and Dad are bickering as they attempt to carry the pram in.

'Lift your end up.'

'I am. Stop talking so loudly, you'll wake her up.'

'Me? Me? It's *you* who has a voice like a foghorn.'

'WE'RE BACK!' she shouts up the stairs.

'Shit, Nick, get up!' I hiss. 'They're home!'

We both leap out of bed, throwing the duvet back in a frantic search for pants, socks, trousers, T-shirts.

How is it possible that as an adult I am on my hands and knees trying to find my knickers having just done it with a boy at my parents' house? I'm meant to be a grown-up now.

Before opening the door, Nick pulls me to him, holds my face and kisses me deeply like he used to when we first met. For a split second it is just the two of us in our bubble.

Then Mum shouts up, 'She's awake, and it smells like she's done a poo. Shall I change her or do you want to?'

And we're back to being parents, but something has shifted. I almost instantly feel less annoyed with Nick. It's so obvious, but maybe the trick to not killing each other is to find time to do something that's just about us once in a while.

'Can you hear me, Emily? Sorry if we've woken you but can you let me know where the wipes and the bum cream are?'

And just like that, the moment has passed.

Chapter Fourteen

'Now, you remember which bus you're getting?'

'Yes, Mum, I have been into town before, you know.'

'I know, I'm not fussing, it's just things might have changed since you last got the bus into town.'

'Nothing in Lincolnshire has changed, Mum, believe me!'

'Right, fair enough. Well try to be back for five as I'm making baked aubergine for tea.' Mum's signature dish. My most hated meal. Something got lost in translation over the last three decades and now I can't tell her.

'Fine, yes, can you just help me get the pram out of the door?' She grabs one end and we lift it through in one go, a choreography we have perfected during the last few days.

'Ooh, the house is going to be quiet tomorrow without you all here, isn't it?'

'We'll be back soon . . . BYE!' I shout through the door to Dad and Nick who shout 'bye' back in unison over the dull cheer of whatever football match they've found to watch on Sky Sports.

Mum has given me fifty pounds and encouraged me to go into town to spend it. 'It'll only get eaten up by house stuff and nappies otherwise, and this money is a treat just for you,' she'd told me as she pressed it into my palm.

So Lucy and I are heading into Grimsby on the bus. Mum's second cautionary word was not to take the car as everywhere will be heaving with sale shoppers, but that the bus would be a more relaxing alternative, which I know is untrue as it takes about an hour longer as it winds through all the villages scooping up OAPs. But this is her treat and I'm not going to turn it down.

The bus driver gets off at the final stop to help me lift the pram off.

'She's a big one, isn't she?' he comments as he puts the wheels down on the pavement.

'She's fourteen weeks.'

'What's that in real terms, six months or something? Anyway, it's better to have a solid baby than one of those fragile little things. Well, have a good day, girls.' He sparks up a fag and strolls off.

'You're absolutely perfect, aren't you?' I coo at Lucy as we head towards the precinct.

Mum was right. It's absolutely solid with shoppers. The shopping centre reeks of teenage perfume and sweat. I scan the selection of shops and quickly come to the conclusion that nothing in any of them is going to fit me. The Topshop window mannequins are sporting crop tops, for fuck's sake. In December!

'Let's just get a coffee, shall we?' I say to Lucy and we head for the door. As I try to turn the pram around I bash straight into the person behind me, ramming her ankles. 'Shit, I'm so sorry,' I fluster.

'Goodness, you should look where you're going!' says a voice from the past that stops me in my tracks.

I look up to see Mrs Chapman, Rachel's mum.

I hardly recognise her, she's about a fifth of the size I remember her being, with dyed blonde hair cut in a smart bob instead of the long, unkempt brown hair she used to scrape back into a bun.

'Well, Emmie Jones, this is a surprise!' She still has the

ability to make me feel like I'm doing something wrong, even after all these years. 'I'd heard you were back for Christmas and bringing your new baby. This must be her, what an angel face. Your parents must be delighted.'

'Yes, Mum adores her.' My eyes are darting behind her and all around. Is she on her own? I can feel the panic rising. My hands are clammy, which isn't helped by the heater near the entrance blasting hot air straight in my face.

'She's in Burtons buying something for Callum if that's who you're looking for.'

'Yes I just . . . yes.'

And then I see her. Rachel. It's like looking at a ghost. I think about running out the door but that would be ridiculous. Besides, Mrs Chapman has blocked the entrance, arms folded over her chest like a bouncer, clutching her Boots bag.

Rachel locks eyes with me and stops. Frozen. A beat passes, she composes herself and then walks towards us.

'Emmie. Well, this is a surprise.' It's like they've rehearsed their responses.

My heart is beating too fast and my mind goes completely blank.

'So . . . what are you doing here?' she asks matter-of-factly.

'Oh, right. Yeah, Mum gave me some Christmas money for clothes but I can't find . . . Fuck, sorry. Sorry. I just hadn't expected to see you. You look great, Rach. You've had your hair cut. It looks great short.' Mrs Chapman is shaking her head in disapproval, she always despised swearing with a passion. 'Sorry,' I mutter again.

'Well, a lot has changed since I saw you last, Emmie, not just my hair.' She shrugs coolly.

'Of course, of course it has.' I nervously push the pram back and forth as we stare at each other; the distance between us is only about a metre but it feels like miles. I'm lightheaded. It's like coming face to face with your first love and not being able to think of one thing to say. Looking at a face you know better than your own because you saw it growing and changing every day for the best part of eighteen years.

Rachel breaks the trance by peering into the pram and very softly stroking Lucy's face. 'Look at her; she's so beautiful.'

'Thanks, I know every mum must say this, but she is amazing.' Thank fuck for Lucy.

'How does she sleep?'

'Really badly, actually. We're never asleep at the same time, I don't think I've ever been so tired. I feel mental,' I laugh nervously. I desperately want to tell her everything. I have to almost physically push down the desire for it all to just bubble up and spill out messily all over the place. For me to rip myself open and show her all the confusion and the hurt and the anxiety, and to show her the massive fucking gaping hole next to my heart where she should be.

'And how are you? How's everything?' I ask.

'Good, we're good, aren't we, Mum?' she answers without emotion, the way you'd respond in an interview.

'Yes, we've just had a lovely Christmas. Very low-key, just a relaxing couple of days, isn't that right, Rachel?'

'Yes, it was . . . nice.'

'We had Rachel's friend Natasha over, do you remember her from school, Emmie? Lovely girl.'

'Yes I remember her,' I whisper, trying to swallow down the burning jealousy that grips my throat.

'Well, we had a few people over, not just her, for Christmas Eve, like always.' Rach is picking a hangnail on her thumb as she speaks, like she used to when she felt uncomfortable. I want to hug her.

103

'Yes. Yes, just a low-key affair for close family and friends.' She emphasises the word friends. 'And how about you, Emmie? Did you have an enjoyable Christmas?'

'Great. It was great. It was really good, thanks.'

We all stand in awkward silence. I want to say so many things but I don't know where to start and my mouth has dried up. I want to find out everything she's been doing beyond the second-hand information from Mum. I've got a thousand questions for her and a million things to tell her in return. I wish Mrs Chapman would leave us alone for two minutes; I've never been able to speak confidently in front of her.

The silence becomes unbearably loud. I want to say, I miss you. I miss you every day, it's like an ache. And I love you more than I thought it possible to love a friend, that I only realised how much when it was too late. And most importantly, I'm sorry. Please forgive me. Guilt pulses through my body like a heartbeat.

'Well, shall we get off then, Rachel?' Mrs Chapman looks at her watch. 'See if we can catch the 2.23 bus?'

'We could always catch the next one, if . . .'

'No, I've got to put the chicken in.'

'Sure. OK, Mum. Nice to see you, Emmie.' She smiles at me but it doesn't reach her eyes.

'Rachel, I—'

'Callum is waiting,' she cuts me off.

'Of course, well give him my love.'

'I will, but he doesn't know who you are.' Her words sting like acid but I deserved that. 'Congratulations on Lucy again.' She briefly squeezes my arm. 'Enjoy her.' She picks up her shopping and they both head out of the automatic doors.

I want to weep as I watch them walk away. I haven't been called Emmie for over fourteen years.

1997 age 16

'You haven't forgotten your bum bags, have you?'

'Shut up, Ryan, they weren't our idea.' He has his hand on my thigh while he drives, occasionally having to retrieve it to change gear.

'It's good. Practical,' he smirks.

Mum bought me and Rachel flesh-coloured bum bags that are meant to go underneath our jumpers for safety. I hadn't meant for Ryan to see it but he caught me clipping mine on this morning.

'You're just jealous,' Rachel pipes up from the back seat.

'Of your bum bags? I doubt it.'

'That we're going to Glastonbury and you're not.'

'I've been hundreds of times, Rach. You need to have your virgin experience with someone else who hasn't been.'

My face instantly glows beetroot at the mention of virgin. Did he say it on purpose? He squeezes my knee. Yes, he clearly did. I wish we could get to the station faster. I need to be out of this car and talking everything through with Rachel immediately.

Kylie's 'Confide in Me' plays on Radio 1. 'Fucking Kylie,' Ryan mutters and pushes his Rage Against the Machine tape into the car stereo. One of his dreadlocks comes loose as he leans forward and I unselfconsciously move it from his face. He smells of a heady mix of Lynxx Africa, joss sticks and bonfires.

Rachel glares at me in the mirror, eyes wide with unanswered questions. She'll just have to wait.

Ryan pulls up in front of Market Rasen railway station. He slams the car to a halt on the gravel, drawing attention from all the OAPs who are heading into Lincoln for their Friday shopping.

'See you in a few days.' He opens my hand and presses something into the palm, curling my fingers around it. He leans in and whispers, 'Put that in your bum bag and think of me when you're coming up.'

I look at what he's given me. A small jiffy bag with four what look like ecstasy pills in it. I hastily stuff them in my combat trouser pocket. Rachel has already walked to the platform and I jog after her, weighed down by my ridiculously heavy rucksack.

Rachel and I find two window seats facing each other and check we have our tickets for the millionth time.

'So, when are you going to tell me? Did you or not?'

'I don't know.' I fiddle with my train ticket, folding it in half one way and then the other.

'What do you mean, you don't know?' Rachel's voice has grown loud and high-pitched. The old couple sitting across the aisle both turn to look at us.

'Keep your voice down, Rach. I just mean, when do you know, like actually know?'

'Did you bleed after?'

'A bit, on the sofa. I tried to get it out with Vanish but it made it worse, so I've just put a throw over it and hope Mum doesn't notice.'

Rachel pulls a face. 'Was it romantic, though?'

'Ummm . . . He put "Little Fluffy Clouds" on the stereo while we did it.'

'Ah, now that is romantic, actually.'

'I know, isn't it?' This is a bit more like the 'Losing Your V Plates' summit meeting I was hoping for.

'Do your bits hurt?'

'What do you mean?'

'Does it hurt to sit down or go for a wee?'

'I think it did, I can't remember.'

'OK, well just be prepared, Emmie, cos it will sting a bit.'

'OK. Thanks.' We both look out the window as the train pulls into another busy station. The train has made a few stops now and is starting to fill up with young people with rucksacks and tents. The conductor is making his way through the carriage with difficulty.

When he checks our tickets he stops. 'These both say child's tickets.'

'That's because we're both thirteen,' we lie.

'Well you're either thirteen or you're eighteen, girls, you decide.'

'We're thirteen!' I protest.

'Then you won't need these, will you,' and he takes the cans from the table and puts them in the bin behind the seat.

'Not a great start.' Rachel shrugs.

'It's fine.' I keep my eye on the conductor and when he's disappeared into the next carriage I retrieve the half-drunk cans from the bin, giving them a wipe on my cardy, and pass Rachel hers. She lets out a small snort of laughter: 'I love you, Emmie Jones.' I grin as I squeeze in next to her and continue swigging from my can, which now smells slightly of beef sandwiches.

These are our best moments, when it's just me and Rachel. Us against the world.

We disembark the train with hundreds of other people and are shepherded along a track. There are several buses waiting in the car park but no one seems to be getting on them so we just follow everyone else.

We walk along for another ten minutes; my rucksack's getting heavier and it's my turn to carry the tent, which is digging into my fingers.

'I'm desperate for a wee again, I wish I'd gone on the train before we got off.'

'Me too.' Rachel stops a woman with multicoloured dreads and a Free Nelson Mandela T-shirt. ''Exuse me, do you know how much further it is to the entrance?'

'Where?' I notice now her eyes are dilated and I get a strong whiff of weed and patchouli oil from her. The waist strap of my rucksack is pushing right down on my bladder and I feel like I'm going to piss myself right here and now.

'The entrance to the festival,' I snap.

'Yeah, you can get in down here. Just follow everyone else and queue up. It's a fiver to crawl under the fence but last year someone'd done a shit in the tunnel so better to spend a tenner and climb over the ladder, I'd say.'

Rachel and I look blankly at each other. What is she talking about?

'But where do we show our tickets?'

The woman lets out a horse laugh that turns into a wheezy cough. When she's caught her breath she shakes her head at us, 'That's what the buses were for at the station. Fucking idiots.' She shakes her head at us again and walks off muttering, 'Posh twats.'

We turn around in the direction we've just come, but all we can see are hundreds of people walking down the hill we now need to walk back up again.

'What do we do?' Rachel is starting to panic. I can feel it too, that tightening in my chest and the underwater feeling. But we can't both start panicking our faces off, we're not even at the festival yet, there's plenty of time for that over the weekend. One of us needs to make a decision and looking at Rachel who has now started to wring her hands like Lady Macbeth, it's not going to be her.

'We'll just jump the fence.'

Rachel looks at me like I'm a total mental.

'But what about our tickets?'

'We can frame them at home. It'll be cool.'

I sit down on my rucksack and light an Embassy Number 1. The ends of my fingers have gone completely white on my right hand now from carrying the tent and I'm strongly considering just weeing in my combat trousers.

She joins me on my rucksack. 'OK. But we can't tell anyone about this.'

'Obviously.'

'What a couple of idiots!' she laughs and leans over unselfconsciously to light her fag from the lighter dangling around my neck, a familiarity born out of sixteen years of being best friends.

We tag team an emergency wee behind a bush along with tens of other women, help each other put on our extraordinarily heavy rucksacks, and rejoin the crowds heading towards the infamous Glastonbury fence.

*

From where we're camping you can see straight down the hill to the Pyramid Stage. Radiohead are on in an hour but Rachel and I both want to see Massive Attack on the Jazz World stage. We sit outside the tent and open a Foster's each; she takes a big gulp and tips half of it down her top. 'God's sake, I've only bought two T-shirts with me.' She flaps it wildly.

Someone shouts 'bollocks' from somewhere in the

campsite. It's met by another call of 'bollocks'. Within seconds the whole of the campsite is shouting 'bollocks'. Rachel and I join in self-consciously, then more loudly. We're starting to enjoy ourselves.

'Cheers!' We smash our cans together.

'Salute!' Someone shouts from inside their tent.

'Tschüss!' A shout comes from somewhere else.

'Tack!' Comes a call in response.

We've started an international chant! Rachel and I grin at each other; we're really starting to get the hang of this festival lark.

'Do you feel anything?' We've both taken half each of one of the pills that Ryan gave me and washed them down with mouthfuls of warm lager. We didn't want to take a whole one as we're both feeling a bit apprehensive. That said, it doesn't feel like anything's happening, but then I have no point of reference so I could be completely off my head but not realise it.

We're weaving our way through the tents towards the Jazz World stage, making our way down the hill arm in arm, which is virtually impossible.

'Nothing. Maybe that's normal?' Rachel suggests.

'Or we're totally hardcore.' We both laugh nervously. Previous attempts at smoking weed and pulling complete whities would suggest otherwise.

'They must be really weak then, that's fine with me.'

We walk along in silence, stepping over guy ropes and smouldering disposable barbecues.

'Can I ask you something?'

''Course.'

She takes a deep breath. 'Are you worried at all about your GCSE results?'

I hadn't expected that question. In fact I'd pretty much forgotten about the exams the moment I walked out of the last one a month ago.

'A bit, I suppose,' I lie, 'I'm not convinced I did all that well in any of them apart from drama, but then that's all I need if I'm going to be an actor, isn't it?' and I bow theatrically.

'Yep, you'll have nailed drama, guaranteed.'

'I thank you,' I respond in my finest RP voice.

We walk along for a while longer before Rachel pipes up. 'Sorry, Emmie, I don't mean to go on about it, and I know that it's really uncool to talk school here. It's just, well, Dad has been giving me a really fucking hard time about doing well and I can't stop thinking about it. About what will happen if I do badly.'

'Nothing will happen, you'll be fine, you know you will. And your dad has always been a dick about school stuff.'

'I know you're right, it's just, OK don't think me a total fucking spod OK if I tell you this.'

'OK.'

'Promise?'

'OK.' I sign a cross over my heart.

'OK, so before the end of term, I was called into Sir's office. . .'

'Which one?'

'The Head. . .'

'What for? And why haven't you told me?'

'I'm telling you now.' She gets her fags out of her bum bag and lights two, passing one to me. 'So he's asked me if I want to go on the school trip next year to visit Oxbridge.'

'Where's that?'

'You know, Cambridge and Oxford.'

I must be staring at her blankly.

'About applying for university there.'

'Bloody hell, Rach.'

'So. . .' Rachel starts to speak but I'm just trying to make sense of the last thing she said.

I'd just assumed me and Rach would obviously choose the same universities or ones that are so close to each other we'd be neighbours so that it would be like now, only somewhere else. 'Shit that's such a long time away that's all, we haven't even started our A levels yet.'

'I know, but he' − the Head I think − 'says it's important to get into the mindset or something, and it's a good motivator. That's partly why Dad's being such a twat about it.'

We walk along in silence for a bit.

'Why didn't you tell me before?' I sound irritable. I'm not sure why I'm making this all about me.

'It only happened last week, and you had some big news what with sleeping with Ryan and everything, so I just. . .' She shrugs to end the sentence. 'He doesn't even know I'm here, it's ridiculous.'

'Who?'

'Dad. He'd go fucking ape shit if he knew. Mum lied for me, said I was going with her to stay with Auntie Sharon for the weekend. I just couldn't do with all the bullshit. He'd just assume I was off my head the whole time.'

I suddenly remember we've taken the pills. 'I still don't feel any different, do you?'

'Nope, they must be duds.' She sighs, looking troubled. 'Look, it's all going to be fine, you just can't tell anyone about this. It might not happen and I don't want to have to hang out with the prefects for the whole of the sixth form if this gets out.'

As I turn my head to look at Rachel, my vision follows

in a series of colourful freeze frames. I blink and my sight refocuses.

'Rach. I feel weird, do you?'

I furl and unfurl my fingers; they feel rubbery, not like my hands. And wet, my left hand feels wet. I look down to see a dog licking it. Where did he come from?

Rachel's pupils are suddenly enormous. She opens her mouth to say something but no sound comes out, so we reach for each other's hands, intertwine fingers and walk unsteadily towards the masses.

The bass feels like a heartbeat. We fall into dancing with the Massive Attack crowds; everyone is moving as one. Someone is standing so close behind me that their body is propelling my body to move. I turn around to see a woman balancing a little girl on her hip who must be no older than about three. She's wearing tie dye trousers and a bright red knitted jumper that's far too big for her with a yin yang symbol on the front. The girl has her head nestled into the woman's neck with her eyes closed.

'I fucking love you!' she shouts to no one in particular as she catches my eye and squeezes me with her free arm.

'Who's the girl?' I bellow.

The woman bumps her up on her hip, kisses her on her forehead and continues to dance. I notice the girl isn't wearing any shoes and her feet are filthy.

The sun is now sinking low in the sky and the final rays of the day's light stretch out like fingers. Dust twinkles and dances in and out of the rays. It looks beautiful.

Everyone has a bright glow around them. The woman and child push in between Rach and I, and she shouts, 'Lucy!'

I can't remember the question.

'My daughter, her name's Lucy.'

Lucy. Lucy. Lucy. I like the way my mouth moves when I

say it aloud. The girl opens her eyes and smiles at me.

I wish my mum had taken me to festivals when I was little. I wish I had a daughter right now who would love me as much as Lucy loves her mum. I look at Rachel who grins at me, her jaw jutted out and arms raised in the air in total ecstasy. My favourite person in the world.

I don't want anything to change, ever.

Chapter Fifteen

'Come in! Come in!' Dennis opens the door wearing a Father Christmas hat.

I've never understood why Dennis has to say everything twice. He embraces Nick and slaps his back like a football player.

'Cathleen, Cathleen! They're here, they're here!'

Cathleen emerges from the kitchen wiping her hands on her apron. 'Welcome, and a very Merry Christmas. I'm making goose for dinner, but then Dennis reminded me that you're a vegetarian, Emily, so we've got a Linda McCartney lasagne for you. It says . . .' and she wanders off into the kitchen and re-emerges with the packaging, 'it says . . . hang on, let me put my glasses on . . . right. It says, layers of free-range egg pasta which contain soya mince ragu and rich béchamel sauce topped with cheddar cheese. Will that be alright for you, Emily?'

We still haven't closed the front door and I'm awkwardly holding Lucy on one arm and the change bag on the other.

'Sounds lovely.'

'You still eat bacon though, don't you?'

This is going to be a long New Year.

'Come in! Come in!' Dennis repeats and we follow him through to the reception room. They do have a sitting room, but we're just not allowed to sit in it as the décor is different shades of white and the sofa still has its plastic packaging

115

on it to 'keep it nice', so the whole room has a kind of post-forensic murder-scene feel to it.

'And here's my favourite little granddaughter, Luce.'

I shoot Nick a look. I've told him I hate it when his parents call her Luce and have asked him to ask them to stop it, but he obviously hasn't.

Dennis takes her out of my arms and walks towards the kitchen with her. 'Cathleen, Cathleen, here she is. The main attraction. Luce the goose about the hoose.'

'Really?' I mouth to Nick who shrugs apologetically in response.

Cathleen scoops her up from Dennis and starts making clicking noises, similar to the sounds you make to attract the attention of a horse.

'Leave all the stuff in the car for now, let's get comfortable and have a drink, shall we?'

Cathleen walks off with Lucy, clicking at her, and Dennis guides Nick to the sofa with his arm around his shoulder. 'How's life, son, how's work going?'

'All good, Dad.'

'But that's not what—'

'Not now, Dad,' he hisses at Dennis.

'Aah.' Dennis taps the side of his nose conspiratorially. 'Understood.' He then turns to me and asks with all the enthusiasm of a car salesman, 'Baileys? G and T? Vodka and Coke?' like he can somehow erase the fact that I was in earshot of their conversation with pure exuberance. I try and catch Nick's eye, but he purposely avoids my gaze.

'Or a sherry, Emily? A nice festive sherry?'

'Do you know where Cathleen's gone with Lucy?'

'She'll just be showing her the vegetable patch, Emily. Don't you worry, she's in safe hands. Now, what about that drink?'

The truth is, I don't want any of those, I just want Cathleen to come back with my baby and to have five minutes to ask my boyfriend what's going on in his life that he can talk to his dad about but not me.

'She'll be fine with Mum.' Nick gesticulates outside.

'I know,' I snap back.

'I think someone needs a loosener. I'll pour you a glass of Chablis to get this party started.' Dennis wanders off into the pantry, whistling 'Santa Baby'.

I know he is trying to be hospitable but I have an overwhelming urge to get up, grab my baby and drive straight back to Mum and Dad's where I can relax.

'Nick?'

'Let's talk about this another time, Em. We're here to celebrate. Mum's cooked a goose. This isn't the time.' He's cracking his knuckles nervously as he talks.

'OK, OK, well just let me know when,' I try to reassure him, sliding my arm around his waist.

''Course.' He slinks away and follows Dennis into the pantry. 'Need some help, Dad?'

There is not one part of this house I feel at home in. Until I was pregnant, Dennis and Cathleen insisted Nick and I slept in separate rooms, which seemed a bit odd when we were both thirty, but also felt like a challenge. We had sex all over their house and garden unbeknownst to them. The irony being if they'd actually let us share the same room, we probably would have just gone to sleep. Anyway, now we are parents we have been honoured with the responsibility of sleeping in the same room. This means we are all crammed into Nick's old bedroom, which has a bunk bed. The bottom bunk was only ever used when Nick's weird cousin came to stay so that's where I'm to sleep, and Lucy will be in the travel cot next to me.

'Can I tempt you to a Scotch egg, Emily?' Dennis offers up the plate.

'She's vegetarian, Dad.'

'That's why we bought them, with Emily in mind.'

'It's got sausage meat in it, Dennis.' Give me strength.

Dennis slaps his forehead. 'Apologies, apologies. I will instead ceremoniously open the Quality Streets. Drum roll, please!' And with this, Nick starts beating the kitchen table with his hands and wolf-whistling. What happens to him when we get to his parents' house? It's like he has a complete cool-bypass.

'I'm just going to go and feed Lucy.' I locate her and Cathleen in the garden.

'I'm showing her granddad's veg patch,' she explains.

Lucy is still in her Babygro with no coat on and her lips have started to go blue. I take her back from Cathleen.

'A bit of cold is good for babies. It toughens them up. I used to leave Nick outside in the pram when he was a baby so that he got some fresh air.' This is one of countless pieces of 'experience' Cathleen shares with me.

I wrap up my freezing-cold daughter in my coat, her icy hand fitting perfectly inside mine, and go and sit on the bottom bunk with her, wondering how long I can stretch out the feed.

Nick knocks on the door. 'I come bearing gifts.' He's even started to sound like Dennis, and we've only been here for an hour. He presents me with a handful of Quality Streets. 'Just don't leave the wrappers lying around though, as we're not allowed to eat upstairs.'

He sits cross-legged on the floor next to the bed. 'Is she still feeding?' Lucy has gone to sleep cuddled into my chest. Her clammy face is pressed against my bare breast and I want to say yes as I don't want to move her.

'If not, can I hold her? I haven't held her in ages.' I peel her off my skin and pass her over, all floppy and creased.

'Dad's opened a tin of Celebrations as well, as he wasn't sure if you'd prefer them – a vastly different beast to a Quality Street, is a Celebration.' Nick grins mischievously. I'm pleased he can see how ridiculous his family is sometimes too.

'Can we just stay up here for a bit?'

''Course. Hitch up.'

I shuffle over on the bottom bunk and Nick carefully squeezes in next to me, Lucy sleeping with her mouth wide open on his chest. I rest my head on his shoulder and close my eyes. He smells faintly of the aftershave I bought him for Christmas and clean washing. I breathe him in and put my arm gently on Lucy's sleeping back.

As if reading my mind, he whispers, 'I love you guys.'

I feel my body getting heavy, relaxing into them both and realise these are my most treasured moments. When we're not really doing anything other than being together, the three of us.

As I start to drift off to sleep, Dennis bellows upstairs, 'COME ON EVERYONE, IT'S SECRET SANTA TIME!'

We leave Lucy asleep on the bottom bunk with the baby monitor facing her, surrounded by cushions in case she suddenly learns how to roll in the time it takes us to unwrap some mediocre presents and put the travel cot up, and head downstairs.

I retrieve my gifts from the car, wrap them individually in the Lidl bags that are stuffed under the front seat, and add them to 'Santa's sack', which is an old pillowcase.

'Right then, can I refresh anyone's glass?' Cathleen giggles as Dennis fills up her Baileys. She only really drinks at Christmas and funerals so will be absolutely hammered after this one.

'I will be the ringmaster, if there's no objections,' Dennis says, rolling up his sleeves like a doctor scrubbing in.

He holds out the pillow for me first. I pull out a small parcel and start to open it.

'NO!' Dennis, Cathleen and Nick shout in unison.

'You have to wait until we've all got a gift, then we have to guess what it is first before opening it, that's half the fun!' Nick explains.

I wish Lucy would wake up.

'OK! You next, Nick!' Nick pulls out one of the Lidl bags. It's so transparent you can clearly identify the *Radio Times* and the Mars bar.

'Ooh – that one was meant for Cathleen.'

'That's not how the game works, Em.'

'No, no, it's fine, Nick. Emily is new to our little shenanigans and she's obviously bought something with Cathleen in mind, so, Nick, you give that one to Mum and choose another.'

He does as he's told, then pulls out the other Lidl bag.

'And that one's for Dennis,' I mutter.

'Spin again, son!' Dennis has completely got into the role and is borderline delirious.

Nick finally chooses a present that's not in a supermarket bag and then we all sit in silence feeling and shaking our presents.

'Gifts down. Contestants ready!' Dennis bellows. I'm not sure if this makes him the gladiator. 'Emily, you first!'

I look again at the misshapen package. 'A scarf?'

'Open it!' Cathleen squeals.

It's a packet of Marks and Spencer's handkerchiefs.

'Ooooooh,' they all chorus. 'Good guess.'

And around we go.

Nick guesses a diary. It's *Harry Potter and the Philosopher's*

Stone. He's delighted. Apparently, he's been in a literary vacuum for the best part of twenty years and hasn't read a single J. K. Rowling.

Cathleen guesses the *Radio Times* and a Mars bar.

Dennis guesses a car air freshener and a bottle of dandelion and burdock. 'Tremendously thoughtful, Emily. Shall we crack this bottle open and see if we've got something stronger to add to it?'

After this we have to go around again, but Cathleen has fallen asleep and so Dennis is guessing for her as well. I assess the scene. These are good people, there's no question about that. They are kind, and their hearts are in the right place. They have always just been Nick's parents. I've never had to consider how our lives would fit together as they've never really had to. I'd visit with Nick from time to time, but they felt one removed from me. That has now all changed. They are my daughter's grandparents. They will now always, always be in my life. This is it, the goalposts have shifted. I am a grown-up and will now have to start thinking about other people. I will have to learn when their birthdays are and buy a card for them from Lucy. I'll have to ring Cathleen to give her updates about her granddaughter. This is a whole other layer of responsibility I hadn't considered until now.

'Come on, Emily, don't keep us in suspenders.' Dennis chortles loudly at his own joke, waking Cathleen with a start.

'A pencil case?'

'Open it, open it!' Dennis and Nick chant.

It is a pencil case. They cheer. Lucy's crying comes through the baby monitor: my tiny saviour.

*

'You alright down there?' Nick whispers loudly from the top bunk.

'Yes. You?'

'I think I've eaten too many chocolates. My stomach's making really weird noises.'

'I think it's more likely the seventeen whiskies you had with your dad.'

'Maybe.'

'I'm just going to pop my head in the cot.'

'It's OK. She's fine, I can see her from up here. She's fast asleep.'

We hear someone cheering outside.

'Do you wish we were out?' Nick sounds almost wistful.

'No. A bit, maybe . . . but I'd never stay awake even if we were.'

The cheering outside has turned to shouting and it sounds like someone has broken a glass.

'Same. I thought I would miss it, but I can't be arsed. It's nice just being with you guys.'

'I was thinking, next year maybe we should have Christmas at home, the three of us.' I have been thinking about this a lot today, I can't wait to be back in our own home in a couple of days' time.

'What, like just you, me and Lucy?'

'No. Three other entirely different people, Nick.'

'Sorry, I just meant— I'd never really thought about . . . well, it just feels very, I don't know . . .'

'Grown up?'

'Yeah.'

'Well, we are.'

'Who gave you the sensible attitude for Christmas?'

'Let's just think about it, that's all I'm saying.'

I can hear him breathing loudly on the top bunk, he does

that when he's concentrating. He'd be the worst person in a poker game. I'm starting to fall asleep when he asks, 'But who would cook the goose?'

'Night, Nick,' and I roll over and pull the Laura Ashley duvet up under my chin. A group of women pass the house singing 'Dancing Queen', an old favourite of mine.

'Remember when you sang that in Bangkok?' Nick whispers.

I smile. 'I was just thinking about that too.'

Nick and I were running low on money and we'd seen a karaoke competition in one of the bars on Ko San Road. The prize for the best singer was fifty dollars. I was dreadful but what I lacked in talent I made up for in enthusiasm, and all the other acts were worse so I won. Nick had spun me around like Richard Gere in *An Officer and a Gentleman* and told me he loved me with early-romance intensity.

'Can I just come down to you?'

'Yes OK, but try to do it quietly.'

Nick slowly climbs down the ladder, creaking each rung as he goes, and I shuffle up in the single bed. 'Lift your head up,' and he puts his arm around me. I bury into his neck. I love the way he smells, it's reassuringly homely.

As the weight of the day starts to pull us into sleep, I suddenly remember the conversation I'd heard Nick and his dad have when we'd first arrived.

'Is everything OK with your work, Nick?' I can feel him tense next to me.

'Yeah, it's all fine.'

'But what about what your dad said?'

'What did he say? Has he been talking to you?'

'No. No. Just what you two said in the kitchen earlier. Why would Dennis talk to me?' I scoff. I don't mean to, but the idea of Dennis and me sitting down for a heart to heart is beyond ridiculous.

He takes my hand and interlocks his fingers with mine. 'It's just that restructure they've been talking about for ages. It's all fine, it's just, you know, they could do with making their minds up about what they're doing. So that we all know where we are. But it's all fine.'

He keeps saying the words 'it's all fine', like a mantra. 'Is your job safe, Nick?'

'Yes, yes, 'course,' but his voice sounds thin and unsure. Then again, we're both whispering so it could just be that. I pull him closer to me and wrap my arms around his chest as we listen to the fireworks outside. It must be midnight.

'Well we made it, we're awake!' I kiss Nick. 'Happy New Year!'

'Happy New Year. I love you,' he murmurs.

'I love you too.'

Just then someone sets off a particularly loud firework and Lucy jolts awake with a scream.

'Fuck,' we both chorus.

Chapter Sixteen

It's now 3.20 p.m. and I said for people to arrive from 3 p.m. I've just rechecked the text I sent, it definitely said 'from' not 'at', which I'm now regretting. How much after 'from' is acceptable? It there a 'fashionably late' when you are day-time drinking with children?

It's the day everyone's coming over and in a fit of social anxiety I've gone totally over the top with the food and drinks. Tania and Spiral are vegan, and Helen's husband, Chris, is gluten-intolerant, so I have basically spent a month's worth of child benefit in the Marks and Spencer's food hall trying to accommodate a range of dietary requirements. But now I've got it all out on plates it doesn't look like very much at all.

'Nick, stop eating them, just have a piece of toast if you're hungry.'

Nick goes to take the gluten-free cheese straw out his mouth.

'Don't put it back, just don't eat any more.' This was such a bad idea.

'Fuck's sake,' Nick mutters under his breath.

'What? WHAT?'

'I just don't know why you're being all weird about this. It's not like you even really know these people.'

That's the whole point. I don't really know them, and they don't really know each other, or me, but this is what you do when you have children, isn't it? Repeatedly put yourself in socially awkward situations for the sake of your kids.

Maybe we should have invited some of Nick's mates to bump up the numbers a bit, but then they'd just spend the whole afternoon smoking by the back door and talking about football, and that is not the kind of New Year gathering I had in mind.

There is a loud knock on the door.

'Right! They're here. Look relaxed.'

Nick leans against the worktop and strikes a nineties Kay's catalogue model pose as I pick up Lucy from her playmat and head to the door.

'Happy New Year!' Helen and Chris chorus.

'Come in, come in!' Oh my God, I've started to sound like Dennis.

'Polly's asleep in the pram, is it OK to carry it through?' Chris asks.

'No problemo,' I reply. I don't know what's happened to me – someone ban me from speaking. 'Nick, can you come and help?'

Nick emerges from the kitchen with a beer in one hand and a mouthful of vegan pate, which he tries to quickly swallow.

Nick and Chris briefly introduce themselves, shake hands then carry the pram through to our bedroom while Helen follows me and Lucy to the kitchen.

She looks more relaxed, younger almost.

'Oh, before I forget, this is a little something for Lucy,' she pulls out a wrapped present from her handbag.

Seriously? We are giving each other's children presents now? Why didn't I know this? I do a quick mental audit of everything Lucy has been given for Christmas, like a

126

speeded up version of The Generation Game, wondering if there is anything I can rewrap and give to Polly.

'Thanks so much. The boys have put Polly in our room now, so I'll get her present when she's woken up.' Nice save for the time being.

I help Lucy unwrap the present; it's a cardigan from White Stuff.

'The receipt is in there, just in case it doesn't fit.' Helen gently strokes Lucy's cheek. Riiiiiight. So I can't exactly give her the *Where's Spot?* book from Mum's next-door neighbour as this cardy must have cost the best part of forty quid.

Nick and Chris walk through, laughing like old friends.

'You didn't tell me Chris was from the Wirral!' Nick exclaims, part surprise, part accusation. Of course I didn't, I've only met him for about two seconds before today, and he was half naked and had just been shagging his wife. It's easy to forget the smaller details in those circumstances. What's so special about the Wirral, anyway? It's not like Nick himself comes from there . . .

'Beer, Chris?'

'Don't think I'm a dick but I've brought some gluten-free ones, otherwise I get the most crippling stomach aches.'

''Course not, mate. Totally understand. Knock yourself out.' Nick claps him on the shoulder. That was definitely not what he was saying when I told him how much I'd spent in the M&S free-from aisle. And when did he develop a Saaaf London accent? Looks like I'm not the only one who's trying to impress. Nick leads him away to the kitchen, talking about all the bars he used to go to in Liverpool when visiting one of his best mates who went to university there.

Two glasses of Prosecco later and I'm starting to relax into being the host.

Helen and I are sitting on the sofa with Lucy sleeping on her chest, and she is baring all.

'It's like we have to make up for the six weeks he's been away, it's a bit intense. Like we'll plan places to take Polly most days, even if it's just going out for lunch. We try and have date nights, but they're mainly at home as I haven't found a babysitter. And we're having sex a lot, which is knackering, but I keep thinking that there's only two more weeks and then he's going to be gone for another six weeks again, so we just need to get those moments in where we can. Do you know what I mean?'

'Yes.' I have absolutely no idea what she's talking about. We've done it once since Lucy was born and in all honesty, if given the option, I would prefer to have a snooze on the sofa while watching *The Good Wife* instead of doing it again anytime soon. Feeling brave after Nick comes over to top up our glasses for the third time, leaving us the bottle, I cut to the chase. 'Do you still enjoy it though?'

'What?'

'Sex.'

Helen takes a big gulp of her drink and snuggles her chin into the top of Lucy's head. I think she's ignoring the question and I start to regret asking, until she turns to look at me. 'I'm not sure, you know, that's a tough one.' She downs the rest of her drink and purses her lips in thought. 'I guess I like it when it's happening, when we're actually doing it. I like sex. I always have. It's just different once you've pushed someone out of your vagina, isn't it?'

I nod in agreement. 'Completely, totally different.'

She shrugs. 'But given the choice I think I'd prefer to watch a bit of telly or have a bath.'

'Me too,' I sigh with relief.

I fill up Helen's glass and she takes another gulp before

continuing. 'I used to love sex, you know. I had a much higher libido than Chris when we first met.' She gesticulates behind her at her husband who is laughing like a drain with Nick. 'It was quite a problem for a while to be honest – I had to buy all manner of sex toys and so on. We even got our old next-door neighbour involved once for a threesome. But that was just hugely awkward afterwards when we were all out in our gardens and whatnot. But as I say, not so much now.'

'Bloody hell,' I exhale.

'Sorry, Emily. Did I shock you?'

'Not at all, God no,' I lie, and then blurt out, 'Nick and I once did it in the disabled toilets in a Burger King in Peterborough!'

'Well there you go then . . .' Helen takes a big gulp of her fizz. 'We've all got up to mischief at one time or another, haven't we?' She pats my arm encouragingly. 'Shall I top you up?' She fills my glass and then hers and relaxes back into the sofa.

Crikey. As I get older I realise that my life experience isn't nearly as worldly as I thought. Maybe Nick and I should have had a threesome when we were younger. We talked about it once after several bottles of wine but it all seemed a tad messy and a bit of a logistical nightmare. I didn't really want to watch Nick getting off with another woman, and he wasn't mad keen on the idea of me bonking someone else while he lurked around watching. And how would we decide who the 'trois' in our ménage would be in the first place? It was far, far too complicated so we filed it in the 'maybe' pile, never to be reopened. But surely we've had a more exotic sex life than shagging in the Burger King loos though?

Nick and Chris stand shoulder to shoulder as they watch

something on his phone. He catches my eye, gives me a thumbs up and I reciprocate. On the whole I'd say this is going well. Helen and I are happy-pissed, bonding over our current disinterest in sex with our partners versus her previously insatiable sex drive. Both children are asleep and Nick and Chris are getting on like old mates. Win.

I've all but forgotten about Tania, Spiral and Falcon, until I hear a woman shout, 'Why couldn't we have got a fucking taxi? No. No it's not about your fucking carbon footprint. You're just tight. No, I didn't wake him, you did.'

Tania stomps down the path with Falcon tied to her front in a brightly coloured sling, Spiral walking a couple of metres behind with his arms tightly folded round his chest.

'I'll get it,' Nick makes his way to the door. Chris comes over to the sofa and kisses Helen gently before turning to me.

'This is exactly what we needed, Emily, thanks for inviting us over.'

'My pleasure,' I beam. I am the hostess with the mostest.

'Sorry, sorry, sorry!' Tania announces loudly, and Polly starts to cry in the other room. Helen passes the sleeping Lucy to me; she's floppy and warm and smells faintly of Helen's perfume.

'Shit,' Tania hisses, 'I didn't realise anyone was asleep.' She waves behind her. 'This is Spiral. He's the reason we're late!'

He raises a hand, half in greeting, half in defence. Nick and Chris are introduced, then Helen and Polly when they emerge.

We all stand around in a circle slightly awkwardly.

I wonder if I should bring over the tray of vegan cheese and spinach tarts, when Spiral gets out his rollies and asks, 'Is it OK if I go out for a smoke?'

'Yes!' Nick and Chris respond in unison and follow him outside onto the patio.

'Hi, hi.' The women greet each other with a warm hug and a kiss, Helen hands Tania a glass of Prosecco and I offer her a vegan tart.

Her eyes dart over to the patio door. 'Do you have any meat?' she whispers.

I point at the gluten-free sausage rolls. She reaches for one, not taking her eyes off the door for a moment and pushes an entire sausage roll into her mouth in one swift move.

It dawns on me that I'm feeling more like myself than I have since giving birth. Nick, Chris and Spiral are smoking what smells uncannily like weed in the garden while Helen, Tania and I mind the children, mainlining sausage rolls in secret and drinking our body weight in Prosecco. It's not how I'd envisaged my soirée but fuck it, everyone looks like they're having a good time.

'You have no idea how good it is to be here, Emily,' Tania sighs heavily. 'This has been the worst Christmas ever. Can you pass me another one of those?'

Helen holds out the tray of sausage rolls obligingly.

'You look amazing by the way,' Tania gushes to Helen as she takes the tray off her and settles it on her lap.

'Thanks!'

'But your posture is all over the place,' she adds, spraying crumbs. 'You'll get a crick in your neck standing like that. You should come to my yoga class.'

'Well maybe I will.'

Fuck. If Helen goes I'll definitely have to go. You can't have your new friends becoming better friends with each other than they are with you, especially if they originally met because your mum had bought fizz and you'd hosted the party with all the posh food.

'Why don't I start a WhatsΛpp group for us?' Hclcn gcts her phone out. 'Put your number in, Tania,' who obediently types and seconds later both mine and Tania's phones beep. 'There. Done.'

'So why was it so shit?' I switch positions with Lucy so as to not have bad posture too.

'What?'

'Christmas.'

'Urghhhhh,' Tania groans, 'because my fucking parents bought us a car.'

'That's amazing!' Helen and I chorus.

'How is that amazing? Our whole "thing",' she says, making quotation marks with her fingers, 'is that we walk when we can, get public transport blah blah blah, taxis now and then but only in electric cars. They just did it to piss me off. Well, to piss Spiral off.'

'I wish my parents were so minted they pissed me off like that.' I laugh, but actually I'm completely serious.

'Me too,' Helen chips in. 'My mum sent me a card with twenty euros in it and wrote that I could spend them when I can be bothered to visit her in Spain.'

'I got some hankies from Nick's folks and a pencil case.'

'Wow.'

'Yep, but then I had bought them the *Radio Times* and a bottle of dandelion and burdock so I kind of deserved it.'

'Wow. That is shit. You win!' Tania high fives me. 'We're going to send it back, obviously.'

'Obviously. Have you had a spin in it though?'

'Yes, of course. It drives like a fucking dream.'

'That's tough. Happy New Year, guys.'

We chink our glasses as the boys come back in.

*

Two hours later, Nick is attempting to do the washing-up but has already dropped and smashed two of our champagne flutes. Everyone left about half an hour ago. Lucy is asleep in her cot, but she has just started to make whimpering noises and Nick and I are both pretending we can't hear her in the hope that she might, by some miracle, learn how to self-settle in the next two minutes. I am pumping out a feed's worth of milk to throw straight down the sink because I realised I had drunk over a bottle of fizz. My head is pounding and sucking the very last bit of moisture out of me is not helping. A hangover at 6.45 p.m. just seems so unbelievably unfair.

I bring Lucy in and she attempts to feed from my empty boobs. 'Do you think everyone had a good time?' I call out to Nick.

'Yes.'

'Do you think they liked the food?'

'Yes.'

'Do you think Helen and Tania like each other?'

'Yep.'

'More than they like me?'

'Yes.'

'Yes?'

'I mean no. Look, you did well.' He comes and sits next to me on the sofa and puts his wet washing-up arm around me. 'You did good. They seem like nice people. Spiral's a bit weird but I've met weirder. And Chris is a top guy.'

'Do you think they'll invite us back to their house?'

'Probably. I'm going out for a beer with Chris next week to watch the football, so I'll ask. It's OK, I'm not stealing your mates,' he says, reading my mind. And then to wind me up, 'He just probably likes me more than she likes you.'

I playfully slap his arm, and snuggle up next to him.

I feel contented, calm. Until the branches of anxiety start to splay and weave through my brain. An image of Rach's Christmas drinks for her family and friends creeps in like an unwanted visitor. I wonder who else was there. Was it at her parents' house, were they all sitting around on the old brown sofa and matching armchair that I know so well? Were they still using the massive Argos CD stack system to play Christmas songs? I remember every inch of their house; I only have to close my eyes to transport myself back there.

Our own festive drinks suddenly feel shallow and meaningless.

'I'm going to put Lucy down and then go to bed myself.' I kiss Nick on his cheek.

'Do you want company?' he asks mischievously.

'No, not tonight.' Nick's smile falls. 'Sorry.'

I can't make everyone happy all the time, I have to try to remind myself of that.

Chapter Seventeen

'Do you want me to hold her while you take your coat off?' the nursery worker at Apple Eyes reaches out for Lucy who is clinging onto my neck like a baby chimpanzee as I try and take my arm out my jacket. Gemma looks about ten, even though she says she's been working for Apple Eyes for three years. Maybe it's just that everyone looks pre-pubescent since I've had Lucy.

'She's fine. Thanks, though.' I unselfconsciously sniff the bit behind Lucy's ear as she holds my neck a little bit too tightly. I imagine someone else looking after her for eight hours a day and the thought makes me feel sick.

This is the fourth nursery we've looked around. Nick has lost the will to live. He says he can't use up any more of his holiday. He says he needs to be more 'present' at work, whatever that means, and taking half a day off a week to look round nurseries that I'm only going to pick holes in before we've even got through the brightly coloured front door is not a 'good use of his time'. So now I'm looking around them on my own. I can't believe I have to do this already anyway, it's ages until I go back to work, but it turns out some people sign their children up with nurseries before the babies are even born. I can't quite get my head around the logistics of that. Anyway, Lucy's showing no signs of stopping breastfeeding. Unless we can find a nursery within a boob's distance of my office, I can't see it actually ever happening.

The thing is, when I was growing up I was looked after by my Granny. When Mum went back to work when I was just four months old, Granny moved in with us, much to my dad's absolute horror, and cared for me during the day. I'm not entirely sure what she did in the evenings; I personally would prefer to kill myself than have to spend every night making polite conversation, but my memories aren't punctuated with nervous laughter or slightly passive-aggressive judgement as I imagine they would be with Cathleen. I remember the fun stuff growing up with my family, going on the top deck of the bus to the precinct in Grimsby and eating knickerbocker glories on Cleethorpes seafront.

So nursery just feels like a total foreign concept to me; a bit like baby prison.

'Is this the first nursery you've looked at?' Gemma asks as she guides me down the corridor.

'Yes,' I lie.

'After you two . . .' She opens the door to a darkened room filled with wall-to-wall cots. Two women who look younger than Gemma are doing the mum-rock with babies not much older than Lucy.

'This is the room for the under-ones, it's called the Seedlings room. As in seeds of apples,' she whispers in a hoarse voice.

'What activities do they do in here?' I whisper back.

'They sleep in here, and play in the room next door. It's gorgeous in here though, there are night stars on the ceiling, and we play soothing music like Sade and Pavarotti to calm them down.'

The whole ceiling is covered in the glow-in-the-dark stick-on stars, like a massive meteorite has exploded.

'We try and work to mummy's schedule,' she whispers.

Did she just call me mummy in the third person?

'But we normally recommend a sleep mid-morning, a play with the key worker until lunchtime, then an afternoon nap, and a quick play before mummy picks her up.'

She totally did.

She closes the door on the women, who continue to rock with a fierce determination. I change my hold of Lucy as she's starting to give me a dead arm.

'Are you sure I can't take her from you?'

I've got to get used to her being with other people, I've got to woman up. I try to pass Lucy over, but she grips my neck and arches her back like a cat.

'It's OK, Luce, come here, babe.' Gemma unpicks her from me and Lucy pushes against her with her arms and feet while making a loud screeching noise. I last about three seconds before the hormones kick in and I swipe her back.

'Do you want to see the yard?' Gemma asks. 'We've got a sensory area, a little veg patch and a relaxation area for the older children when they need a time out.'

But I've seen enough. I mumble something about needing to get home and thank her for the tour. I push the green automatic release button and emerge into the fresh air.

'So, what did you think of that one, Lucy?' I ask as I pick up the pace.

Almost on cue she does a loud wet fart and I couldn't agree more.

'Mummy's so picky, isn't she? Isn't she?'

Nick is lying next to Lucy in the front room, blowing raspberries on her stomach as she kicks her legs in the air and squeals with delight. 'I bet you liked one of the nurseries, didn't you?' This is his new thing: he's started talking to Lucy about things instead of having a conversation with me.

Raspberry.

'Didn't you?'

Raspberry.

'Was Mummy just being picky again?'

Lucy throws her legs up and down excitedly and inadvertently kicks Nick in his windpipe.

He rolls onto his back with an almost silent 'Fuck's sake', and I want to fist-bump Lucy.

'I just want to get it right, Nick, this is a huge responsibility.' I try and ignore his whimpering. 'We are choosing who to entrust the most precious person in our life to. Stop being such a dick about it.'

'Well what was wrong with the first one we looked around?'

'The one with bars on the windows? It looked like a baby prison.'

'Or the one near your work, that would be convenient, what was wrong with that one?'

'It was completely filthy. There was a dog shit in the playground for a start.'

'Or that one you looked at near Helen's?'

'It was titchy. The kids were practically sharing seats to eat their lunch, it looked like a scene from *The Evacuees*.'

'But that one was the cheapest, wasn't it, by a mile you said?'

'Yes, but you can't put a price on childcare, Nick.'

'Well you obviously can, Em.'

He's such a smartarse sometimes. 'You know what I mean.'

'No, I don't really. They can't all be that bad. What about the one today?'

'Everyone who worked there all looked about five.'

'Come on, Em.'

'And they play Sade to get the kids to sleep.'

'We need to choose one so that you can go back to work. I don't think any of them are going to be good enough for you.'

'I don't know what the rush is anyway, Nick. It's not like I'm going back next week or anything.'

'I know, but we have to consider all options.'

'What options? Can you stop talking in riddles.'

'I just think we need to be realistic. About money. About what we're doing. I know we said you would have a year off work, but maybe we need to look at the bigger picture.'

'What bigger picture? Really, Nick, you're starting to do my head in. Can you just speak in plain English?'

'Maybe we just need to find a nursery and commit to it. So we know what the long-term plan is.'

I fold and unfold the tea towel that's strewn on the back of the sofa to do something with my hands. 'What's this all about, Nick?'

'The point is, Emily, that we just need to be careful with money. OK?'

The washing machine starts to shudder into the final stretch of its cycle as I try and decode what Nick's telling me. He's not one for exaggeration, that's always been my department. In fact he's always brushed off the big stuff. If de-exaggerating was a word, that's what he does. He takes the hot air out of a situation, that's one of the reasons we've always balanced each other out so well. I inflate, he deflates, and somehow, we keep afloat.

Nick is cracking his knuckles, working one joint at a time on each hand. I need to know what we're dealing with here. What the facts are: how careful do we need to be? But just then I see Lucy move from the corner of my eye.

'Did you see that?' I ask excitedly.

'What?'

139

'Lucy. Did you see what she just did? She rolled over, she just rolled over, Nick!'

Lucy is indeed now lying on her stomach with her head craned upwards, cooing, with spit dribbling from her mouth.

'Put her on her back again,' Nick enthuses.

I gently roll her over, where she immediately slams her legs down, before grabbing both feet and rocking her body from side to side until the momentum takes her all the way over. She grins with the achievement as we clap and congratulate her with a sea of kisses.

Nick picks up Lucy and holds her above his head. 'You clever girl.' He looks at me; his face has softened, the previous conversation parked for now. 'Look, just do what's best for Lucy. Everything's going to be OK. I'm just tired. Everything seems more of a big deal when you're tired. Isn't that right?' He looks up at his daughter whom he's holding in the air and she responds with a wide-mouthed gurgly grin, as a long string of spit drips out and lands in Nick's eye.

Chapter Eighteen

Nick and I have decided we need to plan some activities as a family. When I say Nick and I, I obviously mean me. He, half-complying, half-talking to me like I'm his mother asking him to tidy his bedroom (which is his latest thing), agreed.

I'd had a middle-of-the-night-feeding-Lucy panic, when I realised that the last time we'd consciously done anything 'together', instead of drifting from day into night into sleep-deprived day, was when we pretended we needed to go into Nottingham for nappies at New Year and then spent the afternoon wandering around the shopping precinct to have a break from Nick's parents. We're not exactly the Waltons. But what is there to actually do?

I turned to WhatsApp for some answers:

2.05 a.m.
Me: What can Nick and I do with Lucy together?
Tania: You better have a baby awake or you're wasting precious sleeping time worrying about this.
Me: She's asleep.
Tania: Then go to sleep.
Helen: Swimming?
Me: Is Polly up?
Helen: Yep. She's been feeding for hours. I'm on my third episode of Suits.

Me: I just want to do something together as a family that isn't watching The fucking Lion King.

Helen: I LOVE The Lion King. I hate swimming.

Me: How can you hate swimming?

Helen: I can't stand getting my hair wet.

Me: Then mum swim.

Tania: Yeah mum swim. I've been taking Falcon since he was four weeks old.

Me: Really? With Spiral?

Tania: Fuck no. Spiral can't swim and I don't want to have to look after two babies in the pool.

Me: He can't swim?!

Tania: I know.

Helen: Is it an environmental thing?

Tania: Nope. He's just lazy.

Me: L's just woken up so got to go.

Tania: Told you. Now you'll never get back to sleep. Night.

Helen: Night.

We've (I've) decided on swimming. It's also about time I started to do some exercise and my plan is that perhaps, once we're into a routine, I will be able to sneak into the big pool and do forty lengths while Nick and Lucy have a play. I know this kind of undermines the group activity ambition, but I saw myself in the full-length mirror this morning with the big light on, and it wasn't a pretty sight.

Since Lucy was born I have attempted a swim and had sex once. That is the sum total of the exercise I have done, and I didn't put much effort into either activity, if truth be told. I'm going to sort it out: I'm going to get back into my skinny jeans if it's the last thing I do, which it might possibly be, given the struggle I had to take them off last time I gave them a go. A photograph of me taken at our New

Year's drinks party made me realise that I can't use Lucy as an excuse anymore. In it, I've got my arms tightly wrapped around Tania and Helen's shoulders like a quarterback. My features look like my own but it's almost as if they've been Photoshopped onto a much rounder face with no neck.

Lucy is five months old now. That's five months of four rounds of toast with Nutella as a mid-morning snack. Of getting the bus to the local Spar which is so close I can see it from my front door. That's eleven goes on the Slendertone I bought off eBay in an attempt to acquire a six-pack while sitting on the sofa drinking wine and eating a large Dairy Milk as I electrocute myself.

I've got to get some control, make the switch from existing to actively making decisions. So I'm going to cut back on the peanut Trackers, because even if Dad used to eat them and was relatively healthy, he also used to do mountain walking with his friend and was probably about to tackle Scafell Pike after his snack, not settle down to an afternoon of *Murder She Wrote* with a sleeping baby on his chest.

I also think Lucy could probably do with a bit more stimulation. Watching Ryan Gosling films at the cinema down the road is definitely more for me than her, and being jiggled up and down for two hours in semi-darkness can't be that much of a laugh for her anymore. It was fine when she was a newborn, but now it's just an endurance test for us both as I desperately try and reconnect with any kind of pop culture.

So here we are, on an enforced family-fun day out. Nick and I get the bus to the pool. I don't know why we've both made this into such a big deal: for me it's about us making the effort, I suppose. For Nick, it seems to be more about survival – but that's probably because he googled 'babies drowning in municipal swimming pools' minutes before we left the flat and got about five-hundred-thousand results.

'It can be really dangerous, Em,' he'd said in a bid to talk me out of going.

'Well let's try not to drown her, that's got to be a start.'

'Have we got all the right kit, though? Armbands, goggles, that kind of stuff?'

'She doesn't need goggles. Now are you coming with us or do you want to stay here and google doom sites all afternoon?'

He'd reluctantly closed the lid of his laptop. 'I'm coming, obviously. I just want her to be safe.'

'Yes, me too. Now get your shoes on and let's go.'

As we arrive at the leisure centre the woman behind the counter tells us that the little pool is shutting in twenty minutes, so it is up to us if we want to pay twelve pounds or not to go in. I can see Nick's battling with his northern impulse to save his pennies, but then reluctantly hands over the cash. We have been building up to this all day, after all.

We lurk around the changing rooms, noisily complaining about people without babies hogging the family changing facilities. One eventually becomes free and a family of five – two parents, two toddlers and a baby – emerge. I smile apologetically, then squeeze Lucy into the tiniest pair of waterproof pants, and me into my too-small Asda swimsuit. Once our clothes are rammed into a locker the size of a shoe box, we tiptoe through the verruca pool and emerge into the chlorine-saturated room, only to be stopped on our way to the baby pool by a member of staff telling us that it's just about to shut for swimming lessons, even though we know there are still five minutes to go before the twenty-minute curfew.

Nick distracts her, pointing this out at great length, while Lucy and I dart into the water. We enter step by step, for the first time, followed closely by Nick, who's shaken off the woman.

'Hey, this is OK, isn't it? Are you enjoying this, Lucy?' She really looks like she is, smiling and hitting the water with her hands as her body becomes submerged in the just-off-freezing pool.

Nick and I grin at each other. These are the moments to be savoured, the little rays of light when we're all working together and everyone seems to be happy.

'Nice one, Em,' he compliments me, 'this was a good idea.'

Seconds later the lifeguard blows his whistle. 'Every-oooooooone oooooooout the pooooool' (we are the only people in here) 'eeeeempty the poooool, it's swiiiiiiming lessons noooooooooow. Geeeet ooooooooout.'

We reluctantly get out and go through the whole rigmarole in reverse. Moaning about the family changing facilities. Getting out of tiny costumes and pants. (Turns out you just rip off the waterproof nappies, not carefully pull them down and save them for the next time. I'm going to have to start YouTubing everything before leaving the flat.)

Lucy instantly falls asleep on the bus on the way home and Nick and I congratulate each other repeatedly on how well this has gone for a first attempt, and how much we both enjoyed it. I know we are both waiting to see who cracks first and says what we both really mean – it was a whole load of hard work for five minutes.

Nick takes my hand and gives it a squeeze and I suddenly get a swell of pride. I am on the bus with my family and we have just been swimming together. We haven't slowed down global warming or helped with the national debt, but we're moving stuff along. We can put a swim nappy on and take it off in a sweaty changing cubicle without killing one another. Surely that's a result.

Nick unlocks the front door, scooping up the post off the mat and flicking through the envelopes absent-mindedly.

'There's one here for you.' He passes me a handwritten envelope and stacks the more official-looking ones on top of a pile of old newspapers on the table, which is shorthand for these will never get opened. 'Right, kettle on. Tea or coffee?'

'Tea, please.' I lift Lucy out of the pram and carry her through to the front room.

'Normal?'

'Yes please.' I sit down on the sofa, latch Lucy on and rip open the envelope, pulling out the official-looking paper. My stomach flips.

Dear Emily,

We are about to launch several training sessions over the next few months around SMART working and time management. You may wish to consider attending and using one of your Keeping in Touch days. If this is of interest to you, please do let me know and I can give you further details on the various times and dates. You are under no obligation to do so and attendance would not 'break' your maternity leave.

With warm regards,

Liz Johnson
Head of Arts and Regeneration.

'Fuck.'

Nick carefully passes me the mug. 'What?'

'It's work, about keeping in touch days.'

'That'll be a piece of piss. You'll just sit there and show everyone pictures of Lucy and drink coffee.' I get the feeling

146

Nick similarly has no real grasp of my job. Shame I can't get on my high horse about it.

I notice that Liz hasn't even bothered to sign it herself, it's pp-ed by Mags, her office admin.

'The thing is' – I take a sip of my tea and pass the cup back to Nick as I switch Lucy onto the other side – 'I've been thinking. Maybe I don't actually want to go back, Nick. I never really saw myself staying there long term, not really. It was never meant to be permanent, it was just, you know, a stopgap until I did something I wanted to. I can't imagine myself there anymore. I think I need somewhere with more creative people. I think I'd be far better suited working in an ideas job. An agent for a theatre, or an assistant director, that's what I was thinking. Something like that.' The ideas are starting to formulate. Admittedly this is the first time I've thought about any of this, but it just seems to be flowing out of me now. I have a picture in my mind of me in my new role, hair cut in a quirky style, wearing skinny jeans, an oversized shirt and mismatched dangly earrings. 'Then I could finish my own play. I just need to work in a place where I feel supported creatively, do you know what I mean, Nick. Nick?' I strain my head round to check he's still in the room.

He's leaning against the sideboard resting his head in his hands.

'Nick? You OK?'

'Yep.'

'Sure?'

'Of course. I'm just going to nip out and get some more tea bags.' He picks up his coat and as he heads out I see a new economy box of Tetley on the top of the plates cupboard. How could he have missed them? But before I can shout his name he's slammed the front door.

Chapter Nineteen

We're going on a date tonight and it has to be brilliant. This is our first date since Lucy was born. I think I may have put too much pressure on myself, expecting this to be an incredible night, but God I need it. We are, after all, only going to the pub around the corner for a bit of food. But the planning that has gone into it is astronomical. Not by Nick of course, but I have had this in the diary with Mum and Dad since we went up at Christmas.

I haven't been out of the flat past 5 p.m. since I don't know when, so for me, this feels like a massive deal. But for Nick, who goes to work every day, often staying late and no doubt going for a drink with colleagues before coming home, this is just a bonus night out. The balance of expectation doesn't feel quite right. I've been planning what I'm going to wear for ages, but now that I'm getting dressed I realise I haven't actually thought about the logistics, i.e. do any of my clothes that aren't ninety-nine per cent elastic actually fit? My plan had been to look effortlessly hot in the Vivienne Westwood fifties dress I'd bought off eBay on my iPhone during a late-night feeding sesh, but it doesn't fit. Not even close. The zip gapes wide at the top, and the bit I've managed to do up is so cripplingly tight that I'm convinced I'm having a heart attack.

'Knock knock!'

'Come in, Mum, I'm having a bit of a nightmare here.'

She's shown up just at the point I was thinking I might have to call the fire brigade to cut me out of it.

She greets me with, 'Now then, don't you look lovely!' Before I turn around to show her I'm ten per cent dress and ninety per cent exposed flesh.

'Ah!' she adds. 'So, your dad's going to stay at the Travelodge this evening, as we had a look at the TV guide and both wanted to watch different things, so I thought I could watch my programme here and your dad could watch his at the hotel.'

'Great, sure. Can you help me out of this?'

'Ooh, it is tight, isn't it, but such lovely fabric.' She manages to narrowly miss slicing my skin as she lowers the zip and I go in search of something three sizes bigger.

'Are you going anywhere nice?' Mum shouts through from the other room.

'Just the pub around the corner.'

'That's not very romantic; hasn't Nick booked you a table somewhere?'

It hadn't crossed my mind that he should have done, but now it has and he hasn't, I can feel the fizz of an argument starting in my stomach.

'Right, what do you think of this?' I've settled for a maternity dress that isn't bobbling too much over my tummy.

Mum already has Lucy snuggled down on her chest, legs tucked up underneath her like a frog, her mouth wide open letting out little whistling noises every time she exhales.

'You look wonderful,' she says with way too much conviction. 'Just have a lovely night, that's all that matters,' she reassures me.

Maybe she's right. Maybe this is the start of our social life. Maybe Mum could come down from Lincolnshire once every month so we can go out. Maybe we could even consider venturing further than ten metres from the front door.

I'm getting ahead of myself: let's get through tonight first.

As Nick arrives home, I'm feeling borderline smug about how well it's all going.

'Lucy's had a good feed and has gone down in her cot.'

'Great. Hi, Jennifer.' He waves at Mum. 'Where's Richard?' He cranes his neck round the door.

'Dad's watching a Steven Segal film at the Travelodge, there's a microwave meal in the fridge for Mum, and *Midsomer Murders* has just started on the telly.'

'Well, let's get out before it all goes to shit.' Nick doesn't bother changing, and affectionately slaps my bum as I walk out the door. 'You look hot, by the way.' He grins as we leave the flat and I instantly forgive him for not booking a Michelin-starred restaurant for tonight.

We hold hands on the walk down to the pub. We never hold hands anymore, as one of us is always pushing a pram. It feels lovely to have his fingers intertwined in mine.

As Nick pushes open the door of the pub we hear a disembodied voice asking, 'Genuphobia is the fear of what part of the body?' over the PA. It turns out it's quiz night, so the romantic evening looks to be punctuated with general knowledge questions. Several of Nick's friends are sitting round a table scrutinising the quiz sheet. They spot Nick and beckon us over. I stay rooted to the spot.

'This is meant to be our date night,' I hiss.

'I know, I'm just saying hello.' He shrugs at his mates and guides me to the only available table, which is the size of a jam jar lid and positioned next to the gents.

'I'd totally forgotten it's quiz night.' Nick waves at someone I don't recognise sat at the other side of the bar. 'That's Jim, I used to be on a five-a-side team with him.'

'Should we go somewhere else, Nick?'

'No, we'll be grand here. Just ignore it.'

We order our food quickly, as the barmaid says the kitchen is shutting soon. On Nick's recommendation I order whitebait which he assures me I'll enjoy.

When my dinner arrives, it's a vegetarian-who's-recently-started-eating-fish's worst nightmare. It looks like a fish morgue, just loads of little dead fish with their eyes looking up at me from the plate.

'Nick, this looks awful.'

'Oh fuck, I didn't mean whitebait, I meant scampi. Yeah, you're right, I don't think you're going to like that at all. Do you want some of my chips?'

He's ordered rare steak and his chips are swimming in blood so I refuse. I struggle to get the little fish past the gag reflex, so down my wine after each mouthful, and a third of the way through dinner I'm already feeling a bit pissed.

To make matters worse, I can't think of anything to say. Not one thing. Nick casually talks about a phone call he had with an old school friend who would like to come and stay soon to meet Lucy. He switches to a chat he'd had with his mum, and how they are also threatening to visit, but for me not to worry as the chances are they won't and if they do they'll book themselves into the Travelodge. Between mouthfuls he talks about one of the guys sitting on the table near us, whose younger brother has just had a trial for Portsmouth FC. He chats effortlessly and confidently, floating from one subject to another with ease. He's easy company, that's what everyone says when they first meet him, how instantly likeable and approachable he is. Whereas in this moment I've never felt less approachable. My face feels tense and I can't find a way to sit that looks natural.

Nick drains the last of his pint. 'Another?' I nod, and I

watch him chatting to the barman like old friends. He returns, clumsily putting our drinks down, and I just sit there in silence.

If anything has happened with Lucy during the day, I give him a ring for an update. Is it dinner etiquette to talk about the hard time Luke's having bonding with his dad on *One Tree Hill*, or the woman who took the DNA test on *Jeremy Kyle* and found out her long-lost sister was actually her mum?

I've insisted that we don't talk about Lucy, that this evening is about us, but I don't feel like there is anything else I can offer up to talk about. And right now, I miss her. It's ridiculous as I can probably see our flat from the pub if I crane my neck, and we've only been gone half an hour, but I miss her smell. I check my phone again.

'She'll ring if there's a problem,' Nick reassures me.

'I know, I was just checking I had enough battery, that was all.'

'Bernie at the bar said there's a hundred-pound jackpot for the bonus round tonight.' I shake my head disappointedly. 'I'm just making conversation, Em.'

'I didn't say anything!' I protest.

'I know you didn't. In fact you haven't said more than about two words since we got here.'

'I know! I know I fucking haven't,' I whisper. Why does he have to always state the obvious? Why does he have to make me feel like shit with just one throwaway line? I'm not choosing to be Silent Mike. I'm not in a huff. I just can't think of a bloody thing to say.

Nick shoves an unnecessarily large forkful of steak into his mouth and then continues to talk while chewing. 'So, have you seen anything of Helen recently?'

'Yeah, a bit.'

'Chris is back, isn't he?'

'Er, yes, I think so.' I have no idea.

'I just saw him on the walk home from work the other day, so we had a quick pint. I can't remember whether I said.'

'No. No you didn't mention it.' I'm not sure why this is so annoying. Is it because Helen's never invited me out?

'And what about the other mate?'

'I have got more than two mates, Nick.'

'I know, I know. Yoga thingy.'

'Yoga Tania.'

'How's she doing? Did she keep that car she was bought?'

'I've no idea.' I shrug and take a large gulp of my wine.

One of Nick's mates emerges from the gents doing his fly up. 'Why don't you come and join us when you've finished your food?' he asks.

Nick looks at me expectantly.

'Of course.' By which he surely knows I mean, 'Of course not.'

'Great, see you both in a bit.'

As Nick stabs at his chips I whisper, 'You're unbelievable.'

'But you said . . .'

The next round starts. 'Who owned the *Daily Mirror* newspaper between 1984 and 1991?'

'Robert Maxwell,' Nick replies without even looking up from his plate.

The evening couldn't have been further from what I'd wanted it to be. Tears threaten to roll down my cheeks. Nick looks up and gives me a strained smile. I burst into tears at least seven times a day at the moment, so it's not necessarily a good indicator of a bad situation; I could've just watched the Oxfam advert.

I take a deep breath and change the subject. 'How's work going?' I venture.

'Em, are you genuinely trying to sabotage this evening?'

'No. 'Course not. I was making conversation.'

'Sorry. 'Course you were. I didn't mean to snap. It's fine. It's all OK, I think. There's nothing really to add to that. I get up, I go there, I work my arse off, I come home. That's all there is to say. Nothing to worry about.'

But there is something, there's clearly something worrying him. Why can't Nick talk to me anymore? Everyone's got to have someone to talk to, haven't they? Who does Nick talk to if it isn't me?

'Another?' he asks. He's got the edge to his voice of a man who's not exactly pissed but you wouldn't ask him to operate heavy machinery.

Just then Mum rings.

'I hope you're both having a good evening.'

I can hear Lucy screaming in the background and my body reacts immediately as my milk comes. My breast pads must have slipped down as two circular wet patches appear on my chest.

'I'll be home in a minute.' I feel hugely relieved that the decision has been made for me and I can just get back to her.

Nick gets up to leave too. 'Just stay, there's no point us both going back.'

'Do you genuinely mean that this time?'

'Yes, I mean it.'

He leans in to kiss me but I'm bending down to pick up my handbag and we clash heads with a thud.

'Shit, sorry.'

'Forget it.'

'Look, I won't be long, I'll head back after the quiz.'

'Just come back whenever.' I shrug.

As I push open the door I hear a cheer from his mates' table as he joins them. It starts to spit as I power-walk back home on my own.

This has to be up there as one of the least successful date nights ever. Definitely not worth a 500-mile round babysitting trip for Mum and Dad. I can't even bring myself to tell Mum how it went. I can't shake the feeling that something has shifted with me and Nick. That it's more than just my inability to hold a conversation, it's something more fundamental.

I compose a text to Rachel.

I've turned into a mute with no conversational skills, and Nick would prefer to hang out with his mates than spend any time with me. Any ideas? Xxx

I don't have a mobile number for her, only a landline, so I can do this in the quiet confidence that it will never get sent. But I do it from time to time, I find it settling. Writing a text to Rachel that will never get sent. I imagine her receiving it, laughing to herself and then composing a response. To this it would be something like:

You've always got something to say about EVERTHING, Emmie. Xxx

I will, of course, never know what she'd say until I have the balls to actually contact her. And even then, there's absolutely no guarantee that she'd respond.

What a shambles of a date. But on the plus side I've learnt that 'genuphobia' is the fear of knees and/or kneeling, so the evening hasn't been a total washout.

Chapter Twenty

It's the eerily quiet 3 a.m. feed when I first start fantasising about what it would be like to not have a child.

The world feels like it has ground to a halt. The only light comes from the full moon seeping through the paper-thin IKEA bedroom curtains and there's the occasional noise from a car driving by. I'm in bed with Lucy latched on, Nick asleep next to me, and I let my mind wander.

By not having a child, I don't mean not actually having Lucy. It would be better described as leaving this life in some kind of *Doctor Who*-style freeze-frame ready to come back to, while hopping into another, which is exactly the same, except it's just me. And possibly Nick, unless he's being really annoying, and then the daydream just involves me. The dream predominately revolves around sleep. Full, uninterrupted, deep sleep. I would trade every potential holiday or meal out I might ever have in my future life for a night of pre-child quality sleep.

All the baby books say that by now a baby should be only waking once. In fact, one particularly irritating e-newsletter I received, and have now subsequently unsubscribed from, told me 'now your baby is having longer, possibly all-night-long sleeps, you should find some time for yourself during the day with your new-found energy'. I can only assume it was written by a man, or a mother of ten who just wants to fuck with us first-time mothers' minds.

Tania says that Falcon sleeps anything up to ten

consecutive hours a day. Mind you, she also says that almost all ailments can be cured by eating boiled nettles, so I'm in two minds whether to believe her.

I wonder how many other mothers are quietly feeding their babies around the world at this very moment? I try contacting two of them.

3.10 a.m.
Me: *Anyone up?*
Helen: *P's dropped off but I can't get back to sleep.*
Tania: *Me. Falcon in our bed. He's taken up all of the space like a human starfish.*
Helen: *Is he asleep?*
Tania: *Snoring. What baby snores??*
Me: *Nick's snoring too.*
Helen: *I wish I had someone snoring next to me.*
Tania: *Bollocks.*
Helen: *OK. Not snoring.*
Tania: **news* We're keeping the car.*
Me: *What about the environment?*
Helen: *Fuck the environment, it's a free car.*
Tania: *Spiral's looked into it and it's more environmentally friendly than the bus, as long as we're all in it. New rule – we can only go out if there's at least three people in it.*
Me: *What kind of car is it?*
Tania: *Dunno. It's got a Panther or cheetah or something on the steering wheel. I don't know anything about cars.*
Helen: *It can't be a fucking Jag, can it?*
Tania: *Dunno. It's black. It's got digital radio so I can listen to Lauren Laverne.*
Me: *I love LL.*
Helen: *Me too. Night.*
Me: *Night.*

Why can't Dennis and Cathleen buy us a bloody Jag to drive round in like a huge expensive baby walker? Why are everyone's babies asleep? What the fuck is wrong with my baby?

The thing is I don't even think Lucy's hungry. She's just using me as a massive woman-shaped comforter. I lie down with her next to me so that she can feed and I can sleep, but instead she just painfully chews on the end ten per cent of my nipple, while kneading her feet into my stomach like a cat. This can take up to an hour before I fall back into a light restless sleep, while Nick continues to gently snore undisturbed like a disgusting pot-bellied pig.

He puts the kettle on in the morning with the enthusiasm of a full eight hours rest and says, 'She did really well sleeping through last night, didn't she?' and it makes me want to smash him over the head with the high chair.

I appreciate that parents of babies talking about being tired must be up there with hearing someone banging on about their dreams in terms of the boring-o-meter, but it's all I can think about.

As I sit in a fug at the table sipping my tea I wish for the first of about 198 times today to sleep for more than four hours at a time. This wish doesn't involve a posh hotel room, or even a comfortable mattress. I'd happily sleep on a bed of rusty nails if it were eight undisturbed hours.

At 8 a.m. the doorbell rings. It's the Hermes guy with my latest eBay purchases. As I open the door with Lucy on my hip he asks, 'Is this for you then?' and tries to unsuccessfully pass the package to her. 'Is he sleeping through yet?'

'No.'

'Never mind. The time goes so quickly. The days are long but the years are short, as they say.' As who says? I think, but I can't be bothered to ask. 'My son's thirty-four now, it feels like only yesterday that he was the same age as this little lad.'

I don't know why everyone thinks she's a boy; she's wearing a pink Peppa Pig Babygro, for Christ's sake.

'OK. Thanks, do I need to sign for this?'

'Yes, just put your autograph there. Now, my grandson, that little firecracker is a sleeper. He's always been like that. He's four now and we just can't get him up in the morning. He'd happily stay in bed all day playing his Xbox if we'd let him when he comes to stay with us. Kids, eh? Anyway, enjoy your day.'

I rip open the parcel. It's a size ten Topshop vest top in lime green which is never in this lifetime going to fit me and just holding it up against my face makes me look like I have jaundice. I can't even remember bidding on it.

I feel the prickle of irritation with the delivery man, partly for delivering this overpriced top that smells of cheap market aftershave, but mainly for not asking about me, about how I am today.

See, the second thing I dream about is having a conversation with an adult in which a) I am asked questions about anything other than Lucy and b) I can get to the end of a sentence in one sitting. I like talking about her, that's a given. I clocked up over 1,500 pictures of her on my phone within the first two months of her life. I can't imagine the world without her in it. But I would love it if once, just once, someone would ask a question that didn't start with Lucy.

I don't even know if people are genuinely interested in her or just feel they should be asking questions. Family have to be, of course, but people I used to work with or the woman behind the counter in Boots or the man who makes toe-curlingly strong coffee in the park café can't all genuinely want to know how heavy she is, can they?

I used to have a job where people listened to my opinion. I wasn't exactly chief adviser to the prime minister, but if you wanted to know about arts education for under-elevens in East Sussex, then I was your woman. Now that feels like someone else's life.

When I talk to Mum on the phone, she wants to know, in this order: how many poos Lucy is doing a day (four, at least); how the bottle feeding is going (abysmally, I think she's going to be breastfed until she's at university); how she's sleeping (see above); and finally, how I am (fine, thanks for eventually asking). I feel such a dick for being grumpy that I don't get a look-in, but in my parallel child-free life, I sit around and discuss things. I remember Nick and I used to debate, to put the world to rights. We'd discuss books, music, world politics, but when I remind him of this he says, 'You're rewriting history, Em, we just used to get pissed.' He's probably right, but I would like a guilt-free day to get pissed, eat pizza, dance my tits off to music that's too young for me, talk shit, then teleport myself back to my life now, feeling hangover-free and like my old self.

Nick thinks I'm being childish when I try to talk to him about it, like Lucy is stealing my limelight, or I'm not the centre of attention anymore. But it's not that; I just want to feel like me again. I genuinely don't know who I am half the time.

I mean, I know I'm 'Lucy's mum'. The health visitor calls me Lucy's mum. Our Hot Doctor calls me Lucy's mum. Auntie Jan sent me a card addressed to 'Mummy' the other day, which is frankly a bit weird.

In my parallel life I am confident, I can talk on a range of subjects and I'm more fun than the average person can handle. I'm known for it:

'You know Emily . . .'

'Oh, the really fun one?'

'Yes, that's her.'

Yep, that's me.

But the reality is I can't even string an understandable sentence together. When was the last time Nick and I talked about something, anything, properly?

'I've got to go in a minute, do you want to have a shower before I head out?' Nick wanders into the kitchen with wet hair and a hand towel wrapped around his waist instead of the large bath towels that I had quite clearly hung on the back of the door. What if we have visitors? Are they expected to dry their hands on the towel that he's rubbed his scrotum all over?

'Yes, 'course I do.'

'OK, I was just asking. You don't always.'

'When have I not wanted to have a shower, Nick? When have I not wanted to wash?'

'Keep your hair on, Em. Who was at the door?'

'It was the postman.'

'Anything for me?'

'Nope. Just a top for me.'

'Going to give me a quick preview before I go?' He grins.

'It's not a sexy top, Nick, obviously.'

'Right. 'Course.'

'What do you mean, 'course?

'I didn't mean anything by it, I was just saying . . .' He's shaking his head at me in a way that I can only interpret as patronising.

'Well don't.' I have no idea why he's irritating me so much this morning but everything he says feels like a dig.

'Look, if you're going to have a shower, I suggest getting in it now. I have to leave in seven minutes, so be quick.'

161

He's not even dressed so I don't know where the seven-minute deadline has come from. My skin prickles with annoyance and I try to suppress yet another early morning argument with him. This is about the extent of our transactions these days.

I stand in the shower and think about what Mum said over Christmas about Mario and wonder who my Mario would be. He'd probably have the looks of Ryan Gosling, the sense of humour of Peter Kay and the intellect of Brian Cox.

He'd be an infamous theatre director called Tom Smith, or something like that, who was entranced by the incredible script I'd written, and we'd be collaborating on a production at the National. I'd be cool in an 'I can just put on jeans and a grey sweatshirt, tie my hair up and look like I'm modelling for Urban Outfitters' kind of way. He'd be stomach-churningly gorgeous, the kind of guy who makes your fanny fizz just by smiling at you.

We'd be the perfect creative team in the rehearsal room, then spend the evenings eating in quirky restaurants before fucking in the toilet cubicle because we just can't wait to get home to take each other's clothes off.

I am just trying to work out if I fall pregnant with Lucy after the show transfers to Broadway, or if I already have her from an unknown father and Tom adopts her, when Nick bangs on the bathroom door.

'Em, did you put a wash on yesterday?'

'I'm in the shower, Nick, can't you just give me five minutes?'

'I can't find any boxers.'

'No, I didn't put a wash on. I'm not your mum, Nick. Do your own washing.'

'I didn't say you were, I just wondered if you did put a

wash on if any of my stuff had gone in too. Chill out, Emily.'

I give him the Vs to a closed bathroom door.

'Oh, and Lucy's done a poo by the way, I don't have time to change her so just saying. She's not upset by it or anything so should be OK for a bit.'

I try and picture Tom Smith again, but I can only see Nick standing there in a dirty pair of boxers with his hands on his hips in the infuriating stance he adopts when he thinks he's right. I rest my head against the tiled wall and let the water run down my head and neck, hoping it will wash some of my irritation away with it.

Chapter Twenty-one

'I saw another nursery yesterday.' I've stopped telling Nick about my weekly visits to nurseries until today. But, I think I might have found the one. Probably. Possibly.

'They have a big playground and all the staff were over twenty,' I continue, 'and I handed Lucy over to the key worker when I took off my coat without even thinking about it.'

'Great!'

'It's called Laugh 'n' Learn Academy, though.'

'But you liked everything else about it? And Lucy was happy?'

'Yes. But it was called Laugh 'n' Learn. It has an 'n' in the name. Wouldn't you find that massively irritating every time you saw it?'

'We just need to suck it up and choose one.' He says this like he's been helping too. Like he's been pushing Lucy all over Brighton to look around nursery after crèche after childminder's house for weeks on end. Laugh 'n' Learn Academy is the first place I've seen that I haven't wanted to leave the moment I walked through the front door, so we should just do it, of course we should. I don't know what's holding me back; I don't know what or who it is I'm looking for really. Someone like me, I guess, just better.

'Just do it, put her name down.'

'OK.' I feel relieved that a decision has been made. I'm

not sure if it's the right one, but a decision has been made nonetheless. The microwave pings and I remove our dinner of Spar's own-brand vegetarian curry.

'I'm going to have to go into work early every day this week, Em, I know it's a ball-ache, but bear with me. It's not going to be forever.'

'As long as it's not, Nick.'

'It won't be, I promise. I meant to ask, have work been in touch again about going back?'

'No, not since that letter a while ago.'

'Right, so there's no more indication as to when they need you to start back?'

'Nope. Well, yes, but it's up to me. I told them a year like we agreed but I could go back sooner, I guess. Or not at all if I get around to writing the play that's going to make us rich,' I joke, pausing briefly to think about Tom Smith and what we'd be having for dinner in my other life, before removing the plastic lid from the food and dividing the greasy contents onto two plates. Nick's drumming his fingers with a nervous energy that's putting me on edge as I pass him his plate.

'Why are you asking?' As I fill the kettle up I can feel the weight of his stare on my back and I can picture the look of worry that has settled on his face.

'No reason, it's just work are now saying they're looking to create a more streamlined approach to the business.'

'What does that mean?' I sit down opposite him.

'It means that they are looking to downsize, to develop a more economically viable model.'

I raise my eyebrow. I still have no idea what he's talking about, this is just a load of words crudely clubbed together to make a sentence that sounds like it has been put into Google translate.

'Nick. Speak English.'

'They're looking to make redundancies, that's all. But it could be a long way off and might not affect me at all. There's also talk of a merger as well, which could actually make everything loads better, so this is all just what ifs at the moment. I just think we need to, you know, plan for the worst, hope for the best.' He smiles weakly.

'Is this serious, though, Nick?' I put my fork down. He has my full attention.

'No more serious than anything else in life.' He shrugs. Why has he started talking like a Hallmark greetings card?

'What can I do, Nick, what can I do to help?'

'Nothing. It will be fine.'

'Stop saying it will be fine if it's not going to be fine. Let me help. And stop wringing your hands, you're making me nervous.'

He folds his arms, tucking his hands under his armpits.

'I just want to support you. We can work this out together, Nick. We're a team.'

'Well unless you can get me three new clients by the end of the month then there's not much you can do,' he laughs, but it's a hollow laugh. Mean.

'Nick, you don't have to be like that, I was just—'

'Sorry. Sorry. That wasn't meant to come out like that. It's just . . . Look, Em, this might not be anything, but maybe we just need to put you going back to work earlier that we'd anticipated out there as an option.'

'Like when?' I splutter.

'Well, I don't know. It might not have to happen at all if I work really hard and show them how good this guy is,' and he prods himself in the chest with two thumbs, trying to make light of the situation.

'Come on, Nick, stop fucking about.'

He sighs, deflated. 'Look, it might just be a chat with work to see what the deal would be about going back early. Just a chat to see if it's possible.' He drains his glass. 'And it's not like there's a recruitment freeze or anything, they've just employed a new consultant, so that's got to be a good sign, right? You don't go employing people if you're about to shut up shop, do you?'

I feel nauseous, not helped by the artificial sweetener smell wafting from our dinner. I'm a planner. I like to know what's going on, I like to be at airports the moment the check-in desk opens, or at the train station with time enough to buy a drink and a magazine before the platform number has come up on the board. This is starting to feel like we're going off plan.

'She's great as well. It's reassuring to have that level of experience in the office, to see what we're all doing. I think she's confident in my ability, she's said as much so that's a good thing.' Nick shovels slimy courgette and hard white rice into his mouth as he explains how she has 'brought a much-needed lightness to the office'.

'Who are we talking about?'

'Shelly.'

'Who the fuck's Shelly?'

'Oh, the consultant they've brought in. She's hilarious, you'd like her, Em,' Nick tells me. 'Honestly, she does the most amazing impressions . . .'

'Like Michael McIntyre?' I mock.

'No. Not really, I don't know who I'd compare her to.'

'Right.'

'Right, what?'

'Nothing. It's just I thought we were talking about your job, but now we're talking about . . .'

'Shelly?'

'Yes, but—'

'But this is the job, part of it. Shelly is coming in to do an audit on the company, like a health check, and so we all need her to know what a good job we're doing, so that she can report back. Up. To my bosses.'

It's rained all day today. Lucy and I have spent the entire day in our tiny flat. Helen was going to come over with Polly, but Chris came back home to surprise her for their anniversary, so they're probably shagging the day away. Tania is teaching on a two-day yoga retreat somewhere in Surrey, and there isn't really anyone else on my phone-a-friend-and-hang-out-with-a-baby hit list.

Without a back-up plan we just watched daytime TV and I did about four loads of washing, because one of Lucy's favourite things at the moment is watching the spin cycle. Today was frustrating, for both of us, and I've been hanging out for Nick to come home. And now we're talking about Shelly, bloody gorgeous, hilarious Shelly, when I think what Nick is really trying to tell me is that he might lose his job and I may have to go back to work asap, but we've lost the basic levels of communication to even talk about that sensibly.

'Look. Tell me more about what's going on with you, Nick, I didn't mean to be rude, I'm listening, I'm all ears.'

'OK. Well, she's moved down from London for the job but it's only a short-term contract . . .' I didn't mean tell me more about bloody Shelly! '. . . so we thought we'd go out for some team drinks with her on Friday to welcome her to Brighton.'

'Hasn't she got any mates of her own?'

'Emily, I don't know what's happening here, but can it stop? Can you stop?'

I want to. I want to be carefree Emily again. I want to

feel funny, confident, sexy. I want to be a listener, an empathiser. I want to say the right thing. But I can't. It's like I have a brain full of cotton wool and it's all I can do to remember the pin number for my cash card.

'Shelly is . . .'

He's seriously going to be wearing his curry in a second.

'Shelly is in her fifties, Emily. Her kids are all grown up and she's recently divorced so has gone into consulting.'

'Well good for her. I'm sure she'll do a splendid job.' I try and keep my voice calm but inside I am a mixture of rage and relief. Why didn't he say that in the first place? Is he intentionally messing with me? I'm going to have to find a way to steer myself through these emotions, because between this and the exhaustion I genuinely feel like I'm cracking up.

I wish I could call Rachel. She would know what to say, she would give me some well-needed perspective. She is the most adaptable person I know, she's had to make changes I couldn't even imagine were possible.

I'm looking at Nick, who is pushing an unidentifiable vegetable around his plate, and wonder if it is the way I am that has meant he couldn't talk to me about his work worries sooner. Have I always expected too much of people? Not in a 'high standards, dream big' kind of way, but more that I have a set idea of how things should be and a prescriptive way of how friends should fit into that idea, and if it doesn't work out like that then I'm disappointed, or worse, I distance myself.

I want to ask Rachel this alongside a million other questions. I want to ask her if she thinks I have made it hard for Nick to talk to me. If I have pushed him away like I did her.

'I'll just go and check on Lucy.' Nick moves his plate away.

'I did it before dinner, she's fine.'

I clear up the virtually untouched meals and think back, for about the twentieth time today, to bumping into Rachel at Christmas. I rerun every bit, from twatting Mrs Chapman's ankle with the pram to the pair of them walking out of the shopping centre together. I think about what I could have done differently. About the squeeze she gave me on my arm. How I should have pulled her into a bear hug. Asked if we could start again, start from today. Reboot our friendship with a simple control alt delete.

I know I should just pick up the phone to Rachel, I know the ball's in my court. But what I don't know is whether I've left it too late.

I look over at Nick. He looks miserable. He's got a grain of rice stuck to his mock-hipster beard. I think about mentioning it, but he'll only take it as a criticism of his ability to direct food into his own mouth.

The thing is, you can't expect everything from one person, I do know that. Nick can't be my everything, he just can't. But this just isn't how I imagined being an adult would be when I was growing up.

How the fuck did we get here?

1998 age 17

'Knock, knock!' I wish Mum would actually knock instead of saying it. She has a pile of clean washing for me, which she puts on the end of my bed, then slowly sits down, as if she's trying to gather her thoughts as she does.

'Now . . .'

Oh God. Here it comes.

'I trust you and Rachel . . .'

Please fast forward to the end.

'Don't leave your drinks unattended at any time. Don't take anything that anyone gives you, even if you know them. And don't go back to anyone's house.'

'OK, Mum. I do have a boyfriend you know.'

'I know. It's not that I don't trust you and Rachel . . .'

'You said.'

'And of course I want you to have a lovely time. It's just I've had Rachel's dad on the phone again. He's really not happy with you going away so close to your exams.'

'Our exams aren't until next year, Mum. Next bloody year,' I hazard a swear word. She doesn't react. 'It's half-term and we're only going away for two bloody nights.'

'Language, Emmie.'

'But, Mum, we're going to look at Rachel's colleges, how can he object to that?'

'I know. I know. It's just some people aren't as laid-back as me and your dad.' I'm desperate to say something but bite my tongue since she is, after all, on our side.

'Rach can revise every other day. What is his problem?'

'I know, I know, love. He is a difficult man. And I said to him, it's just a weekend. You're youth-hostelling in Cambridge, not clubbing in Ibiza.'

I let out a snort.

'What, Emmie?'

'It just sounds weird when you say clubbing.'

'Well, anyway. He seems a little happier now. So I'm trusting you girls, as I've given him my word that you're going to behave.'

'Mum. How much trouble can you get up to in Cambridge anyway? It's full of posh kids and punts.'

'Emmie!'

'I said punts, not . . .'

'OK, well I've said my piece now. You'll have an amazing time, I'm sure. King's College Chapel is meant to be spectacular.' She sees me roll my eyes. 'But maybe that's more up mine and Dad's street.' She gets up and ruffles my hair like I'm four. 'Let me know if you need any help packing.'

'I don't.'

I look through the pile of clean clothes to see if my Miss Sixty crop top is anywhere.

'Knock, knock!'

'WHAT?'

Rachel pops her head round the door. 'Can I come in? Your dad said to come straight up.'

'Sorry, I thought it was Mum, she's doing my head in a bit at the moment. Have you finished packing your stuff?'

'I'd swap her for my dad any day of the week.'

'Mum said he's been ringing up about us going away again.'

'I can't stand it, Emmie. Why can't he just leave it alone?

172

No one else gets this much shit from their parents, like literally no one. It's just not worth the hassle half the time.'

'Don't say that, we're going to have an amazing weekend.'

Rachel picks up different shades of my nail varnish and starts to sort them into a neat row on top of the chest of drawers, lightest to darkest.

'Mum's completely useless as well, making excuses for him all the time. If I was her I'd just tell him to do one.'

'Just think, this time next year we'll be at uni and you'll never have to come home again if you don't want to.'

Rachel looks away quickly, not making eye contact.

'What? What did I say?'

She picks up my copy of *Prozac Nation*. 'Bit of light reading while we're away is it?' She puts the book down and starts picking at a hangnail.

'Mum says she'll pick you up at nine tomorrow morning to take us to the station, you probably won't have time to pack your stuff after breakfast so you definitely need to do it this evening, Rach.'

'Yeah, I know. It'll be fine.'

'I don't mean to go on, it's just we want to make sure we get to the station early enough that we can get snacks from the shop.'

'I know. We will.'

'It's just good to get there a little bit early, you know, because we don't have seat reservations.'

'You said.'

'And Costcutters—'

'GOD'S SAKE, EMMIE!' she explodes. 'STOP GOING ON ABOUT IT!'

The silence between us weighs heavy. I can taste it, sour and angry. My skin prickles with confusion and embarrassment.

173

Rach picks up my tartan miniskirt that Mum had just brought in. 'Are you going to take this one? You should, you look really good in it,' she says, as if nothing's happened.

There's a look in Rachel's eyes I don't recognise. She looks different. Weird. It's not anger, or frustration. It's something else.

Fear.

'What's the fuck is going on, Rach?' I whisper. Scared to speak any louder in case my voice cracks and I burst into tears.

Rachel perches at the end of the bed. I shuffle along next to her.

She lets out a long exhalation, like a slowly deflating helium balloon. 'I don't know where to start.' She drops her head into her hands and her shoulders start to gently shake as she weeps.

'Is it because of your dad?' I soothe. 'He is a prize prick but you've got nothing to worry about. You're predicted A-stars for all your A levels. And you'll get them obviously, you got about a million As at GCSE, didn't you? I know you give yourself a massively hard time about school work, but that's because you're so clever. You're going to breeze through your exams because you already know it all, I promise you, Rach.' I stroke her hair, tucking the loose strands behind her ear. 'And then you'll go to Cambridge and you're going to have the best time. We'll still see each other every weekend, obviously, while you're training to become an international journalist, which, of course, you'll be brilliant at. Then . . .' I pause to let my imagination take over. 'Then you'll get assigned to an amazing paper and will live abroad writing. We'll live together of course, because I'll be a much-sought-after actress by then. We'll have a penthouse suite in New York and you'll be a world-acclaimed correspondent and I'll be on Broadway. We'll drink cocktails every night on our roof terrace and throw exclusive parties for hot men. What do you say?'

'What about Ryan?' she asks through sobs.

'Oh, Ryan will be long gone. I'm not going to take my crusty boyfriend to New York with us and ruin our scene, Rach!' A little chuckle escapes her and I think, I can always make her laugh. Always. 'And we don't need to see your dad ever again if you don't want. We can make sure the concierge at our fabulous apartment knows to ring the police if he turns up, that'll fettle him. What do you think, Rach? It's all going to be OK, I promise. You just need to get through the next few months and then school, family, everyone, they can all sod off, what do you say?' I'm hugging her tightly and feel her relax slightly.

'Sounds amazing, Emmie.'

'See? See? It's all going to be OK.'

And then she says in the tiniest of voices so that I'm unsure whether I heard her correctly, 'I'm pregnant, Emmie.'

'Sorry, what?'

She looks up. Big drops of tears are rolling down her face. Her nose is running and she wipes it on her sleeve. 'I'm pregnant.'

I can't think of anything to say. Not one thing. She looks at me expectantly. But my mind's gone blank. It's whirring about a million miles an hour trying to compute what Rach has just said but none of the thoughts seem to translate into words or sentences.

'How?'

Rach rolls her eyes at me, and looks out the window.

'I don't mean how, I mean . . . how?'

'I'm such an idiot. How could this happen to me? What am I going to do?'

'Is it Gary's?'

'Yes of course it is, I don't just go around shagging anyone, Emmie,' she snaps.

'I know, I'm sorry, it's just, sorry.'

'But that's fucked now as well isn't it? It's not like he's even my boyfriend, not properly. I can't tell him I'm pregnant. I can't tell anyone. You can't tell anyone, Emmie, promise me?'

'I promise.'

I burn with hatred for Gary Riley; it fizzes like acid in my stomach. He is a total slag. He shags everyone. Nearly everyone. He doesn't 'do' relationships. He just 'sees' lots of girls. He's a complete penis and his eyes are way too close together in my opinion, but now's probably not the time to bring that up.

'When was it, Rach?'

'That stupid end of summer party at Natalie's house. I knew we should have used a condom but he promised me he wouldn't come inside me. Fuck. How could I be so stupid? What am I going to do, Emmie?'

'Hang on, that was ages ago, Rach.'

'I know.'

'How did you not know?'

'My periods have been all over the place, the doctors told me it was stress. So I didn't think for a second that it could be . . . shit. This is such a mess.'

We sit in silence with Rach occasionally sniffing loudly.

'Do you still want to go to Cambridge tomorrow?'

'Are you serious, Emmie? I'm telling you my life's over and you want to know if I'm up for going youth-hostelling with you?' She's furious, wringing my tartan skirt into a rope one way and then unravelling and wringing it the other. I want to ask her to stop, it's one of my favourites but it's only from C&A so is likely to fall apart. I guess it's not important right now. I guess most things aren't important right now.

We sit in silence. A car drives by outside playing 'Wonderwall' at full volume and I think briefly about Glastonbury. I thought we'd go again, that we'd do it properly this time. But that doesn't look likely now, does it? The guilt immediately takes hold: I'm not sure I'm particularly good in a crisis.

'What are you going to do, Rach?'

'Honestly? I have no idea.'

'When is it due?'

'I don't know.'

I pull my Salvador Dali calendar down from the wall and look at the month-by-month overview on the back. 'OK, so if you shagged Gary then' – I point to a date in late August – 'then we're counting nine months from then, aren't we?' I trace nine months on with my finger, then look up at Rach. 'May.'

'And the start of our exams.' She buries her head in her hands and slumps.

'You could get rid of it, Rach, there's still time. Why don't we go to the doctor's on Monday? We can go together.'

Her hands fall to her stomach and it dawns on me. This might not be just an unwanted pregnancy. Has Rachel started to think of this as an actual possibility? This is getting completely out of hand.

'Rachel, why don't we go to the doctor's anyway, we can just see what they say. What do you think?'

She's looking out the window. She doesn't answer for such a long time that I start to think she hasn't heard me, and just as I open my mouth to ask again, she nods. 'OK. Let's go on Monday then, after Cambridge.'

I squeeze her hand and silently rejoice in the fact that we're still going away, then it dawns on me that she isn't going to be able to drink or smoke while we're away and that all the plans we'd made for the weekend will probably have to change now. My stomach flips with the uncomfortable realisation that one way or another, everything has changed today.

How the fuck did we get here?

Chapter Twenty-two

'Have we got everything we need?' Nick asks as I push the pram onto the street. We are on our way to meet Tania and Spiral in the park with five or so food-filled plastic bags dangling from the pram handle. I choose to ignore him as I know I will end up making a smart remark about how he wouldn't know what we needed as he hasn't done anything to help. I'd like to at least give the illusion of harmony when we turn up for the picnic.

Well, I say picnic; once at the park we arrange the food on the blanket and it looks like an episode of *What Not to Eat*. Our contribution is shameful – two Ginsters Pasties, one steak and kidney, one cheese and onion, a family packet of Quavers, some party sausages, Bourbon biscuits and a token bag of supermarket cut carrots. In contrast, Tania has bought a healthy-lifestyle spread of homemade hummus, pomegranate seeds, rye bread and some kind of kale and sesame seed salad.

The boys push the children on the baby swings while we sit on the blanket and Tania shouts over, 'Not too high, Spiral, he'll fall out.'

'Spiral, did you even wash this kale before you put the dressing on? It's completely gritty.'

'Yes,' he replies and gets back to talking to Nick.

'And did you not put the wet wipes back in the change bag?'

'No,' he replies.

'What a cock,' she murmurs. 'Could I borrow some of yours?'

Spiral seems totally unperturbed by the constant stream of criticisms and demands.

'God, it's times like this I really fancy him.'

She's completely taken me by surprise. 'What, when he's at the park?'

'Just look at him.' Spiral is pushing Falcon with one hand and smoking his vape with the other. 'I wouldn't tell him, obviously, that would be too easy.' She shrugs, while pushing half a steak and kidney Ginsters into her mouth.

'Has he always wound you up a bit, though?'

'Yes, 'course. He's called Spiral, for fuck's sake. I'm not an idiot, I knew what I was getting into when I met him. You should have seen the look on my parents' faces when I first brought him home. It was absolutely priceless.' At the mention of her parents I remember their gift.

'Where's the car?'

'Over there.' She points towards the road near the park.

I look over. Oh my God. It is a fucking Jaguar.

'I'm not sure if it's working out for us, to be honest, though. We've been pulled over in it about ten times now, I think it's cos Spiral looks like he's nicked it.'

I sometimes forget that Tania's parents are 'conventional' adults, if owning half of Surrey is classified as conventional, and I wonder what they must have thought when their only girl, the heir to their hotel empire, brought back a tattooed stoner and announced that he was the person she was planning to spend the rest of her life with. I'm going to choose all Lucy's boyfriends for her.

'He's not going to earn us a million or run the country, but we balance each other out.'

I look over at Nick, who's absent-mindedly texting while pushing Lucy, and I wonder how we balance each other out. We don't seem to see enough of each other at the moment to feel like there is any balance. He's left the flat really early every morning this week before I've had time to have a shower, so I bring Lucy into the bathroom in the baby bouncer so I can watch her while having a wash. We haven't spoken properly in days, other than passing on jobs lists of what we think the other person should be doing.

'You should try tantric yoga,' Tania remarks. 'Can I open these?'

''Course, help yourself. I should try what?'

'I could live on party sausages.' She sneaks a peek over to Spiral to check he's not watching before opening the packet and shoving two in at a time. 'Tantric yoga. It works miracles.'

'What's that?'

'Oh, it's great. It's a sensual way to reconnect. Through touch and spiritual growth. It's about creating a deeper bond spiritually.'

'What, you and me?'

Tania spits out half a sausage. 'God no, that would just be fucking weird. No, no, you and Nick. It feels like you've got an energy block between the two of you.'

'Oh, OK, that makes more sense. I thought you meant, well, never mind.'

'Your energy's all wrong, anyone can see that. You just need to align it. Preferably naked.'

'Really?'

'Yep, absolutely. And Nick could do with working on his posture and it would help with that too, so that would be two birds with one stone.'

I look across at Nick stooped over his phone. Stress seems to radiate off him.

'Sorry, I've finished these off. You don't get many in a packet do you? Can I offer you some kale and pomegranate on rye?'

'No, I'm good.'

'I don't blame you.' Tania watches me watching Nick. 'Be kind to each other, Emily. It's tough enough being parents without wanting to murder each other every other second. I've got a number for a local tantric yoga guru if you're interested?'

'I'm not sure it's us.'

'But driving each other mental is "you" is it?'

'Is it really that obvious?'

'Can you take over, Em? I'm getting cramp,' Nick shouts across, dramatically shaking his arm.

I tut loudly as Tania answers, 'Yes. Yes it really is. Remind me before we leave and I'll dig out that number.'

'Thanks.' I don't think sex yoga is the answer, but she's definitely on to something.

As we both get up to swap over with the boys I unselfconsciously brush down Tania's jumper of Ginsters' evidence.

'Thanks . . . God, I don't know why I don't just tell him I love meat.'

'Because sometimes it's good to have something just for yourself, even if it is sausage rolls?'

'Yes, I guess. Right,' she shouts over to Spiral, 'I'll push for a bit but don't eat everything, OK?'

'Were all your boyfriends posh before Spiral?'

'Why do you ask?'

'Well, just cos of your parents. I just thought . . .'

'Yes. I'm such a cliché. God. You wouldn't believe me if I told you their names.'

'Go on then.'

'OK. So let me think. Fergus, Montgomery, Gerald, and Rod.'

I burst out laughing. 'Rod doesn't sound too posh.'

'Short for Roderick.'

'God that's awful.'

'Yep, I know. Posh school, posh kids, total sense of entitlement. You can see why I got out the moment I could. What about you?'

'Nope. No posh boyfriends.'

'No, I mean, life before Nick.'

'Oh I see. There was a guy, Ryan, who I was with throughout school, but it kind of fizzled out when I went to uni. Then a few randomers. Then Nick.'

'Very straightforward there, Em, a baggage-free history.'

'Yes and no.'

'In what way?'

'Well there was someone, my first love you'd say, and I behaved like a total shit.'

'How so?'

I stop swinging Lucy as I struggle to find the words. 'I was really selfish when I was younger.'

'And? Who wasn't?'

'I let someone down that I loved very much, and I think about it every day.'

Tania stops swinging too. 'You can't carry around guilt for stuff you did when you were younger, Emily, it eats away at you and makes it more difficult to be a good person now.'

'That's a lovely thought, Tania, but I can't just switch off my brain and forget about what a shit I've been in the past.'

'Well sometimes you have to. We're all shits sometimes,

but you nccd to acknowledge you've been a shit and then try not to be a shit in the future.'

'Very profound.'

'I guess all I'm saying is you might have been not very nice to a boyfriend in the past, but you are a good person.'

'It wasn't a boyfriend.'

'Emily Jones, you dark horse!' We each take our children out of the swings. I hold Lucy close to me, wrapping her in my cardigan and inhaling her neck. 'So who was she, Em?'

'It wasn't like that. She was my best friend, and I abandoned her when she needed me.'

'Well why don't you ring her? Say sorry?'

'It's not that easy, Tania.'

'You know what?' She's holding Falcon at arm's length, the distinct smell of shit rising off him. 'Sometimes it really is. Right, I've got to change this guy before I puke.'

Is it though? Is it really that easy to be forgiven?

Chapter Twenty-three

'Shall I just do it?'

It's the just that makes me want to kill him. Like I have been buggering about all day and now Saint Nick has come in, he will be able to dry Lucy's hair and get her into her sleep suit in triple time. I step away from the change mat on the living room floor and gesture to Nick with a sarcastic bow.

'No need to be like that, Em, I'm just trying to help.'

And now it's the trying that is making my blood boil.

I open the washing machine door to put in a load of Lucy's clothes and there, already waiting to be washed, is Nick's work shirt and a couple of pairs of boxers.

'Who are you expecting to sort these out, the washing fairy?'

Oh my God, I said 'the washing fairy' out loud. What's happened to me? What have I turned into? I'm a cliché, a bad Channel 5 sitcom cliché.

'I just thought if you were already sticking a wash on, then . . .'

'Then what? WHAT, NICK?' I raise my voice. As I spit out Nick's name, Lucy jumps with a start and starts crying. Nick shakes his head slowly and lifts her off the mat, holding her head on his shoulder, and all I can think is, your shirt is now covered in Sudocrem, am I going to be expected to wash that too? And then it happens, the wave of guilt.

It washes over mc like a tsunami. I look at Lucy sobbing on Nick's shoulder, upset because of me, of my shouting. Nick comes over and puts his arm around me but I tense up, shoulders shooting up to my ears.

'Everything's OK.'

Everything is not OK. I am a shit mum, I dislike my boyfriend, I have lost the ability to speak properly, think properly, write properly. I don't have any mates. Where have all my friends gone? I'm sure I used to be popular, or if not popular, at least I knew more people than my yoga instructor and the woman from the cinema. Friends from work, from the pub, from random nights at clubs that were way too young for me. What happens when you have a baby, do people just think you're too busy, or happy, or that you have your own family now so you don't need them?

The thought of just having Nick as my only friend until Lucy goes to university makes me want to punch myself in my own face. I suddenly resent my family for living so far away even though it was me who decided to move 250 miles down south. Where has all this anger come from?

I miss being able to go to the cinema, or the pub or the shop around the corner, just because I want to, on my own. I miss all the people I used to see out who I thought were my friends but now I'm not really sure as I haven't seen them for six months and I don't really remember what we used to talk about. I miss being fun, and drunk and smoking fags. I miss eating slices of pizza for a quid from Aladdin's at 2 a.m. It was the best pizza ever. Or was it? Was it just good because it was 2 a.m.?

I miss going to the hairdresser's, I miss the smell of my hair when I came out and it was shiny in a way I could never make it look. I miss looking good, because I did, sometimes. Not all the time, but when I could be bothered, when I'd put some make-up on and straightened my hair and was full of anticipation and gin with a carefreeness about me. God, I miss being carefree, of only having to have my handbag to leave the flat. To only think about me. I miss just thinking about me.

I miss being in a relationship with Nick, I miss talking to Nick about stuff other than nurseries and how bad or not bad his work is and the nutritional value of formula milk. When did my hot, easy-going Nick tap out and leave me cohabiting with this frustrating know-it-all? I'm not sure if it's because he's changed his aftershave to the one Cathleen got him for Christmas, but he doesn't smell very nice. I'm not sure I like the way he smells at the moment. In fact, I am going to bin that aftershave and then pretend I know nothing about it.

But mostly I feel so, so guilty for feeling any of these things, because I have Lucy. And I should be grateful; she should be enough.

No one tells you how shitty you might feel after having a baby, or if they do, how long that shittiness might last, on and off.

I have Lucy and she is perfect. I made a baby who is healthy and happy and doing everything she's meant to be doing according to the BabyCentre weekly e-newsletter. I love her in a primal way. In a way I've never loved anything or anyone before, like I want to wrap her in my skin to protect her as just holding her doesn't feel safe enough. I love her with a depth of love I didn't know existed; it's so raw it makes me nervous. So why isn't that enough to make me Mr-Tumble-style happy with my life?

When mums say how contented they are with their babies, how they could just watch them all day, are they lying? Could they really just watch them all day? Wouldn't they get bored? Am I a bad person? Am I a selfish woman who just doesn't know how good she's got it? Is it wrong that I sometimes see men on TV and wonder what it would be like if they were my boyfriend, like Paul Robinson from *Neighbours* or the guy from the Sure for Men advert? Is it wrong that the Tom Smith fantasy has started to take over a bit, so that sometimes Nick will say something annoying and I think, Tom Smith would never say that, like he's an actual person, a living breathing person in my life instead of a figment of my imagination? I daydream about the house we'd live in, and the sex we'd have and the family holidays he'd book as a surprise for the three of us because he was just that kind of guy, and I don't even feel remotely bad that I've just tippexed Nick out of the story. Is that normal? Am I normal?

I just need to stop the constant chatter in my brain, the constant self-evaluation, the endless guilt. The guilt is so overwhelming, I feel like I'm drowning in it. I kind of want to talk about all this with Nick, but don't know how without getting angry with him. I also think that maybe I just need a good night's sleep.

If I drank water, slept a bit and ate at least one of my five a day then maybe I'd start to feel more normal again.

'Just breathe, Emily,' Nick whispers. I slowly exhale and realise I've been holding my breath for ages while my thoughts flash through my mind at a hundred miles an hour. 'Sit down and I'll put the kettle on.'

I sit on the sofa. My body feels so heavy, I wonder if I'll ever get up again.

'Why don't you give Lucy her night feed then I'll put her down. You just sit here and relax.'

My instant response is he's testing me; he's tricking me to see if I say yes and then it will prove to him what a rubbish mother I am. But instead he passes Lucy to me and slowly rubs my shoulders. It feels so nice to be touched. When did I become so suspicious of him? He kneads his fingers deep into the knots around my neck. I can't remember the last time he touched me, and my muscles ache somewhere deep inside in response.

'You're doing an amazing job, Em. I know I don't say it nearly enough, but you are.'

'Has Mum been speaking to you?'

'What? No. Why?'

'Nothing.'

'Well she did ring the other day, but that's not why, that's got nothing to do with it, I just wanted to let you know that . . . you're amazing. Do you want normal or herbal tea?'

'Herbal.'

I hold Lucy's hands, pulling her gently forwards and backwards, silently singing 'Row Row Row Your Boat' as Nick clanks around in the kitchen. My skin still tingles from his touch and I think momentarily about Tania's suggestion. Was it such a stupid idea? Could we do sex yoga together? I can't even touch my toes so I'm not sure how sexy it would be. Maybe I'll suggest it to Nick as a joke and see how he reacts.

As I turn to face him he says, 'Look, Em, I need to speak to you about something and I'm not sure how you're going to react, so before you react, let me finish.'

'OK,' I say cautiously as he gently sits down next to me, moves the pile of unopened bills on the coffee table to one side and puts down my cup.

'I've been crunching some numbers and, look, don't look at me like that.'

'It's just, who says "crunching numbers", Nick?' I snort as I take a huge gulp of tea. 'Bloody hell,' I splutter, 'didn't you put any cold water in this?'

189

'Shit, no, sorry. Just water from the kettle and a tea bag. Shall I get you some cold water?'

'Yes, please!'

He comes back with a pint of water and I down half of it in one go.

'Sorry, sorry about that. Bad start. OK,' and he sits down next to me again and takes Lucy from my arms, as protection I think. His small human armour. 'So, so I've been doing some sums . . . better, Em?' I nod apologetically. 'And I think you might need to talk to work to ask about going back earlier.'

'What? Since when, Nick?'

'We spoke about this before, and—'

'I know, I know, I just thought that since you hadn't really mentioned it since then, that everything was getting better.'

'Well it is. And it's not.' His face looks tired. Not late night tired, but worried tired. How had I not noticed this before?

'What's changed?'

He exhales slowly and runs a hand through his curly hair. 'The company is losing money. There are too many head-hunters' – I knew that was what he did, I make a mental note to look up exactly what that means on Wikipedia when he's next out – 'and not enough business for all the clients. It's a joke. My job is a joke. Everyone just uses the fucking inter-net now. I knew this would happen, I should have started looking for something else ages ago. Anyway, it looks like they're going to get rid of some of us, I don't know who, but I don't want to find out it's me and then neither of us are at work.' He kisses Lucy on her head, passes her back to me then rubs his forehead repeatedly with the palm of his hand.

'Shit, Nick. How long have you known it was this bad?'

'A while I guess. I just hoped that something big would

happen to make it all alright, I don't know what . . .' his voice trails off to a whisper.

'It will be OK, Nick.'

'I know.' He mirrors my faux optimism.

I take his hand from his head and hold it in mine. It's cold but familiar. 'I'm sorry you weren't able to talk to me Nick.'

'Me too. But I'm sorry you're not able to talk to me either.' He looks so downbeat. Lucy starts to tug at my top, making a clicking noise with her tongue, which is her newest way of communicating with us.

'Sorry, sorry, Lucy, you must be starving,' I give both my boobs a squeeze to see which one is the most full then latch Lucy on.

'What's happening to us, Em? Why is it that we don't talk to each other anymore?' he says in a voice so small he sounds like a child. The question hangs between us; the longer the silence, the more complicated the question becomes.

I don't know where to start. How do you tell the person that has loved you for over a decade, who you have started a family with, that there are some days where you feel like you're losing your mind? I have no point of reference; I can't give him any context for how I'm feeling because there is none. It's irrational but it feels so painfully real when it's happening that it's almost physical.

I can't expect Nick to understand what it feels like to be one minute overwhelmingly happy looking into the eyes of your daughter and the next feeling incapable of making a doctor's appointment because that assertive confident person you used to be feels like she's slipping away.

How do I explain to Nick about the pendulum of emotions, going from complete calm to skin-prickling rage in seconds, and how the catalyst is almost always, with few exceptions, him? How do I tell him that sometimes I fast-track in my

191

head to being a single mum, and play out the whole scenario to see if I have the patience for it? I don't, of course I don't. Because by the time I've reached the end of the daydream I feel sick to my stomach that he's not with me, because I can't imagine a future without him in it, but I've no idea how we get ourselves unstuck from this sticky point we're in.

I can't tell him any of these things.

But I tell Mum. Because she understands without judgement. She will listen, and then wipe the slate clean for our next conversation like it's never happened. She knows how hard this can be because she's been there. She's had a tiny baby, a little daughter; she was that woman sitting at home not knowing what the fuck to do with her day or her life.

Tania's words pop into my head. Be kind to each other. I nestle my head into Nick's neck and close my eyes. He kisses my forehead and I feel him relax too.

'I'll email work when Lucy's in bed. It'll be OK, Nick. It'll all be OK.'

'Will it though?' he whispers.

'It will, I promise you. I love you, Nick, and I promise you we'll make it all alright.' I look him in the eye, emphasising every word for added conviction.

'I love you too,' he sniffs, wiping his nose with his sleeve. I kiss Nick's wet cheek and wonder how long he's been silently crying.

Chapter Twenty-four

All the baby books and forums advised not to begin weaning until Lucy was six months old. So six months to the day I re-open that chapter of one of the countless barely read baby books we own. At which point I read, 'If you have waited until six months to start weaning . . .' Waited? Waited? YOU TOLD ME TO WAIT.

Parenting feels like a constant battle of contradictions. One health visitor will tell you one thing; the next will tell you the complete opposite. I put Lucy down to sleep on her back, and Cathleen tells me that when Nick was born children had to sleep on their fronts. I'm told I have to choose between breastfeeding or formula, then told that combination feeding of both is fine. I let Lucy sleep in bed with us as co-sleeping is good for bonding – but then read an article that says I definitely shouldn't let her co-sleep or she'll be a victim of cot death. The list is endless.

So, I've waited for over six months as advised/in opposition to the advice I've been given and it turns out it's quite a stressful, pungent job. Stressful because Lucy has quickly realised that if she sucks her lips in like she's gurning, then nothing will go in, and no amount of singing, zooming of spoons or enthusiastic clapping will unclamp them. This is a bit depressing when she's quite happy to lick the rusty metal chain that holds the swings up at the playground, but not the sweet potato mash I've lovingly made for her.

I'm trying my hardest to be totally fun about the whole process. That's what the health visitor said: 'Have fun with it, make it fun.' I'm smiling through gritted teeth as I put on my fun-face, but I'm convinced I'm just projecting my own food anxiety onto her. Every time she clamps her mouth shut I imagine I'm channeling a thirteen-year-old girl who is refusing to eat breakfast for fear of being fat. But this is fun, right? We're having a right laugh.

Me: Help! Anyone else finding this weaning bollocks fun?
Helen: It's not fun. It's gross.
Tania: And your house will start to smell like a school canteen from boiling all the veg.
Helen: Have you tried sweet veg like carrots?
Tania: Or sweet potato?
Helen: Has she done a proper poo yet?
Me: Nope.
Helen: Oh.
Tania: Yep.
Me: What?
Tania: Then the trouble really starts. *gross times infinity*

How can a person so small and beautiful produce something so disgusting? I'm talking 24-hour-benders poo, where you forget to eat anything other than pub nuts and the closest to a glass of water you get is watered-down lager.

The smell is unbelievable, it sits in the air long after everyone's been hosed down and the nappy bags have been put in the neighbour's wheelie bin. It's like tar and it dyes everything – clothes, changing mats, bums, hands. Apparently Jennifer Aniston lives on jars of baby food, which is why she's so skinny. Well good luck with that I say, you deserve to look absolutely fantastic after putting yourself through that every day.

Poogate starts on Monday when we're hanging out in the kids bit of the library with Helen and Polly. There's an almighty smell, so we routinely sniff the girls' bums.

'Mine!' I call like a pro doubles tennis player, and without thinking, stick my finger inside her nappy to confirm my suspicions that it's just a trump. The slow motion voice comes out. 'It's a poooooooo. It's all uuuuup her baaaack. And all ooooover my fiiiinger . . .'

We rush to the disabled toilets as the baby changing ones are, as always, engaged with a middle-aged man who has gone in for a leisurely sit down. Helen takes her coat off for Polly to lie down on while Lucy holds her feet and rocks from side to side on the carry change mat for maximum coverage of poo over her whole back. The carry mat is instantly ruined with a large turmeric-coloured stain. We strip her down and Helen clamps both her hands to avoid a poo to mouth incident. It dawns on me how much time I spend squatting down on the floor in public toilets since having Lucy.

'This is beyond a wet wipe job,' Helen sighs. 'We're going to have to get her in the sink.'

'OK, let's give it a go.' We try to dunk her in the sink to get the worst of it off, attempting to hold her under the tap. This is virtually impossible as there's not a baby-sized gap between it and the bowl.

'Here, let's try this instead.' Helen uses a blue paper towel to scrape the worst of it off while I hold Lucy under her armpits. The sink slowly blocks and fills to the brim with yellow greasy water. This is not going to work; it was never going to work. We just need to go home.

I look in the change bag.

'Shit, I've only got age three- to six-month-old Babygros in here, I can't remember the last time I cleaned this out.' I also spot an uneaten Twirl at the bottom of the bag, so that's a small win.

'Just wrap your scarf around her?' Helen suggests.

So I wrap my only decent pashmina around her body, put her back into the pram while Helen tries to strap Polly to her without actually touching her skin. Helen's fingers have turned a sixty-a-day smoker's yellow from where she's come in contact with the poo and there is nowhere to wash them as the sink's so full it is now sloshing dirty water onto the floor.

'This is rank, let's get out of here sharpish.' As I open the door, I see the queue has grown of mothers with little babies and toddlers. I give an apologetic smile as we hold the door open for the next unsuspecting woman.

'She's going to hate us,' Helen whispers.

I deposit Lucy's nappy, clothes and change mat in the bin outside the library. Feeling slightly traumatised I say goodbye to Helen, who assures me she's had a fantastic afternoon, and head home for a snooze in front of *Murder She Wrote*, writing off the rest of the day.

Tuesday comes and we meet up with Tania in the park. There is a similar stench, and sure enough, poo everywhere.

'Is it meant to be that colour?' Tania is peering into her nappy.

'I don't know, is Falcon's not?'

'No, his are like actual adult human shits. Proper logs. It's like he's thirty-eight years old.'

'Wow. OK, I don't know then. This looks pretty grim, though, doesn't it?'

'Yes, yes it does.' She shrugs, not even attempting to hide her mild disgust.

Everywhere I look there seem to be mothers effortlessly feeding their children. It's like when you first find out you're pregnant and the world suddenly fills up with women in their third trimester. How had I never seen it before?

A woman is pushing her daughter on the swing. She can't be much older than Lucy and she's holding a slice of avocado in each hand, smashing them into her face.

'Is she actually eating those?'

'She loves it; I can't get her to put them down. Not even to go on the bloody swing!' She smiles as she pushes her baby.

'How old is your daughter?'

'Twenty-nine weeks.'

Two weeks older than Lucy. 'And does she just like avocado or . . .?' Just say yes. Please say yes.

'God no, she'll eat anything. She was interested in food from about seventeen weeks. So we'd just put out bits on her high chair when me and my husband were eating so she felt like she was involved. Now she eats three meals a day.'

'What do you mean, three meals a day?'

'Well she just has some baby rice for breakfast, and mashed up fruit for lunch, then I just give her a little bit of whatever we're eating in the evening. It's obviously a bit blander than what ever we're used to eating, but you know, it's nice to eat together.'

'Such as what, what do you eat together?'

The woman is starting to look a bit uncomfortable, like the conversation might be switching from mum playground chat to mental woman interrogation.

'Oh, I don't know, fish pie, something like that?' She's stopping the swing now.

'Fish pie? Your daughter eats fish pie?'

'Well not always, of course,' she apologises. 'You know what they say, though, just have fun with it.' She laughs nervously.

'But it's not fun. Not really, though, is it?' Has my voice got louder? I'm not sure. I didn't mean it to.

'It's been really nice to meet you but we've got to get back,' and she lifts her daughter out of the swing, covering herself in avocado as she hastily straps her in her buggy.

Tania saunters over with Falcon as the woman is wrestling with the child lock on the gate. 'Right, I'm off, *Loose Women* starts in a bit.' She follows my gaze. 'Wow, she's in more of a hurry to leave than me! What did you say to her?'

'Urgh, I just went on a bit about weaning.'

'Well, don't expect a play date with her anytime soon.' Tania laughs.

And I wonder why I only have two mum friends.

Chapter Twenty-five

Taa daaaah! I'm a mum who goes to swimming lessons with her daughter. That's moving things along, that's taking control.

'You're only allowed in the changing rooms ten minutes before the lesson?' Tania asks the receptionist in disgust the first time we turn up. 'Are you serious, ten minutes? Do you have any idea how long it takes to get a pair of tiny water-proof pants on a baby?'

It turns out that it's only Tania, me and the kids signed up to the lessons due to an admin error. Wendy, the instructor, has been running the swimming lessons for about fifty years and has lost all enthusiasm by the looks of things. She asks Tania and me to face each other, clutching our babies in front of us, and sing 'Ring-a-Ring o' Roses' to each other. It's painful. What Tania makes up in flexibility, she definitely lacks in rhythm and tone. Wendy also says she isn't much of a singer, so she starts us off, then sits down on a plastic chair and checks her phone, leaving us to it.

She looks at her watch after we've finished 'Grand Old Duke of York', 'Twinkle Twinkle Little Star', 'If You're Happy and You Know It', and 'Zoom Zoom', which isn't even a proper song, and barks, 'get out now. It's time for the next class!'

'I don't do singing,' Tania grumbles as we retrieve our bags from the lockers.

'You were great!' I lie.

'I probably wouldn't have signed up if I'd known it was going to be mainly singing.' We all squeeze into a family changing room with the prams and Tania starts to undress.

'Please don't leave,' I say, panicking, 'otherwise it will just be me singing a solo to Wendy!'

'OK, OK, but you must be a pretty good friend you know, I wouldn't do this for just anyone.' She has no idea how happy this has made me.

'You're a good friend too.' I grin and I think I catch Tania rolling her eyes.

'Well, there you go then,' she responds, standing in front of me completely naked. Her body is incredible. She has actual stomach muscles. She sees me looking at her.

'It's yoga, Emily. You'd look like this too if you could be bothered to come to my class,' she says as she whips her fisherman's trousers on, not bothering with underwear to 'let everything breathe'.

'Fancy a coffee after this?' I suggest.

'Sounds good, Spiral's got my cash card though so you'll have to get them.'

'Fine,' I begrudge. Will I ever make a friend who will buy me a coffee?

'I don't think Wendy likes us,' I mention as I bring the cappuccinos over to the table.

'She's an angry woman with bad energy,' Tania explains. People have one of two things in Tania's mind: those with good energy and those with bad, and she can sum them up in a second.

'What have I got?' I ask as I take the coffees off the tray.

'Good energy on the whole' – she opens her bag and empties a variety of pots onto the table – 'otherwise I wouldn't spend time with you, obviously.'

'Obviously,' I agree. Thank fuck for that.

Falcon is opening his mouth like a baby bird waiting for Tania to spoon in a lump of mushed-up carrots. 'He's like a fucking gannet, he's never full.' She opens another Tupperware tub.

'What is that?'

'Whizzed up broccoli and broad beans,' she explains.

'It smells disgusting.'

'I know. He'll eat fucking anything, it doesn't matter what it smells like.'

I look at Lucy wedged in her high chair; she has her mouth clamped tightly shut as I just smear butternut squash over her lips in the hope that some will be ingested by mistake.

'Don't be jealous,' Tania says as if reading my mind, 'I'd much prefer a picky eater. She's not going to starve, Em, they never starve, but at least you don't have to spend the whole fucking day feeding her. I swear I've built up muscles in my right arm I didn't know I had.' The spoon hovers near Falcon and he swipes at it in frustration, knocking it out of Tania's hand and onto the floor. She mutters something under her breath, picks it up, licks it herself then carries on feeding Falcon. 'Germs are good for them, builds up their immunity, apparently.'

I sip my coffee, wipe Lucy's mouth with the napkin and then get her out of the chair for a cuddle. She tugs at my top to try and get to my boobs.

'That's why she won't eat food. Why would she when she's got your lovely milky instead?'

There's something a bit unsettling about the way she says lovely milky.

'I know. But she still won't take a bottle, and then she won't eat anything, and by tea time I've totally given up so I just feed her myself. It's not like she's going to still be breastfeeding when she goes to school or anything.'

Tania raises her eyebrows. 'What?'

'My cousin did with both of hers. She fed them both until they were six. She is fucking weird though.'

Tania opens the third tub of slop. 'I didn't get my libido back until I stopped breastfeeding, I couldn't stand being around Spiral, but now I don't mind it so much. And I like sex; not always with him, but I just think of someone else and it's fine.'

'How often do you do it?'

'About once a week. You?'

'Twice.'

'Well there you go; twice a week is going some. No wonder you look knackered.'

I think of Helen and her neighbour. She and Chris are probably back to shagging twice a day when he's home now.

'No, twice since Lucy's been born.'

Tania lets out a long, high-pitched whistle. 'Did you not get in touch with my tantric guy?'

'No, I thought about it but . . .'

'You're so fucking British, Emily. Sex is never going to be how it was before you had Lucy, but it doesn't mean it's going to be worse, just different.'

'I just don't feel very . . . well, sexy these days.'

'Who does? It's all in the mind. You need to start feeling hot about your own body, Em. You're gorgeous.'

'My tits dangle now, they actually dangle. And I tuck my stomach in my pants like it's a vest. That's not gorgeous.'

'You also need to work on taking a compliment. Jesus. You know Helen rang my tantric yoga guy?' My eyes widen with surprise. 'Don't look so shocked, she's very in tune with her sexuality.'

'I want to be in tune with my sexuality,' I demand, sounding very much like my teenage self and definitely out of tune with my sexuality or anything else for that matter.

'Well do something about it, then.'

'Like what?'

Tania pulls a knowing face at me.

'I'm not seeing your shagging yoga guy, I'm just not. There has to be another way.'

'Just get back on the horse, Em. Just crack on.'

Lucy, fed up with being ignored, sticks her squash-covered finger in my ear. 'Do I really look knackered?'

'No.'

'Honestly?'

'You look fucked, Emily.'

*

I've just received the email from work inviting me to arrange the time to come in for my keeping in touch day, and I feel like I'm going to puke. I knew this was coming. Of course I did. It was me that emailed them to ask for this, but I'd filed it away in the 'too big a deal to cope with so I won't' compartment of my brain the moment I'd pressed send.

How am I meant to make the transition from maternity-leave brain to 'I'm a mum who works, goes out, and has a flat that doesn't look like it's been condemned' every day? I've been dreading this pretty much since I left work but have been quietly confident that over maternity leave I would somehow become an award-winning playwright; that I would be earning more than I ever earned at the council, and that I could just send a polite, liberating email back explaining that I would not be returning as I had a trilogy of plays opening at the Royal Court. This has not happened.

How did Mum go back to work when I was only four months old? I know it was the olden days and you popped into the hospital at 9 a.m. to have your baby and were home by 3 p.m. to put the tea on. But seriously, four months? I was still congratulating myself for getting out once a week to the cinema at that stage. Lucy's now seven months old and I give myself a hearty pat on the back for leaving the house before 10 a.m. or getting us to the swimming class once a week to sing at Tania. Even with all the best planning in the world it sometimes feels like days are full of half stuff; that nothing actually gets completed or done properly and with that comes the guilt again.

I sit and stare at the laptop on the kitchen table, minimise my emails and open a blank word document with the intention of starting to write something. By 'write something' I mean type my name in different fonts to see which one looks the most creative and inspiring to write the amazing, mind blowing, 'I can't believe she wrote that with a seven-month-old-baby' play. Lucy is sitting on the floor surrounded by a WWE-style ring of cushions with a selection of toys stacked up in front of her that she was given at birth and she's definitely outgrown; she looks bored out of her brain and I feel guilty again.

I save the opening two lines of my potentially award-winning script and close the laptop. We start to play together and make each other laugh, which has to be up there with one of the best things ever, as she chortles like a drain now, and then I remember that we're meant to be getting into some kind of routine.

So I sit Lucy up in her high chair, offering her some rice cakes and a strawberry. She pushes them around the suction plate and I feel guilty that I'm not taking it seriously enough. After ten minutes I take her out and breastfeed her because then at least I know she's not hungry. The Annabel Karmel book I enthusiastically bought off Amazon at 2 a.m. in the hope it would give me some inspiration is currently being used to prop up the wonky chest of drawers in our bedroom.

I put Lucy down for her afternoon nap and turn the computer on again. Google 'good first lines of plays' and choose one at random, then drift into the unavoidable Facebook black hole, bidding for crap on eBay, and sifting through emails from Gambian princes who just need my bank details to complete the transaction to transfer two million quid of tax avoidance money into my name.

I open the email from work again; even the council's official font makes me feel nervous, like it represents another life. How am I meant to type every day in that font and have a baby as well?

Lucy wakes up; I turn the computer off, convincing myself that updating my status and uploading another picture of her is, kind of, like writing. And there it is as always, the niggling guilt.

I look outside and it's still raining. Lucy has turned her nose up at the sweet potato I lovingly peeled and overboiled, so I just clear a space on the floor, have a cuddle with her and stick on the DVD of *Sex and the City* series three.

This is, of course, the moment when Nick gets back from work. 'Busy day, girls?' he asks as he takes his jacket off and throws it on the back of the sofa. He picks up Lucy, nestles himself into her neck for a sniff, then kisses me on the top of my head. 'Looking sweeeet, Em!'

I look down at my strawberry-stained jogging bottoms and the T-shirt from my sixth-form twinning exchange trip to Dortmund.

'How's your day?'

'Greeeeeeat!' he does his best Tony the Tiger impression for Lucy.

'I've had the email about going back today.'

'Really?'

'Yep,' I sigh.

'It'll be good, Em, it'll be fun.'

'When has arts education ever been fun?'

'You know what I mean. Change of scene, it will be good for Lucy too. Cuppa?'

'Go on then.'

'Normal or weird?'

'Normal.'

'Coming up. I'm going to have a beer.' He flicks on the kettle. 'It's been a good day today, Em, things feel like they might be turning a corner.'

'Does that mean I don't have to go back to work?' I ask optimistically.

'Not that good. But Shelly said in the team meeting this morning that things are definitely improving. I'm keeping my eyes peeled for other stuff, but anyway, that's the first positive thing that's been said at work for yonks.' He sounds lighter in his voice.

'That's great news, Nick. Really brilliant.' I take a deep breath and casually drop in, 'I was thinking . . .' I noisily clear my throat. I know that this probably isn't the best time to bring it up, but I announce with as much confidence as I can muster, 'I think we should have sex more, Nick.'

He doesn't respond. I'm not sure if he's heard me so I go back to watching Carrie Bradshaw. The kettle boils loudly. Maybe it's because of the jogging bottoms. I don't look my best, I really don't. I'm not sure I'd want to shag me. But I've said it now. It's out there.

'Good idea,' he says when he eventually turns around.

He's grinning. 'Fantastic idea, Emily.'

'Good. Glad you think so.' For some reason I give him the double thumbs up and surprisingly he does the same in return.

OK then. Well that's good news. In fact it's almost like actually doing it, having the conversation. What a relief. So that's one less thing to feel guilty about. There. We are a normal functioning couple again, who can talk about sex but might not get round to doing it any time soon; but that doesn't matter.

Who needs sex yoga? I've got this one covered.

Chapter Twenty-six

The building looks different from how I remember it. It's massive; I don't remember it being so big. I can see Frank, the old guy on reception, sat behind his desk. He's the kind of man who's been old since he was born, who would have called you 'duck' or 'love' when he was in his teens. We would have eaten him alive at school but right now, as he catches my eye and waves, I've never been happier to see him.

I walk through the revolving doors and up to the desk.

'Hello, duck, how are you? How's the little 'un? You just popping by to see us all?'

'I've got a keeping in touch afternoon, actually. I'm coming back soon, though,' I try to say casually as I fill in a temporary pass.

'Sounds very official. Well, don't you go working too hard; you need to keep your strength up for your baby. What did you have?'

'A girl. Lucy.'

'Lovely. Like Lucy Stone.'

'Yes!' I have no idea who he's talking about. I tap the pen absent-mindedly on the desk.

'It's floor three.' He points towards the lift.

'Yes. Right. Thanks.' Shit. I can't even remember the bloody floor, how am I going to remember what my job is? I feel nervous, like first-day-at-school nervous, or that feeling you get when you walk into a room and you know people have just been talking about you. I'm really sweaty. I couldn't decide on what to wear today. I've spent the last eight months in the middle-class mum uniform of ill-fitting jeans, Breton striped T-shirt and a pair of white Converse. I wanted to look grown-up today, professional. But I must have woken up thinking I worked as a stockbroker in the early nineties. I am wearing a heavy woollen trouser suit from Next that hasn't seen the light of day since about 1992 and is a bit short on the leg, teamed with an unintentionally off-white T-shirt. I look at my reflection in the mirror in the lift; I look like Diane Keeton in *Baby Boom*. I could kill Nick for letting me leave the house like this.

He took the afternoon off work to look after Lucy. As I left they were both at the window waving at me, and I felt a mixture of total excitement at leaving the house to go to work, reconnecting with the old 'me', and complete fear, as I don't know who that person is anymore.

The lift doors open to a hive of activity. The open-plan office is still as drab as it has always been. Royal-blue partitions segregating the large room are intended to slice up the space into departments and give a sense of personal space, but all it has really done is mean you can hear people speaking loudly to each other or on the phone but you just can't see them. There are bursts of colour on people's desks with pot plants, photos of family and friends, cards and general tat that's built up from years of working for a local authority. There must have been a push in the seventies to make every council building feel completely soulless, as anything beautiful might ignite happiness which could in turn start a revolution.

I'm not sure where I'm meant to go or whom I'm meant to see. The email invitation was a generic one from HR. I hadn't really read it properly, and now I'm wondering if there was some crucial information I'd skim-read and forgotten that would give me an idea of what to do next. I hate myself for feeling so indecisive and small. I am actually wet sweaty under my armpits and it is starting to heat the wool up a bit as well, creating a kind of rural England aroma. I fiddle about with my phone to relocate the email, while scanning the office for a familiar face. There has been a restructure since I left, with several departments merging onto the same floor to save money, and as a consequence nothing looks familiar. I don't recognise most of the people. Why didn't I just write that award-winning fucking play? Then I could be at home with Lucy drinking coffee on the sofa reading my Lyn Gardner review instead of self-consciously being ignored in an office full of strangers.

'Emily?'

'Hi!' I shrill. It's Mags, the office administrator. She is Mum's age and has worked for the council since councils began in the 1800s. I hug her. She awkwardly hugs me back and I realise in all the years we have worked together I don't think I have had any physical contact with her other than passing a piece of paper or a cup of tea, so this comes as a bit of a surprise to us both.

'I thought I'd see if I could find you. Liz has been waiting for you in the meeting room.'

I follow her through the sea of booths towards the meeting room, which is a glass-walled construction in the middle of the room, built with the intention of letting in light as none of the walls are external, but which gives no privacy. You are in a fishbowl in a middle of a sea of worker bees. Mags opens the door for me. 'Tea?'

'Yes please,' and I nod my gratitude this time, like a karate sensei. I feel so completely self-conscious; my upper lip is sweating. What has happened to me? Why are my physical reactions so totally out of control? It's like managing a large puppet.

'Emily, so lovely to see you, sit down, sit down.'

There are no windows and with the glass door shut, the room quickly starts to warm up.

'So, how are you? You look very . . . smart.'

Liz is in her late fifties. She is a serial civil servant, having worked here for the best part of thirty years. As the fable goes she started as a receptionist and worked her way into a comfortable senior role where she is paid well, will have a generous old-school pension, and can never be sacked. She manages the Arts and Regeneration Department, of which I am one. It's a team of two, three if you count Mags, which no one does. She also manages Events, which puts on all the outdoor activity in the city, and is much bigger, with about fifteen people. They do all the things that bring in money, like Little Mix concerts in the park, so are deemed more important.

'How's your little one?'

'Great. She's great.'

'What did you call her?'

'Lucy.'

'Ahh, like Lucy Maud Montgomery.'

'Yes.' Again, no clue, but who knew there were so many famous, obscure Lucys in the world?

'Did you get the flowers?'

'Yes, they were beautiful. Thank you.' And the card which was signed by a load of people I don't know, one of whom had wished me a 'quick and painless labour' which seemed a bit over-familiar as I don't remember ever meeting 'Karen from Accounts' before.

'Great. Great.' I'd never noticed her Dennis-like repetition of words.

211

'So, this afternoon is really your opportunity to touch base with us before you come back. To feel connected with work and so it doesn't feel like a shock when you return. We can use the afternoon however you would like. Is there anything specific you'd like to do?'

My mind has gone completely blank. I can't pull together enough words to formulate a sentence. I think I am high on the overpowering stench of warm wool and I have *The Night Garden* theme tune on loop in my head. I realise I have just been staring intently at Liz with my mouth open.

'Or know? Is there anything you'd like to find out about that's been happening since you went on maternity leave?'

Liz juts her chin out to indicate it's my turn to talk.

'Ermm . . .'

'Tea!' Mags pushes the door open with her bum and saves me from further professional suicide. I gratefully sip the drink and then, for the reason that it is the only thing I can think to ask, I say, 'Could I have a tour of the new office layout?'

'Of course, of course. Mags' – Liz exhales a sigh of relief – 'would you mind showing Emily round? I'll be at my desk, Emily, so come and find me when you've had a look about, and then we'll introduce you to Simone, who's been your maternity cover.'

The next thirty minutes are a painful exercise in introductions and small talk with people who a) don't know who I am and b) don't care. I meet the full Parks and Countryside team, Refuse and Accounts, including Karen, who cocks her head to one side and asks, 'How was it?' while looking towards my vagina. She has photos of about twenty kids stuck to her booth so that accounts for her concern; she probably hasn't sneezed without pissing herself for the best part of a decade. And to complete the grand tour, we finish in the

212

corner of the room. 'And here's your team!' The booths are empty apart from John, who's about Liz's age and has worked for the council for a similar length of time, although his career trajectory is vastly different, given he is on the same pay grade as me.

'Good to scc you, Emily.' John nods and then awkwardly turns back to his screen. At least his lack of enthusiasm is reassuringly consistent.

'And this . . .' Liz's voice bellows behind me, 'is Simone.'

Our paths have never crossed because I went on maternity leave the week before she started, and all she knows of me is a scrappy list of handwritten handover notes. Liz has her arm on her shoulder, like a proud parent. This isn't a good sign.

Simone extends her hand. 'Lovely to meet you, Emily. I've heard lots about you from your team.'

God she's irritating. And good-looking. And I love what she's wearing. She smiles and asks if I'd like to catch-up on what's she's been doing on my projects, and that she hopes I think she's been doing a good job of looking after them. She's so fricking considerate and thoughtful – what is wrong with this woman? We sit down at the spotless desk; there's a photo stuck to her booth of her and a man who is glossy-magazine hot.

She notices I'm staring at him. 'That's Harry. We're getting married soon in Italy.' She gazes wistfully at the picture for a second and I wonder if I've ever, in all the time I've known Nick, looked at him like that in real life, let alone a photograph. 'I hope you don't mind but I had a bit of a reorganise of your folders. I can put them back to where they were before, though, if this system doesn't make sense to you.'

The computer filing systems she's devised are incredible.

She's dated all the documents, put them in neat folders and sub folders, created systems for contracting artists, made spreadsheet after easy-to-understand spreadsheet logging conversations with schools. She's worked with Karen in Accounts to develop financial targets and created a red, amber, green system to see how she is measuring against these targets and set up monthly meetings with Liz to talk through the progress. What have I been doing for the past six years other than emailing Nick and googling pictures of Ryan Gosling? This is an absolute professional disaster.

'Ask me anything you want about what I've done, I really don't want to be treading on your toes or doing things you don't think are necessary.' I've no idea what to ask, other than, would you mind fucking something/anything up before I come back to make me look good?

People from other departments make a detour by our desk to say hi to Simone on their way to the kitchen. She's made friends with everyone; several of them introduce themselves to me, assuming I've just started.

As I leave Simone hugs me. 'It's been so lovely to meet you. Do get in touch if there's anything I can help with, although you must be run off your feet doing the most important job in the world at the moment.'

I look at her blankly.

'Motherhood?' she clarifies.

'Ah yes. 'Course. See you later.' And then I shout, 'BYE!' to no one in particular in the open-plan office. To which not one person replies or even looks up from their booth except John, who raises an arm in acknowledgement but doesn't even bother to turn around.

'Don't worry, Emily, your job has been in a very safe pair of hands. Isn't she wonderful?' Liz asks as she walks me towards the lift.

I look back to where she's sitting and John, who has chronic social anxiety and doesn't bother speaking to anyone, has wheeled his chair over to hers and is smiling and laughing. Actually fucking laughing. I hate Simone.

I check my phone on the bus. Nick has sent me a picture of him and Lucy at the park and she has her arms wrapped tightly around his neck, grinning. The text says, 'Don't hurry back, we're having a great time!'

A superwoman has taken over my job. Lucy doesn't need me. Today is officially a shit day. I do the only thing I can think to do, and burst into a snotty-nosed, mascara-dripping cry, leaning my head against the greasy window of the number 40 as it takes me home.

Lucy is in her cot when I get in.

'I put her down as she was so worn out that I didn't even bother with the bath,' Nick gloats.

My shoulders slump in disappointment. I've been dreaming about sniffing her all afternoon.

'And you will never guess what.'

'What?'

'Guess. Guess what she did.'

'Nick, I'm too tired for this, what did she do?'

'What has she never done before?' He's literally hopping from one foot to another.

'I dunno. Walk? Write?' I flop down on the sofa without taking my coat off, which is uncomfortably tight around my woollen suit.

'Come on, Em, seriously. Guess what she did today. With me.'

I sigh. 'Please, Nick. I just want an obscenely large glass of wine and a catch-up on *Corrie*. I don't have the brain space for this.' I shut my eyes.

'OK, she, drum roll please . . .' He waits for me to fill the void but gives up after a couple of seconds. 'She took a bottle.'

'WHAT?' I sit bolt upright.

'I know. She drank from a bottle. A whole one-fifty mil, the whole thing. Can you believe it?'

'No. What do you mean, she drank from a bottle?' I'm wrestling to get my coat off as I've suddenly become extremely hot. 'Why didn't you tell me?'

A wave of panic sears through me. How is this possible?

'I know!' Nick misinterpreting my distress for excitement. 'A whole new chapter, eh?'

'But she can't have!'

'But she did!' Nick grins.

I should be relieved. I know I should. We have spent month upon stressful month trying to get her to take a bottle. But I don't feel happy. I just can't. Is it because I wasn't there to witness it? That it's been me who's seen all her firsts and have always told Nick? No, this isn't jealousy, I know what that feels like and this isn't it.

'How did it happen?'

'Well, I knew we'd agreed that you'd feed her before work and then I'd give her tea and everything, but I just thought, why not pop into town and—'

'Hang on, you popped into town? What do you mean you popped into town? How?'

'I just put her in the pram and we jumped on the bus.' Nick passes me a glass of wine. 'Anyway, we went to Boots, I bought some formula, and then we gave it a go. And she downed the whole thing like a total pro, it was amazing. She was amazing.'

'And then what?' I can't quite belief that he just 'popped' into town with her with such ease.

'Then we went to the park, and then we came home.'

I take a large gulp of the wine and it hits me like a truck. This feeling. This uneasiness. It's the kernel of the thought that she doesn't need me anymore. This is what we've wanted to happen for months and now I'm not so sure. Soon my milk will dry up and my boobs will look even more like empty sausage skin than they do now.

'Do you want to have a cuddle with her before she goes to sleep?' Nick whispers.

'I thought she was already down?'

'I'd only just put her in the cot, she's not asleep yet.'

Nick wanders out of the room and returns with Lucy curled over his shoulder.

'She's nearly off.' I feel like I've come home as he passes her floppy warm body to me, her hair smelling of his aftershave.

Nick moves the oversized ornamental cushions off the sofa and squeezes in next to me. 'So' — he pats my thigh — 'tell me, how was your afternoon?'

This is the first time in months I can answer the question without talking about Lucy but I don't want to talk about work. I don't want to talk about Simone and Liz and John and Karen from Accounts. I don't care enough right now. I just want to be with these guys. 'Fine. It was good. Good to be back. Why don't you get us fish and chips from round the corner and we can watch *Masterchef*?'

I look down at her sleepy, creased face and Nick slots his arm around my shoulder.

'She'll always be your baby,' he whispers before kissing my ear.

'Promise?'

'Promise.'

I forget he knows me better than I know myself. That, right there, is true friendship.

1999 age 18

Rachel's house smells different. I can't put my finger on it. Cleaner maybe.

'Come through,' Mrs Chapman whispers, beckoning me towards the sitting room, 'they're in here.' She looks at me accusingly, arms firmly folded over her large chest, as the bottles in the carrier bag clink. 'She's not going to be needing those, Emily. Do you want to leave them by your shoes?'

My cheeks burn with embarrassment. 'Of course.' I put the Oddbins bag in the entrance hall next to my Doc Martens and follow Mrs Chapman through the open door. She wears a floral skirt that hangs off her massive bum, swaying as she walks like a huge, human lampshade.

Rachel is lying on the sofa with eyes closed and the crocheted blanket that normally hangs off the back of the armchair is covering her, pulled right up underneath her chin. Next to her is a Moses basket. I peer inside and there he is. Callum. He's absolutely tiny, fast asleep with both arms raised above his head like he's surrendering in a shoot-out. His little chest rises and falls so fast he looks like he's panting. He's wearing the baby-blue knitted hat and cardigan that my mum had made for him. He could be a baby from a home crafts magazine. He's perfect.

Rach stretches and opens her eyes. 'Emmie. How long have you been here? Mum, why didn't you wake me?'

'Sleep when the baby sleeps. That's what the midwife said, isn't it?'

Rach groans. I assume it's at her mum and her irritating comments but then I see her trying to pull herself into a sitting position.

'No sudden movements, Rachel, or you'll end up back in hospital.'

'I've had a caesarean,' Rach tells me by way of explanation, although I'm not entirely sure what she's talking about. 'Sit down, sit down next to me. God, I'm glad you're here.'

I perch on the edge of the sofa. 'So this is him, then?' I point at Callum and instantly feel stupid.

She nods, smiling. 'Do you want a hold?'

'You shouldn't wake him while he's sleeping, Rachel. He'll never go down later otherwise.' Mrs Chapman hasn't moved from her position as gatekeeper.

'Mum, I'm dying for a cuppa. Would you mind making one for me and Emmie?'

'Of course, of course I will. Milk no sugar, Emily?'

'That's right, thanks.' She reluctantly leaves, but not before saying, 'Just keep your voices down, you girls don't realise how loud you get sometimes,' then waddles out.

With the room to ourselves, Rach lets out a loud sigh. 'She is driving me fucking mental, Emmie. Can we come and live at your house?'

'I bought some Cava but your mum told me to leave it at the door. Sorry.'

'Thank you.' She shifts slightly on the sofa and winces. 'I can't drink at the moment but hopefully before too long, eh?'

'So, how's it all going?'

'I don't really know, I've got nothing to compare it to really. Callum sleeps for about an hour at a time and then wakes up to be fed, day and night, so I'm pretty tired.'

'You look amazing,' I lie.

'Thanks. I haven't looked at myself in a mirror since bringing him home a couple of days ago. Mum has to help me in and out the shower cos of my stitches, which is mortifying but hopefully I'll heal quickly and then I can start doing stuff on my own.'

I want to ask her about her stitches, about what it's like to actually have a baby. Did she poo everywhere? That is my absolute worst fear about giving birth, that I completely shit myself and everyone including my husband sees. But then Rach didn't have her a husband there, did she? It was just her and her mum. There are so many things I want to ask her, but it feels like something has shifted, something massive. I don't really know how I'm meant to be with her anymore. I mentioned this to Mum and she'd told me to just be myself, that Rach needs her best friend right now and that nothing has changed between us. That she'll need me more than ever now and for me to keep things as normal as possible. But I can't think of anything to say that doesn't sound stupid or immature in my head. Is it OK to talk about how Natasha Clarke from our year apparently got fingered by the bald bouncer with a face tattoo at Ritzy's, and now she gets in for free every Saturday? The old Rach would want to know about that, but is it even relevant when you have a baby?

I'm just about to ask Rach if she wants the gossip when Callum starts to make squeaking noises like a small animal.

'Hello, little one,' Rachel coos in a tone I've never heard her use before. She leans forward and quickly sucks her breath in in pain. 'Emmie, could you pass him to me, I can't get close enough without pulling my stitches.'

'Umm, OK, yes of course.' I lean into the Moses basket

and am met by a huge pair of blue eyes. He's kicking both legs in the air and I wonder how I'm meant to pick him up.

'Just put your hand underneath his bum and the other one underneath his head and lift him out.' How does Rach know all this stuff already?

I tuck my hands underneath his tiny body. He's warm and soft as I gently lift him up. He's so light. His tiny hands reach out and his fingers furl and unfurl, springing open like a mechanical toy. I hold him in front of me as if presenting a gift to someone, mesmerised by the smallest person I've ever seen. How has Rach grown something so utterly perfect? How can her body have known how to put all the cells in the right place to make a beautiful, perfect boy? I gently lower him into her arms.

'You're a natural!' Rachel compliments me and my face burns with pride. She lifts up her top and unclips the strap of her ugly, skin-coloured bra, revealing a massive nipple. I've seen Rachel's tits millions of times over the years but they've changed shape. She guides her huge nipple into Callum's mouth and as he sucks, Rach shuts her eyes and leans back against the sofa.

'Thank God he feeds properly. There were posters everywhere on the ward saying "Breast is best" and if I'd heard a midwife say it to me one more time I was genuinely going to kick off.'

'How's your dad been?'

'How do you think? He's virtually ignored Callum since he's been born. Calls him the baby like he doesn't have a name. Mum says he'll come around and fall in love with him like she has, but I don't give a shit to be honest, I'll be out of here as soon as I can get a flat of my own. Dad's even talked about going round to Gary's house to see if he could convince his dad that we should get married. Can you imagine?

221

It's not the sixteen hundreds, Dad!' Rach snorts at the prospect and Callum's head flops back. 'Shit, sorry, Callum,' and she guides his head onto her breast again. 'Anyway, that's enough about me, what's going on with you, how are your exams going?'

'Oh you know, OK. I've never been good under pressure. I just panic. I'm not good at exams, Rach, I'm not like you,' and I instantly wish I could swallow the words.

'Sir has sent a stack of mock exams for me. He thinks I should carry on revising and do my A levels next year and that the universities might consider extenuating circumstances and defer my conditional offers for a year.' She nods at a pile of official-looking papers stacked up on the table.

'That's brilliant news!'

Rach rolls her eyes at me.

'What, that is good news, isn't it?'

'Emmie, seriously, you're sounding like Dad. What would I do with Callum? I can't exactly take him to lectures, can I? Should I just leave him here with Mum? Pretend that none of this happened? Is that what you think?'

'Sorry, I just thought . . . sorry, Rach.'

'No, I'm sorry, I shouldn't have bitten your head off. I'm just tired. So tired. And everything hurts.' She lets out a long sigh. 'And I know that on Saturday you'll all be in the pub celebrating the end of exams and I'll be here with Mum watching *Noel's* fucking *House Party*. And I wouldn't change him, Emmie, I wouldn't change Callum, but I just wish . . . I don't know what I wish. I just feel a bit sad.'

Rach starts to quietly sob, and I budge along to sit next to her, putting my arm round her shoulder gently so as not to disturb Callum. She rests her head on me and whispers, 'Just don't forget about me, Emmie.'

'I won't.'

'Promise?'

'Promise.' I stroke her hair in response and a reassuring silence falls between us, only broken by Callum's suckling noises.

Part Three

'I'm going to take up some new hobbies over maternity leave and learn a new language.'

Chapter Twenty-seven

I feel sick. Today is Lucy's first full day at nursery and my first full day at work. I've just dropped her off at Laugh 'n' Learn academy with two jars of baby food and three bottles of formula.

She's had a couple of settling-in sessions already, where I'd unpicked her grasp on my T-shirt and neck and reluctantly passed her to Kimberly, her new key worker (which in itself makes her sound like a teenage gang member who's on probation). I'd waited in a greasy spoon round the corner for two hours. I couldn't shake the feeling of dread, as if I'd just done something really stupid like handing her over to a child murderer or a paedophile. Completely irrational thoughts I know, but why was I sat in a shitty café with fading pictures of Cindy Crawford in clip frames all over the walls instead of being with my baby? The bald man behind the counter had asked me when I came in, 'First day of nursery is it?'

I nodded. 'How can you tell?'

'Cos it's the only time a woman under eighty comes into my café – when they're waiting for their little'uns. At least you're not crying, they're normally crying.' And he'd gone back to drying cups with a tea-towel that looked as if it had never seen a washing machine.

When I picked Lucy up after what felt like the longest two hours of my life, Kimberly had told me what a pleasure she'd been, how developed she was for her age, how 'cute' she was (which made my toes curl a bit) and how much they were looking forward to having her at the nursery. She'd waved at Lucy as I'd carried her out and Lucy waved back; I'd felt a slight pang of jealously and betrayal. I want her to be happy, of course I do, but she's not allowed to like anyone more than she likes me.

Today is not going to plan.

Lucy wouldn't settle last night; she point-blank refused a night-time bottle, even though she's been taking them every day since Nick 'cracked the case', as he keeps reminding me. As a result, she used me as a kind of human dummy all night. She wasn't really feeding, just using me for comfort, but I caved because at the time I thought it would buy me the most sleep. If you've ever tried to sleep with a large nipple clamp attached to you, which might be the case for a niche percentage of the population, then you'll know how impossible it is to get comfortable. As a consequence, I feel like I've had about ten minutes sleep and am so tired it's like being in a slow-motion film. Nick, on the other hand, had snored his way through the night and even started actually laughing in his sleep at one point, which made me want to push him out and onto the floor. Then he was up and out before 7 a.m. for his Monday morning meeting, leaving me and Lucy to fend for ourselves.

And today, after eight months of watching crap telly in the afternoon and endlessly pushing Lucy around the block to get her to sleep, that all changes. I need to be a fully func- tioning adult again. I am handing her over to a nursery full of strangers while I go to work. It is only two days a week to begin with, but that will soon become three, and then I will spend nearly half the week without her. Nick's life has changed very little since her arrival. Of course he loves her, and plays with her, and gets up with her in the night, but the main changes in his life are that he's more knackered, we don't binge drink as a couple anymore and we have sex once a year instead of once a week.

Today is massive. It's huge. Today signifies 'the next step', and Nick leaves me to sort it all out by myself? I'm furious and send him a text to say so, almost exactly the same time as I receive one that says how sorry he was he had to leave so quickly, and how much he loves us both and how proud he is of me. I feel completely guilty, and start to cry, before seeing the time on the kitchen clock and realising that today I don't have the luxury of crying at will.

We get to nursery almost half an hour late. I apologise to Kimberly and she tells me it doesn't matter; we have to pay for the half-hour regardless. She also warns me that Pat, the nursery manager, charges a pound for every minute we're late picking up. A pound. Are you shitting me? I pass Lucy to Kimberly and she starts crying. Big tears. She's pushing her away with her feet and hands, trying to flip over in her grasp.

'She'll be fine, Mummy, if you want to go. I'll text you to let you know she's settled.' I don't think I'm ever going to get used to adults calling me mummy.

'It's probably easier if I take her.' I put my arms out and she strains against Kimberly to get into my hold.

'Whatever you would prefer, but it might take her a lot longer to settle.'

I feel completely torn. I kiss Lucy on the top of her head as she makes a grab for my shirt, holding on like a koala bear. I'm in a kind of clinch with Kimberly too, like a Lucy sandwich.

'Come on, lovely.' Is she talking to Lucy or me? 'Here we go, let's go and have a look in the sensory room, shall we?

Let's leave Mummy to go to work. Come on.' She unpicks her from me and promises, 'I'll text you a picture when she's settled, she'll be fine. They all have a wobble on the first day, it's completely natural.' She smiles reassuringly, presses the buttons on the keypad for the door, and then they're gone. I watch Lucy through the latticed window screaming, like a scene from *One Flew Over the Cuckoo's Nest*.

I step out into the morning air and the main security door shuts behind me, just as I realise I've left my scarf and hat on top of the pram. Fuck it. I can't go back now.

The bus into town feels like looking at the world through someone else's eyes. Everyone's on their way to work. I haven't done this journey in over a year and it's so busy yet quiet because it's just grown-ups. People are reading books, listening to their music. I check my phone for the fourteenth time and there's nothing yet from Kimberly. Maybe I should phone her?

Frank on reception greets me with a grin. 'What time do you call this!'

The large clock behind him reads 9.47. What? How has it got so late? I started getting us ready to leave the house nearly three hours ago.

The lift doors open just as Liz is striding past purposefully. She sees me, stops in her tracks, over-acts looking at her watch and says, 'We didn't think you were coming. Simone thought her job was being made permanent!'

I ramble an excuse about nappies and buses as her eyes glaze over.

'Well Simone has kindly written up a list of where she is with all her projects, she can take over when she comes back in on Wednesday.'

I hate Simone. I hate Liz. When did I agree to job-share with Wonderwoman? Why am I not at home watching

One Tree Hill with Lucy? And when did I become such an angry woman? Tania would definitely describe this as 'bad energy'.

It's about 10.30 a.m. when my milk comes in, which is unusual, as Lucy has had her morning feed as normal so I don't know why my body has decided it's time to lactate. It must be because Kimberly has just sent me a photograph of Lucy sitting in a high chair holding two plastic spoons covered in what looks like Weetabix and grinning at whoever is behind the camera. She's settled in fine!!!!!! the text reads. I ignore the multiple exclamation marks and try to feel relieved that she's happy.

I, on the other hand, have spent the best part of an hour staring blankly at a screen trying to remember my password. The curser is blinking menacingly next to the statement 'password incorrect'. The work set-up is that I come back on Mondays and Tuesdays, and Simone will work the rest of the week until I take back my third day, then she will be out of a job and I will have to squeeze what is meant to be a full-time post into three days, which, even with my poor maths, doesn't seem to add up. She has left me a handwritten note, welcoming me back and outlining the things that she has done. She's also left me a big bar of chocolate and a bottle of Lucozade as she said her sister was completely knackered when she came back to work after having her nephew. She's lovely, she's completely lovely and thoughtful and considerate. She probably doesn't swear and takes her make-up off every night before bed. Her handwriting is beautiful and artistic. I imagine this job is just a pit stop for her while she builds up her collection to go into the National Portrait Gallery. I hate myself for being so awful about her so I eat the entire family-size Dairy Milk in one go.

*

10.47 a.m. I'm starting to feel a bit nervous. I've made six failed attempts at logging in and now the computer has completely locked me out. I can't remember the number for the service desk and even if I could, I can't remember my pin number for the phone so there is no dial tone.

11.10 a.m. Mags rings the IT helpdesk for me who reset my password. I am now staring blankly at a very well-organised desktop of folders instead. I am none the wiser.

'I think you've spilt something on your jumper,' Mags whispers as she passes me a tissue.

I look down: two small rings of milk have appeared on my chest. Shit, I didn't even think to wear breast pads.

1.30 p.m. I step out into the sunshine and head to an over-priced, artisan sandwich shop. I sit at an impossibly small table near the window just because I can, and enjoy eating on my own. I can't remember the last time I've been able to drink a coffee warm. This is going to be OK. I might even go and have a look around Topshop afterwards.

1.50 p.m. I'm in the Topshop changing room when my next load of milk comes in. What's happening to me? My boobs are ginormous and have started to drip milk. The tissues Mags gave me are sodden and I've managed to leak onto the pile of clothes I was trying on. I put my jumper back on, hand the assistant the pile of slightly damp clothes and head to Boots to buy breast pads and Paracetamol as I'm starting to feel a bit under the weather.

2.30 p.m. I'm in the disabled loos at work attempting to hand-pump out some of the milk. My ducts are starting to block and you can see my veins protruding. A thread of milk shoots out of my breast, which I aim into the sink. I massage as much milk as I can out, but it's getting really sore. Trish Lane, the only wheelchair user in the whole of the council, is of course waiting outside the toilet as I leave, and mutters about how able-bodied people should use the toilets on the third floor. I apologise and consider telling her it's because I can't milk myself into the toilet bowl in a small cubicle, but decide against it.

It's 3.30 when my third lot of milk comes in. I have had a productive-ish hour of reading spam emails and circulars from the last six months and I've decided that today isn't the day to attempt to understand Simone's list. I'm starting to feel really sweaty; my nipples are red raw and I can feel a golf-ball-size blocked milk duct under my armpit.

And it dawns on me. Lucy was feeding throughout the night instead of her usual twenty-minute feed in the morning and before bed and my body has gone crackers. It thinks it's feeding a newborn and has adjusted my milk production accordingly. Stupid, stupid body. Does it not know I am two hours away from seeing my baby and have no idea what I'm meant to do until then? I suddenly feel very cold.

'John,' I call over, 'are you chilly?'

'Nope. I'm roasting.' He doesn't look up from his desk. This is the most he's said to me all day.

I put my coat on and continue to read about the Tunisian prince who would like to give me $4,000,000 if I email him my bank details. Maybe I should email him John's info, the mardy bastard.

'So how are you getting on?' Liz is leaning on the back of my chair reading the screen. 'Busy?'

As I turn around in the spinny chair, Liz takes a step back. 'Are you OK, Emily? You don't look OK.'

I wipe the sweat from my forehead on the sleeve of my

coat. How can I be sweating when I'm shivering?

'Maybe go and sort yourself out in the toilets and we can have a catch-up afterwards.'

'Thanks, Liz, I'm absolutely fine, it's just a bit warm in here.'

'It's not. Give your face a wash and then come and find me.'

Back in the toilets, I look at myself in the mirror. I look absolutely dreadful. I'm grey and blotchy and incredibly sweaty. My breasts are now throbbing and feel so heavy with milk I need some kind of extra support to hold them up.

I have felt like this before. When Lucy was days old.

Oh shit, I have mastitis. Who gets mastitis with an eight-month-old baby?

I take off my coat, use the hand drier to dry the armpits of my jumper and my face and go back to my desk.

'Better?' Liz asks.

'Much,' I lie.

'Are you sure you're up to this?'

Now, the thing about Liz is she has absolutely no interest in children. In fact I would go so far as to say she actively dislikes them in a Cruella de Vil kind of way. She made a conscious decision to never have children herself so that she could spend her money on expensive holidays and a Georgian town house in Hove. As a consequence she has no sympathy with any issues that may arise about, with or because of children. I have seen her reduce women to tears with her lack of interest in their photos of their newborns.

So, long story short, I can't tell her I have lactated myself into a fever and need to go home. But I have, and I do.

'Would you mind if I just came in early tomorrow and had a short day today?'

She shrugs, unimpressed. 'Just make sure you do,' and she turns on her heels.

A long bus ride and a short greeting with Kimberly later, and I am sitting on the bench outside the nursery feeding Lucy. It's excruciating and I have to bite the inside of my mouth to distract myself from the pain, but twenty minutes later and I have deflated both breasts and Lucy has fallen asleep in my arms.

This working mum thing is a piece of piss.

Chapter Twenty-eight

'You looked fine in the last thing.'

This is the seventh outfit I have tried on. I hate all my clothes, nothing fits properly and the things that do are so mumsy I want to shoot myself in my own face.

'I don't even know why you're getting all worked up about this.' He shrugs his slim shoulders on the body that is exactly the same size as it was when we met. Of course he doesn't get it. 'You're only meeting Helen and Tania. It's not like you're going to try to get off with them.' He laughs at his own stupid, pre-pubescent joke.

'Well maybe I might,' I retort for no reason at all.

Nick walks out muttering something under his breath and I look at myself in the full-length mirror. My jeans fit, just, but half my waist is uncomfortably squeezed over the top. I am wearing a floral blouse that wouldn't be out of place in *Abigail's Party*; I don't even know where it came from, I'm not convinced it's actually mine. I just can't wear that bloody stripy T-shirt again. I've worn it every day for the last week, putting it in the wash in the evening and then drying it on the radiator. I want to impress Helen and Tania and I don't think the floral blouse is going to cut it.

'Taxi's outside!'

Fuck, fuck, fuck. I quickly pull off the shirt and give in, putting on my trusty stripy T-shirt, some red lipstick and voilà. I pop my head around Lucy's bedroom door. She is lying on her front with her bum stuck in the air, her back rising and falling as she gently sleeps. I kiss the top of Nick's head as he watches *University Challenge*.

'You look nice,' he tells me without hardly looking up, and I head out.

Tonight was my idea and now I'm regretting it a bit.

I'd WhatsApped Helen and Tania to see if they fancied a drink, expecting they'd both make an excuse, which would mean that I wouldn't actually have to leave the warm flat but would imply to them both that it was totally normal for me to go drinking of an evening. Double win. Except they both called my bluff within seconds, the two blue ticks indicating they'd read it.

Helen: It's a 100% yes from me.
Tania: And me. I don't care if we meet on a park bench with a bottle of cider. I really need a night out.
Helen: Can we meet somewhere nice and not on a park bench? I haven't been out for months.

It dawns on me that we haven't seen each other without children and feel momentarily panicked about how we will fill three hours of chat without the distraction of a baby when conversation dries up. Do I need to do all the chatting to make things more comfortable? What do we actually have in common other than the children? I make a mental list of 'conversation starters' in my head.

7 p.m. The taxi pulls up outside the Hare and Hounds. The security guard opens the door for me without a second look; I guess my days of being ID'ed are well and truly over.

I scan the pub. It's absolutely heaving, the bar must be seven deep, and the DJ is playing dance music at a ridiculous volume. Was pub music always this loud?

I see Helen and Tania sitting in the corner of the room, leaning in to speak to each other and laughing. I feel a pang of jealousy. They're not actually allowed to be friends unless I'm there, that's the rules. Both of them have got dressed up, like properly dressed up, too. I consider jumping back in the cab and whizzing home for a quick change but Helen spots me and waves.

'I like your . . .' her eyes dart up and down as she holds me at arm's length, 'lipstick. Red suits you.' Nice save and she gives me an awkward hug.

'So this is what Friday nights look like.' Tania is specifically pointing at the crowd of hipsters with handlebar moustaches huddling around the DJ booth. I hadn't even realised it was Friday night: my working week finishes on a Tuesday so I am totally out of touch with the outside world.

'When did beards get sexy?' Helen asks. 'I've been off having a baby and all the fit men now look like Mr Twit.'

I think of Nick with his fluffy beard and completely agree.

'Right, shall I get us some drinks?' I ask.

Tania drains her glass of wine. 'It's my round. Shall I just get a bottle? Seems daft to keep buying glasses.'

7.40 p.m. We've drunk the first bottle of white wine in record time and are now cracking into the second. We're talking through our labour in blow-by-blow detail which, it transpires, in all the time we've known each other, we haven't actually done. And it's amazing. Like stepping back in time, describing an experience that you see from a bird's-eye view. Time, pain and the physical act of pushing out a baby feels like they happened to someone else. There is something so incredible about revisiting it. We listen intently as we each take a turn to describe it. By the time Tania has finished, we're all in floods of tears.

I nip to the loo, and when I come back Helen is talking about how hard she found it to get pregnant, and that she'd had five miscarriages before she got pregnant with Polly through IVF. She tells us how she feels so nervous all the time with Polly, like it's a temporary situation, like something might happen to take her away. She looks so sad, like core sad, the kind of shift that happens in someone when they lose a loved one. I reach out and hold her hand. Tania does the same. Helen grips them both tightly.

Tania tells us about how difficult she finds parenting with Spiral. How they're just not on the same page. How he has an ideal of what it is to bring up a child but it doesn't translate to real life. She talks of how she dreams of another life, and I think about Mum and Mario and me and Tom Smith.

It might be the wine, it's almost definitely the wine, but I hadn't expected this kind of evening. We're quite different women and I didn't know if it would work, the three of us out together. We have very different backgrounds, and jobs, and partners, and possibly every life experience now I think about it. But we do have something that binds us together. We're all mothers. We're all trying to work out how the fuck you do it. How you look after a little life and also, somehow, still be yourself.

I feel quite emotional about how connected I feel to them both, the depth of understanding, and think this would be the perfect time to talk to them about my ongoing worry about Lucy getting carried away by seagulls. I tell them how I look at the world as a series of potential death traps, a catalogue of 'what ifs'.

Their faces are blank at first but then Helen squeezes my hand and says, 'I think that's completely normal. I do the same. But it's about the bath and drowning.'

I hadn't thought of that. Now I will. I go up to the bar to buy another bottle of wine. They have an offer on Tuaca so I buy three shots of that as well. It tastes like cough syrup so can't be that strong.

8.30 p.m. My milk's come in. My right boob is particularly full. I've also forgotten to wear breast pads so my bra is soggy. I sit on the toilet holding on to an empty pint glass and attempt to hand-pump the milk. It's not easy to start with, and my breast is getting really sore, but suddenly a jet of milk squirts out, spraying the back of the toilet door. It's incredible the distance it can reach. I aim it in the pint glass and massage the milk ducts as a small puddle of milk appears at the bottom of the glass. Fifteen minutes later and there is an inch of milk. I stuff my bra with tissue and rejoin the girls. Tania has bought another bottle and lined up a shot of tequila each. She's taken her shoes off and has put them on the table so she doesn't forget them.

9.15 p.m. We've now done four shots. Or five. I'm not sure. Helen has bumped into a woman whom she used to work with at the bank. She kept hugging her really tightly and telling her how much she used to love working with her. The woman looked a bit uncomfortable. I've found half a packet of fags on the floor in the toilet and Tania and I are in the beer garden smoking them. I haven't smoked for over two years now and probably wouldn't have bothered but they were just sitting there in the loos, like a sign. A guy in a Gay Bikers on Acid T-shirt lurks near us. He could be forty or sixty, it's hard to tell; his face is so weathered, framed by lank, long grey hair. A timely reminder to not smoke after this evening.

'Have you got a light?' he asks. He's clutching one in his

hand, which I point out. 'What do you girls do?'

I a) object to being referred to as a girl and b) want him to bugger off so I can carry on talking to Tania about how painful it is to get the coil fitted.

'We're both mothers actually,' Tania responds with pride. She later tells me this isn't pride, it's confusion, as she'd forgotten what I did for a job, and hates telling men she's a yoga instructor and massage therapist (I didn't know she was) as they make jokes about 'extras'.

'MILFS,' he replies with a kind of Beavis and Butthead laugh.

'MILFS? Fucking MILFS? What are you, thirteen?' This bursts out of me, taking us all by surprise. 'You know what –' I'm really coming into my stride now, hello outspoken Emily, I wondered where you've been hiding all these months – 'you know what, it is totally unacceptable to just approach women in this way and then to say shit like that. You're an embarrassment, this situation is completely embarrassing. For you, I mean,' and I point at him. 'If you want to talk to us, fine. Ask. See if we want to talk to you. Don't just fucking come and . . .' I'm losing my thread here. Come on, Emily. Keep it together.

'Think we want you to invade our personal space,' Tania has picked up the gauntlet. Brilliant. 'Now fuck off.'

He mumbles something under his breath as he picks up his rollies and heads back in.

'Gay Bikers on Acid were shit!' I shout after him. I probably should have left it at Tania's 'fuck off', but I was enjoying myself. We high five each other. And someone claps, and then someone else, and then we have a kind of feminist standing ovation, and it feels like we need a power ballad to accompany this moment as Tania and I put our arms around each other. And then I hear it. 'Man in the Mirror'.

241

'COME ON!' I drag Tania back inside. 'This is our song!'

This isn't mine and Tania's song. It's mine and Rachel's. But she's not here and Tania says she's up for anything.

10 p.m. We've been asked to leave, as apparently I was being argumentative. I don't think it was argumentative. I was just giving the bouncer a different perspective on the same situation. He said dancing on tables was unacceptable and dangerous. I told him that I am a legend at miming to 'Man in the Mirror' and he should have just let me finish the song and then I would have got down. Anyway, it turns out it doesn't pay to argue with bouncers.

Thankfully there is another pub over the road that plays equally loud music and has considerably lower standards and doesn't seem to mind three very drunk mums pulling back a few of the tables to create a makeshift dance floor.

It turns out Helen can breakdance, like properly break-dance. She tells us her mum sent her to street dance classes when she was younger to make up for not ever being around and she got really into it, county competitions and every-thing. I went to tap and jazz classes, not so cool to pull out the bag now but I give it a go anyway. The DJ puts on some JayZ for Helen and people start to form a circle around her, watching her dance. Someone else comes into the ring and then Helen steps out. She's created a dance-off, a real-life dance-off. I could die happy.

I thought she was slightly boring when I first met her, what with working in a bank and everything but now, with the sex addiction and the breakdancing, I think I'm a bit in love with her.

'WHEN I FIRST MET YOU I THOUGHT YOU WERE A BIT BORING WITH WORKING IN A BANK AND EVERYTHING,' I shout over the music at her, wrapping my arm around her neck in a kind of headlock, 'I DON'T MEAN THAT IN A BAD WAY, JUST, YOU KNOW, THAT'S WHAT PEOPLE THINK ABOUT BANKS. AND ACCOUNTANTS. AND COMPUTER PEOPLE.'

'Thanks.'

'NO WHAT I MEAN IS YOU'RE TOTALLY NOT. YOU'RE TOTALLY NOT BORING AT ALL. I DIDN'T MEAN YOU WERE. I MEAN'T YOU WEREN'T. AREN'T.' I think she's taken the compliment in the spirit it was intended.

I wander into the beer garden to smoke a fag. Tania is there getting off with the Gay Bikers on Acid guy. She still hasn't got her shoes on so must have left them in the other pub. I think about saying something but they're really going for it, so I just rest on the wall and smoke.

10.40 p.m. I've been sick. It wouldn't have been so bad but I mainly missed the toilet and I've got it on the sleeve of my T-shirt as well.

'Emily, are you in here?' It's Helen.

'Here,' I croak and stick my foot under the door so she knows what cubicle it is.

'Is this your foot?' and she pulls it. I think she's trying to get me out by tugging me through the six-inch gap under the door. 'I think Tania is still outside with that old guy. I've got to go home, I can't drink any more.'

I retrieve my leg and unlock the door.

'Wow, what's happened to you?'

I catch my reflection in the mirror behind her and see what she means. I've also got sick in my hair, and my eye make-up has run down my face like Kiss.

'I'm good, I just need some water and then I'll be fine again and we can go somewhere else. Thanks, Rachel.'

'Who's Rachel?'

'I mean Helen. Did I say Rachel? You know Rachel, she's my best friend from home.'

'I don't think I've heard you mention her before ever.'

'Yes you have. You must have. I'd marry her if I wasn't with Nick, you know that?'

'Nope. I don't know who you're talking about.'

'Yes you do. Rachel, you know, Rachel. Fucking Rachel, Helen, do you know who I mean?'

'Nope. Come on, let's go back to the bar.'

'I don't know her either. It makes me so sad. So sad, do you know that, Helen?'

'I know.'

'But do you? Do you really?'

'Yes. I know,' she lies and puts her arm around me to prop me up. 'Don't get puke on me.'

We guide each other out of the loo, and we're back into the thumping bar. The barman comes over and tells us there's a taxi stand over the road and he would prefer us to leave without making a fuss. We stumble out to the back garden, tell Gay Bikers on Acid to get off our friend and the three of us walk out of the pub, arm in arm. We squash into the back of the taxi.

It's been less than four hours since we all met and I can genuinely say I don't think I've ever been this drunk.

6 a.m. I hear Lucy crying. I try and lift my head off the pillow and it feels like I've been hit with a massive iron bar. My eyes are stuck together and when I prise them apart the small shaft of light coming through the curtains feels like it's burning my retinas. I'm lying on top of the duvet wearing all my clothes including my shoes and I've still got my handbag around my shoulders. I can smell sick really

strongly. I'm lying on my front and my boobs are throbbing with the weight of the milk for her morning feed. I know I'm going to have to express it and bin it but the thought of extracting the very last bit of moisture from me right now might genuinely finish me off.

I can hear Nick talking soothingly next door to Lucy, singing her a little song and I get a wave of nausea and guilt.

All I can think of is, please don't bring her in, please don't bring her in. Followed by, if I stay really, really still, maybe I can trick my body into thinking it's not hungover?

Too late. Here's Nick with Lucy.

'She's refusing the bottle, I think she just needs a hug.'

'Can you please hug her?' I croak.

'I'll bring you a cuppa. You've survived worse, Em,' and he ruffles my hair affectionately. My brain feels like a pea inside a bucket and ricochets off the sides of my skull.

Tania: HELP. I'M DYING.

Helen: Me too.

Me: I'm feeding.

Helen: Oh God. What an awful thought.

Me: And I can feel her top tooth coming through.

Helen: Urgh.

Tania: Did I????

Me: Yes.

Helen: Yes.

Tania: Fuck. It's the tequila. He was about 70 wasn't he?

Me: Yes.

Tania: Wow. OK. Don't tell Spiral.

Helen: Never.

Me: Agreed.

Tania: Fun though. Can we do it again soon?

Me: Deffo.

Helen: When I feel normal again. Which might take some time.
Tania: Right, I'm crawling back to bed to die and feel really bad about myself. Speak later.

However awful I'm feeling today, at least I didn't get off with some middle-aged guy who looked like Keith Richards.

Chapter Twenty-nine

Lucy has chosen now as the perfect time to abandon sleeping in long stints, just as I'm finding some kind of routine after three weeks back at work. It's like she's completely regressed, like she's been waiting until I started relaxing a bit and then thought now, now, would be a great time to go on some kind of dirty sleep protest. All the forums say she should be sleeping for at least five-hour stretches. That's 'at least'. Not in total over the course of the whole night. Nick tries to help.

When I say tries, I mean he brings her into our bed after trying to settle her for about four minutes and says, 'She only wants you, Em, I've been trying for hours,' before rolling over and instantly going back to sleep. He's like a machine, a really fucking irritating machine. Right now I'm looking at her and she's smiling and playing with my hair and babbling away. It's 2 a.m. How am I going to function at work tomorrow?

We go in the front room and I put the Peppa Pig DVD on, pile all her toys on the play mat then lie down on the sofa under a throw and try and watch her with one eye open. I must have picked her up at some point and snuggled down with her because at 6 a.m. Nick starts noisily clanking about in the kitchen and I see Lucy's asleep on my chest. I feel sick from lack of sleep. My brain throbs and I have a pain behind my eyes that makes it uncomfortable to focus on anything.

Nick leans over the sofa and clumsily kisses my cheek. He reaches out to Lucy and I hiss, 'Don't wake her or I'll kill you.'

'Alright, Em, chill out.' Chill out, chill out? I'm not sure which part of the day I hate him most at the moment. The middle of the night when he's snoring and taking up eighty per cent of the bed like he's a single man, or the morning when he's full of beans and plays the 'I'm such a laid-back person, you just need to take a leaf out of my book on uber-relaxed attitudes and then you'd be happier' card because he's had eight hours sleep while I've been functioning on an average of two?

The mental distance between this moment, as I'm lying pinned to the sofa by our girl, and the moment in three hours' time when I will be dressed and sat at my desk ready for work, feels like a lifetime away.

I reset my phone alarm for 6.30 and close my eyes.

'Cup of tea?' Nick shouts in his outdoor voice and Lucy lifts her head, her face crumbling as she starts to cry.

He scoops her off me as she bucks and kicks. 'What's wrong with you, pumpkin?' I wish he'd stop calling her that. Cathleen and Dennis call her that. It's their generic name for small animals and anyone under the age of ten.

'What's your plan today, Em?'

'I'm working. I've got to go to work, same as you.'

'Ahh, yes, sorry, I forgot.'

'It's massively easy, Nick. I work three days a week now. I'm with Lucy the rest. What's difficult to remember about that?' I'm standing up now, rising like a phoenix from the ashes, except I'm wrapped in a child's pram blanket with my hands on my hips in a rage. I'm not sure where it's come from but I'm furious.

'OK, Em, chil—'

'DON'T TELL ME TO CHILL OUT!'

Lucy is full-on screaming now and my voice is matching hers if not louder.

'Em, I've got to go to work in a minute, can you stop shouting at me?'

He doesn't have to go to work in a minute. If he left the flat in forty minutes, he'd still be the first in. I worked this out at about 3 a.m. last night and the more I've thought about it, the angrier I've become. I know he's having to prove himself at work at the moment, but who proves themselves at 7.30 in the morning? What has he actually been doing for the last few months? He never used to leave the flat this early before we had Lucy. We'd drag our hangovers out of bed to get to work for nineish. But now, now that I actually need some help, Nick just gets up and fucks off.

'What time do you actually need to be there?'

'Where?'

'Work, Nick. What time do you actually need to be sat at your desk?'

'I don't have a desk.'

Seriously, what do they do at their work? 'You know what I mean.'

'Eight, Em. I try to get in for eight.'

'Exactly.'

'Exactly what?'

'Why do you need to leave now? You're like a part-time fucking dad, Nick. Just helicopter in for the good bits and then leave me to clear all the shit up.'

'That's just not . . .'

'I don't remember the last time you changed her nappy.' I've really found my stride now. I know I am being unfair but the tiredness and the stress propel me on. 'You give a load of chat, Nick, but you don't actually do anything.'

'I'm not listening to this, Em.' He passes Lucy back to me gently, puts his coat on and picks up the last banana from the fruit bowl.

'That's exactly what I mean.'

'What??'

'That banana is for Lucy,' I lie. 'You don't think about anyone but yourself.'

Nick puts it back, mutters a sorry and heads to the door. I bury my face in Lucy's hair and start to sob. What is happening to me? I sound like a cross between Cathleen and Hyacinth Bucket.

Lucy's not a baby anymore. I've had months of parenting – why haven't I got my shit together? I put Lucy down on the floor in the kitchen, with a range of 'interesting' things for her to crawl around and play with. Two wooden spoons, a saucepan and a pile of Duplo bricks. I race into the bedroom to give myself a quick wet wipe wash and put on the only half-decent pair of work trousers I own that still fit. This isn't how I imagined it, not one bit. I thought we'd all be more, I don't know, happy by now.

Some days I just don't want this life. There, I've said it. Some days I just wake up and think, not again. Not another Groundhog Day of clearing up, feeding, washing, watching a bit of crap telly then going to bed. Not another day of trying not to lose my shit with Nick. Of looking at him and trying to turn off the inner voice that says, 'He's just doing that to annoy you.' I don't even know if I love him anymore. That makes me feel sick to my core to even think it, but is it possible to love someone who makes you so consistently angry? I don't want to be an angry person. I don't think I used to be, did I? I don't think I am with anyone else. I can't imagine being with anyone else, but is that just because we've been together for so long?

You go through so much with a person that your life experience binds you together instead of your love. I don't even know if we have anything in common now except Lucy. What is actually keeping us together?

I pop my head into the front room. Lucy is happily banging a wooden spoon on the top of the saucepan. I nip into the bathroom to brush my teeth and take a good, long look at my face in the mirror. I look old and I think my eyes have sunken into my head a bit – does that happen?

And then I hear her, coughing then crying.

I run back to the kitchen to see the cupboard door under the sink open. Lucy's clutching an open bottle of washing-up liquid. It's dripped all over her arms and it looks like there's some on her face too. I scoop her up and she feels weightless but I think that's the adrenaline pumping through my body.

I wash her face and try to get her to drink water directly from the tap but I'm just making her hysterical. This might be because I'm holding her too tightly. She stinks of washing-up liquid but I don't know if it's just because it's all over her, or because she's actually drunk some. Why hasn't Nick put the fucking door locks on the cupboards?

But it's not his fault, it's mine. I left her in here while I went to feel sorry for myself. Shit. Shit. Shit.

I ring NHS Direct who ask five million questions before advising me to take her to A&E. By this time Lucy seems perfectly happy again, banging her spoons together. I call a taxi as I don't think I can drive, and rush around sticking some stuff in a bag.

I hold Lucy on my lap in the back of the cab. I don't know whether it's her shaking or me. What if she's damaged on the inside?

I ring Nick.

'This better be an apology, Em, I'm getting sick of your moods.'

'I'm on my way to A and E as Lucy's drunk washing-up liquid.'

'Fuck. OK, OK. It will be OK.' That's not what his tone is saying, his voice is pure panic. 'I've just got in to work so I'll tell them what's happening and then jump in a cab. Is she alright?'

I look down at Lucy who is happily drinking milk from the bottle she's found in the change bag, snuggled tightly to me with the seatbelt wrapped around her. It's like nothing's happened, other than the fact she absolutely reeks of Fairy Liquid.

'She seems fine, but see you in a bit.'

The taxi driver catches my eye in the rear-view mirror. 'My niece drank contact lens fluid and had to have her stomach pumped.' He must see the horror in my eyes. 'She's fine now. And they give you a hospital bear at the children's hospital. So that's nice.'

I text Liz at work to tell her I won't be in until later, if at all. She sends one back instructing me to tell HR and take it as holiday. I fucking hate my job.

As I explain to the receptionist on the children's ward what has happened, she rushes us through to see the doctor, who speaks calmly and firmly to me. He looks in Lucy's mouth, takes her temperature and listens to her heart.

'How much do you think she drank?'

'I'm not sure she even did. I just left the room for a minute and came back and she was covered in it.'

'Hmmm.' Is that a hmmm, she'll be fine or a hmmm, you've broken her?

'And has she been sick or had diarrhoea?'

252

'No. Nothing.'

'OK. Well I would like to keep her here for observations, so we can check that her condition doesn't change. If you want to make her comfortable and I'll come back to see how she's doing in an hour. If anything changes at all then you ring the buzzer and someone will be over straight away, OK?'

'OK.'

I must look awful, as he adds, 'Don't worry. We've seen much worse.'

Lucy and I are sitting on the hospital bed with the blue partition curtain drawn, watching Peppa Pig on my mobile when Nick pops his head in.

'How are my girls doing?'

My face crumples with relief and fatigue.

'Budge over.' He snuggles in next to us. 'What have you been doing to us, pumpkin?' Lucy crawls over me and curls up with Nick.

'Sorry,' I whisper. Nick kisses me on the forehead.

'Nothing to be sorry for.' He slips his arm round my neck and I feel my whole body untense.

Shortly after ten o'clock the doctor pulls back the curtain. 'So how's the patient?'

Lucy is watching what must be the fortieth episode of Peppa Pig, now on Nick's phone as we've used up all the data on mine.

'She seems fine, totally fine.'

The doctor goes through the process again, checking her throat, temperature and heart. 'Yes, she seems perfectly well,' he reassures us, 'so I think it's fine for you to take her home, but if anything at all changes, bring her straight back in. Give her lots of fluids and keep an eye on her stools for any change.'

He ruffles Lucy's hair, picks up his clipboard and redraws the curtain.

'Let's go home.' Nick picks Lucy up and offers me a hand to get off the impossibly high, narrow bed. 'Shall we bunk off work for the rest of the day and watch *The Lion King*?'

I look at the face that I know as well as my own. It's like looking at home, and I put my hand up to his cheek.

Nick smiles with relief, and says, 'Everything's fine, isn't that right, Lucy?' He kisses her repeatedly on her cheek until she's squealing with laughter. 'Now, shall we go via the hospital shop and pick up some chocolate?'

I love him so much right now it aches.

Chapter Thirty

There is literally nothing to do with a baby when the weather's rubbish and you have a flat the size of an old 50p. Lucy's got her own cupboard, which is the only one now without an uber lock on it. It's filled with a no-expenses-spared collection of Tupperware and old magazines, which she empties, I refill, she empties, and repeat until she's bored. That's fun for about ten minutes, and then there's the thirty-second cruise around the flat, a visit to the bathroom for her to pull herself up on the tub and to chuck all her toys in, as well as trying to get her hands on the Jo Malone candles I used to use in another lifetime when having a soak. Then finally, and I usually hold out until things are really reaching breaking point, a play on the TV remote control. The TV isn't actually on, she just likes pressing the buttons, or holding it up to her ear and babbling like she's on her mobile, which gives an indication of what she sees me and Nick doing ninety-seven per cent of the time.

All of that takes a total of about twenty-three minutes, then we've got about another eight hours to fill before Nick gets home from work.

I've just put the washing machine on in a last-ditch attempt to entertain her for a couple of minutes as she likes leaning against the glass as the machine rumbles, when Helen WhatsApps.

Helen: I'm losing my mind. Does anyone want to go to the soft play?

Tania: Which one?

Helen: I don't care.

Me: I'm in. I'll go anywhere.

Tania: A woman from my Tuesday class caught herpes at the one near Sainsbury's.

Me: Not that one then, but any others.

Helen: Great. Let's go to the one near Asda. Why are they always near supermarkets?

Me: Great.

Tania: Great.

Helen: Remember to hide your packed lunch on the way in.

I've never taken Lucy to a soft play before, as it all seems a bit of a waste of money for a child who can't walk yet. At three quid fifty, I wasn't expecting luxury on tap, but it's still a bit of a culture shock. If I owned a disused air hangar, and could reasonably stick a ball pool in it, wrap scaffolding with foam and drop leaflets round all the mums' groups advertising a new funplex, I would be minted.

Tania and Helen have already baggsied a table in the café. By café, I mean that garden furniture has been arranged in a circle next to a trestle table selling KitKats and Pom Bears with a guy stood behind it who can't be older than twelve.

Tania waves and shouts, 'Get a coffee – it's fucking freezing in here!'

She's right, it's so cold you can see your own breath, and when I look up, it's clear why. Half the roof is missing. There are literally cracks in the corrugated plastic panels. You need to keep your coat on inside, unless you're sitting under the strip heaters that are turned up so high you'd at best get a sun tan, at worst melt all your skin off.

Both Polly and Falcon are sitting in stationary plastic cars.

'I tried Falcon in the ball pool but he kept eating the old food he found at the bottom like it's a lucky dip. This place is disgusting.'

Helen is rubbing the lipstick stains off her cup with a wet wipe. I prop Lucy up in a car made of foam and line her up next to Falcon and Polly's cars next to the table. They look like they're at a mini drive-in for babies. We all take pictures of them, upload them to various social media, and then sit down to drink our coffees.

As is always the way, we commence the competition of who is the most tired.

'Falcon was up at five this morning. My eyes are so bloodshot they're the same colour as my skin.' Tania has shifted her seat under the strip light and does look a bit flushed under the UV rays.

'I thought he slept for ten hours straight?' Helen jokes.

'Yeah, well . . .'

'Five? That's a lie-in. Lucy has been up and down all night. She's back in bed with us and will only sleep on my shoulder so I wake up with a dead arm. Nick's absolutely no use, he just lies there snoring and tells me the next morning about what a good night we've had with her. It makes me want to Chinese burn his face. I was at work on Monday and in the middle of emailing a school and I closed my eyes, just for a minute. I swear that was all it felt like, until my prick of a colleague John clicked his fingers next to my ear and shouted wake up! He actually clicked his fingers, like I was a dog or a horse.'

'What a wanker,' Tania mutters.

'Isn't he? It's bad enough that I have no idea what I'm doing ninety per cent of the time. I don't need people catching me having a power nap there as well, do I?'

'You should train as a yoga instructor.' Tania helps herself to one of Lucy's party sausages out of one of the Tupperware boxes I'm unloading on the table. 'I could go to sleep at the end of every session if I want to, and everyone would just think I was in a deep state of relaxation.'

'Well at least you've got some help if you need it.' Helen's turn now. 'Chris isn't back from offshore for another three weeks. We FaceTimed him the other day and Polly kept chanting something that sounded like "Bob, Bob Bob."'

'Who's Bob?' I ask.

'No idea. Chris looked like he was going to burst into tears. We'd been practicing "daddy" all day and then she pulls that one out the bag at the last minute. I mean, honestly, I feel like a single mother most of the time.'

Tania and I nod sympathetically. Helen wins this round.

Just then I hear Lucy scream and we see a boy about three times her size trying to get into the car with her, or get her out, I'm not sure which. Quick as lightning I whip Lucy out of the car, pushing the boy out of the way in the process. Now, when is it acceptable to tell off someone else's child? When they grab a toy from your daughter? When they push her over? Or when they literally launch themselves through the window of a foam car, potentially squashing your baby because they can't wait two minutes for me to get her out? I try to explain there are lots of empty cars more suitable for his age that he can play with, while barely managing to disguise my fury.

The little boy shrugs me off, looks me directly in the eye and whispers, 'Bitch,' and then runs off and throws himself in the ball pool on top of a boy half his age.

'Did you hear that? Did you hear what he called me?'

'Little shit,' Tania mutters.

Lucy has immediately forgotten the incident, so we continue drinking our coffee and fiddling with our phones.

'Soooo.' Helen looks up. 'I have some news.' She shifts in her plastic seat uncomfortably.

She glances from Tania to me and back again and then announces, 'I'm pregnant!'

'Congratulations!' Tania hugs her.

'How?' I am genuinely astonished.

'It's a bit unexpected, to be honest. I'd always hoped we'd have another, but after the difficulty we had conceiving Polly I didn't think it would be possible. But. You know.'

I realise I've just been staring at her with my mouth open. 'Wow!' Come on, Emily, you can do better than that. 'Congratulations! When are you due?'

'I'm fourteen weeks at the moment. I can't really get my head around it.'

'Did Ditra help?'

'He was great. I think, yes, he definitely got us into a different headspace.' Helen turns to me and explains, 'He's the tantric yoga guru Tania recommended. He's quite something.' She sighs contentedly and I make a mental pact with myself to follow through with my promise to Nick of more/any sex.

We dislodge the other children from the cars, sit them on our knees and open up a range of Tupperware containers of raisins, chopped apples and cheese chunks. I might as well cut out the middleman and put ours straight in the bin, for all the interest Lucy shows in them.

I have about a million questions for Helen, like, what does sex yoga entail? What are you meant to do with two children? How will you afford it?

'I haven't told work. I've only been back a couple of weeks. I know they can't stop me of course, but I feel like a bit of a shit letting them down.'

'It's a bank. They're always letting everyone else down, give them a bit of their own medicine,' Tania replies while wrestling with Falcon who is trying to empty the entire box of Mini Cheddars into his mouth in one go.

'Well that really is wonderful news.' I don't know why I don't sound more sincere. 'It truly is.' What is this feeling? It can't be jealousy: I can't be jealous, can I?

But she's planted a seed. A second child. I'd never thought beyond Lucy, beyond the end of the day, the next sleep. And here's Helen doubling the number of children she will have.

'I've told Spiral to have a vasectomy.'

OK, so this is the other end of the parenting spectrum.

'And what's he said?' I ask.

'He told me to fuck off. But he'll come round to the idea when he realises the alternative is to never have sex again.'

Lucy is chewing raisins, spitting them into my hand, and then eating them again. Progress.

'I thought you had loads of sex?' Helen ventures.

'He doesn't believe in condoms.'

'Who doesn't "believe" in condoms?' I scoff.

'I know. He says it's because of the non bio-degradable materials they're made from. And' – at this point she starts to laugh – 'he says it's cos his cock's too big for them.'

She's howling with laughter now, which is infectious, and we all crease up until Falcon hits her in the face with the Tupperware lid.

Lucy spits out a raisin for the umpteenth time.

'You're going to have your hands full anyway, Hels.' Tania shrugs. 'But good luck to you.'

'Thanks, I'm really pleased, absolutely delighted in fact.' Her voice sounds sincere but there is a glint of panic in her eyes.

We pack up the kids and all their belongings and head out. I try to give the mean boy's parent the 'look' as we exit, but chicken out at the last minute and disguise it as a sneeze.

When we get in, Lucy and I watch *Back to the Future* and dream of wine o'clock, but in the back of my mind there is a niggle. I can't quite relax now.

Chapter Thirty-one

'Did you see Simone's wedding pictures on Facebook?' John has wheeled his chair over to my desk. I try to ignore him and minimise Explorer as I am currently bidding on a pair of bright red Mary-Jane shoes, and quickly replace it with the internal emails.

'No, I'm not friends with her on Facebook.'

'Oh, oh right. I just thought you would be, she's friends with most people here.'

I don't even know what Simone's surname is, or most of the people from work's for that matter, unless I have to email them. Why would I want to know what John, or Liz, or Mags or Karen from Accounts are doing on their weekends? Why would I want to look at pictures of what they've eaten and their #blessed families? That said, I hadn't realised that everyone from work was linked in on social media. If John, the biggest social recluse of them all, is, then most people must be.

'Anyway, I just ask because she looked incredible. It was this gorgeous Vera Wang dress . . .'

'How do you know who Vera Wang is, John? You buy all your clothes from Primark.'

'She'd posted about it. And I wear Atmosphere actually.'

'That's Primark.'

'Whatever. I was just trying to make conversation.' As he wheels his chair back to his desk he adds, 'As you hadn't signed the card that had gone round on Friday.'

'I don't work Fridays, John,' I mutter. 'And why are people sending her a card?'

'Not just a card, there was a whip-round. She got sixty quid in John Lewis vouchers.'

'Good for her,' I huff, thinking about the flowers I'd received from everyone when I went off with Lucy. They couldn't have cost more than fifteen quid and I've worked here for six years. Simone wasn't even here for twelve months.

I open up eBay again. Fuck. Sold for £10.21, I'd bid £10.20. Thanks, John.

'How's it all going?'

I jump out of my skin. How does Liz do that? I hadn't even heard her approaching. 'Fine.'

'Busy?' She points to the screen.

'Sorry, Liz, I was just . . .'

'Never mind. Can I have a word?' My stomach lurches. A word at work could easily turn to two: 'You're fired.'

'Of course.' I catch eyes with John, who's smirking, arms folded, just watching unashamedly.

We head into one of the fishbowl rooms.

'How are you finding everything?' Liz asks with her head cocked to one side in faux empathy.

'Great! I'm really enjoying myself,' I lie.

'And the projects? Anything new coming up?'

'Just mid-evaluation of everything that's coming to an end, but yes, lots of interesting prospects in the pipeline. I'm developing some fantastic partnerships to get things off the ground.' Words. These are just a load of words strung together that mean absolutely nothing.

'Great. Great that you've grabbed the bull by the horns, Emily.' She's looking at me as if it is my turn to say something.

'And I'm really enjoying it,' I add.

'Great. And the wider team? All going well within the team?'

'What, Arts and Regen?'

'Yes. Yes. Everything running smoothly?'

It's only me and John. And Mags, if you count her too, which no one does.

'Yes, like clockwork.'

'Good. Well you know where I am if you need to talk anything through, or if anything comes up.'

'Yes. Thanks, Liz. I feel a hundred per cent supported.'

'Great. Great. And how's . . .' she leans forward, urging me to finish her sentence.

'Lucy?'

'Yes. Yes. Lucy. How is she getting on? She must be walking and talking by now is she?'

'She's nine months old.'

'Fantastic. Good for her. OK, well I will send you over the outline of this meeting and then if you can electronically sign it off and send it over to HR, that would be great.' She opens the door. It initially looks like she's holding it for me so I go to leave but she walks out first and we do a sort of awkward sideways shimmy.

I sit back down at my desk.

'Anything wrong?' John sneers nosily.

'No. Thanks for your concern, John.'

I open a spreadsheet and am starting to make columns for all the Brighton-based schools, before realising I'd already started this last week but can't remember where I saved it, when an email pings in my inbox from Liz.

Subject: back to work meeting

It's an outline of what we'd discussed, although it wasn't what we'd discussed at all. It was a list of all the things Liz should have spoken to me about but hadn't. This is clearly something she should have done weeks ago. I read it, sign it, then send it to HR before locking my computer and heading out for a long lunch.

Sitting in Costa over a large latte and toasted cheese sandwich, I search for Simone on Facebook. It doesn't take long. She has got all the privacy settings in place of course, I wouldn't expect anything less, but her profile picture is from her wedding. John was right. She does look incredible. Her life must be amazing, filled with freshly squeezed orange juice and midweek facials.

Without thinking I type Rachel's name into the search engine. It's like a reflex; I do it from time to time without thinking. She also has all the settings in place, but she regularly changes her profile picture so I just have a quick look at that.

Her pictures are mainly of her and Callum, who is considerably taller than she is, but today she has changed it to a photo of her and Natasha, a girl we both went to school with. The photograph is of the pair of them at a party, dressed as the Pet Shop Boys at someone's thirtieth with their bomber jackets and pork pie hats. They have their arms around each other, grinning, both of them with red-wine-stained lips. It kills me. That should be us. The feeling of jealousy wraps and chokes its way around my throat.

I wish Rach hated me, because if she did then it would mean that she felt something towards me. But seeing her having fun, looking relaxed, looking happy at the party, means something far worse. It means that she's moved on. I have people I could ring to go out for a dance with, but I don't know who would turn up as the other half of my nineties band. Who would be my Neil Tennant?

There is no one to blame for this but myself. I have to live with that. I have to live with the weight of never having a proper best friend again. I hope she's happy. She looks happy. I hate myself for begrudging her friendships because she, of all people, deserves a good life with excellent people around her. She deserves better than good, she deserves everything. She was about to have everything and then her life changed and I wasn't a good enough friend to be there for her. So if I'm occasionally lonely then that's a choice I made. But I now know that best friends don't come around very often. If I could speak to my eighteen-year-old self, I'd say, don't be a selfish dick. Look at what you have. Because if you don't then you will have a massive Rachel-shaped hole in your life that will be impossible to fill.

Maybe I need to stay away from social media altogether. I never come away from it feeling relieved that everyone's having a shit time and my life is sorted.

I go to put my phone back in my bag, but have one last look at Rach and Natasha laughing together before I do. Before I've had chance to think it through I press Friends Request. Fuck. My hands are shaking as I put the phone away. It's done now. It's out there.

Chapter Thirty-two

Nick is playing five-a-side football with colleagues. This is a recent development, but now it's his 'thing' on a Saturday morning. He says it's good team building. The Director of Development is on the team so it's very important to show willing, he tells me.

'You have your thing, Em, football's mine. You know I always used to have a kickabout on a Saturday morning before . . .' the sentence drift off.

Before we had Lucy. Before we became parents. Before we had to make changes in our lives, or more specifically, before I did.

'What's my thing then, Nick? What's the thing I do?' I'm cross now. It takes over so quickly these days that I don't know if there is even a transition between calm and cross; it flips in the outtake of a breath.

'Oh, Em, I'm not going to fight with you, I just need to find my shin pads or I'll be late.'

It's not posed as a question but I know it is. He leans against the sitting-room door, waiting, before I mutter, 'They're in the cupboard under the sink in an Aldi bag.'

'Thanks!' he chirps and I realise, not for the first time, that my moods have ceased to have any impact on him.

I hear him rooting round in the cupboard before he shouts, 'Bye, Em, hope you both have a good morning!' then the front door slams.

He hasn't even kissed me. We always used to say whatever happens, whatever we've argued about, however bad our moods were, we would never a) leave the house without giving each other a kiss, however tight-lipped it might be or b) go to sleep without saying 'I love you' in case one of us unexpectedly dies during the night and we'd regret it forever. Somewhere over the last few months we seem to have forgotten about both of those rules.

I instinctively wander into our room and look at Lucy sleeping. She now sleeps for up to two hours in the morning, which should be bliss and a chance for me to get on with things. But I'm not sure what to get on with.

I open my laptop and consider the title of my new play, then google it and realise it has already been written. I close it up again, check my phone: no messages. I scroll through the WhatsApp group to double check I haven't missed anything from Tania and Helen. An arrangement I might have made during a middle of the night conversation. I haven't. I check Facebook for the twentieth time today to see if Rach has responded to my friend request. Still pending. Suspended in the digital ether, taunting me.

I wipe crumbs from the sideboard into my hand and tip them into the bin; it needs emptying but I can't be bothered to do that now. I neatly stack Lucy's books on her dedicated shelf, then pick up the framed photograph of me and Nick on a beach in Thailand from the shelf above. It's thick with dust and I wipe it off on my cardigan sleeve. We are holding each other so tightly that I remember our skin made a kind of squelch noise when we untangled ourselves from each other to retrieve the camera. We're grinning. Wide grins beaming from wrinkleless faces.

It was taken after the first time Nick had upset me. We were in Ko Samui walking along the white sandy beach, hands intertwined, and he'd made a throwaway remark about a woman who was sitting in a hammock reading to a child, who couldn't have been any older than about three. The little girl was snuggled into her mum's neck, playing with one of her dreadlocks.

Nick caught me staring at her and whispered in my ear, 'She leaves her in her room at night so she can go out partying.'

'Who?'

'Sandra in the hammock, she waits until her daughter's sleeping and then goes out for the night and gets fucked up.'

'But she looks like she's a great mum.'

'What. Because she reads her books?' Nick had made a kind of snorty noise and shook his head.

I'd thought, how dare he? How does he know what her life is like? How does he know if she had her baby at seventeen while all her friends were finishing their A levels? How can he know that she's not doing her absolute best for her daughter?

I remember looking at Sandra and seeing Rachel staring back at me, curled up with Callum in her little flat, spending her days avoiding the judgemental stares of her dad and her old school friends.

'Shit, I'm so sorry, what did I say?' he'd asked when he caught my eye.

'Nothing.'

'No, go on, please; shit, I didn't mean anything by it, I just meant . . .'

'I just think you need to give people a chance, Nick. You never know what shit people are going through.'

He'd stopped and cupped my face in his hands, kissed me firmly and reassuringly and replied, 'You're right. You're so right. Sorry. Don't ever let me become a judgey old bastard.

Fuck, that's why I left Nottingham in the first place. So I don't end up driving around in a Ford Fiesta thinking I'm the fucking nuts.' He kissed me again and this time I kissed him back.

'The last thing I want to do is upset you, Emily. Don't ever let me become a dick,' and we'd both laughed, then someone had asked if we wanted our picture taken.

I replace the photo on the shelf in the ridge of dust it sits in. The feeling in my stomach rises again. It's like nerves, but it somehow comes from a deeper place and feels more like hunger. I know what it is. This feeling has grown and taken hold more intensely since Christmas.

I miss Rachel. I miss her so much it feels physical. It's always been there, bubbling away under the surface, hiding behind smiles and laughter, but now it's ever present. I try to ignore it on a daily basis, but it creeps in, like when I thought I'd caught nits at school and couldn't stop itching even though it turned out I hadn't. It has been with me ever since the moment I found out I was pregnant with Lucy. But what kind of a crap friend would that make me? What kind of a woman would that make me, to get back in touch because I need her now, when for all those years she'd needed me?

I take a gulp of lukewarm tea and shut my eyes for a moment. Lucy won't wake for another hour or so and Nick won't be back for two. What advice would I give Lucy if she was a grown-up rubbish friend? I can't really imagine what she'd look like as an adult. I'd also have to imagine myself in my sixties, which is just weird. But the idea of Lucy being unhappy I can imagine, and that is my greatest fear. That she will grow up to be unhappy or find life difficult. That she will have challenges that aren't actually challenges but problems, and she can't find a way to overcome them.

If that was ever the case, I know with all my heart what I'd say. I would tell her to do whatever she could do to make it right. That it's never too late to say sorry. Like a reflex I check Facebook again. Pending. Obviously.

My stomach knots with nerves as I make a decision. I scroll through to her number and then think maybe I should ask the universe if today is the day. This is a phrase we used to use with gay abandon at university, as if we were all seers and had some kind of divine power. We'd ask the universe if we should go to lectures or not that day, or spend our money on beer or wine, or buy a new dress or a pair of shoes. All the important stuff. Then chose an 'either or' situation, and wait for the universe to answer.

I don't know what made me suddenly think of it, but I decide to give it a go.

So. If Steve Wright's next song is by a woman then I should ring her.

Whitney Houston's 'Gonna Dance with Somebody' plays in. Fuck. OK.

So, best of three.

If the top of the toothpaste is on then I have to ring her. Nick never puts the top back on, he says it's a waste of time as you only have to take it off again next time you go to brush your teeth. I push open the bathroom door, and there is it standing tall, lid on and even in the toothbrush cup. Seriously? Why today, Nick?

OK. Best of five.

I see the postman walking down the path. Some days he greets me with 'Good morning' and other days it's a simple nod. If he says 'Good morning' then I have to one hundred per cent ring her. This is the last go. This is the definitive round. There is no getting out of this one. I swear on Lucy's life I'll do it. I even say it out loud to no one: 'I swear on

Lucy's life.' My voice sounds loud and empty in the quiet flat.

The doorbell rings. I answer it.

'Good morning,' he chirps as he hands me the Boden catalogue and a stack of junk mail.

'Urgh.'

'Not a good morning for everyone, I see.' He shrugs and virtually skips up the path to the next letterbox. I'll have to make it up to him by being extra friendly on Monday.

So, that's it. I've sworn on Lucy's life, so there is absolutely no way I can back out now.

I'll just make another cup of tea and then set myself up. Lucy is still sleeping soundly. I pop my head around her door and hear her making little whistling noises as she inhales and exhales.

The kettle boils and I pour the water over a tea bag, squeeze it and put it in the kitchen composter, which is full to overflowing and lets out a puff of rotten vegetable smell. I add a splash of milk to the mug and position and reposition myself on the sofa. I take a deep breath and look at the screen for the seventeenth time.

'Just do it, you fucking idiot,' I scold myself and dig my nail into the palm of my hand for good, painful, measure.

My heart is pulsing loudly in my ears as I press call.

It rings twice, three times, four. I hadn't prepared myself for the fact that she might not be in. It's been so long since I last rang a landline that I'd half forgotten that you're ringing an actual house, but it's the only number I have. It's not a tinny melody carried around in a back pocket or handbag to be answered or ignored at your leisure. She won't know it's me on the other end.

It rings for a fifth time. Then she picks up.

'Hello?' her voice is so familiar it's like hearing my own

voice played back to me. A beat. 'Hello? If this is a sales call don't bother, I—'

'Hi, Rachel.'

The line goes quiet and I wonder if she's hung up, but then I hear the radio crackle faintly in the background. She is listening to the same station I am.

I hear her sigh. 'Emmie. It's you.'

1999 age 18

Dear Emmie,

How's it all going? What's your course like? What's Brighton like? I've got so many questions, I don't know where to start.

Sorry I haven't texted for a while. I've never got any credit or any money to top it up, so it's easier to write, and anyway, who doesn't love getting letters?!

I saw your mum in Morrisons the other day. She said she was getting the stuff to make your dad baked aubergine for tea – shame you missed out on that one! Anyway, she asked me if I'd like to go to the cinema with her. Is that a bit weird, me going to the cinema with your mum? To be fair she's the only person to ask me out in months, so I said yes! We're going to watch There's Something About Mary *next week at the Odeon in Grimsby.*

She said that you've got some nice flatmates, that one of the guys has blue hair (shock horror) and that there are a couple of nice girls. Not too nice I hope, don't forget who your best mate is (joke/not joke).

Talking of nice girls, I heard that Natasha Clarke is pregnant by that minging bouncer from Ritzy's who has a spider's web tattooed on his cheek. I feel sick even thinking about it. Without being a total cow, it's quite nice that people are gossiping about someone other than me for a change. My mum suggested I pop round to talk to her, that it would be the right thing to do. I don't know why. We didn't really know her, did we? She sat behind me in General Studies and that's about it. I don't want to be mates with someone just because we both have babies, that's beyond tragic.

I still haven't heard anything from Gary since Callum was born. Apparently he's gone to uni at Leicester to study Sports Science. He's such a massive knob. Mum said she bumped into his mum in the big Asda in town and she blanked her, like literally pushed the trolley straight past her as if she hadn't seen her, although she clearly had (it's hard not to!). Anyway, who needs men? If J.K. Rowling can be a single mum and write Harry Potter, I can certainly do it and sit on my arse watching daytime telly.

Callum is mega gorgeous at the moment. I've sent you a picture, he's wearing another cardie your mum knitted for him! Everyone says he looks like me, but I can't see it myself. He just looks like a baby! But it's nice that people say that. No one says he looks like Gary which is a relief, but then I don't know whether they just don't say that so as not to upset me.

Right I've got to go. Mum's taking Callum and me into town so that I can buy some non-maternity jeans. Yay. Kill me now.

Write back soon,

I love you,

R and C x

Dear Rach (and Callum),

How are you both? How was the shopping trip? I saw some gorgeous jeans in Topshop the other day with embroidered flowers on the pockets and thought they'd look nice on you, but then I remembered there's only a BHS in Grimsby. You should come down and stay with me here then we could go shopping. I found this little second-hand bookshop the other day and thought of you, I bet you could spend a fortune in there, I'll take you when you visit.

Mum said it was nice to go to the cinema with you. I went to see it with some of the guys from my course last week. I LOVE Cameron Diaz, what I would do to look like her. Was it a bit cringy to watch the jizz bit with Mum? I guess you've had a baby so she must know you know what spunk is, but still! At least she didn't bring virgin Auntie Jan, now that would have been awkward. Remember when she was over for the night and Dad rented Showgirls from Blockbusters when he meant to get Show Boat? Oh my God, it was wall-to-wall fannies. Dad looked like he was going to die of embarrassment and Auntie Jan just pretended she was asleep through the ENTIRE film!

I wonder what you're doing at the moment? I often do this when I'm on my own, I think of what you're doing and if we're doing some of the same things, like listening to the same radio station, or watching the same thing on telly. I guess your routine is a lot different to mine now, with Callum and everything. It's 7.30 here and I'm sat in my room in halls (I know you're not doing that) and I've just eaten beans on toast with cheese for dinner (but you might have done that!!). I haven't really unpacked my stuff properly, you'd be appalled by how shit I've made this room look! I have put up the picture you sent of you and Callum though. It is in a nice frame on the wall above my desk and makes the room feel more like home. People are right, he does look like you, he has your mouth and nose.

The girls I live with are really good fun, but they're not you, so don't worry, I'm not going to be replacing you anytime soon!

I wish you were here now. I know that's a stupid thing to say, but it would definitely be better if you were here. Life's a lot funnier when I share it with you.

I feel like I'm putting on a bit of an act here, which is lucky as I'm doing theatre! But it's like I'm not being myself, not yet anyway. Everyone's trying to impress each other, trying to show how cool they were before they came to uni. Where they've travelled to, how many drugs they've taken, the music they're into. It's all a bit boring. I haven't (obviously) told everyone how much we love Michael Jackson yet. I think I'll keep that one in my back pocket until I've made some real friends!!

How's everything going at your end? Have your stitches healed? Is it OK to ask about that or is that really personal?? I totally understand how you don't want to hang out with Natasha. The only things I know about her are that she was a brown belt in karate in the first year and learnt to play the flute when she was four. Bore off.

Right, I've got to go. We're all going to an 80s night at the student union in a bit. Apparently Paul Robinson from Neighbours is meant to be there as the 'celebrity guest!' Please let that be true, I'm going to make it my mission to get off with him if he is!!

I'll write a longer letter soon, give Callum a big kiss from me and write back when you've got time,

Lots of love,

Emily x

Dear Emmie (since when did you start calling yourself Emily?!)

It sounds like you're having a totally brilliant time. I knew you would. I'd love to come and stay and you know I'd be there in a heartbeat if I could. It's just tricky while I'm still feeding Callum and he doesn't take a bottle. I'll be weaning him soon though so that should make life easier to get out and about.

I'm waiting for a flat to come up at the moment. I ring the council nearly every day, I think they're totally fed up of me. I am second on the waiting list, so I just need two people to either move out, or die, and then it will be my turn.

Mum's been in hospital. It turns out she's got type 2 diabetes, mainly because of all the crap she eats and her being so overweight. They scared the shit out of her by telling her that

277

if she doesn't get it under control, she could have kidney failure or lose her eyesight or a leg. She's got to take medication to start with and I'm making sure she does. She's got to manage it herself when Callum and I move out, but we'll cross that bridge when we come to it. I can't imagine Dad being that much help.

I went out with Natasha the other week. Well, I say 'went out' — we went to the park with Callum. She asked me about a million questions about having a baby. I told her it might be different for her, because I had a caesarean and she might have a normal birth, but she still wanted to know everything. It was quite nice to talk about it to be honest. And she's not as boring as I had remembered. Did you know she got her grade 8 in flute when she was seven, that's incredible isn't it? I don't think I could even read properly then, let alone play an instrument!

Anyway, I'm going along with her to her antenatal classes, you never know, I might meet a hot single dad there! Natasha said Gordon (that's the name of the spider-faced bouncer — fucking Gordon! You couldn't make it up!!) is keen to be involved in the baby's life, which is good. But she also says it's difficult because she finds it really awful to look at him when she's not drunk (which she obviously isn't with being pregnant) and she only really shagged him to piss off her ex-boyfriend, who also worked at Ritzy's. Long story short, she's asked if I'll be her birthing partner, as she doesn't have anyone else. I think I'll probably do it.

When you wrote about thinking what I'm doing, I do the same with you. Like when I'm bathing Callum I wonder if you're getting ready to go out with your mates, or if you're already in the pub. I do eat a LOT of beans on toast, so chances are when you're having it for tea, I am too!

Whenever I think about you, I imagine you having the best time. I know you said about not feeling like yourself in the beginning, but that's just normal. That's just doing something new. Everyone who meets you loves you, Emmie. But not as much as me – don't forget that!

I've got to go now. Callum needs changing and is screaming the house down. He can roll over now so I can't take my eye off him for a second.

Write soon,

I love you,

R and C xxx

Dear Rach and Callum,

How are you both doing? How's your mum now? My mum said she saw her in town the other day and she looked like she'd lost loads of weight, so that must be good, right? The diabetes thing must have been a bit of a shock, but that's great that she's doing something about it.

Things are really good here, I'm going out loads at the moment and barely getting any work done, but everyone says the first year is just about settling in, so if that's the case then I'm on track for a first! There is a brilliant bar that only makes cocktails named after exotic birds, you'd love it! I'll take you there when you come down.

I'm seeing this guy at the moment, he's called Ted and he's an activist. He's really interesting and completely passionate about climate change. We have deep chats about politics, but he went completely mental at one of my flatmates the other night when they threw away a wine bottle, saying they should be re-cycling it. He actually got it out of the bin (which was minging because we hadn't emptied it for days) and took it home with him, so I don't think it's going to last as he's a bit too serious.

Do you know what you're doing for Christmas? I break up at the beginning of December (I know right!) but I might stay down here and work for a bit. I can't remember whether I told you that I've got a job in a pub?? It's called The Shaman and it's just down the road from halls. It's a total dump full of crusties but I love it. They've asked if I'll do some shifts over Christmas and I've said yes because I really need the money.

I'm glad you're spending time with Natasha. I'm sure she's really nice, I just didn't know her that well at school, that's all. She's very lucky to have you and I can imagine that you'd be an amazing birthing partner. Does that mean you will see her baby actually being born? Won't that be the most incredible, gross thing ever?!

Right, got to go. I'm on my way to a Halloween screening of Lost Boys at the art house cinema and I'm wearing a PVC catsuit. The feminist in me is weeping, but I've squeezed into a size ten, so I don't care!

Write back soon and I love you,

Emmie x

Dear Emmie,

How's it all going? I left a message on your mobile last week, I don't know whether you got it, but it was from my new land-line! (I won't be doing that regularly by the way, apparently it's 50p a MINUTE to ring a mobile!)

That's right, I've got a new flat! It's nearer Cleethorpes than Grimsby, so that's good news. It's small, but there is a room for Callum, which is brilliant, and a small front room and separate kitchen. The garden is more of a yard, but it's big enough for a little bench and I thought I'd put some pot plants out as well.

It's just such a relief to be out of the house. Mum is coming round every day at the moment, which is way too much so we might have to have a chat about that! I know she is just trying to help though. Your mum's popped over, she brought a spider plant as she said they are impossible to kill – she knows me so well!

It's weird, I go from thinking one minute, this place is great

*and how I can't wait for you to come up and we can sit on
the window ledge when Callum's asleep, drink red wine, smoke
fags out the window, and laugh at how ridiculous everyone is
on my new street. To thinking, fuck, this is actually my life. I
actually live in a council flat with a baby instead of going to uni
in Cambridge. My best mate is out with her new friends, living
her new life, and I'm stuck in watching* East Enders.

*Sorry, I don't mean to sound all depressing. My period
started again yesterday for the first time since Callum was
born and I'm a bit of a wreck. I'd forgotten how awful they
can be, or maybe they're worse now. Either way, everything's
good. Apparently there's an English teacher who lives opposite, who isn't at retirement age yet, so you never know, I
might even have a conversation with someone about literature
after all!*

*How are things going with Ted? And when did you get into
talking about politics?? You'd literally leave the room if I ever
tried to talk about it — you've changed!!*

Write soon, I need to hear all your news,

All our love,

R and C xxx

Hey Rach,

*Quick postcard to say hi to you and Callum. Just on my way
to work. Double shift, groan. The picture on the front is of the
starlings flying over the West Pier. We all sat on the beach
drinking wine and watching them at dusk the other evening. It
was magic.*

Speak soon,

Em xx

*PS what do you mean I was never into politics?! Just because
I don't watch* Newsnight!!

Hey Emmie,

I haven't heard from you in a while so I thought you might have misplaced my new address, so I'd write again.

Sorry we missed each other at Christmas. It didn't sound like you were up for long. It's a shame, I would have loved to have shown you my flat. I've painted most of the rooms now and put up some pictures so it's starting to look nice.

It sounds like you're really busy at the moment. Your mum popped around the other day and said you were making a short film about the rise of pop culture, or something like that? She didn't sound very sure and used quotations when she said 'pop culture' which would have driven you mental! Anyway, it was lovely to see her. She brought round a little truck for Callum which he loves sticking in his mouth. Oral obsession, like Mum! I can't believe he's going to be one in a couple of months, it's just mental.

Did I tell l you Mum's going to a slimming group now? She's lost over three stone, you wouldn't recognise her. She comes round here and tells me about nutrition, and how I need to eat more fruit, and drink at least eight pints of water a day. It's annoying, but at least she's not so fat you need to open the double doors for her to get into Wilkos anymore, so that's a bonus. Apparently my dad's started to cheer up a bit too, now he's eating better. Maybe it wasn't Catholicism that made him into such a dick, it was lack of vitamins!! Either way, I'm pleased he's not so miserable, although he's still only come to see me once, and then he just complained about how uncomfy the sofa was, and why haven't I got Channel 5 on the TV, but he's started calling Callum by his name instead of 'the baby', so that's a start.

Talking of babies, bit of goss – Natasha has had hers! A little girl called Sophie, and guess what? She's mixed race, so it is her ex-boyfriend's, and not Spiderman's after all. That was an awkward conversation in the birthing suite!!

Are you still seeing that guy Ned, or Ted? I can't remember his name and can't find your last letter. Mum's probably cleared it away, she's always tidying stuff up so I can't find anything, it's driving me up the wall.

Anyway, I'll keep it short, it's definitely your turn to write to me!

Love you,

R and C xxx

Rach!

It's been ages. SO sorry. I just found your letter and realised I'd never responded. Don't hate me! That's so hilarious you mentioned Ted, I'd completely forgotten about him. That didn't last more than about a week I don't think, I can't remember, it was so long ago. I'm single at the moment, after a series of traumatic love encounters with unsuitable men! I'll fill you in next time I see you (are you EVER going to come down and see me??).

I'm moving out of halls soon and into a flat with some mates and there's a spare room. How's Callum doing? Give him a kiss from me.

Speak soon,

Em x

Hey Emmie,

Just a quick invitation to Callum's first birthday party. I know you won't be able to come but I didn't want to not invite you. Thanks for asking me down to see you, it's not really that easy to get down to Brighton from here as it is for you to come up to see me, but maybe if I pass my driving test I could come down. It would be great for you to see my flat and Callum, obviously. You probably wouldn't recognise him now! Don't know whether you've spoken to your mum but she's coming to the party, Natasha too with her new baby.

Rach x

Hi Rach,

Thanks for the invitation. I'm in the middle of my end of year exams so won't be able to come up unfortunately. I've got to pass these as I've not really done so well with my course work as I'd hoped. Glad my mum and Natasha will be there though. Sounds like you've already got a house full so you won't miss me!

I realise that it's not easy for you to come to stay here, I just wanted you to know you're always welcome.

Give the birthday boy a kiss from me, I'll pop something in the post for him,

Em x

Hey Emmie,

Just wanted to drop you a line to say thank you for Callum's birthday present. Your mum gave it to me at the party. I knew you wouldn't forget. The matching bus to go with the truck your mum got him – he loves it! And thank you from Callum. That's a picture of him in his birthday jumper (eating your bus!) on the front of the card. Mum has got into crafts with her newfound energy, and spent all weekend cutting and sticking these fucking cards together!

Anyway, good luck with finding your new house.

Rachel Xxx

Emmie,

How's you? I know you're moving soon so I rang your halls phone the other day and spoke to someone called Horatio (I'm sure that's what he said but surely no one's actually called *that!!) who said he'd pass on a message. Don't know whether he did or not . . .*

Anyway,

Speak soon,

Rx

Hi Emmie,

Just a PostIt note this time. Just wanted to let you know that I've passed my driving test. Maybe I could come down and see you sometime? Let me know what you think.

Rach x

Hi Emmie,

Your mum says you might be coming up for a flying visit soon. It would be good to see you if you do, but let me know when, as I've got quite a lot on at the moment. Callum and I have joined a few classes and I've met some other mums so our days are quite jam-packed. I'm going for a drink with a couple of them next week – see, you're not the only one with a social life now it turns out.

Anyway, check in if you can,

Rach

Part Four

'It's just about getting the work/ family/ social life balance right. Easy.'

Chapter Thirty-three

'You took your time.'

I don't know whether she's joking or not.

'Sorry, I just . . .'

'Emmie. I'm a bit busy at the moment, is there anything that you . . .' the sentence drifts off and I realise that I'm meant to fill this space. She's definitely not joking.

'Oh no, no, nothing's wrong or anything. It's just . . .' It's just what? Why have I chosen today of all days to ring? Why this Saturday instead of all the other Saturdays in the last fifteen years? Why now? Why bloody now, after all this time?

'It's just what, Emmie? Because things are a bit busy at this end,' she repeats. I look at the kitchen clock. It is 9.47 a.m. on an overcast, cold, Saturday morning. Have other people's lives become busy already by this point? I'm still sat in my pyjamas, sipping yet another cold cup of tea. I can't imagine a time when I will have a routine again, or a 'thing', as Nick would call it, to do on a Saturday morning.

'Sorry,' I whisper.

'For what, Emmie?' I hadn't expected her to ask. I'm so unprepared for this conversation, it's awful. I don't know what I thought would happen. Certainly not a hero's return or a tearful reunion, that would have been too much to ask for. But she seems so hugely irritated by me ringing. In fact it's more than that, it's far worse. She sounds cold.

Stupid fucking universe, with your painfully inaccurate predictions.

'I just wanted to say how nice it was to bump into you at Christmas.'

'That was months ago, Emmie.'

'I know, I know, but I've only just got your number again from Mum' — the lie tumbles out my mouth — 'and so I thought now would be a good time to ring with it being Saturday morning and everything, but it's clearly not a good time, so maybe I'll ring another time when it's better for you? Or you could ring me if that's easier? I'm in a lot, well most of the time actually, apart from Thursday mornings when I take Lucy swimming. But I imagine you're at work then anyway, so that wouldn't make a difference . . .' I ramble on. I'm holding a tissue and I look down to see I've shredded it into tiny pieces.

I can hear her let out a long quivering sigh, as if she's trying her absolute hardest to control every action, every word, to keep herself tightly held in place, to not start to unravel. 'No, go on . . .' She pauses. 'I've got a few minutes I guess, before I've got to do stuff.'

The line goes quiet and then: 'I'm listening.'

She has given me the floor. Don't fuck this up, Emily.

I start with the basics. 'I'm so sorry, Rach.'

She lets out a little yelp as if she's trying to swallow back tears, and I realise that mine have started to flow down my cheeks. I wipe my nose on my sleeve. Come on, Emily, get a fucking grip.

'Rach, are you still there?'

'Yes,' she sniffles. 'God, this is just . . .'

'Just what?'

'Just fucking awful actually, Emmie,' she says matter-of-factly.

We rest into an uncomfortable silence. I can hear her breathing. As a serial overthinker, I uncharacteristically haven't thought about what to do next. The void is so huge, any words would just disappear into it. I pace up and down the small front room, stopping to look out the window at the ominous black cloud. I wonder if I should bring in the clothes horse from the garden which is laden with Lucy's Babygros.

I decide to ask the universe what to do next one more time.

Universe. If this is going to be OK, let me know now.

Nothing.

I mean now, I repeat in my head.

Still nothing.

NOW. Let me know NOW.

And then, as if finally answering my question, 'Man in the Mirror' starts to play on the radio. Our song. We have a dance routine to it that only works if we're both doing it. It's a call and response, a dance for two, for me and Rach. I'd do the reach and grab on the first line, she followed with the leg kick on the second, and so it continued until the chorus, when we both danced together.

I can hear it in the background in her flat too as we both say in unison, 'I love this song.'

The huge gap closes, just slightly. 'I miss you, Rachel,' I say in my tiniest voice.

I wait. Was it too soon? Do I even have the right to say it?

She eventually responds. 'You have no idea how much you hurt me, Emmie,' her voice has hardened again, like it used to sound when she was talking to, or about, her dad.

'I know.'

'No you don't. How could you?' The rain starts to fall outside, big wet drops lashing against the window.

'Well tell me,' I hazard.

'Really? You really want to know?'

'Yes, Rach, I really do.'

I can hear her pull a chair out. It scrapes across the floor, and I imagine what her flat looks like. I wonder what she's looking at now, if it's chucking it down in Cleethorpes too?

'OK then, well you leaving was worse than Gary blanking me' – she pauses, and it sounds like she's taking a gulp of something – 'I didn't give a shit about him, I didn't care that he didn't want to be in Callum's life, because he's not important to me or Callum. We didn't need him. We needed you.' The weight of her words knot and twist in my stomach, gripping me like period pains. I knew all of this, but it's one thing knowing it, and a very different thing hearing it.

'You were my best friend, and you fucked off and left me for a better life. One without the inconvenience of a friend with a baby.' Her voice is getting louder, 'And now you have a baby of your own you think you understand, but you don't. You just don't.'

I sit in silence. She's right. Of course she is.

'I needed you, Emmie. I fucking needed you,' she's shouting at me now. 'Well?'

'Well what?' she's taken me by surprise.

'Well what? Well fucking what, Emmie? No, I'm fine.' I think she's talking to me but then I hear another voice in the background, a man's.

'Is that Callum?'

'What? Yes. Yes, he was sleeping. That's what teenagers do. I must have woken him shouting. I'm fine,' she repeats, 'go back to bed, I'll bring you a cuppa in a minute.'

The anger has defused fractionally from her voice thanks to Callum, so I venture, 'What I did was unforgivable. I was young and selfish, but I thought I was doing the right thing, for both of us.'

'By what? Abandoning me?' She's not shouting at me now. That's a start.

Deep breath. 'I got to uni and yes, to start with, I couldn't work out how we fitted into each other's lives.' I'm talking slowly and softly, trying to find the words that I've rehearsed a million times over the last few years. 'But the more I heard about how well you were doing, the more Mum told me about what a great mum you were, I kind of thought you didn't need me anymore.'

'How did you figure that one out?'

'You'd grown up, hadn't you? You were a mum, and I was this stupid immature friend, who was writing you letters about getting pissed at uni, while you had made an entire human being. How could anything I was doing ever compare to that?'

'Don't put this on me, Emmie.'

'I'm not, at all – this is all on me. I just thought . . .'

'You don't get it, do you? You never did. You didn't have to compare to that, to anything. Jesus. You always miss the point, don't you, Emmie? I needed you to not change. That's the whole point. I needed you to be my best mate. Can you imagine how shit it was being at Mum and Dad's when Callum was born? Dad ignoring us both. Mum fussing around me like she does. And everyone else was off having fun. Going out, getting pissed in the pub, or going to uni, while I was stuck at home watching telly with Mum and Dad. Stuck in that house. Sat on that fucking sofa night after night.'

I can immediately picture it. The brown corner sofa and matching armchair, which was Mr Chapman's and had the perfect imprint of his body carved into it from years of sitting, reading the *Racing Post*. The large gilt-framed mirror hanging above the gas fire and bookended by two shelves either side, that were crammed full of Dalton dolls. Woman after ceramic woman carrying parasols and swishing their Victorian dresses. How Rachel and I hated those figurines; we used to dream of smashing every last one of them.

'And you know the worst bit? It wasn't Dad calling Callum "the baby" all the time like he didn't have a name, or spending Saturdays going into town with Mum as a treat. That was OK, those things were OK. But it was that everyone stopped ringing or coming around. Every single friend stopped getting in touch. It was like I'd dropped off the end of the earth. Like I'd had Callum, and suddenly I didn't exist. But the one person I thought I could rely on, the one person who I thought was going to be there no matter what, was you. I could deal with everyone else letting me down, Emmie. But not you.'

The sky has gone a murky grey now, and the wind has picked up. I see that some of Lucy's clothes have blown off the clothes horse and are now pinned to the bush.

'I've thought about ringing you so many times. I've picked up the phone and then chickened out. I just didn't know how to act with you once you'd had Callum. I didn't know what to say to you. It sounds so stupid now, but I just thought you'd moved on, and so I had to do the same. But I've missed you. Every day.'

'You have no idea how lonely I was.'

'I didn't,' I whispered, 'but I think I do now.' I quietly sob into my cardigan sleeve.

She lets out a long sigh. 'It's not easy is it?'

'Nope. No it's not. I love her of course but . . .'

'But it's fucking hard work,' she finishes my sentence like she used to.

294

'Yes. Yes it is. And Nick and I don't see eye to eye on virtually anything these days.'

'Well, that's one thing I didn't have to deal with, I suppose.'

'How did you do it, Rach? How did you do this on your own?'

'I had Callum. He's always been my team.'

I pick up my mug and add it to the countless other unwashed mugs in the sink.

'She's beautiful, Emmie.'

'Who?'

'Who do you think, you idiot? Not you, that's for sure.' She's taking the piss out of me. This is good.

'Thank you. I've got Nick to thank for her long eyelashes. She's got my bum chin, unfortunately.'

'Well, you can't have everything.'

The ten o'clock news starts on the radio. 'Are you still OK for time?' I ask.

'Yes, it's nothing important. Tell me about her.'

'Tell me about you first, Rach.'

'OK then. What do you want to know?'

'Everything.'

'God, I've missed you, Emmie,' Rachel utters.

'I've missed you too, Rach. You've no idea.'

And we start to fill in the gaps of our lives over the last fifteen years. Starting with the birth of Callum, and ending with the arrival of Lucy.

As Nick returns from football, I bat him away with a cheery, 'I'll be on the phone for a while, can you change Lucy?' who has just woken up, no doubt with a full nappy.

My phone beeps to let me know it's running out of battery, so I relocate to the bedroom and plug it in. Over two hours later we finally, reluctantly, say goodbye.

'Ring me on the mobile next time, Emmie,' and she gives me her number. 'No one rings the landline apart from Mum. It's not 1999, you know.'

'Thanks. I love you Rachel Chapman.'

'And I love you, Emmie Jones,' and then she adds, 'but if you leave it another fifteen years before you call again, I'm going to fucking kill you, understood?'

'Understood.'

I hang up and feel lighter and more myself that I have in weeks, months, years probably. I walk into the front room to see Nick holding Lucy on the sofa, playing This Little Piggy on her toes. She giggles with anticipation every time he tickles up her body.

'You look nice.' He smiles. It's gone midday and I still haven't brushed my teeth so I assume he's joking. 'Happy,' he adds and I realise he's not. 'It's good to see.'

I join them on the sofa and snuggle into them both. I feel like I'm floating on air.

Chapter Thirty-four

Liz has called me into one of the meeting rooms. This can only mean bad news. The rumour is that HR are having a bit of a shuffle around, which is a restructure without calling it that, so they don't have to give anyone a pay-off. I'm thinking, right, that's me gone then, and to be fair, I wouldn't blame them. Since coming back I have systematically undone all of Simone's good work. Her filing system is now unrecognisable, with the desktop being ninety per cent pictures of Lucy that I've emailed to myself. I've worked out that, most days, I can get in for 9.30 and leave at 4.30 and no one notices. My lunch breaks can often creep up to well over an hour and a half, once I've been to Boots for nappies, done a shop in Sainsbury's and had a coffee and an overpriced cheese toastie in a café. I would fire me if I was my boss, but how could I tell Nick? He says his work is picking up, but he still looks permanently worried. What would it do to him if I came home and told him that, because of my online shopping addiction, I am now unemployed? He'd combust.

'Everything going well, Emily?' she asks while scrolling through her phone.

'Yes, I think it is, Liz,' I respond and ease myself into one of the metal-backed chairs, then expand, 'the Poets in School project is—'

'Great,' she interrupts, looking up from her phone, 'and it hasn't gone unnoticed.' What hasn't gone unnoticed? That

I haven't initiated one new project in the whole time I've been back, which is quite poor, seeing as that's the basis of my job? That sometimes, I just make spreadsheets for the sake of it to look like I'm busy, and then delete them at the end of the day? Fuck. Have IT been monitoring my emails? Can they tell I've been buying stuff off eBay?

'You're industrious, Emily, you're committed. You have a "can do" attitude, which I like.'

Can do nothing, I think and resist snorting at my own joke. I'll have to remember that one to tell Nick later on.

'We have an opening for someone to develop the annual outdoor summer children's parade. This would mean condensing your current roles into two days, and taking this on as an additional responsibility on the third day. I have complete faith that you would be able to embrace this challenge.' Liz is now half looking at me, half watching what someone is doing outside of the meeting room.

'Isn't that John's job?' I thought I hadn't seen him around for the last couple of weeks.

'John has moved on,' Liz says matter-of-factly. 'We would like you to pick up some of his responsibilities.'

I internally air-punch. I've never really forgiven him for consistently ignoring me, while simultaneously becoming Simone's best friend. After she left he kept the photograph of her and her fiancé pinned to his workstation. I'm not convinced she actually gave it to him.

'So, what do you think, Emily?' she asks impatiently.

My mind's a whirr. 'So you're not making me redundant?'

'No, Emily,' she uses her best patronising voice, 'should we be?'

'No. God no. Sorry, I just thought . . . never mind.' Relief washes over me like a tidal wave.

'Well.' She claps her hands to signify the end of the

meeting. 'Are you in agreement with this arrangement?'

I stumble to find the words. Fuck. Don't just agree to anything. Think, Emily. You're an assertive, independent woman. Act like it.

'Will there be any additional salary to accompany the new role?' I ask in my smallest, least assertive voice.

'Just to be clear, this isn't a new role we are asking you to do. It is an addition to your existing role. You will not be asked to take on additional core hours, but will be condensing your existing hours and shifting your focus on day three to the children's parade. I will, however, as a goodwill gesture, speak with HR about renegotiating your salary onto the next pay point in recognition of your commitment and long-standing service to the council. Would you find those terms more acceptable?'

This does sound remarkably like just doing more work, instead of being formally promoted. Come on brain, work with me.

'Yes, that seems acceptable – providing I can leave work early on some days to pick up Lucy.'

'Who's Lucy?'

'My daughter.'

'Ah. Yes, yes. Just make up the time.'

I'm on a roll. Fuck it, Em, just ask.

'And I'd like to work from home one day a week.' I bite the inside of my mouth with anticipation. No one works from home. Ever. Apart from Clive in Events, and that was only after he'd fallen down the escalators at TK Maxx and broke his leg in three places so couldn't walk because of the pins. He had to come back the moment they put him in a half cast and he was able to shuffle into the lift.

Liz looks furious. She glances at her watch and then at me.

'Fine. Fine. But just don't tell everyone about this, Emily. I don't want people thinking this is acceptable.'

'I won't. Thanks, Liz.'

'Speak to IT and they'll set you up remotely. So that's a deal?'

'Yes, that's a deal, Liz.' I can't stop grinning. I bet this is how Sheryl Sandberg felt when she negotiated her contract with Facebook.

'Fantastic,' and she offers me her bony, gold-ring-encrusted hand to shake. It feels paper-thin and dead-person cold. 'I'll get HR to draw up the paperwork and email it over today.'

They must be keen to get me to sign. Everything takes years in the council to get signed off. Nothing happens in one day, not even a reply to a straightforward yes/no email.

I nip into the kitchen to make myself a congratulatory hot chocolate. The children's parade would be a brilliant thing to manage. John never looked like he did anything other than play Solitaire so I'll easily be able to pick up where he left off. The extra money would also be nice, however much it is.

'Did you hear about John?'

Where the fuck did Karen from Accounts just come from? She's like a hybrid car. Since Simone left, Karen has transferred her friendship effortlessly to me, like we're the same person. She has no idea what my name is but sees me very much as a kitchen confidante.

'That he resigned?'

'Well' – and she looks over both shoulders to ensure the empty kitchen is, in fact, empty – 'we discovered a discrepancy in his accounting, shall I say.'

'Sorry, Karen, you've lost me.'

She sighs, rolls her eyes and says, 'John was stealing

money from the council. He has been doing for years. I was one of the people who uncovered it.' Her neck blotches with pride.

'No, not John!'

'Yes.' She is now beaming with self-satisfaction.

'But how? It's not like he wore nice clothes, or bought himself good lunches.' John didn't even get himself a posh coffee on payday, and he brought his own meat-paste sandwiches in every day.

'I can't really go into it in much detail because of confidentiality, obviously.'

'Obviously.' I suddenly feel sad for John and wonder what could have possibly happened in his life that meant he had to steal from the council. All those years we've known each other, and not really known each other at all.

'So . . .' and she shrugs, then just stares at me and I realise that was the end of the conversation. I pick up my hot chocolate as she taps her nose again. 'Mum's the word,' she whispers in a creepy voice.

This woman is nuts.

'That's fantastic, Emily. I'm so proud of you,' I'm talking to Nick on the phone as I've taken myself off for an expensive coffee and diabetic-inducing-size piece of chocolate cake in the Italian restaurant as a late second lunch/congratulatory treat.

The waitress comes to clear my mug and I signal I'd like another latte.

I can't remember the last time Nick said he was proud of me. Probably when I gave birth to Lucy.

'So I'll be managing the children's parade on top of my current responsibilities.' Liz didn't exactly say manage, but I think it's fair to assume that's what I'll be doing. I can feel a shift in me. I can't explain what it is, but it feels good. I think it might be confidence.

This isn't the job I want to do forever. It never was. But for now, it suits us all fine. I don't get the impending sense of doom on a Sunday night. On the whole, I get to speak to relatively interesting people and have a manageable work-load, which has, in all honesty, been quite light of late.

See, I'm more tired, yes. Less motivated, possibly. But I can now get done in twenty minutes what would have taken me two hours prior to having Lucy, because I see a window of time and can fill it. Lucy's asleep and I can clean the flat, put a wash on, and do an online shop in that hour. Before having her, that would have taken the best part of a day. I can get the majority of my day's work done before 11 a.m., if I just crack on. If I was going to set up my own business, I would positively discriminate in favour of recent mothers, as they are the nation's most undervalued resource.

'Why don't you see if Tania can babysit this weekend and we'll go out to celebrate?'

We are starting to behave like a normal couple. I have a promotion at work, I'm going out with my boyfriend. This feels nice, this feels like progress.

'Great idea. See you at home.'

Me: Can you babysit on Saturday?

Tania: Yep no probs. Do I have to bring my own wine and do you have Netflix?

Me: No Netflix. I'll get wine and party sausages.

Tania: OK. I'll just bring my iPad. I'm halfway through series six of Suits and I've got a huge crush on Mike.

Me: He's called Mike??

Tania: Yep, I know. Dad name. But I'd live with that to see him naked.

Me: Thanks. See you Sat.
Tania: XOXOXOX

As I finish up the last crumbs of my celebratory cake, I look out the window and see a mother pushing a pram along the pavement. She walks slowly and purposefully with a determined look on her face, using the pram to take some of her weight. She stops when she reaches the café door, mentally evaluating how to open it with the pram. I leap up and push it wide open for her.

'Thank you,' she responds gratefully, her breath coming out in dragon puffs of cold air.

'No problem.' I peer in the carriage as she pulls it in. 'How old?'

'Two weeks. She's called Nancy.' Her sleeping baby is tiny, tucked up under a beautifully crocheted blanket. I move one of the chairs for her so she can park up.

'Congratulations. She's utterly beautiful, and what a gorgeous name.'

'Thanks. It's after my grandmother.' Her movements are slow and considered as she lowers herself into the most comfortable-looking armchair, 'God, that was hard work.' She sits down with a huff. 'It's our first time out the house today.'

'Oh, well done, that's quite an achievement!'

'Thanks. It really feels it.' She leans over to look in the pram and instinctively places her finger under Nancy's nose to check she's still breathing, then sits back again with a sigh. 'Thanks again for your help. I've had my heart set on coming to this café, I used to come here all the time. And now I've got here I just want to go home. Ridiculous, I know.' An awkward laugh slips out that turns into a sob in her throat.

'You're doing brilliantly,' I reassure her. 'What do you

want, now you've made it here?' I grab my handbag from the neighbouring table and sit opposite her.

'Ah' – she closes her eyes – 'a cappuccino with chocolate sprinkles, and a piece of Victoria sponge.'

'Righto, you stay here and I'll go and order for you.'

'Really?'

'Of course,' I say and I give her arm a quick squeeze.

'Hang on' – she roots around in her change bag – 'let me find my purse.'

'It's fine, it's my treat.'

'Don't be so nice to me, I'll never stop crying,' she jokes as the tears start to spill down her cheeks.

As I walk up to the counter, I look back at her, nervously checking her baby every few seconds and trying to sit uncomfortably on one bum cheek. I think back to mine and Nick's first outing with Lucy, and how long ago that now feels. How your brain can only deal with the moment you are in with a child, and lets go of all previous knowledge to make way for the new stuff. I only know exactly what a ten-month-old baby does, but have absolutely no idea what to do with a newborn anymore.

'Cappuccino and a Victoria sponge,' I order.

'And for you?' the waitress asks in a soft Italian accent.

'Another latte, please.' This could be a bad decision, it's my third here and they are like rocket fuel.

'Coming right up.' I offer her my cash card and she dismisses it with a shake of her hand. 'Your money's no good here today.' She nods in the direction of the new mum and says, 'It's important we all look after each other.'

I thank her, feeling a swell of pride and then instant regret at not ordering another piece of cake for myself, as I pick up our tray.

'Thank you so much.' The new mum beams as I hand

her the coffee and cake. 'Do you have children yourself? I'm assuming you do.' She tucks into the cake with large forkfuls and I realise I should have mentioned that I hadn't actually paid for them myself, but I seem to have missed the window now.

'One. Lucy. She's ten months.'

'Wow. Ten months. How's that?'

'It does get easier,' I say non-committally and then re-member the words of the midwife before leaving hospital.

'God, I hope so. We've only got the bus into town and I was petrified all the way here.' She smoothes down her wild curly hair and ties it in the hairband she has around her wrist.

'The amount of stuff you need to get out of the house is completely ridiculous, isn't it? An hour was the fastest I could get out the flat when Lucy was very little.'

'It took us an hour and a half, so that's fast,' she chuckles with a mouthful of cake.

'Did you have an episiotomy?' It's amazing how you can talk to a complete stranger about their vagina if it involves childbirth.

'Yes, how can you tell?'

'The way you're sitting. I was the same.'

'Yes, sitting down is a bit uncomfortable at the moment. My husband's bought me a rubber ring thing that you're meant to sit on, but I don't really want to bring it out with me.'

'Have you tried arnica tablets?'

'What are they?'

'They reduce the swelling. They really worked for me, anyway. They might not be for everyone,' I add, not want-ing to sound like a total fucking know-it-all.

'Thank you.' She gets a little pad and pen out from her

change bag. 'I'll write that down as I won't remember it otherwise. What was it called again?'

'Arnica.' I take a big swig, immediately feeling slightly anxious as I buzz with caffeine. 'Do your family live close by?'

'No, they're all Bristol way. My husband's don't live far away, but it's not the same as with your own mum, is it?'

'No, not at all. My mum's miles away as well. Sorry, I'm Emily.'

'Lottie.' She extends her hand.

Just then Nancy lets out a small mewing sound and we both lean forward to look in the pram. Her tiny arms are stretched out in front of her, all skinny and bird-like. Lottie gently lifts her out. Nancy is opening and closing her mouth with a smack.

'Wow, I forgot how small they are at her age.' She is utterly mesmerising.

'Do you want a hold?'

'Oh my God. Are you sure? Yes please, I'd love to.'

Lottie passes her over to me. I support her head and hold her in the crook of my arm. She is weightless and her newborn baby smell is intoxicating.

We sit in comfortable silence, both staring down at Nancy, lost in our own memories.

Lottie finishes her coffee with a slurp, 'I really need a wee, Emily. I know I've only just met you but . . . no, forget it.'

'I can look after her while you go?'

Lottie looks from Nancy to me and back to Nancy again, assessing the situation. Does she want to leave her brandnew perfect baby with someone she's only just met for fifteen minutes?

'I promise she'll be OK.'

Lottie laughs nervously. 'It's not that, it's just . . . Well it's totally that. OK, great, thank you. I'll just be a minute.'

As she unsteadily pushes herself to standing I say, 'When you go for a wee, lean forward as if you're touching your toes.'

'Sorry?'

'If you lean forward while you're weeing, it doesn't sting so much.'

'OK.' She smiles. 'I'll be right back,' and she weaves her way through the chairs, looking behind her every few seconds to check on us.

I stroke the palm of Nancy's hand and her reflex opens it up then she closes her hand around my finger like a Venus flytrap. I thought Lucy was still little, but looking at Nancy, it dawns on me how much she's grown. How far we've come. Lucy is crawling and babbling. She plays games with us, she covers her face with her hands and thinks because she can't see us that we can't see her. She laughs like a drain, and when she does, she opens her mouth to reveal a handful of teeth, like tiny Tic Tacs. I gently rock Nancy. She has locked eyes with me, although I think I'm still upside down to her at the moment.

I think of pregnant Helen. Since hearing her news, I have considered having another baby at least once a day. That's a lie. It's more like once an hour. Not right now, it would be too much now, but soon maybe? How wonderful would it be for Lucy to have a little brother or sister? I never had that. But then I had Rachel, she was like my sister, and I hers. Maybe Lucy doesn't need a sibling, she just needs her own Rachel.

I look up and see Lottie gripping chair after chair as she makes her way back to the table.

'That' – she grins – 'was the best piece of advice I have ever been given. Ever.'

'What?'

'The weeing. I've been breaking out in a sweat every time I think about going. That was the first time that I've been for a wee without crying since she was born.'

'I can't take credit for that one. It was a woman on the maternity ward who told me about it.'

'Well she is my hero.' She eases herself back into her seat. 'What do you do?' She gestures at my suit. She probably thinks I work in a bank.

'I work at the council.' God, that sounds just as bad as working in a bank. 'But I'm also writing a play at the moment.' It's not a complete lie. I think about it all the time, I just haven't written it yet.

'Really? What's it about, or can you not say until it's finished?'

'It's a work-in-progress at the moment.'

'Well, when you're finished you should email it to me. My husband works for the National in the literary department. I could pass it on to him to have a look if you want? Unless you're already working with a theatre?'

A high-pitched noise escapes from my mouth, 'Are you shitting me?'

'Well, it's the least I can do after you've been so kind to me today.'

'Well I will definitely, definitely do that.' I'm so excited I think I'm speaking faster and louder.

'Great, well put your email address in my little book' – she nods towards her change bag – 'and I'll email you my details when I get home.'

I write it down, then check the time quickly. My extended lunch break has now taken a record two hours. 'Shit, I've got to get back to work, Lottie. I can't tell you how brilliant it's been to meet you.'

'You too, and thanks again for being my saviour.' She smiles. 'I'll email you tonight.'

As I walk out into the bracing wind, I wrap my coat tightly around me, and head in the direction of work. My face aches from grinning.

My brain is going twenty to the dozen. It's not the possibility of someone from the National reading my play. It's the possibility of the play itself. For the first time in months I have had an idea. A proper idea for my play, and it's taking shape so fast and furiously in my head that I'm desperate to get in front of a computer to start writing it down. I think about all that's happened in the last year, the things I now know so well. The ups and downs, the funny bits, the challenges, the arguments with Nick, how we have simultaneously grown apart and closer in the same breath. The friendships that have blossomed, the brutal honesty of those friendships and how they are based on survival more than enjoyment. The love. The absolute love you feel for your baby. The gut-wrenching, guilt-inducing, sleep-depriving, worry-creating, raw, brutal love you feel for the human being you have made.

This is what I know. This has to be my play.

Chapter Thirty-five

Me: Should I organise a party for Lucy's birthday?

Tania: No.

Helen: Yes.

Tania: It's just pointless consumerism. She's not going to remember it.

Helen: That's not the point. You will. You'll have survived a year. You deserve it.

Tania: It's ages away.

Helen: It's not ages away. I'm planning Polly's now.

Tania: SERIOUSLY??

Me: What are you going to do?

Helen: Not sure. I've started a Pinterest board so far.

Tania: FFS. Do I have to do one then?

Me: Nope.

Helen: Yep.

Tania: Who are you inviting @emily?

Me: Dunno. You guys. Rachel. My folks. Nick's parents.

Tania: That's the problem.

Me: ???

Tania: Parents.

Me: Yep. Me too. Ours haven't met each other before.

Helen: WHAT??

Tania: WHAT??

Me: I know. Bit awkward.

Tania: But you two have been together forever, how did you avoid that?

Me: Luck and good planning.

Tania: In that case. Do it. Grab the nettle.
Me: But you said??
Tania: Change of plan. Face your fears.
Helen: And do it in a pub.
Tania: Yes. Do it in a pub.

It's about time I owned a bra that isn't a nursing one, bought second-hand from eBay or originally purchased in 1999 before I headed off to university.

Lucy and I are waiting in M&S to get measured. The shop assistant has made a big production of slotting me in, as apparently bookings are usually made months in advance for fittings. It does, however, look like she's just chatting to her friend behind the counter, and texting while she waits for my appointment, which is a bit irritating. Lucy and I are passing time wandering around the food court. A WhatsApp message from Tania pings, asking if either of us are free. I haven't seen either of them for a few days, as I have been using every available moment to write. When Lucy is having her nap, when Nick is bathing her, I've even been writing instead of watching *One Tree Hill*, which has to be the greatest, most selfless, sacrifice. It feels brilliant. I am inspired, and better still, my muse is my little buddy, Lucy.

I'm making great use of my time at work as well. eBay has been replaced with dialogue, Ryan Gosling pictures with plot development. Liz thinks I'm doing a fantastic job as I always look so busy and my lunch hours have now been reduced to a more-than-acceptable half-hour. The children's parade has been pretty much running itself. It turns out Simone had Simoned all over John's filing system as well, so everything is very easy to find. I can copy everything she did and then claim it as my own. That's excellent management skills.

I absent-mindedly pick up a packet of cheese straws, open them and give one to Lucy. I need to remember to pay for them on the way out. Just then I think I catch sight of someone I used to know. He's some distance ahead of us, but I recognise the familiar broad shoulders and Mr Soft-style bounce in his step. By the time I've pushed Lucy round to the gluten-free aisle, he's gone.

We head back up to floor three to be greeted by the woman looking purposefully at her watch.

'I'm Kate-Marie and I'm going to be your underwear technician, please follow me.' I realise that I've still got the half-opened cheese straws on top of the pram. Fuck it, what are they going to do, arrest me?

'Have those been paid for?' She points at them. God, she's good.

'Not yet.'

'Make sure you do,' and she ushers me into the disabled changing room, so we can wedge Lucy and the pram in with me. This is going to be a fun experience. I self-consciously take my T-shirt off and she wraps the tape measure around my chest and boobs with the efficiency and precision of a woman who's done this for years.

'I'll just go out on the shop floor and bring some back in your size. Are we looking for practical or something a bit special?'

'Practical,' I respond without hesitation. She says she'll be back in a minute and, meanwhile, asks me to remove my bra.

'I haven't been asked to do that in over a year!' I joke, and she visibly flinches. When did I turn into Sid James? She returns with armfuls of bras and looks at my current one with a mixture of utter shock and complete disgust.

'How long have you had this for?' She's stretching and pulling at it.

'A couple of years, maybe?' I lie. It's more like five.

'Well, this is offering you zero support. Zero,' and she passes me the first of about thirty bras to try on. I give Lucy my old one to play with, as there isn't enough room for me to bend down and retrieve any of her toys from underneath the pram.

Kate-Marie finally settles on a beige bra with no lace. It makes me look naked without nipples, but she's satisfied that it fits correctly, and after half an hour in this hot changing room I'll settle for anything.

As I'm paying at the till I think I see him again. This time in the male knitwear section. I catch a profile shot and yes, it looks just like him. I grab my bag and push Lucy in that direction, but I'm too late.

Lucy and I get the lift to the café for a pit stop. I live in a town with a thousand cool cafés. Most of them child friendly, all of them the kind of places that play cool music, have list upon list of fruit teas, smell a bit of joss sticks and are staffed by sickeningly gorgeous people, despite a face full of piercings and dreadlocks. But I have always favoured Marks and middle-aged Sparks. They do a fantastic pot of tea and scones. As Lucy is pulling the ham out of her sandwich and lobbing it all over the floor, I check out my purchase. It really is very sensible. And by sensible, I mean the kind of thing you definitely wouldn't wear on a first date. Or second. In fact, you'd probably go for a shit with the bathroom door open in front of your boyfriend before you dragged out this sexless boulder-holder. But it looked great under my T-shirt.

As we sit among the table-hogging grandmas and foreign exchange students, I spot him again, and this time I know it's not my mind playing tricks on me.

The man is sat on his own, having a similar afternoon snack. He's wearing a hoodie and jacket, even though it's totally sweltering.

Ridiculously, it is his hands I notice first. The fingers that are curled around his mug. Those hands that had touched my body in a different lifetime. Then the curve of his shoulders, and as he turns to get something out of his rucksack it's confirmed. It's Ryan. My first proper boyfriend, whom I lost my virginity to. It must be over fifteen years, at least, since I saw him last. He has crossed my mind from time to time, but seeing him in real life is odd. I hadn't really imagined he'd age. I thought he would still have dreadlocks and combats, with a half-smoked joint dangling out of his mouth. But he looks old, his face looks lined and tired. I make a decision to go over and say hi, and it's only when I'm nearly at his table that it dawns on me that he might not actually recognise me. As I stand indecisively, he looks up from his cream tea and exclaims, 'Emmie Jones. My fucking God.'

'Bloody hell, Ryan. Hi!' I kiss him clumsily on his unshaven cheek.

'So who's this?' He points at the pram, grinning.

'My daughter. Lucy.'

'Wow. Massive congratulations!'

'Thanks!' I shrug. I've always found it strange when people congratulate you for procreating. I mean it's hard work being pregnant and giving birth is hell on earth, but the only real decision you've made is to have unprotected sex. It's not like I've trained to be a neuroscientist or anything.

Ryan hasn't aged well. His dreads have been replaced by a number two cut with a receding hairline and prominent bald spot, which I can see from my standing position.

'Do you want to sit down?'

314

I check my watch like I have somewhere else to be, which of course, I don't, before saying, 'Yeah, go on then.'

'I can highly recommend the scones. Fuck, this is so weird. You look good, Emmie. You haven't changed a bit.' We both know that's not true. Lucy entwines her fingers in my hair and I try to detangle her as I sit down.

'What are you doing here?'

'Oh, just getting some lunch.'

'Not here, here. Brighton. What are you doing in Brighton?'

'Oh, yes, of course. There's a food festival and the company I work for has a stand, so I'm cooking.'

'You cook?'

'Yep. I've been a chef for nearly eighteen years now. God, that makes me feel old.'

'And are you still . . .'

'I live in Leeds now, working in a restaurant in town. It's fun; hard work but fun most of the time.'

'And are you, have you got . . .'

'Kids? No. Doesn't really go with the job to be honest. Shame really, I think I would have been good at it. What about you? Married?'

'Nope, Nick and I have been together for years, though. We might one day, I dunno.'

'Good for you. And what do you do now? Other than this, of course' – he points to Lucy – 'did you go off and become an actress? I always wondered, I sometimes think you'll rock up on *Casualty* or *EastEnders* or something.'

'No, I never really got into it after uni.'

'Shame, Emmie, you were good.'

I can feel myself flushing. No one's mentioned me wanting to be an actor for decades. I'd kind of half-forgotten that was what I'd dreamed of doing when I was younger.

It's strange to be sat opposite a man who knows me from a different lifetime. A carefree time of dreaming and scheming. Of free parties and festivals. Of hazy, hot school holidays that went on for weeks, filled with sitting in parks listening to someone's radio, smoking spliffs and putting the world to rights. Of friendships you thought would last forever. Of first kisses, first fumbles, first times. I suddenly remember what his penis looked like and feel my neck blotching in embarrassment, as if he can read my thoughts.

'And how's Rachel? Are you guys still best mates?'

'Yes. Yes we are actually,' I can say that now with all confidence. If I'd seen Ryan a month ago, it may have been a very different story but now we are. Or getting there. We speak regularly and text every few days. We haven't seen each other yet, but that's the next big leap.

Ryan knocks back the last of his tea. 'That's brilliant news. I liked you two together. You were fucking trouble. Right, sorry to love you and leave you, but I've got to pick up an industrial fridge for tomorrow. Exciting stuff.' He smiles, and the years fall away. I can see the seventeen-year-old boy who used to mosh to Rage Against the Machine. 'It's been so great to see you.' He leans over and kisses my cheek. 'Emmie Jones. The one that got away!'

'See you, Ryan,' and off he goes, weaving his way through the sea of old women and prams.

'Mummy was going to be on stage,' I whisper to Lucy. 'I was going to be an actress. I was very good, you know.'

Lucy gurgles back. She's picked the napkin up off the table and is chewing on the shredded strips, which I retrieve with my finger. I reel through the memories with Ryan, like watching an old black-and-white film of a time when I used to be impulsive and responsibility free. I know I can't necessarily be those things now, but surely some of that person is still there?

I spend a lot of my time fretting and fighting with Nick. But I don't want to. That is not the life I chose. That is not the person I am, or the couple we are, for that matter.

Nick and I need to start living for now, start doing stuff together again, start enjoying life a bit more. We need to break the routine and remember who we are.

Things have moved on. I have moved on, but my life hasn't really caught up with me. If I don't get out there and start living with Nick and Lucy, then we'll just drift. Marks and Spencer's lunches will become a treat and we'll end up looking like old, tired versions of ourselves, who have forgotten how to have fun.

I'm not going to let that happen.

'Come on,' I squeal at Lucy, 'I've just had a brilliant idea!'

I push Lucy out onto the high street and text Rachel as I walk purposefully.

Me: You will NEVER guess who I've just seen.

Rachel: Please let it be Ryan Gosling.

Me: Nope. Another Ryan.

Rachel: Noooooooooooooo. What does he look like now? Still a crusty?

Me: No, a chef. He looks old, but still like him if you know what I mean.

Rachel: Still got a cock shaped like a carrot, then?

Of course Rachel remembers that too. She knows everything.

As we head in the direction of the record shop, I remember I've left my granny bra under the table in the café.

Fuck it. I'll buy one from Agent Provocateur online. Be the change you want to see, I remind myself, one bra at a time. On the plus side I have inadvertently stolen the cheese straws.

'Two tickets to BeachFest, please.'

'Are those adult tickets or is it for you and your baby? You don't have to pay for her.'

Who takes kids to festivals? I'm not mental. No thanks. 'Yes, they're adult tickets.'

'That's two hundred and forty quid. Are you paying by cash or card?'

Shit. That is a lot of money on a whim. But on the other hand, we haven't been away just the two of us since Lucy was born. We need this. I need this. I want to get my fake fur coat out, to wear a festival Bardot top, wellies and un-flattering cut-off, camel-toe-inducing denim shorts. I want to traipse around a field half-pissed on weak lager that cost me seven quid, watching some band that I should know, but clearly don't as my cultural references ground to a halt around 2005.

I hand over my card and hold my breath, hoping there's enough money in the joint account to pay for it.

'There you go, have a good one,' and he hands over the tickets. It was that easy. It took ten minutes to go from middle-aged mum to cool-as-fuck festival reveller. All I need to do now is find someone to look after Lucy for two nights, and explain to Nick why we don't have any money for groceries until payday. Easy.

As I push open the front door I am met with an overwhelm-ing smell of burning.

'Em, is that you?' Nick shouts from the kitchen.

'What are you doing home so early?' I shout back as I negotiate the wide pram through the narrow door. It always takes about six attempts to line it up so that we don't become wedged. I don't know why we didn't measure it before buying it.

'Come through!' he calls back excitedly.

I scoop Lucy out of the pram, prop her on my hip, grab my handbag and make my way to the living area. Nick is in the kitchen half of the room, a tea towel slung over his shoulder and spatula in hand. Layers of smoke hang in the air like waves. Nearly every surface is covered in pans or bowls or cups.

'Here.' He pours and passes me a glass of red wine and I resist the temptation to comment on the mess. He must have used every utensil in the flat, even the ornamental dish that Auntie Jan gave us one Christmas that we normally keep the house and car keys in.

'What are we having?' I ask, trying hard to keep the irritation out of my tone.

'My own special recipe. It was going to be a veggie moussaka but I forgot to buy aubergine, so it's kind of a stew-come-lasagne. Don't pull that face, Em, it's going to be delicious. Sit down, ladies.' He mock bows and indicates the table, which, in stark contrast to the kitchen, is set beautifully. All the crap that has been piling up for months, the unopened bills, the children's books, the unread newspapers, have all been removed, and in their place is a vase filled with yellow roses. Three places are set, two grown-up and a baby bowl on Lucy's high chair. A bottle of Prosecco is chilling in a mixing bowl full of water and ice.

'Nick, this looks amazing.'

'Good. And don't worry about the kitchen, I'll clear it up later on. Get Lucy set up in her chair and I'll bring her over her dinner.'

I ease Lucy's legs into the high chair and give her a plastic spoon to bang around.

'For you, mademoiselle.' Nick now has the tea towel over his arm like a sommelier and is offering Lucy a sippy cup of water. 'Excellent vintage and full-bodied flavour. And for you, madam.' He refills my wine glass.

'What's the occasion, Nick?'

'Can't I just cook for the wonderful women in my life?' he chirps as he presents Lucy with sticks of cooked cooled carrots, sweet potatoes and cheese.

'I'm not complaining, I'm just surprised. This is nice. Thank you.'

'For you.' He squeezes my shoulder as he places a plate in front of me. It doesn't look like particularly appetising but it smells amazing. 'It tastes better than it looks,' he reassures me.

'So, how was your day?' I ask him when he sits down opposite me. I take a mouthful of the stew. It's absolutely delicious, so much so I break my own rule and close my eyes while eating. 'God, that's tasty, Nick.'

'Good, glad you like it.' He eats a forkful himself and nods in agreement. 'I have had a good day actually,' he says, emphasising the good and I raise an eyebrow. I have given up asking him specifics about his job, as it only seems to wind him up, or make him look stressed. 'So the mid-year management accounts came in and . . .' he pauses for full effect, 'it looks like we've managed to get the company out of the shit.'

'What does that mean?'

'It means that we're no longer in the red, Em, that all those late nights and early mornings have paid off. It means my job's safe.' He grins.

'Fuck, that is good news.' I chink glasses with him.

'And that's not all. They've been monitoring our progress, and it turns out I'm pretty fucking good at this job,

Em. Seems my gift of the gab and overwhelming charm are well placed.'

'If you do say so yourself.'

'If I do say so myself. So you are now looking at the Head of Regional Recruitment. I will, as you can imagine, expect an awful lot more respect at home of course.'

'Of course, Head of, what was it?'

'Regional Recruitment.'

'What does that actually mean?'

'Really? I have no idea. But what it does mean is an extra five grand a year. So you can call me Head of Regional Brilliance if you like.'

'Head of buying the drinks tomorrow.'

'And that.' He passes me an empty champagne flute.

'Nice one, Nick.'

'Nice one us.' His voice softens as he passes Lucy a carrot stick that's got wedged in her bib. 'I know I've been a bit stressed.'

'A bit?'

'Yep, OK, but you've not exactly been zenned out of late, Em. Anyway, that's going to change, I promise.' He squeezes my hand.

Nick pops the Prosecco and I wonder if now is the time to tell him the best good news of the day. I have bought us tickets to the coolest festival this side of Glastonbury. But then I decide to wait until we're out; he's going to be so excited about this.

'Why are you being such a dick about it?' We're sat in the beer garden at the Setting Sun on our celebration night out and I've just presented Nick with the tickets.

'Keep your voice down, Em. I'm not, it's just we could have spoken about it first.'

'We could have spoken about it but then it wouldn't have been a surprise. And that's the whole point of surprises. That you don't know about them.' I can feel my neck starting to get hot in anger.

'You don't have to get all arsey about it, Em. I'm just saying that we should have spoken about it first. This is our money, and it would have been good to make a joint decision, that's all. The car is due to be MOTed in a couple of weeks and it will definitely need new brake pads as the warning light flashed on the other day, and that's not cheap, Em. We're talking a couple of hundred quid I'd say.'

Oh my God, could Nick be any more of a doom lord? OK, I had completely forgotten about the car, but still, he could at least pretend to be excited about a weekend away with me.

We sit in silence, sipping our drinks. A couple on a table nearby are whispering to each other and giggling, and then start properly getting off with each other. I can't stop watching them.

'Look, Em, it will be fun, it'll be great. And I think it's a brilliant idea. I'm just saying let's talk these things through in the future.' He raises his pint to me and smiles apologetically. 'Deal?'

This wasn't how I'd imagined the conversation going.

'OK, deal.'

'So who's playing, anyway?' I notice he has drained half his pint in two gulps.

'Orbital,' I sulk.

'Are you shitting me, Em?'

'And the Chemical Brothers, I think.'

Nick leans over, cups my face with his hands and presses his lips against mine. 'Forget what I said, forget the car. Oh my God. You are amazing,' and when he kisses me again, this time I kiss him back.

He smells of clean washing and my posh shampoo and that momentarily annoys me, as I bought him his own sub-standard brand from Poundland, but then I let it go.

That's something I'm getting better at, letting go. Not in a massive way, not in a hipster 'Don't sweat the small stuff, cos everything's small stuff' kind of way, because I do sweat the small stuff, daily. Just not all the small stuff. That's the difference Lucy has made in me: she has pushed out some of the selfish, some of the fret, some of the day-to-day worries, to make way for her and a whole filing cabinet of new frets and associated worries.

I never expected that being a parent would be so hard. There, I've said it. I thought Lucy would somehow slot into our lives. That there was a baby-shaped gap waiting for her to fill. The final piece of our jigsaw puzzle. But the reality is it's a completely different board game, a new one with complicated, small pieces and no rules.

I was so used to being the centre of my own world that it came as a complete surprise how much the focus shifts, and most importantly that it's a permanent shift. I can never again look at a clock at 7 a.m., 12 p.m. and 5 p.m. and not think, right, it's meal time.

But the greatest surprise of it all is I never expected I had the capacity to love another human being as much as I love Lucy. It's not a kind love. It's not a soft-focus love. It's fierce. It's core love, jump in front of a bus if it meant she'd live love. I'd take any terminal illness, any heartbreak, any suffering in a moment if it meant she would avoid experiencing it.

I could bury my nose into her neck and just smell her, just breathe her in and I can feel my heart rate slowing, the tension in my chest loosening. They should bottle the small-child smell and sell it at Neal's Yard, they'd make a fortune.

Nick fills up my glass from the bottle of red. 'Thank you.' I take a large gulp. 'How's about we have these and go home?' I suggest.

'Are you not having a good night?'

'It's not that.' I interlock my fingers with Nick's. 'I just thought, if Lucy's still sleeping, we could go straight to bed?'

Nick flashes me a quick look to check I don't mean to sleep, which ninety-nine per cent of the time I do, but not tonight. Tonight I am celebrating my promotion and Nick's. I am out with my boyfriend, and we are going home to have sex.

This is more than progress; this is the start of our new and improved grown-up life.

Chapter Thirty-six

'I thought she'd be walking by one. Nick was walking when he was ten months, do you remember, Dennis?'

I hand Cathleen a cup of tea and resist the temptation to pour it straight down her coral-coloured cardigan. She is queen of the passive-aggressive dig.

'Well, this really is lovely, Emily. So cosy, we often struggle to fill the rooms in our house but this is perfect for the three of you, isn't it?'

I genuinely don't know how she does it. 'Did you find your hotel OK?'

'Yes, it's basic but clean. And the woman on the reception was so thoughtful, wasn't she, Dennis? She couldn't have been more helpful. She gave us a map of Brighton and rang a taxi for us to get here.'

'Well if you came down more often you'd know where you were going,' I mutter. Nick shoots me the first of many looks.

'And Nick tells me you're writing a little play now, is that right, Emily?'

'Yes, yes, that's right, Cathleen.'

'Well it's good to have a hobby, isn't it? I've always found crocheting relaxing, which is similar to an extent. Both creative pursuits.'

It really fucking isn't though, is it, Cathleen? I say in my head, while my mouth says, 'Yes, kind of,' and make a mental note to not invite her to the opening night.

'And any words yet? Has our little Luce said what she's thinking?'

Nick goes to say yes but I cut across him, 'No. Nothing yet, but I'm sure it will happen soon.'

She has started to speak, apparently. According to Kimberly, her vocabulary is now up to three words – shoe, spoon and no. The thing is, I haven't heard her say any of them. The other morning she said something that sounded a bit like 'yes boy', in a Jamaican accent. As I asked her if she was enjoying her tea the other day she said what I thought was 'shit'. But maybe I was looking out for that one, as it was crumpets and cucumber, which, let's be frank, is a shit tea. She babbles all the time and I think she might understand what I say a bit. 'No' has definitely gone in, not that she takes any notice, and when I say 'nose' she sticks a finger up her nostril, but I don't understand what she's saying to me.

I instinctively know when Lucy wants something, but that's just being her mum and knowing her. I can't decipher words, actual words. We haven't developed some kind of language that only the two of us understand. We blow raspberries at each other, which is kind of like chatting, and Nick, Lucy and I sometimes all shake our heads at the same time, Beatles style. I'm desperate to find out what she's saying, what's going on in her head, because I suspect she's going to be a really strong-willed person. I can't wait to have a proper conversation with her, and I think I'm going to have the mother of all cries the first time she tells me she loves me, but right now, I'd just be happy to hear her say spoon.

'You've done so well with the flat, Emily. It really is lovely. It must be so difficult to find the time to keep on top of it all with a baby now you're working.'

'Of course! Of course!' Dennis pipes up as if someone has just plugged him in. 'How is life in the fast lane, Emily? Is it all, "buy, buy, sell, sell"?'

'I work in Arts Education for the council, Dennis.' He looks at me completely blankly. 'So yes, it's a bit like that.'

'Good, good.' He settles back into the armchair and continues reading his copy of the *Daily Mail*. I'm going to have to put that in someone else's recycling bin when he's finished with it.

'I don't know how you do it, Emily, I really don't. Working and rearing a child . . .' Cathleen pauses for full impact. 'There's absolutely no way I could have gone back to work after having Nick.'

Boom. There it is.

I leave the room to check if Lucy's still napping in the hope that Cathleen and Dennis will have magically disappeared when I return. She's lying on her front with her bum in the air, her hands tucked under her chin and a string of spit spilling out of her mouth, creating a puddle on her sheet. Her party dress is hanging on the back of the bedroom door, identical in colour to the dress I bought for myself on eBay, which was completely unintentional, so we will look a bit like Danny DeVito and Arnie in *Twins*.

The doorbell rings and I rush to get it before Nick. Mum and Dad are stood there, arms laden with gifts and a bunch of flowers.

'Are they here yet?' Mum hisses.

Her whispering voice is infamous in our family for being louder than her actual speaking voice. I put my finger to my lips and nod.

Nick and I have been together for over a decade, yet somehow we have managed to avoid ever getting our parents together. We are launching this Montague and Capulet-style event at our flat, then seamlessly moving, as suggested by Helen and Tania, to the pub. The obvious first choice for any one-year-old's party.

I am, however, wholeheartedly regretting the entire thing. I wish beyond wishes that I could go back and retract the invitations, put on *The Goonies*, drink fizz on the sofa and cuddle up with Lucy.

Dad squeezes my arm and mouths, 'It's OK,' as they follow me into the kitchen.

Cathleen and Dennis are standing awkwardly in the kitchenette, Cathleen's hands clasped in front of her like the Queen, and Dennis is leaning uncomfortably against the fridge door with his arms folded.

'Hi, hi!' Nick enthusiastically kisses Mum on both cheeks, surprising them both by his sudden switch to the continental. He then pumps Dad's hand before announcing in a newsreader's voice, 'Can I introduce you to my mother and father?' this level of formality being another first. 'Cathleen and Dennis.'

There's a moment of hesitation before they all dive in, kissing, shaking hands and patting backs, everyone at one point displaying shock that they've never met before and joy that it's finally happened. This goes on for several minutes, but once they've exhausted this conversation, the room falls silent, eyes darting nervously from one to another. Someone say something. Anyone?

'We've brought Prosecco if anyone would like a glass?' Thank God for Dad and booze.

'And the table's booked at the pub for one,' I add.

'You didn't tell me the party was in a pub, Nick?' Cathleen's voice is an octave higher than usual and she's smiling through gritted teeth.

'It'll be great, it'll be great,' Dennis enthuses unconvincingly.

I hadn't realised that Brighton and Hove Albion were playing a match today. I just knew the pub was roomy with lots
of space for prams. Funny that Nick hadn't mentioned it
when I told him where I'd booked a table. During the day,
I've often met Helen and Tania here for a coffee and a bowl
of chips, or if the babies are all asleep and it's after midday,
a pint and a packet of dry roasted. But the atmosphere today
is a bit more . . . lively.

'Nice to see you again. Your little one an Albion supporter
then?' the barman shouts over the din.

'How come you know him?' Nick looks mildly concerned.

'It must be from uni or something,' I lie to Nick. He already compares my days with Lucy to being on holiday;
there's no point in adding to his theory by telling him I hang
out in pubs during the day.

I've reserved a long trestle table for us all, but the 'Reserved for Lucy's birthday' sign has been cleared away by
the bar staff. The pub is starting to fill up with blue and
white striped shirts, and the group of men who have sat
down at the end of our table are chanting 'SEAGULLS,
SEAGULLS, SEAGULLS.'

Dad comes back to the table with a heaving tray of drinks.
If there is one thing you can rely on with Dad, it's that he
keeps the drinks flowing. He passes Cathleen her half of
lager and I notice her familiar red-neck booze-flush: she's
already exceeded her one drink quota and it's not even 2 p.m.
Perhaps this is the only way we are going to survive this
afternoon.

A couple of football fans open the double doors to the
pub so Helen and Tania can push their prams in. They are
followed by Chris and Spiral, who walks in smoking, before
remembering himself and rushing back outside to put it out.

'Sorry we're late.' Tania wrestles Falcon out of the pram. He has a banana in each hand and is the size of a four-year-old. 'The buses are full of Albion fans. And it looks like they've all come here! There's the birthday girl. Ooh, nice outfits!' She points out mine and Lucy's matching attires.

Lucy is sat on Mum's lap pulling at her necklace. Cathleen is squashed next to them, trying to get Lucy to hold her finger, but she keeps shouting, 'No, no, no, no,' and shaking her head furiously. Cathleen, disappointed, downs the rest of her lager and heads to the bar, returning with three bottles of Prosecco and more glasses than people.

I beckon Nick over. 'Shall we go somewhere else? This is awful.'

'It's atmospheric,' he shouts back, as a pissed guy trips over our pram, spilling ale on the hood, 'like parties should be. And everyone's having a good time, so let's give it a few more minutes?'

I look around the table. Dennis has his mobile phone out and is showing something to Dad, who tells me later that it's an ancestry website and that they both now share a predictable old-person's interest in mapping their family trees. Lucy has finally let Cathleen hold her, although she is sitting on the edge of her knee and playing with Mum, so is using her more as an elaborate armchair, but Cathleen seems happy with this compromise. Tania is clutching her own personal bottle of Prosecco as Helen reluctantly sips her lemonade. They've put Falcon and Polly back in their prams and are rocking them back and forth even though neither child looks remotely like they're going to fall asleep.

'How pregnant are you?' Cathleen leans over, pointing to Helen's protruding stomach.

'Twenty-six weeks.'

'Goodness, you're going to have your hands full, aren't you?' she exclaims.

'So everyone tells me.' Helen shrugs.

'I only had our precious Nick. I don't know how people find the love for more than one child to be honest, but they do, of course.' Cathleen takes a rather large gulp of her Prosecco for a teetotaller, before filling her glass up from Tania's bottle without asking.

'Sorry,' I mouth at Helen and she playfully gives me the finger. I'm not sure if it's intended for me or Cathleen.

Chris and Spiral emerge from the beer garden looking sheepish, with tell-tale bloodshot eyes.

Chris raises his pint to Nick and shouts, 'Great party, mate!'

We light the candles on the sugar-free cake I've made. It's a badly cooked mix of dried fruit and nuts and looks like something that should come out the other end. Cathleen, who prides herself on the lightness of her Victoria sponge, tells me later that it's because I hadn't sifted the flour properly and that she would happily have made me a cake if I'd only asked as she has, after all, been baking children's birthday cakes since her own child was born. We start to sing 'Happy Birthday'. The men at the end of the table join in, and then the crowd behind them. The song spreads and before we've got to the end of the first line, one hundred Albion supporters are singing happy birthday to our girl. The noise is deafening, overpowering and incredible. Lucy is bouncing up and down on my lap excitedly. I look at Nick and see he has tears streaming down his face. Actual tears. The man who didn't really cry at the birth of his daughter is crying at his fellow Seagulls chanting with him. He has his hand patriotically raised to his chest and his arm around the guy next to him. As we finish the song, there is an almighty roar, followed by 'SEAGULLS, SEAGULLS, SEAGULLS.'

'Well that was quite a performance!' Dennis bellows.

I get a wave of emotion that takes me by surprise. Lucy isn't going to remember today; it's like any other day for her, only better, as she has her family and friends making a fuss over her. But for Nick and me, today means we have survived an entire year of parenting. I look at him weeping and accepting congratulatory pints from strangers and realise that it is almost a year ago to the minute that the midwife passed me my tiny, pink, bloody baby and laid her on my chest, all sticky and slippy, her breath coming out fast and panty like a mouse. She looked so fragile, so vulnerable, but now somehow here she is propped on my hip, throwing her head back, laughing at Spiral who is turning his eyelids inside out for her amusement.

We've done it. We've been parents for a full year and by some miracle, we're still together. We've started having sex again, been on three dates and driven up and down the A1 seven times. I've read two-thirds of a book, watched countless Ryan Gosling films, learnt how to purée butternut squash, started back at work and been promoted. I've started writing, properly writing. I have a first, very rough, draft of my play, and I would, at this stage, prefer to die than share it with anyone.

But Lucy, she has had the most incredible year of us all. She's had her tongue snipped and her body weight has doubled. She has gone from seeing everything in an upside-down haze to clarity of vision. From being a babe in arms to crawling around and pulling herself up and about. Nick and I may have had our first year of parenting but Lucy has had her first year on this planet, and, on the whole, she looks like she's having a pretty good time of it. She has transitioned from living inside my womb to out in the world. Lucy is the only person who has heard my heartbeat on both sides of my skin. The magnitude of this feels overwhelming, so I try to turn my brain off and drink another glass of Prosecco instead.

We down our drinks, round up the multicoloured plastic plates and cups, and make our way out of the pub. It's now one in, one out, with a huge queue developing round the block. The front ten people look both delighted and puzzled as we all emerge with our babies and prams and grandparents.

We kiss and hug on the pavement. It feels more sincere than the kitchen meeting, probably because it's fuelled by about seven pints of Prosecco. Mum and Cathleen have both got their address books out and are exchanging numbers. Dad and Dennis pat each other's backs enthusiastically.

'That went better than expected,' Helen whispers as she kisses me goodbye.

I bump Lucy up on my hip and ask her, 'Have you had a good day, sweetheart?'

'Spoon.'

I freeze. 'Say that again.'

She looks at me blankly.

'Helen, did you hear that?'

'Hear what?'

'Spoon. She said spoon. Did anyone else hear that?' I'm excitedly shouting now. 'She said spoon, SHE SAID SPOON!' I squeeze her too tightly, the clever, clever girl.

Nick slips his arm around me. 'I heard it,' he lies, as the never-ending queue of football fans start to chant, 'SPOON, SPOON, SPOON, SPOON.'

He pulls me close to him and whispers, 'I'd totally do this again.'

I'm not sure if he means the party or having another baby, but right now, I'd absolutely do both.

Just then my phone rings. It's Rachel. I consider ringing her back when everyone has left, but at the last moment, answer it.

'Are you still there?' She's breathless, like she's running.

'Where?'

'The pub, are you still there? Fuck,' she mutters, followed by 'Sorry!' to someone at her end.

'We're just leaving, it's been so brilliant, you would have—'

'DON'T MOVE,' she shouts. And I hear her on the phone and simultaneously in the real world.

I look around and then my heart thuds in my chest. I see, running in the most inelegant way, clutching a large bag under one arm and a coat under the other, my best friend in the entire world.

*

'You didn't tell me he was funny.' Rachel is curled up on our sofa snuggling with Lucy and drinking wine. Nick fills up her glass, grinning.

'That's because he's not!' I tease. 'Although he likes to think he is.'

'I'm definitely the more chilled-out one, isn't that right, Em?'

'I can well believe that,' Rachel laughs.

'Right, you two, that's enough. You're absolutely, categorically, not allowed to gang up on me.' But I am loving this. I have my three favourite people together on the sofa, and really, they can say whatever the fuck they like to me, because I couldn't be happier. It feels like it's going to burst out of me; my chest hurts trying to contain the feeling.

'Did Mum know you were coming down?'

'I'd mentioned it to her, but really, I wasn't a hundred per cent certain I was coming myself until this morning. I needed to make sure that my mum could check in on Callum and she'd been threatening to do a 5K in Newcastle tomorrow morning.' I must look utterly shocked. 'I know! The woman who couldn't walk up a flight of stairs without having a heart attack now runs. Anyway, she's got a bit of a cold so sacked it off.'

'Can't he look after himself?' Nick asks.

'A fifteen-year-old boy? Nick, think back. Would you leave you in a house on your own overnight without anyone checking in on you?'

'Good point.'

'You have aaaaall this to come.' Rachel smiles at Lucy and pushes a curl of wispy hair from her forehead.

'Are you sure I can't convince you to stay here? I could make you a really comfy bed on the sofa?'

'No. You really can't. If I'm honest I haven't been away on my own for years and I've been dreaming about a hotel bath. Also, no offence, but I don't want to be woken up by you at some ungodly hour, however beautiful you are,' and she kisses Lucy's cheeks repeatedly and noisily. Lucy giggles loudly in appreciation.

'Another glass before you go, then?'

'Weeeell' – Rachel looks at her watch – 'go on then. One more can't hurt.'

'We have fifteen years of drinking to catch up on,' I enthuse as I pop the cork on another bottle.

'You don't have to do it all in one night though,' Nick's voice of reason butts in.

'Wanna bet?' Rachel and I chorus. We both kiss Lucy as

Nick takes her off for her bath and bed, and I curl around Rachel under a blanket on the sofa.

This feels like coming home.

Chapter Thirty-seven

This hangover is worse than most. It's like my head is in a vice. The lady upstairs is cooking bacon and the smell is making me retch. I sit on the cold bathroom floor with my cheek resting on the toilet seat. There is a stale smell of wee. That, combined with the close-up of the inside of the toilet, which could do with a good bleach, makes my stomach heave again and I hold back my hair as I retch up bile, foamy and acidic.

Nick calls through from the bedroom, 'Are you still throwing up?'

'It's green now,' I croak back.

'Why do you always do this before we're doing something good? You always peak too soon. You could have at least waited until we were on our way to the festival before you caned it. You're a prat, you know that?'

I'm not sure if he's calling me a prat in an affectionate way or if he's cross. It's hard to tell the difference as my ears are ringing so loudly.

I try and recall how things got so messy.

Mum picked Lucy up at about five. The military-style planning for her to go to Lincolnshire for a weekend was on a par with invading a small country. You couldn't see out of the back window, once I'd packed all her paraphernalia into Mum's Corsa. Lucy clung on to my neck and made it impossible for me to put her in her car seat, screaming, 'NO,

NO, NO,' and tensing her body into a plank so I couldn't get her arms through the straps.

'It'll be fine once we get going,' Mum kept saying in a shrill, nervous voice. Eventually, Lucy drew breath and I pushed her bum down and clipped her in before she started the purple-faced meltdown again.

As they drove around the corner I started to panic about Mum crashing the car. She's a really erratic driver and people are constantly beeping her and giving her the wanker sign for cutting them up, or being too heavy on the brake, which is fine when it's just us in the car, but what if she drives like a twat with Lucy? What if she pisses someone off so much that they get out of their car and kill her, or steal Lucy? Have I just made an awful mistake?

Did I tell Mum about not feeding Lucy whole grapes because she might choke on them? That you can't just cut them in half because that's just as bad, you have to cut them longways? Should I text her to let her know? But what if she then checks the message while driving and crashes, then it would be all my fault. My hands have gone all cold and clammy. I pace the kitchen, clutching a pack of wet wipes. What's happening to me? What have I done?

I ring Nick.

'Why don't you start packing our stuff to take your mind off it?' He's good at giving me a job as a distraction. 'And then you could come and meet me after work for a beer?'

I agree. It's weirdly liberating to think that we can go for a drink at teatime instead of having to feed someone.

I remember meeting Nick and his work buddies in the pub. We were in the beer garden and I sat next to Shelly, who was absolutely hilarious and could do the best Simon Cowell impression I've ever heard.

I knew I should take it slowly, so just thought I'd have a

pint. Or two, but not overdo it because of going to the festival today, that's the whole point. Then someone suggested doing a shot, Shelly I think, which seemed like a totally reasonable idea, given that we were childfree for the weekend and everything. One never hurts. Victoria Beckham has tequila as her drink of choice and she never looks hungover.

Another wave of nausea takes over but there is nothing left in my stomach, so I am just dry retching. Another flashback. Getting a lift on the back of one of Nick's friend's bikes home, and falling off. Where was Nick? I glance at my knees. They are both grazed and instantly start stinging.

'Did I get home on someone's bike?' I ask in my loudest voice, which is nothing more than a pathetic whisper.

Nick emerges, leaning on the bathroom doorframe in just his boxers, arms folded. 'Fuck, Emily. You look horrific.'

'Thanks.'

'No seriously, you look awful. You're white as a sheet. Maybe some breakfast would help? Do you want me to make you a fried egg sandwich?'

Even the suggestion is too much and I throw up the last bit of stomach acid.

'Was I embarrassing?'

'No more than usual.' Nick shrugs, leans over and ruffles my hair affectionately. 'I'll make you a cuppa. Brush your teeth and get in the shower, you'll feel much better. We've got to leave in half an hour.'

I can't imagine having to get in a car, let alone drive three hours to a festival; the thought makes me feel anxious beyond belief. A massive field full of people off their heads. Having to sleep in a hot, airless tent. This all sounds horrendous.

I pull myself up, undress with caution, as I don't have the strength or balance required to take off yesterday's underwear, and step into the shower. As I lean my head against the porcelain tiles and let the water run down my back, I allow myself to indulge in self-pity. I think about the phone conversation I had with Rachel before heading out yesterday. She talked about how Callum will be in his final year of GCSEs in September. I can't picture him as an actual teenager, however much I try. She told me she's been offered a job teaching English at our old school, which doesn't seem right at all because it feels like only yesterday since we left ourselves, two friends with their whole lives ahead of them.

She gives me all the gossip, of which there isn't much, apart from that Natasha Clarke from school is pregnant again, even though her first child is now fifteen.

'Fuck that,' Rachel exclaims, 'there is absolutely no way I'd go through all that again now I'm well out the other side of it.'

'God, poor woman.'

'Yeah, I know. She's not coping well with it either. She's really sick, like Kate Middleton sick, and is completely white as a sheet all the time, poor girl.'

'She's lucky to have you as her friend, Rach.' I mean it with all my heart.

The power of female friendship is an extraordinary thing. I couldn't have survived my childhood without Rachel, or navigated through the first year of motherhood without Tania and Helen.

Your women are the people who give you strength. Who will get you drunk when you need it, tell you how fab you are and never let you go out in an outfit that makes you look shit, providing you have a back-up dress. They make it totally acceptable to burst into tears for absolutely no reason in the middle of the street. Your female friends are the ones who phone you on a date to check if you need a get-out, who inform your teachers you're ill when you're skiving, and who sit in a doctor's waiting room with you for hours while you wait to pick up emergency contraception.

They give you the strength to carry on when you are so life-weary from having a small baby that you don't think you'll get through the next five minutes, let alone the next hour or day. Your women are the ones who let you rant and rave and then forgive you. Who steer you through the shit bits and tell you what you need to hear, not necessarily what you want to.

I want to say all this to Rachel, and to tell her how amazing I think she is. But she knows. I don't need to keep telling her. She was and will always be my first love.

I think about poor Natasha. I wonder if the dad is the bouncer from Ritzy's and if so, if he's still a bouncer. Surely there's a shelf life to being a bouncer, like being a ballet dancer.

Then something Rachel said jumps out of the conversation like a meteor.

I stand bolt upright, hitting my forehead on the shower head. How did Nick just describe me? Horrific. Yes. Awful. Yep. White as a sheet. Isn't that what Rachel said about Natasha?

I clamber out of the shower and root around in the bathroom cabinet. My heart thuds as I try to steady my shaking hands, reaching for the pregnancy test that has been gathering dust in the back of the cabinet for the last two years.

I hover over the toilet, holding the stick in my hands. My legs shake under the strain.

'Em, you haven't even packed your stuff. Come the fuck on, we've got to leave in twenty minutes!' Nick shouts through the keyhole, sounding like someone talking underwater.

I am so dehydrated, I have to turn the sink tap on and

run my finger under the faucet to convince my body to pee. Eventually a pricklingly strong urine squeezes out and I aim the end of the stick in it, weeing on my hand in the process.

I can't be, though, can I? We've only had sex a handful of times in the last few months and I've started taking the pill again, so I just can't be. But what about Lucy's birthday? It was a mental day, what with all the relatives coming down, and then seeing Rachel. The day we truly reset over about seventeen bottles of wine. But what about when she went back to her hotel?

Nick and I had celebrated one year of Lucy with Auntie Jan's champagne, followed by sweaty, breathless, wrist-holding, skin-grabbing, lights on sex on the sofa, like we used to have before Lucy. But I would have been taking my pill like clockwork, wouldn't I? I mean I just would have done, I must have done.

When did I last have a period? Was it four weeks ago?

Four. Five. Six. It was six weeks ago.

Time stands still.

My eyes focus on the towel hanging on the back of the bathroom door. It's Nick's from school. His mum had sewn his name into it, so no one would steal it.

A minute. How long is a minute? Mississippi one, Mississippi two, Mississippi three, Mississippi four, Mississippi five, Mississippi six, Mississippi seven, Mississippi eight. And is it a minute from the moment I started weeing on the stick, or when I stuck the lid back on it?

I daren't look down.

My fingers and thumb are clutching the test so hard I have cramp in my wrist.

The door opens. 'I've made you a cuppa . . . Em, what are you doing?'

I'm naked. Soaking wet, sat on the toilet. Both knees are

covered in scrapes and I have a mouth that tastes like the inside of a brewery. The picture of maternal vibrancy.

I lock eyes with Nick. I can do this. We can do this. We can totally do this.

I look down.

Two blue lines.

'Does that mean . . .?' His words hang in the air as I nod.

I have no words. I feel like I have been holding my breath for days, and then . . .

'Fuck me, Em! FUCKING YESSSSSSSS!' He air-punches, he actually air-punches. Then he squats down, holds my face and kisses me.

I know I taste gross. But it is the best kiss of my life.

Oh my God.

There are going to be four of us.